The Monster Within

Johan Thompson

Science Fiction and Fantasy Publications

THE MONSTER WITHIN
JOHAN THOMPSON

Science Fiction and Fantasy Publications

Science Fiction and Fantasy Publications
HTTPS://SCIFICANTASYPUBLICATIONS.COM
An imprint of DAOwen Publications

The Monster Within / Johan Thompson

ISBN: 978-1-928094-85-2
EISBN: 978-1-928094-86-9

The story, all names, characters, and incidents portrayed in this production are
fictitious. No identification with actual persons (living or deceased), places, buildings,
and products is intended or should be inferred.

Edited by Douglas Owen
Coverart by MMT Productions

10 9 8 7 6 5 4 3 2 1

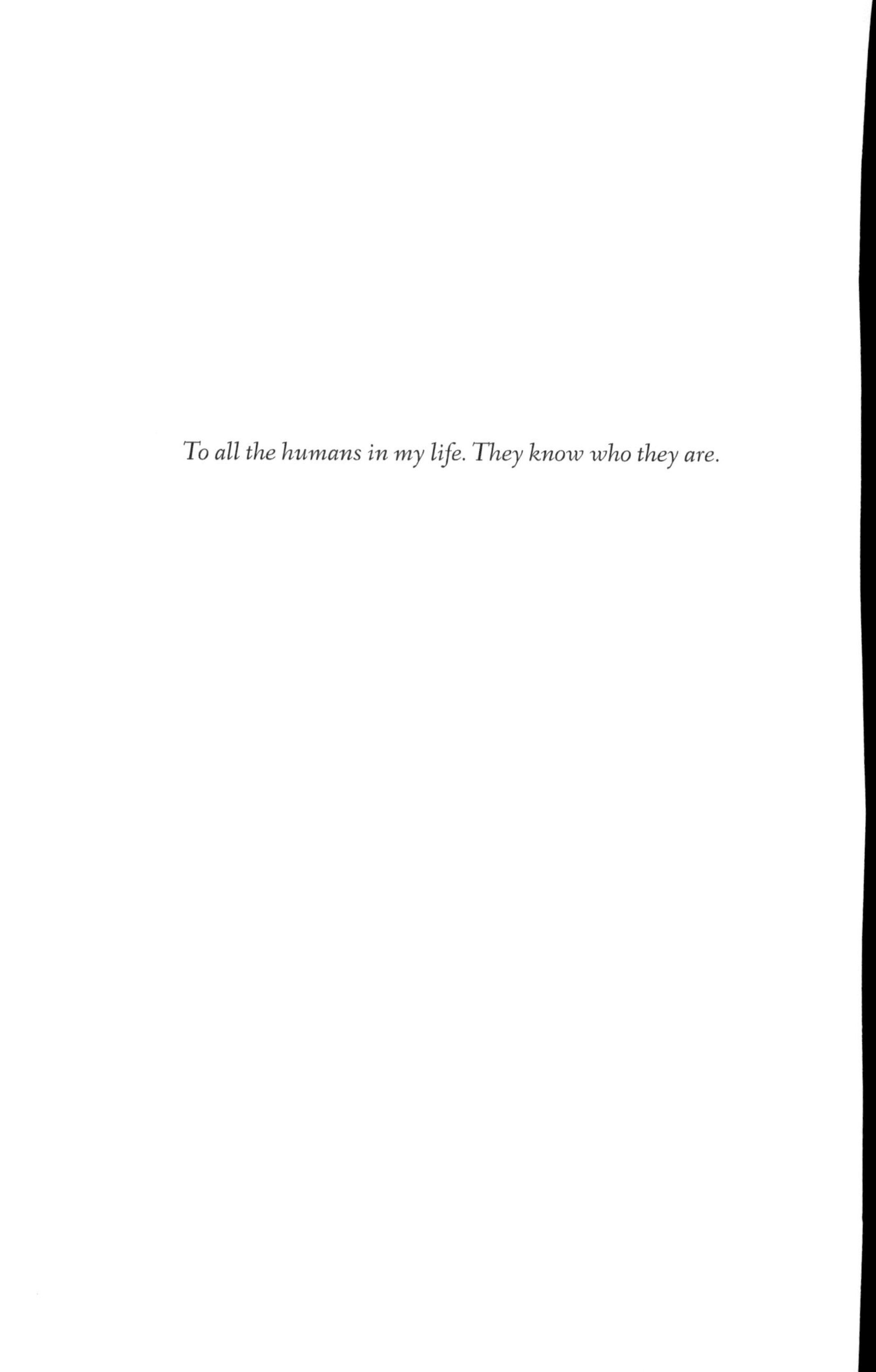

To all the humans in my life. They know who they are.

Prologue

Mom always hurried, as if she knew about the beam-god. After Joshua's birth, she rushed, but only with me. She took her time with him. What angered me most were the whispers between her and the Captain. The stares. Joshua took my stargazing place next to mom. When she told us stories, she told it more to him - and he was just a baby! The captain gave up on me when I turned twelve. If I could have stopped the thing I became, I would have. Mom still tried ruffling my hair, kissing me goodnight. But she couldn't hide the three telltale signs of a woman's fear: grey skin, blackening eyes, and the smell – that hurt me the most. The beams took her after my twelve birthday. At night I prayed to mom's God to make the hunger go away, take away the evil thoughts of what I wanted to do to the captain, and sometimes, Joshua. When I couldn't bear it anymore, I killed our livestock – silencing the hunger and urge to kill. That's when the captain brought out the whip. He wanted me to snap, taunting me to kill him, vindicating himself by showing the world that nurturing and caring for a monster was pointless. At the end, nature would win. My heart can't absorb love, like bone can't absorb blood. They punished me for being born. Or was I punished for being what I am?

2

1

It was a sign of surrender when the captain shook city man's hand: two generals acknowledging each other, one victorious, the other my father. No more blisters, no more sweating before dawn, no more shit between my toes, no more trudging dust, and no more hungry whips. I could handle everything this God-forsaken world threw at me. But I loathed stepping in the same shit, breathing the same suffocating dust, and dreading the same dawn.

But what now? I'm just a farm boy.

The captain stared at his worn boots – the farm's next victim. The city man, dressed in his black suit and red tie, scanned the soul-destroying horizon. He should smile; he won. I stuffed my hands into my pockets as he approached. Each step stirred up a puff of white dust, lingering before settling, inescapable - like everything else. I hadn't spoken to a stranger in two years, and even then, we didn't say much. Father didn't know a stranger visited. A brief green patch by the broken windmill, the only sign he'd never left.

I waited, ignoring the sun in my eyes.

"What's your name, son?" city man asked.

Johan Thompson

I studied his black suit, ending at my reflection in his sunglasses. The scar on my cheek killed whatever pity I had for the captain.

"It's impolite not to answer."

"Next time, look a man in the eye when you take his farm," I said. He frowned.

That's right; I'm not my father.

"What happened to your cheek?"

"I talked back."

City man jerked a thumb over his shoulder. "You're double his size."

"He's my father." I glanced at his fly mobile. "And you're not my father." He was four fingers shorter but pale and lean, like the stickmen my brother drew. A big pointy nose and high cheekbones held his sunglasses in place.

"Size only matters if you have the heart to back it," he said over the rim of his glasses. "Why do you stay in this place?" He looked me over. "We can use a big guy like you in the Dome."

"From the looks of you, there's not much food or sun. And why do you want this place?"

He sighed, shaking his head. "Your father told you I want this place?"

"Don't you?"

"You'll understand soon enough if you're still alive."

"Still alive? Death is afraid of me."

City-man laughed, airing his white teeth. "You are something else."

"You're not sweating?" I asked.

He frowned, running his fingers through his wavy black hair. "Where have you been?"

"Take a guess."

He cleared his throat. "This is a nitro-suit, keeps me cool when I leave Nirvana."

"Nirvana?"

4

"The name of my city." He looked right and bobbed his head. "Why not come with?"

"I can't leave them."

The hint of empathy evaporated like a teardrop in the dust as he glanced over my shoulder. "Stubborn fool. Your father knew this day would come, and still, he remains defiant." He turned and walked to his black fly mobile.

"But what do we do now?" I whispered more to myself.

He turned, removed something from his jacket, and waved me closer. I stood my ground.

City man shook his head as he walked back. "Take it!"

I accepted the icy rectangular piece of glass, resisting the urge to press it against my scar.

"It's my calling card. Press and hold your thumb on my image for five seconds, and I will send someone to fetch you, wherever you are. I can use you."

"And my brother?"

"You have a brother?"

I nodded.

"How old is he?"

"Six." I think.

He shrugged. "Sure. Hope he's got balls like you."

No, he doesn't.

The doors of his fly-mobile rose like a bird's wings on Grandpa's memory cards. As a child, before the beams took mom, she showed me many animals. But this shiny thing circled like a vulture, waiting for our last breath. I learned about vultures by accident. Mom had searched for a picture of an animal with only one horn when an image appeared of vultures feasting on a field of men, women, and children. "If those people were dead before the vultures got to them, it was okay, all creatures needed to eat," I told mom. "If I starved and stumbled upon a dead thing, I would eat it." She had tears when she sent me to my Rock-of-reflection, as she called it. Suppose a starving woman would die if stumbling upon a dead thing.

The whine of the vulture's engine shoved me from my Rock-of-reflection.

"Press and hold," he shouted. "Don't be as stubborn as your old man. You have little time left."

The machine rose from a cushion of dust, pulled in its feet, and sped toward the horizon. The sand stung my eyes, but I kept looking until there was nothing more to look at.

My father's footprints led to our battered farmhouse. Forgotten. As if God had levelled the desert around it as punishment, not to wonder what lay beyond a dune.

I studied the piece of glass with changing letters and pictures. Commander Darius Von Swartz, United World Federation.

Images flashed across the tiny screen: towering glass buildings with flying cars, scurrying, green parks with smiling people, huge flying ships with happier people. Father never told me about this. I turned back to the horizon, squinting, stroking my scar. I had forgotten about it. But I deserved it – eating my brother's food. But he told me he wasn't hungry. Telling the captain behind my back wasn't right.

Father must see this. I sprinted into the house, clutching the piece of glass. The captain and little shit brother sat at the kitchen table, each with a tall glass of chalk-white water.

"What's going on here?" I said, worried about the three-day supply of water and the captain's shifty eyes. He had the same shifty eyes when I bust open their bedroom door - thought he'd been hurting mom. I was wrong.

"Go check on the cows," he said, hunched in his chair.

"They fine." I took a seat opposite him.

He shook his head with a sigh and did another strange thing.

"Let's pray." The captain closed his eyes.

Mom prayed before bedtime or when she had enough of the farm. The only time father had spoken to God was the night the beams took mom. But he called that god a different name. That was also the last time I'd seen the beams.

My brother focused on the glass. I bowed my head but kept my eyes on the captain.

"Lord, have mercy on my soul." He glanced at my brother. "Hope his heart is good. If not, have mercy for those in the Dome, for the time has come. Amen."

Joshua shifted and reached for the glass as my father opened his eyes.

"Wait." I glared at his hand until he pulled back. "But, Captain, the man who took the farm away, Darius, said we could go to the city."

He glared at me as if those beams that took mom brooded in his eyes.

"Look." I placed the calling card in front of him. "We can go there. He will send someone to fetch us."

"It's a dangerous place," he said, without glancing at the cheerful faces.

"It doesn't look that way."

"Don't believe everything you see. The world you read about in Grandpa's books is gone." He looked at Joshua and said, "Drink up, son."

"No!" I prepared for another scar.

Joshua yanked his hand away and looked at me, confused.

"Don't."

"But I'm thirsty," he whispered and licked his chapped lips.

Father leaned in, hissing, "It's our last water, and we have little time left." He glanced at Joshua. "Let's go on our terms."

"No." I swallowed. "Those are your terms." My heart pounded like that drilling machine searching for water.

Father stirred up dust as he ruffled Joshua's tangled hair. "Drink up, you're going to visit Mommy."

"It's a lie, Joshua. Mommy is dead."

"Mommy?" Joshua beamed.

"Drink." Father pushed the glass toward him.

"Mommy is dead, Joshua, like Snowy."

Father leaped to his feet, knocking over his glass. The water spilled over the table, leaving a muddy streak. He yanked off his belt and rolled the end around his bony hand.

"How dare you disobey me!" He struck.

I grabbed the rusty buckle before it drew fresh blood and rose to my feet. "This is not right," I whispered.

Red in the face and with gritted teeth, he grabbed the belt with both hands.

I pulled him closer with one hand, glaring at him. "I can smell your fear."

The fire in his eyes faded like the stranger's eyes after his last breath.

A burp and a glass hitting the table stopped my heart.

"Don't be mad, Captain," my brother whispered. "See, I drank all my water."

"No!" I pulled father across the table. He landed on his back at my feet. "Mother wouldn't want this! We will not give up!" I grabbed the calling card from the floor and shoved it in his face. "I want to go here!"

I rushed to my brother. "The water was bad, Joshua. I need to get it out of you." I flipped his tiny body over, held his legs, and forced my finger into his mouth.

"Leave him," Father screamed. He stood on the other side of the table, pointing Grandpa's shotgun at us.

I poked deeper, gouging the back of Joshua's throat until the warm fluid soaked my hand and spilled onto the floor.

"Leave him! I don't want him to starve to death."

I lowered Joshua to the floor as he gagged air.

"You leave me no choice." Father moved in and aimed the shotgun at my brother's head. "Don't worry, Joshua, you won't feel a thing."

I turned my back on my father, went down on my knees, and wrapped my arms around Joshua. "Don't do this. I will look after him." I searched for a reason to live but found none. Perhaps this was the easiest way out? No! "Give us a chance, Captain. There's a reason we're still alive. There must be!"

This is it. My brother's embrace tightened around my waist.

"You prayed, and I didn't hear an answer," I whispered. "It's because you cursed your god."

"What do you mean?"

"When the beams took mom, you looked up and yelled, fuck you, Alcantar." A cockroach crawled through a hole in the wooden floor. It stopped, feelers searching. I grabbed it and shoved it into my mouth.

"Please, Wayne, I need to do this," my father said. "Before your brother turns. This farm only breeds hatred."

"Then pull the trigger."

"I can't take the chance. I think you already turned against us because of me. She warned me, but I didn't listen," he rambled on. "I thought I had more time. But you're so stubborn. Maybe we deserve what's coming. But it's impossible to show love if you don't have any left in you."

The man was losing his mind. "You will not kill him while I'm breathing."

He gave a drawn sigh. "Fuck, you're stubborn." Another sigh. "I can't see you starve to death, and I can't take you to the city. Tell mom I was tired. And remember her love and compassion. Her human side. Not mine."

Joshua's arms snatched tighter around my waist as the gun exploded. Something hit the floor with a thud.

A river of blood streamed past me. I swallowed, tracing it – the captain's headless body lay on the floor; his gaunt hands still clamped the shotgun. A beam of sunlight poured in from a fresh hole in the tin roof. Pink flesh, grey hair, and bone fragments dripped from the crumbling rafters. For once, the captain was right – my brother wouldn't have felt a thing.

"Is he dead?" Joshua whispered.

"Yes." The smell of fresh meat twisted my insides.

"Is he with Mommy now?"

"No, he's just dead," I said through gritted teeth.

He looked at me. "Are we going to Mommy?"

"No, Joshua." I struggled to my feet. "Mom and father are dead, like Snowy."

"But I heard–"

"Stop it! It's just you and me now."

His blinking eyes filled with tears.

"You're wasting fluids." I turned Joshua by his shoulders and pushed him toward the back door. "Go pack some stuff."

"Where are we going?" He turned and froze, his blue eyes fixed on the corpse.

"Take a good look at the coward," I shouted. "He left us with nothing. Just a scar on my face! And he made me beg! For you!"

Joshua backed away, chin trembling.

"Go!"

He turned and ran out the door, his cries swallowed by the desert.

My feet stuck to the drying blood; even now, he tried to keep me here.

I gathered the last of our food, which would last us another day, a butcher's knife, and a box of matches. Pieces of the captain still dripped from the rafters as I walked over to the fireplace. I removed a picture of my smiling parents from the frame and tore it in half. I wished it was as easy to remove him from my memory.

Memory. I turned to the headless corpse. Grandpa's last memory card, my coward father, forbade me to look at it. Only his thumbprint opened the safe in the bedroom cupboard. I drew the butcher's knife from my bag.

"Joshua!"

He made two mistakes: running and crying.

"Joshua!"

He was about to make the third, but answered, "I'm here."

"Where!"

He sat on the rusty tin roof, looking down at me, like Snowy, our cat, our last pet. Father served her for dinner one night. A distinct flesh I tasted before but couldn't remember when. Joshua never found out.

"You will die in a minute. You'll fry like a piece of bacon." The thought made my mouth water.

"You mad?" Joshua said.

"Mad like the bees?"

"No, I mean, are you angry with me?"

"If you don't get down in the next" –I glanced at my broken watch–"forty-five seconds I'll get up there and throw your body off the roof before the rats take my piece."

"No, I mean–"

"Get off the fucking roof!"

"You said the F-word!" Joshua placed his hand over his mouth, looking around, searching.

"That's how fucking serious I am! And I can shout it because it's only you and me now. Get the fuck down!"

"Okay," he muttered. "But I can still hear it."

I raised my hands, tilted my head back, and bathed in the sudden rush of freedom, screaming at the top of my lungs, "Fucking! Fuck! Fuck! Fuck!"

Joshua approached with light steps.

"Say it," I smirked.

He shook his head, wide-eyed.

"Say it!" I snapped.

"No!"

"Why not?" I grabbed him by the arm. "We can do whatever we want now. No more, yes Captain, no Captain. I only listened to him out of respect for mom."

He frowned. "She wanted us to be good. To be free doesn't mean it's okay to do bad stuff."

I let go of his arm. "Well, I guess we'll find out if I'm good or bad."

"You're scaring me," he whispered.

"Get your stuff and let's go." I picked up my bag, Grandpa's shotgun, a wineskin – that's what mom called it – and walked to the hydroponics tunnel where father had chased our last remaining two cows. The well had dried up three days ago, so my father had the cows devour what remained of our dying crops. He did it for us, he said, and I had agreed. The cows should survive another two or three days, the vegetables only another day.

"Damn," I whispered. Fiona and Emma – Joshua named them – devoured every sprout, vegetable, and root from the channels. They even drank the remaining recycled water from the reservoir tanks.

Remember, nothing is for free. I nosed both cows with a leather strap, then tightened Emma's noose as mom taught me at six. The captain coward never liked it. I removed a metal spike from Grandpa's army steel trunk and wrapped my arm around her neck, holding her still. "You know the drill," I whispered in her ear, rammed the spike into the wound in her throat, just an inch, and pulled it out. Blood squirted from the hole. I positioned the mouth of the wineskin and filled it two thirds. Mom caught me once as I drank the blood straight from the cow. She warned me never to do it again because something terrible might happen to me. I only realised after her death what she meant, but it wasn't a cow I drank from. Since that day, cow's blood didn't taste that good anymore.

I positioned the leather strap over the seeping wound. The rest of the wineskin I filled with Emma's milk. Joshua liked it that way. Me, I loved it without milk – it heals me faster.

After leading the cows out of the hydroponics tunnel, I waited under the dead tree, sitting on my Rock-of-reflection. I removed Darius's calling card from my shirt pocket; I'd always wanted to go there. An invisible force, like a leaf attached to a stem, waiting for the perfect gust. Mother had convinced me otherwise. "It's a terrible place, Wayne," she warned. "They won't like boys like you. You're different. Special." And then her most desperate reason, "They eat their dead." That was not such a terrible thing, I thought. Like my vultures, when they eat the dead. Why waste? On the farm, we recycled everything. And I mean everything. Wasn't that recycling? My thumb hovered over Darius' face. One thing life taught me in my seventeen years - nothing was for free. Nothing. Why did the city want this place? What did city-man tell the captain? How could a farm boy make serious credits in the city? Why did my little shit brother take so long?

"Joshua!" All this reflection hurt my head and butt.

He stood in the doorway. "Aren't we going to bury him?"

"Why? And waste more energy?" I lied; I'll turn into one of those vultures if I go back into the house. There must be a commandment: Thou shalt not consume the flesh of family. It wasn't in the Ten Mom had carried on about. Thou shalt not kill, but nothing about what not to do with the meat after somebody else broke the Commandment. Maybe there was more than Ten. I shook the thought out of my head as I looked into Joshua's judgemental eyes. Mom had the same eyes. If the word fuck upset him, imagine how eating father would have?

Joshua walked back into the house. Another minute crept by before he walked out with a small bag and the big teddy bear mom gave him.

"I threw a blanket over him," he said. "And what happened to Dad's thumb?"

"You can't carry that big thing all the way. Leave it."

"No." He bit his lip. "Grandpa's shotgun is heavier than this." He held up the teddy.

"Okay, let's see what will work best when a wild animal attacks us."

"I wish a wild animal–" The thunderous and crackling roar of a flying machine interrupted. We both searched the blinding sky, squinting. Usually, it was too high to spot. The only evidence that something went over was the white powder spewed by its engines, covering the land as the coward's blood on the kitchen floor. We always took cover in the house before the dust reached us, as it was still hot from the engines. The captain cursed the noise the same way he cursed God.

However, this sound was unfamiliar; it was louder, more intense - my heart shuddered in my throat.

2

Citizens lined the street, dressed in all colours of the rainbow. The government reserved black, grey, and white. The atmosphere sizzled with renewal and kept at sixty-five degrees Fahrenheit – six degrees lower than usual because of the special day. Too hot, and a riot might ensue. The colourful crowd cheered and waved green flags, waiting for their elected president. From within, the shield emulated day or night, but for this special occasion, the Council deviated from the norm – the heavens cascaded glistening stars of silver and gold as if standing in a snow globe filled with glitter. Fighter jets flew in formation, celebrating the joyous occasion.

And then, in a hovering limousine, he appeared, standing proud, waving at his followers, blond hair blowing in the breeze he requested.

Men and women dressed in black, grey, and white gathered around the oval table, silent, eyes pinned on the hologram of earth and the

Four seated around the table. A multitude of red triangles approached Nirvana – a white dot on the northern hemisphere.

All turned their attention to the giant screen on the far side of the room as news of the new president aired.

"There he is, citizens, President Green, at thirty-seven, the youngest elected president ever, a landslide victory... a joyous day for the United World Federation... Let's hope he's not too green behind the ears..."

"Wet behind the ears, you twit, and not a landslide victory," General Steward said in a British accent and reversed his wheelchair from the table. He turned to the enormous screen. His accent was more pronounced when insulting someone. Steward was a gaunt man with eyes as black as his suit and eyebrows as untamed as his grey hair.

"The poor man should enjoy his moment," Commander Whitmore said, tapping the ash from her cigar. "What result did we release, Gabriel?" She turned toward the youngest of the Four, sitting to the right of her.

Gabriel coughed, waving the smoke away. "The correct result was the highest ever" –he glanced at Steward– "a landslide victory of eighty-one percent. We released a figure of fifty-nine." He shrugged. "Don't want him too confident."

She raised a brow. "We had to let him win with that popularity."

Steward returned to the table, shaking his head. "The first bloody time in the Federation's history we had to make the best man win. What a pity."

"Can't believe that fossil that ran against him received only nineteen percent of the vote." Whitmore took a puff. "A three-legged blind skunk with a bladder problem would have received more."

"Probably," Gabriel said, dispersing the smoke. "At least thirty percent sympathy vote." He stroked his gelled hair. "I warned you, the people wanted someone younger, energetic, and breathing."

General Steward shook his head at the cheering crowds. "The bloody sheep genuinely believes his renewal bullshit. Aren't they happy? We've given them all that's required? What renewal are they expecting? They live in a bloody fishbowl!"

"They only voted for him because of his rebellious wife." Whitmore cleared her throat and sniffed the cigar, frowning. "When she died, he gained her followers."

Gabriel leaned back in his chair. "Don't worry. Gray will deflate Green's balls back to size. And with his pathetic daughter by his side, will lose followers faster than the city loses water... and virgins," he muttered the latter.

"Speaking of virgins," Steward said. "We still need to decide if we up the credits for those women who stay pure, or do we increase the credits for those who get an abortion? We have increased the dosage of xenobiotic toxins to the max in their food supply, and still their numbers increase."

"I think to reward abstinence is more humane than to reward infidelity," Whitmore said.

"Excuse me." Gabriel raised his hand. "Fuck, they will fuck. I think we need to nip it in the bud before another vermin takes a breath of our recycled air."

"So, are we in agreement?" Steward asked. "We up the abortion credits?"

Gabriel looked at Steward with a shocked expression. "Are you agreeing with me?"

"The only thing you two agree on is self-preservation," Whitmore muttered.

"Let's vote then." Steward raised his left hand. "Those in favour of increasing the abortion credits by twenty."

Gabriel raised his hand and looked at Whitmore's hands resting on the table.

"We want to be known as pro-lifers," Martha Grace, the eldest of the Four, said. Martha resembled a vulture, with her hunched back, bony shoulders, and sagging head; only her silvery bun towered above her shoulders.

The two men lowered their hands.

"I've got an idea." Whitmore shifted in her seat, tapping her cigar on the edge of a wooden box. "Let's change the constitution that only fifty percent of the vote is required when voting on matters regarding credit." She raised her left hand. "For those in favour."

Steward and Gabriel raised their hands as one and turned their attention to Martha.

"We need a hundred percent to amend the constitution," Whitmore said.

"What the hell." Martha gave the slightest of a shrug and raised a shaking hand.

"So say the Four," Whitmore said.

"So say the Four," all repeated.

Whitmore gave Steward a self-assured smile. "Proceed."

Steward raised his hand. "Those in favour of increasing the abortion credits by twenty."

Gabriel rose from his chair as he raised his hand.

Whitmore looked at Gabriel. "Motion approved by fifty percent. Let the record show those in favour."

Gabriel scowled at the spectators. "If I see another fucking eye roll or shake of the head from any of you, I will cancel every fucking credit in this room."

"I second that," General Steward said with a wave of his hand.

"Especially the scribe!" Gabriel pointed at a heavy-set woman seated behind Martha. Her hands froze above the keyboard as she looked up, shocked.

Gabriel shook his head as he took his seat. "It looks as if she's got Parkinson's disease!" He mimicked her typing, shaking his head.

"Hand me one." Martha pointed to Whitmore's cigar with a gangly finger.

Whitmore smiled and plucked one from the wooden box on the table. "One of the farmers gave it to Darius." She slid the cigar, snipper, and laser lighter to Gabriel, who pushed it to the next, each examining the rare items until it reached Martha.

Whitmore shrugged. "I thought, what the hell, I might as well go out smoking, enjoy whatever time we have left."

"Shouldn't we preserve these relics of the past?" General Steward with raised chin and brow.

"For what?" Whitmore snapped.

"We are doing an all-right job with you," Gabriel whispered.

Whitmore sputtered smoke as she burst out in a coughing chuckle.

An elderly man, standing behind Martha, reached for the relics and said, "May I assist Madam Secretary?"

She covered the relics with trembling hands. "I circumcised my great-grandson a week ago. I think I can handle it."

Whitmore, Gabriel, and Steward shared a worrying glance as Martha struggled with the snipper. Her bony fingers worked the procedure like a spider worked its prey. Murmurs and gasps spread through the War room as Martha snipped a third of the cigar.

Gabriel flinched. "How's your great-granddaughter doing, Martha?"

After Martha avoided third-degree burns and exhaled the first toxic breath, General Steward pointed at the waving president. "When are we going to tell that fool?"

"I can't believe that we are at this stage," Martha said, licking her lips.

"Just make sure our fleet and reconnaissance drones are back before we send in the Sweepers," Whitmore said.

"ETA fifteen minutes," Gabriel said, pointing at the approaching triangles on the hologram.

"I wonder, after all these years, how many are still alive out there?" Whitmore whispered.

"A few stubborn ones." General Steward glanced at the digital clock counting down. "We have thirty days left to cleanse the earth."

"Can't we allow a few more?" Martha said.

"No," Gabriel snapped. "The Domes are filled to capacity, and we're running out of food."

Johan Thompson

"We cross that bridge when we get there," General Steward muttered. "Enough talk." Gabriel sat up. "We can't postpone this any longer. We need to vote. Send in the Sweepers. The cleansing will take roughly three weeks."

Whitmore stubbed out the cigar in an ashtray. "Our children will understand one day."

"We are completing what our predecessors started thirty years ago." Steward said.

Gabriel shook his head. "Why are there still people out there? They have nothing to live for. Why did they not kill themselves? Now we must waste ammunition on these pests."

Martha exhaled a thick cloud of smoke, staring at Gabriel over her glasses. "In the words of Adam Bede, he was like a cock who thought the sun had risen to hear him crow."

Gabriel smiled. "You want to see my cock rise, Martha?"

"Don't bother, Gabriel. I forgot my magnifying glass at home."

***

The Vortex glider cut a dusty line through the barren landscape. The city's shield, resembling a giant water droplet, rose from the horizon.

"Authentication," Lieutenant Stacey Norman's voice broke the silence within the cockpit.

"Are we going through this every time, Stacey? Isn't the signature of my craft enough authentication?"

"Because you're not tagged, I need to confirm that it's you, Commander. The old-fashioned way."

"I still have to encounter a human or alien capable of taking something that belongs to me." Darius chuckled. "Believe me, they've tried."

"It's protocol, Commander."

Darius sighed, pressed his thumb against the windshield and said, "Commander Darius Von Swartz." The scanner embedded in the dashboard scanned his left eye.

"Voice, print and retina scan confirmed," Stacey replied. "Thank you, Commander."

"All me, isn't it? Amazing."

"The Four were worried, Commander."

"You mean the puppet masters?"

"They want you in the War Room."

"The War room," Darius scoffed.

"I will open a window in sector eleven, Commander."

"Eleven, quite fitting."

A whirlpool appeared in the shield, swallowing the glider.

"Where were you?" Whitmore snapped as Darius entered the War Room.

Darius sniffed the air. "I can smell that you've enjoyed the spoils of war, Supreme Commander. Took a chance smoking it."

Martha glared at Whitmore.

"We held the Sweepers back because of you," Whitmore said.

"I went out for the last time, tried to convince an old fool to come."

"Why?" Gabriel said.

"Where else is he supposed to go?"

General Steward glared at Darius. "Why did you go, Commander?"

"He was one of the few that stuck it out. I admire the man's strong will, bravery, and I thought we needed a man with those characteristics in the Dome." Darius walked over to Whitmore and fished for a cigar from the bottom of the dusty box. "At the moment, pansies occupy the Dome." He snipped and lit the cigar. "They are raised in a bubble filled with smoke and mirrors." He blew a cloud of smoke. "If they break the treaty, we will need men like that."

"What did the man say?" Martha asked.

"How did he put it?" Darius puffed. "I don't want to be a prisoner in a place filled with cowards. We're making it easy for them." He stared at General Steward. "Like shooting at goldfish in a teacup."

General Steward inched toward Darius and raised his voice. "The Council that signed the treaty made the decision, not us. When we took over, it was already too late."

"We can break the treaty!" Darius shouted.

"Show some bloody respect!" General Steward raised himself from his wheelchair.

"Stop it!" Whitmore said. "We need to stand together with this!"

General Steward lowered himself and straightened his medals.

"There's no honour in those medals," Darius muttered as he turned toward the globe. No triangles were visible.

"How did the old man know about them?" Whitmore asked. "Only the Council and a select few knew back then."

Darius shrugged, "I don't know. Maybe his grandfather was one of the select few."

"All fifty-two members voted," Gabriel said, glancing at the screen with the names of the Council members. "All gave a 'Yes' vote."

Darius glared at Whitmore. "Tell me one thing. When last did we have any communication from them? They could have lost interest and moved on."

Whitmore looked at Steward.

"What?" Darius said.

Steward shrugged. "Okay, tell him."

The President stepped out of his limousine and waved to the crowd behind the fence. His smile vanished the moment he turned his back on them. "Where's Sadie, Bryan!" he snapped at his chief of security. "I warned you about her. She's like a, uh, what do you call those things again? I read about them the other day."

"What, sir?" Bryan asked.

"Man, they lived in caves," he said, flapping his hands. "Flies."

"You mean bats, sir."

"That's it! She's like a bat. She loves the dark, is difficult to catch, and sucks up all my credits."

"My men are searching for your daughter as we speak, Mr President."

"I wanted her to join me on my victory parade. I felt like a sundial." President Green turned back to the landing of the stairs leading up to the presidential residence. "Are my things here?"

"Yes, sir."

"Good." He took a deep breath. "It's time to start the renewal."

"Mr President," Bryan called.

"What?"

"There is someone from the Council waiting for you."

"What Council?" he frowned.

"They will explain to you, sir."

Green shrugged and proceeded up the stairs, whispering, "Hope it's not a bureaucrat." He turned back. "Oh, Bryan."

"Yes, sir."

"Where will I find him?"

"Don't worry, sir, the Council will find you."

"Aren't you coming?"

"No, sir, he wants to speak to you alone."

Green frowned and turned back to his new home. He hesitated for a moment before taking the next step.

The white doors hissed open.

"Welcome, President Green," an automated female voice greeted as he walked into the double volume entrance hall. He stopped at a framed mirror, jiggled both hands as if preparing to draw, then ran his fingers through his blond coiffure. After neatening his green tie, he tore from his reflection.

"Where's everyone?" he whispered. "Hello!"

A door to the right opened, and a tall, dark-skinned man, dressed in a shimmering grey suit, sauntered in. "President Green."

"Yes," Green said, stepping back.

"I have that effect on people," the man said in a baritone voice. "My name is Mr Gray... with an a." He fingered his suit.

Green straightened. "I'm sorry, but I don't see people of your, uh, culture much."

Mr Gray smiled. "Thanks to the unfair selection practices of the Dome fathers."

"I wasn't aware of it, but as elected President, I will look into it."

Mr Gray's smile vanished. "Don't lie, Mr Green. Everyone was aware. But that's human nature – if you don't fuck with my bubble, I don't give a fuck about yours." He approached Green; their eyes locked. "Besides, it's too late now – the billions not deemed pure or wealthy enough died of starvation, their dust blowing against the Dome walls."

Green scanned the empty house, then reached out his hands. "And here you are, through hard work and dedication–"

"You cannot comprehend what I had to do."

Green swallowed. "I'm a busy man, Mr Gray. How can I help you?"

"The Council have selected you to be President. You are working for them now."

"The people elected–" Green gasped and fell to his knees as Gray punched him in the stomach.

Mr Gray circled him. "Only twenty percent of the Dome voted for your ignorant white ass. We control everything – the military, the media, the food. We feed the people what they need to know and when they need to know it."

Green struggled to his feet, stumbling to the front door. "Bryan!"

"Have a pleasant day, Mr President," the female voice said as the front door opened.

Gray grabbed the President by the hair as he reached the doorway.

"Help!" Green called out to Bryan, standing at the bottom of the stairs. Their eyes locked for a moment before Bryan turned away.

"Welcome back, Mr President," the female voice said as Gray dragged him back into the house, kicking and screaming.

He threw the President face down on the marble floor, then lifted his head by his ruffled hair and whispered into his ear, "I detect some resistance. Do the elected President and his daughter want to die in a tragic accident like his predecessor?"

"Okay," Green groaned. "Okay."

Gray released his grip and straightened. "I must apologise, Mr President, but it usually takes a few civil lessons to condition the new president. Unfortunately, we have little time left." He held out his hand.

Green glared at the hand for a moment and then accepted. "Where's my daughter?" he asked as Gray pulled him to his feet.

"She's at Club Gravity with her friend, Monique, table seven, burning credits. Henceforth, two things never to worry about: credits and the whereabouts of your daughter. We will keep a close eye on her."

3

A flying machine rose from behind our farmhouse, bigger than I'd ever seen, even bigger than I'd seen on Grandpa's memory cards. It circled, nose dipped, engulfing our house in a cloud of dust.

"Run!" Joshua screamed, pulling me by the arm, clutching the teddy with the other.

"Stop it!" I picked my brother up under his arms, hoisted him over my head, and set him down on my shoulders. "I'm running nowhere. And don't piss your pants."

Emma and Fiona thought Joshua's plan was best. The roar of the engines and dust followed them as they darted toward the blue mountains.

"Damn it!" I grabbed grandpa's shotgun and chased after our food with Joshua on my shoulders and the teddy on my head.

A mechanical arm extended from the flying machine, grabbed Emma and hoisted her into its belly. Fiona went the same way. The flying machine circled us before heading toward the mountains.

"Fuck!" I stopped the chase, aimed the shotgun, and fired one round at the cattle thieves.

We watched until the blue mountains swallowed the black dot.

Joshua broke the silence, whispering, "I didn't know you liked that word so much."

"Say it," I whispered.

"No."

I removed the piece of glass from my pocket and licked it clean. Nothing is for free, but I'll do whatever he wants. My brother won't survive another day. I pressed my thumb on the glass until I heard a faint beep. "Let's go back to the farm. Somebody will come and fetch us." I didn't trust city-man, but had no other choice. With my brother on my shoulders, the fucking bear on my head, and Grandpa's shotgun in my hand, I walked back to the farm.

"Look how beautiful the sunset is," Joshua whispered.

I glanced at the setting sun; a blanket of bright orange covered the horizon as if on fire. "It looked like that yesterday, and the day before and the fucking days before that."

My tongue felt like a piece of beef jerky sticking to my palate. Can't believe he poisoned our water. I glanced over my shoulder; the cows were more important than us. We were alone. Worthless. Two specs in a desert that nobody cared about. I slowed my pace. My newfound freedom meant nothing. I was tired but not broken.

Joshua covered my eyes with his hands and giggled, but only for a moment. In our tall shadow, I saw him studying his wet hands. I searched for a quick explanation, but it wasn't necessary. He removed the teddy from my head, placed it on his shoulders, and rested his chin on my head. His skinny arm snaked around my neck. He didn't hug me because he knew better.

One step at a time. The pace or size didn't matter as long as I took it. Keep going – for Joshua. I wasn't free.

"Look!" Joshua said. "The cow thieves are coming back!"

He was right. The black dot increased in size; the roar of its engines was more intense than before.

I raised the shotgun above my head. "Take it."

The teddy bear plonked in the dust as his tiny hands grabbed hold of the weapon.

I turned around, hoisted Joshua over my head, and placed him on the ground.

"Stay behind me."

He handed me the weapon and picked up the teddy.

"Whatever happens, stay close." I stepped in front of him and cocked the shotgun.

The flying machine hovered roughly fifty yards from us. The pilot, dressed in black from head to toe, shook his head. I rested the shotgun on my shoulder and waited.

"It's going to land," my brother said as four feet extended from its belly.

The flying machine descended until settling on a cloud of exploding dust. The roar of the engines whined down, and the belly opened, lowering a ramp.

Three masked figures, weapons in hand and dressed in black, ran down the ramp. Joshua's arm snaked around my leg. I aimed the shotgun, waiting.

They skidded to a stop.

"Take it easy!" the small one in the middle said with a hand raised.

"We don't have time for this shit!" the big one on the left snapped. "He can't hurt us with that piece of crap." He dived, rolled, and grabbed the shotgun by the barrel.

I pulled him closer as he hung on and rammed my fist into his mask, shattering the glass. The big one came to a sliding halt at the little one's boots.

He stared at the groaning man for a moment, then looked at me. "Please come with us. Nirvana has dispatched Sweepers, and we have little time left."

The little one was a woman – the voice, chest, and hips gave her away.

"We can take yer lads someplace safe," the man on the right said.

I lowered the shotgun. *Any place is better than this.*

My brother appeared by my side and walked toward the woman, holding out his hand.

She bowed down to him. "Is there anyone else alive?"

He shook his head, hugging the teddy.

"Let's go!" The woman ran back to the flying machine, Joshua in hand.

The other man helped the injured guy to his feet, and they made their way back to the ramp.

I turned back and looked at our farm - hopefully, for the last time. Joshua ran away with the woman without looking back.

"Are you coming?" the woman yelled above the roar of the engines.

I turned back and walked as fast as my tired legs allowed, up the ramp and into the flying machine. I strapped Joshua into a seat and handed him the teddy. He smiled at me. For the first time, I noticed his missing front teeth. The tooth fairy didn't come and visit him as Mom did with me. I took a seat next to him and tapped his leg.

"See? Never give up," I whispered in his ear.

He nodded and wasted more water. I could not allow myself to do the same because the man I'd punched sat opposite me, glaring with one eye, the other swollen shut.

"Sadie!" Monique screamed, bouncing up and down on Club Gravity's dance floor.

"What!"

"One-minute left – we need to leave the gravity room!"

"No."

"Why not?"

"I want to try my luck!" Sadie said, pointing to a boy kissing a girl.

"Ryan? But he's a dick and taken!"

"All the boys are taken, idiot – haven't you heard the Dome ratio? Three girls to a boy."

"I'll give you two reasons not to - he likes cover models, size two."

Sadie raised her arms, swaying her hips. "I'm almost a four."

Monique ceased her bouncing. "More like a six, maybe an eight."

Sadie flipped her the bird.

"Whatever, he's not into this goth thing of yours - fingernails, hair, eyeliner." Monique pointed at the rainbow-coloured ceiling far above. "He wants happy, colourful, fake, slutty."

"I need to try something," Sadie said, eyes pinned on Ryan. "Now that my dad is President, everyone will know I don't have a boyfriend and that I'm still a virgin. I'll die of embarrassment if it ever comes out."

Monique glanced at Ryan; her lips pursed. "Just remember – if you don't score, you will be up there all alone for close to an hour!" She glanced at the clock. "Shit. I'm out of here!"

"Watch me from the outside!" Sadie yelled at her departing friend, monitoring the gravity clock: four seconds remaining. She sprinted toward the couple and crashed into Ryan, ending the passionate embrace the moment the clock struck zero. They slammed into the floor as the dancers levitated. The crowd cheered as gravity decreased, pushing them higher and higher. Sadie hung onto her catch, laughing as they twirled further away from the colour-altering dance floor.

"Let me go, you freak!" Ryan screamed and tried to push her away.

"Don't you want a good time?" She kissed him hard on the lips.

He pulled away and glared at her for a moment. "Okay, let's do this." He grinned. "All the way."

"You mean all the way?" Sadie said, unsure.

"That's what I planned on doing before you interrupted me." He shrugged. "It's the gravity room, or do you want me to go back?"

"Okay..." Sadie looked around and noticed the uncontrollable desire of the other couples, tumbling and twirling as one, trancelike. One by one, with the use of their handheld micro-jets, the levitators disappeared into pods attached to the walls, like birds entering their nests. The beat of the music increased, spurring on the euphoria.

She searched for an open pod. "We need to hurry before they're all taken."

Ryan kissed her on the neck and whispered, "I reserved one. Relax." He nibbled her earlobe.

Sadie closed her eyes, tilting her head back – her body tingled at all the right places.

His hands slithered to her back, unzipping her dress.

"Wait!" she said, trying to push him away, but his grip tightened around her waist. "In private... in the pods."

"Relax," he said, and continued to unzip her dress.

"No, wait!"

Ryan spun her around and ripped the dress from her body. "I want to go all the way, but not with you." He pushed her away. "I can't believe you can float with that body."

Sadie grabbed at her dress, but Ryan snagged it away, laughing as he tossed it over his shoulder. She watched in horror as her garment drifted away. In her hurry to enter the gravity room, she forgot a micro-jet.

"Let's show the President's daughter how it's done!" Ryan yelled above the drumbeat and removed a micro-jet from his denim pocket. He activated the device, jetted away to his girlfriend, and entered an open pod. He showed Sadie the middle finger before closing the door.

The remaining levitators burst out laughing, circling Sadie, all clutching micro-jets in the one hand and a Dome communicator in the other.

"Never enter the Dome without it, idiot," a boy shouted, holding up the device.

Sadie, dressed in skimpy black underwear, struggled like an injured fish trying to swim upstream. She glanced at the clock, petrified – fifty-nine minutes remaining.

"Smile, Miss President," the levitators chanted, catching each embarrassing frame of her pasty figure.

The setting sun draped half the Dome in bright orange as the Vortex glider sped down Ring Road East toward Building Seven, standing tall at a hundred and twenty storeys. It was the most impressive building within the Dome - a dominating glass and steel structure with rotating floors.

Darius sat in the driver's seat, reading an old book. He turned a page and glanced at his watch: 18:02.

"Call Operations."

A woman with fiery red hair and a bright pink eyepatch appeared in the centre of the windscreen. "Yes," she said, glaring with her one emerald green eye.

"When are you going to forgive me?" Darius said.

Her angel white smile filled the windscreen. "When I dip a protein biscuit containing your treacherous arse into a cup of lemon tea."

"That might be sooner than you think, my little dragon."

"Oh, please," she scoffed with a wave of the hand. "The devil will send you back because you pissed on his flames."

"You trying to seduce me?"

"I'll never make that mistake again. You called me."

"Were the Sweepers dispatched?"

"Affirmative, at eighteen hundred hours."

"I'll be there in five–" A flashing light on the console interrupted. "Just a minute, Lola." Darius tapped the screen, opening the message.

"It's Lieutenant Lola. Someone activated your calling card – fifty clicks west of the Dome."

"Finally," Darius whispered."

"The DNA strain received from your calling card is flagged,

Commander. I must notify the Council." She raised the brow of her exposed eye.

"Are our calls still secure?"

"You think I will fuck around with you on an open line?"

"Just checking." He shifted in his seat. "Hold back on notifying the Council."

"Anything else before they ram a fiery poker up my vagina."

"If you insist. Upload the DNA strain into the Sweeper database. And while you at it, make sure mine is still active."

"You know it doesn't work if the tagged DNA is in a group, like a plane or a vehicle."

"You know, if you stop breathing, you die."

"Fuck you, Commander."

"You too, Lieutenant." Darius blew her a kiss before she flickered away. "Switching to manual." He grabbed the steering wheel and turned, speeding west.

4

The little one removed her mask as she stepped out of the cockpit. She didn't look like my mother at all. It was the first time I had seen another woman. She ruffled her short black hair while studying me with her sky-blue eyes.

"You're beautiful," Joshua said, gawking.

"Thank you," she said with a perfect smile. "What's your name?"

"Joshua."

"That's a beautiful name."

"I know." He pointed at me. "This is my brother Wayne. He doesn't talk much."

I scowled at the little shit.

"My name is Juliet." She pointed at the man opposite me, who still glared at me with his good eye. "This bald gorilla is Brock – he's got the same problem as Wayne – and the man flying the plane is Fritz."

"Why did you come back for us?" I asked Juliet, but kept my eyes fixed on Brock.

"We've intercepted a transmission from a calling card and traced it back to you," she said.

"We were right in front of you," I said, glancing at Juliet.

She smiled. "Sorry 'bout that, but we were not looking for more mouths to feed."

"You stole our cows!"

She shrugged. "Sorry 'bout that too, but we've got mouths to feed."

"Again, why come back?"

She strolled over to me and held out her hand. "Where is it?"

"Why?"

"The Council can trace it."

"Trace?"

"Idiot," Brock muttered.

"You want to lose another eye?"

"You want another scar?"

I jumped up, fists raised.

"Take it easy, Wayne," Joshua whispered. "They saved us."

I glared down at him. "I don't need saving."

"Then why did you activate the calling card?" Brock sneered.

Juliet stepped in between us, placed her hand on my chest, looked straight into my soul and said, "I know, you did it for Joshua. Relax."

My heart still pounded in my throat, but not from anger anymore. Her hand was as warm as the sun, but this was a good warmth. I had to sit; it was as if her hand had extracted all my strength.

"Please give it to me." She held out her magic hand. "They will find us and kill us all."

I removed the piece of glass from my pocket and handed it to her. "But the man gave it to me to call for help. If the city wanted us dead, they could have done so a long time ago."

Her expression turned to pity. "What or who do you think caused all this?"

"The sun."

Brock burst out laughing.

I didn't like Brock.

Juliet broke the calling card in two, destroying the cheerful faces and tall glass buildings. "You asked why we turned back for you. The moment you activated the calling card, it scanned your DNA, and it matched a strain we have in our database."

She must have noticed my blank look.

"It's not a hundred percent match, but it looks like you are the grandsons of the great Wayne Johnson. We could not allow his family to die out here."

Johnson was our family name. I had not heard that name spoken since Mother had died. When the coward, my father, did something wrong, she would always use his full name, Howard Johnson.

"What made him great?" Joshua asked.

"If he was so great, why are we starving in the desert?" I added.

Juliet walked over to a box and removed two bottles of water. "Excuse my manners." She handed us each a bottle.

Joshua looked at it, then at me.

I nodded.

He unscrewed the cap with shaking hands and drank the water. A burp, a satisfied sigh, and the bottle hitting the floor completed his annoying ritual.

"Don't you want some?" Juliet asked.

"I'm good." I removed the wineskin from my bag, took a few gulps, and wiped my mouth with the back of my hand.

"What is that?" Juliet asked.

"Wine," I said, glaring at Joshua, hoping he would keep his little mouth shut.

"Wine?" Brock said, confused. "We can't even produce wine. How the hell could you do it in the middle of the desert?"

"Hydroponics," my brother said, glancing at me.

"Never tasted wine," Brock continued.

I handed Joshua the wineskin. "You think he'll be able to handle it?"

"I don't know." Joshua shrugged and took a mouthful. A naughty smile formed as he handed Brock the wine.

"Aren't you a bit young to drink?" Juliet said.

"Maybe in your world, but in our world, we can do the fuck we want."

Joshua hugged his teddy. "He likes that word."

"Say it."

"No." He glanced my way. "I don't like your world."

"Well" –Juliet ruffled my brother's tangled locks– "we're taking you to my world, and there are rules."

"Good," he whispered, beaming up at her.

"I will not like it there," I said, scratching my scar.

Brock held up the wineskin and snorted. "I'm sure I'll be able to handle it... boy." His Adam's apple bobbed only once before he lowered the skin. His face turned ashen-white, like the desert as he held the mouthful.

Joshua nudged me in the ribs with his elbow.

Brock blinked a few times before his Adam's apple bobbed for the second time. He handed the wineskin back to me and nodded with pressed lips.

"So, what do you think?" I asked.

Brock cleared his throat and coughed before replying, "Not bad."

I didn't offer Juliet the skin.

She scrutinised Brock. "Must be an acquired taste."

Brock muttered, "I don't know why the elders made such a big thing about it."

"What happened to your father?" Juliet asked.

Joshua fiddled with his teddy's ears, head bowed.

"He took the easy way," I said.

"I heard your father and grandfather didn't see eye to eye on many things." Juliet unzipped her suit down to where the fleshy crease between her breasts started.

"Like you and Dad," Joshua muttered.

"My father was a coward," I whispered, eyes focused on the crease. "My grandfather, I never met."

"I will tell you what I know," Juliet said and unzipped even further. "But first, you need to clean up. No offence, but you two smell like shit."

"Looks like shit too," Brock said, recovered.

Fritz yelled from the front. "Hold on, laddies! Six focking Sweepers approaching from the west." The flying machine banked to the right, almost throwing us from our seats. I heard Fiona and Emma moan below, their hooves trampling steel.

"What's a focking Sweeper?" I asked as I tightened my brother's straps.

Juliet and Brock jumped up and ran to the nearest window. "The Dome's final solution," she said over her shoulder.

"We shouldn't have returned for these idiots," Brock snapped at Juliet. "I warned you. We would have reached the bunker by now. We don't stand a chance against–"

I only realised what I did when Juliet slapped me across the face.

"How could you!" she shouted, looking at Brock lying at our feet. "He's the gunner!"

"I'm not an idiot."

She shook her head and knelt beside Brock. "He's out cold." She glared up at me. "You should work on your anger!"

I scratched my head. "You stayed the same colour through all this?"

Juliet rose to her feet. "What are you talking about?"

The flying machine rocked as something hit it. I grabbed Juliet before she fell. She was so light, almost weightless, and she smelt clean, fresh, sweet–

"You can put me down now," she scowled.

"Wayne!" Joshua screamed as the flying machine rocked once again.

I lowered Juliet to the floor. "What's a gunner?"

"Fritz needs to fly, so you're looking at one." She shoved me to the side. "Strap yourself in and look after your brother."

I ran to Joshua and knelt in front of him. "Hold on to it." I wrapped his arms tighter around the teddy. "You must give it a name."

"I did."

"What?"

"Malik."

The name sound familiar. "That's a strange name for a teddy bear."

He shrugged. "I know, but it felt right."

"Dammit!" Juliet yelled from the back. "Brock is one of the best! You are an idiot!"

"Keep Malik safe," I said and ran to the back.

I grabbed hold of a strap dangling from the roof as the flying machine shook. Juliet slammed a button, and a door slid open, revealing a small room encased in glass with two chairs.

"I told you to strap yourself in!" Juliet punched me hard in the chest.

"Here are two chairs."

Juliet threw her hands in the air. "Strap yourself in and don't fucking touch anything!" She removed one helmet from the wall, climbed into the left chair, and secured the straps.

I plucked the other helmet from the wall and jumped into the right seat.

Juliet grabbed the stick between her legs and pressed a button on her helmet. A piece of glass fell from the top and covered her face.

I mimicked her every movement. "Wow." I saw everything as the glass covered my face, the red horizon, the mountains to my right – nothing blocked my view. In the centre of my screen was a green circle with a cross rushing from side to side. The Sweeper was the shape of an arrow, shiny as one too – beautiful. One sweeper broke formation, flying low over the barren earth toward two running specs. It returned to its formation after a flash from its wings and an explosion of sand and fire.

That could have been Joshua and me, I thought as a cloud of dust crept up in the windless sky.

Juliet paid no attention to me as she was too busy pushing and yanking at the stick between her legs. I found it weirdly mesmerising.

Fritz's voice exploded in my helmet. "What the fock are you doing, Brock? You are acting like a maggot! Shoot the fockers!"

"Brock is out cold! I'm trying to get them in my sights!" Juliet pressed the red button on the stick.

I gasped with excitement as the big gun below the glass floor on Juliet's side spewed flames. Glowing bullets, as fast as lightning, arched their way toward the five Sweepers.

"Fuck!" Juliet hit her chair as the bullets bounced off the nose of the Sweeper on the far left.

I noticed the gun below me move as I looked down at my stick. It followed me as I quickly glanced right, then left. Wow! I looked up, but although I couldn't see it move, I felt it knock against the glass floor.

Knock... knock... knock... knock... knock.

"Stop that!" Juliet almost burst my eardrums.

"Stop what?" Fritz asked.

"Not you! The child in the chair next to me."

"The big one or the small one?"

"Big one."

"Are you nuts? Get him out of there!"

"You come and get the three-hundred-pound gorilla out of it."

For a long moment, I could only hear the guns firing.

"Don't focking touch anything, Wayne," Fritz hissed in my ears.

The glass covering my face lit up as I grabbed hold of the stick.

"Oh, great." Juliet sighed. "You just told him touch."

I did this before. Impossible, I grew up on a farm. Somehow, when the glass lit up, I knew exactly what to do. The glass is called a visor, displaying targeting, tracking and fire control. The chair and controls were different, but the basics were similar. Did the captain show me how to do it when I was much younger? Did I learn this from grandpa's memory cards?

"Fock!" Fritz nosedived as a volley of rounds slammed into the fuselage above us.

"Target locked," I said as the red circle engulfed the cross.

We were at a thirty-degree angle below my Sweeper, thereby exposing the less armoured underbelly.

"Let go of the stick, damnit." Juliet yelled.

I fired.

My Sweeper's wings folded in like a bird's before exploding into a ball of fire. I'd never experienced such euphoria. I'm living again!

"Yes!" I fist pump.

Juliet stared at me.

"What?"

"It took me eight hours in a simulator to shoot down my first Sweeper."

"And you think I'm the idiot?"

"Well done, babes! Five more fockers to go!" Fritz's strange voice hurt my ears.

"It wasn't me. It was the three-hundred-pound gorilla."

Another explosion rocked the flying machine, engulfing the outside of our glass room in a blanket of fire.

"Shite!" Fritz yelled. "Another direct hit, and we're fried."

Joshua must be scared shitless by now. The Sweepers grew smarter, zigzagging through the darkening sky, almost impossible to hit. Their shape made it worse, as if shooting at an arrow coming straight at you. I lined up one and fired, but the bullets ricocheted off its front.

"Dammit!" Juliet had the same problem.

"Wait!" The memory or dream or something else reminded me.

"What?" Juliet looked at me, fear edged into her beautiful blue eyes. That angered me even more.

"Don't use the targeting system to lock onto the Sweeper. It locks onto the main fuselage. Aim for the centre of the wings."

"But the rounds will also bounce off the wings."

"There is a small opening on either side that funnels airflow to the engine. It's part of the cooling system. At that velocity, if the round hits or enters the cooling duct, it will tear off the wing."

"How the fock do you know that?" Fritz banked right, then left to evade a volley.

"We were looking for a weakness."

"Who is we?" Juliet asked.

"I don't know." I looked into her eyes. "Please, trust me."

Her frown gradually disappeared as she smiled. "Okay."

I readied myself, taking a deep breath, my heart thumping in my chest. "Fritz."

"What!"

"On three, take her up as fast as possible. The air ducts are situated on top of the wings."

The Raptor shuddered.

"What the fuck are you doing in my seat?" Brock yelled behind me.

"Not now!" Juliet warned him.

"Get out!" Brock grabbed me from behind in a chokehold.

"Not now, Brock!" Juliet repeated, wrestling with the joystick.

"Tell ... Fritz," I barely managed.

Juliet glanced at me for a moment. "Fritz, on three, take this baby up."

"Affirmative."

"One."

I pressed the button on my helmet, opening the visor.

"Two."

I twisted my head and sunk my teeth into Brock's neck.

"Three!"

Brock released his grip, grabbing at his neck. "Fucking animal!"

I dropped my visor as the Raptor shot skyward. "We only have a second or two to fire!"

Brock flew past, crashing into the glass wall in front of us. My eyes and heart were about to burst out of my body. I groaned, teeth clenched, still tasting Brock's blood.

The last rays of the sun reflected off the Sweepers' wings, lighting them up as if on fire.

"Fire!" I held my finger on the button, shifting the cross from one Sweeper to the next, aiming at the wings.

"Bastards!" Juliet yelled as her first arrow exploded.

I was already cutting the wings of my third.

"Leave some for me, damnit!" she ordered.

The last Sweeper ascended, following our lead, decreasing the area of concentration. We fired, not releasing the triggers until the fireball disappeared.

"Yes!" Juliet shouted. "Take us home, Fritz!" She reached over and tapped my shoulder. "Seems to me you've got some of your grandfather's blood in you, Wayne Johnson."

Brock's body slid from the glass wall to the floor.

"Brock?" I had to make sure because his eyes were swollen shut.

No response.

"Where were you?" Sadie cried; her face smeared with mascara.

Bryan covered her with a blanket as she stepped out of the gravity hall.

"I'm so sorry, Miss Green, but you were the one who ran away from us."

"But you are the Presidential Guard – you're supposed to find me!"

"My resources were under pressure today with your father. I messed up. Sorry."

"How did you find me?"

"Umm" –he scratched his chin– "it was difficult not to."

Monique ran up to Sadie and embraced her. "I told you he was a dick!"

"Where is this dick?" Bryan said, standing with his hands on his hips, eyeing each person stepping out of the gravity room.

"Let's just go," Sadie said, and grabbed her friend by the arm.

"There he is!" Monique pointed at Ryan as he stepped out.

Bryan turned to Sadie. "Shit, that's Ryan Whitmore."

"So?" Monique shrugged. "Aren't you going to talk to him? Or shoot him?" She pointed at Sadie. "This is the First Fucking Daughter!"

Three armed men dressed in grey suits joined Ryan as he walked to the bar. He glanced at Bryan, smiled, then flipped him the bird.

Monique gasped, placing a hand on her hip. "Look at that. Please shoot him." She flipped him back the bird.

Ryan stopped in his tracks, glaring.

"Monique!" Bryan covered her middle finger with his hand, lowering her arm. "Sorry, but if I don't do it now, he will make us all pay."

"What?" Sadie said, still wiping black tears.

He slapped Monique across the face with such force, she fell to her knees.

"What the fuck!" Monique looked up at Bryan, bewildered, clutching her cheek.

The crowd scurried away as if Bryan had dropped a stink bomb. All grabbed their Dome communicators, filming the shocked girl on the floor.

Ryan gave a smiling nod and proceeded to the bar.

"Let's go, Sadie." Bryan grabbed her by the arm. "Sorry, Monique," he said before ushering the First Daughter through the voyeuristic crowd.

"Your father gave me the authorisation to implant your tracer tomorrow," Bryan said.

Sadie stopped. "I won't take it – my dad promised my mom before she died."

"Everyone in the Dome receives it at birth," he said, guiding her toward the exit. "I don't know how you pulled it off until now."

Comet Halley inched its way across the shimmering night sky, skimming Orion's belt on its way to Sirius. Way past midnight already. Dawn only breaks when Halley rammed the arse of Leo, the time Sadie turned off her bedroom light. She kept her eyes on Sirius as Bryan led her down the stairs toward her father's limo. Sadie tore her eyes from the brightest light in the night sky when she heard the laughter below. People gathered in the streets, pointing at the surrounding skyscrapers.

"What's going on?" Sadie whispered.

Bryan attempted to cover her face. "Just get in the car!"

"No!" Sadie screamed. Her half-naked body was on display against the towering glass buildings. Her shame had replaced her father's triumphant moment. The naked truth of our President's daughter scrolled across the screens as she grappled with gravity – clawing at nothing, like a poisoned spider.

"We are working on it. Somebody hacked the system," Bryan said.

Someone in the crowd pointed. "There she is!"

"Let's go." Bryan grabbed Sadie and rushed her down the stairs. The Presidential Guard formed a tight barrier around the limo. "Get in!" Bryan placed his hand on her head as he shoved her into the vehicle and slammed the door shut.

The mocking mob broke through the barrier, chanting: "Take it off! Take it off!"

Sadie screamed as the crowd reached the limousine. She leapt from her seat, leaving the blanket behind, and crawled through the narrow opening into the driver's seat. "Lock doors. Autonomous. Presidential home!"

The limousine rose from the ground. "Pedestrians blocking the road, unable to comply." The limo rocked from side to side as the crowd swarmed.

A man leapt onto the hood. "You want some of this!" He unzipped his pants, pressing his genitalia against the windscreen.

"Switch to manual!" she cried.

Bryan reached the driver's side door and placed his palm against the window.

The glass flashed red.

"Engaging seatbelt," the voice notified.

"Just hurry!" Sadie let go of the steering wheel, allowing the straps to lock into place.

"O-pen the door!" Bryan yelled, slapping the window with each syllable. The glass lit up a brighter red with each syllable.

The limousine pulled away, forcing a path through the crowd. Sadie stepped on the accelerator as soon as she'd cleared the mayhem. The powerful thorium engine sped up to sixty miles an hour in under two seconds. The man on the windscreen hung on, shouting, "Stop the car, bitch!"

"Okay," she seethed through gritted teeth and slammed on the breaks, the safety straps pulled her into the seat as the limo nosedived to an immediate stop. The man flew off the windscreen as if sucked from an airlock. She covered her mouth, shocked, as the man crashed into a billboard. Sparks shot from the sign as the man shook from the power raging through his body. Stunned onlookers watched as the man's charred body fell to the ground, communicators in hand. "She killed a citizen!"

Sadie sped away, sobbing, "Call Charles Green!"

The President's dishevelled image appeared on the windscreen. His bloodshot eyes and unkempt hair filled half the image.

"Dad!" she cried, tears flowing.

"My baby," he slurred. "Everything I worked for... everything your mother fought for... means nothing... I'm nothing. I thought I could make things right."

"I'll make it right! Please, Dad... I'm so, so sorry!"

"There's... nothing you can do, baby... nothing. President Green,"-he snorted- "no... Charles Green, over and out." He gave a rolling wave.

"No!" Sadie said as her father's image disappeared. "I'm sorry, Daddy," she whispered.

Sadie almost lost control as flashing lights and sirens erupted behind the limousine. She veered across the road, side-swiping a food dispenser, biscuits and green powder exploding over the windscreen.

Bryan appeared in the windshield. "Pull to the side of the road. We will sort this out, Sadie."

"I can't go back," she said. "I've destroyed everything my mother and father worked for."

"You're three klicks from the Dome perimeter! Stop the vehicle! The shield will incinerate you!"

Sadie regained her composure, hands tightening around the steering wheel. "This is the best way," she said, her voice steady. "Disconnect call."

"No! Sadie–" Bryan flickered away.

***

Supreme Commander Whitmore rose from her knees beside her bed. She placed a hand on her wheezing chest. Since smoking that blasted cigar, a worrying tightness gripped her lungs. She approached the window of her penthouse suite in Building Seven, glaring at Sadie Green's image projected on the building passing by. The poor girl's struggle bombarded Whitmore the entire three hundred and sixty degrees. She had even searched for a struggle-free zone of the city. She could then activate the emergency stop. But the shameful image of the woman in pain surrounded her the entire rotation. Maybe that exasperated the tightness.

"Incoming call from Captain Bryan," a female's voice echoed through her apartment.

She turned away with a shake of her head. "Accept."

A statue of a white phoenix on top of a marble fireplace projected a hologram image of him. "I apologise for contacting you, Supreme Commander, but we have a situation."

"I know!" she snapped. "It's difficult not to notice."

"Not that, Commander, but we are working on the—"

"What situation then?"

"Well, it's an escalation of the situation staring you in the face, Commander. Sadie Green is in control of the President's limousine and is heading for the Dome's perimeter. She's extremely distraught."

Whitmore stared at the hologram for a moment. "Can you stop her?"

"It will be difficult. The Presidential limo is designed to withstand—"

"Will she do it?"

"I believe so, Commander."

Whitmore turned back to Sadie's image. "You want me to authorise a window?"

"Yes, Commander. I believe she'll come to her senses and return to the Dome. She's got nowhere to go."

She turned back to the hologram. "You know the rules, Commander, no one leaves the Nirvana. No one."

"I know, Commander, but this isn't just anyone."

"What if she falls into the wrong hands, or the Sweepers get her?"

"Commander!" Bryan snapped. "She's five hundred metres from the Dome wall. If she dies, her father would be useless to you." He raised his chin, glaring. "And guess who caused all of this? Who humiliated her like this? Your son!"

The limousine sped toward the perimeter, trailed by flashing lights and whining sirens. Sadie closed her eyes. "I'm sorry, Mother."

"Perimeter detected," the voice warned. "Three hundred metres to impact. Reduce speed. Two hundred metres. One hundred metres. Warning. Fifty metres."

Sadie screamed, her hands tightening around the steering wheel as she barrelled toward her fate.

The sirens ceased.

Sadie frowned, her eyes still shut. Waiting. She ventured a peek.

"Shit!" she shouted, eyes wide. "I'm outside!"

The road turned to dust, dust to stone, stone to rocks. "Optimum height for terrain," Sadie instructed. The limousine elevated above the rugged landscape without slowing. As the distance between her and the Dome increased, so did her fear. But she didn't look back. She kept going, racing toward fate.

<hr>

"Do you like my décor?" Gabriel asked the three naked women sprawled on his polished mahogany king-size bed, its canopy draped with heavy gold and blood-red curtains.

The blonde girl on the left sat up. "It's very" –she looked around the room– "goldy."

Gabriel dropped his heavy velvet robe to the parquet floor, showing off his toned physique. "It's French Napoleon." With a sweeping gesture of his hand and chin raised, he said, "It embodies power, ostentatious richness, sophistication and" –grabbing his testicles– "balls."

"It's a bit over the top for me," the redhead said, lying on her side, propped up on her elbow, hand supporting her head.

"I think it's cool," the brunette on the right said.

Gabriel kneeled next to the bed by the blond girl's side and straightened out her legs. "The itsy-bitsy spider climbed up the stairs to the waterspout," Gabriel sang, finger-walking up the girl's leg.

She laughed. "I don't think that's how it goes."

"Well, that's how mommy played it with me," he said and licked the stairs clean ahead of the spider.

"When's Itsy-bitsy walking our way?" the redhead begged in a girly voice.

The brunette on the far right started finger-walking up the redhead's leg. "We have our own itsy-bitsy spider."

"No!" Gabriel snapped, flicking them with his walking-fingers. "This is the only itsy-bitsy spider!"

"Incoming call from General Steward."

"Damn it!" He slapped the blond girl's thigh. "Accept!"

A gold statue of a woman - lying on her back with legs raised and knees apart – on an eighteenth-century walnut and gold commode gave birth to a hologram of General Steward.

"Yes, General." Gabriel rose and stepped away from the bed.

Steward sighed with a shake of the head. "Do you need time to get dressed?"

Gabriel shrugged. "No."

"Is the room secure?"

Gabriel glanced at the three naked women on the bed. "Yes."

"Do you know who hacked our bloody system yet?"

"Do you know who destroyed six of our fucking Sweepers?" Gabriel fired back.

Steward forced a smile. "I know we're equals, Commander, but–"

"But nothing, General," Gabriel said. "You do your job, and I'll mine. I think the more pressing issue is the destruction of not one" – he held up his middle finger– "but six A-class Sweepers believed to be indestructible. I think a half-naked fat girl plastered against a building is less than an issue. Close your mouldy drapes if she's not your type."

"Somebody hacked your impregnable firewall," General Steward smirked.

Gabriel ran his fingers through his gelled hair. "Where's Commander Von Swartz?"

Steward averted his eyes. "I sent him after Sadie."

Gabriel frowned. "That's strange. He left the Dome before her."

"I wish you would show as much balls in front of Whitmore as you are flaunting now."

Gabriel laughed, throwing his head back, "Balls and brains, General, balls and brains." He turned away. "Disconnect."

General Steward's image flickered and disappeared.

"Where were we?" Gabriel rubbed his hands together and walked over to the bed.

"Who was that?" the blonde girl asked.

"Who?" Gabriel frowned. "I didn't talk to anyone."

He grabbed the girl by her locks and pulled her head back. "You know the rules, no questions. I'll do my job, and you do yours."

The girl whimpered.

"She's new, Gabriel," the redhead pleaded. "She didn't know."

He released his grip and walked over to a burgundy chaise lounge. "Fine," he said and slumped onto the couch. "Her punishment will be up to you two."

"What do you mean?" the blonde sat up.

"A steak and bottle of red wine for the one who beats her unconscious."

The two girls glanced at each other, then scanned the room. Blondie rose to her feet, backing away. The redhead focused on it first. A butterfly encapsulated in a resin ball the size of her fist. She leapt to her feet, grabbed it from its gold pedestal, and attacked.

"Angel, no!" the blonde yelled, cowering in a corner.

The first blow struck her on the elbow, the second on the temple. The brunette joined the attack on the gold pedestal.

Gabriel sat up, beaming. "Yes," he hissed. His excitement grew with each blow.

"She's mine!" Angel screamed and hit the brunette in the face with the resin ball. The pedestal slipped from her hand as she stumbled away. The second blow struck her behind the head, sending her face-first through a glass-top coffee table. Angel dropped the blood-stained resin ball to the parquet floor and turned to Gabriel, heaving.

"I assume you're not vegan," he smirked.

"I don't like to share," she said through gritted teeth.

"Silly question, but do you like your steak medium or rare?"

5

The rest of our journey to the resistance's stronghold went smoothly. Joshua slept, using his teddy bear as a pillow. I had to carry Brock's big ass back to his seat. Juliet sat up front with the pilot. Fritz had flown the plane all by himself when the Sweepers attacked, so I didn't know why she sat upfront all the time. She told me to clean my teeth with the laser brush and use the steamer, figured she kept her distance until I'm done. Like mom asked every morning, "Did you brush your teeth?" Every dreaded dawn.

The laser brush worked well. My teeth shined like Darius', and it removed the taste of Brock in my mouth. Mother was wrong. Revenge tasted sweet.

"Shit," I gasped as steam burst through the vents. Wow! Every inch of my body tingled. My skin resembled that of a plucked chicken. I hated the farm even more, what else was I deprived of? It was the first moment I had to myself since the coward blew his head off. Why did he kill himself? Did he mean what he said? He couldn't watch us starve to death. Perhaps Joshua, but not me. What's so dangerous about Nirvana? The Sweepers seemed so familiar. How did I know what to do? Searching for my earliest memories was like hunting for a wild animal in a sandstorm – an unclear glimpse washed away by doubt. The questions haunted me as the last remnants of the farm washed away.

"So, how was it?" Juliet asked from behind the door.

"Not bad," I muttered. "Hand me a towel or something."

"A towel? Press the blue button."

Hot air filled the cubicle, drying me in under five seconds.

"I still need a towel."

She giggled. "You shy, Wayne Junior?"

"Just Wayne." I waited, listening. "Juliet? Juliet!" I pressed the button, and the door slid open. She stood with a satisfied grin, her sky-blue eyes studying every inch of my body.

"Not just a pretty face. Just, Wayne, it is."

I wanted to cover myself, but for whatever reason, did not. My ears and face were on fire.

She stepped toward me.

I stepped back.

Why is she doing this? I covered myself with my hands. The tingling feeling returned. I wasn't angry, so why was my heart working its way up my throat?

"Take it easy, Wayne," she said, still with the grin. "I just wanted to know." She turned and walked away. "There's a uniform on the bed." She turned back and looked at my cupped hands. "Should be a tight fit." She winked. "I'll leave you to it."

What does she mean?

"Can I have a suit like that?" Joshua asked as he stepped out of the steamer.

"No, it's not for kids," I said and pointed at his filthy clothes scattered on the floor.

"But they're smelly and dirty and–"

"So?" I shrugged. "It was like that at the farm, and you never complained."

"I couldn't complain," he whispered, chin trembling.

"Suck it up, princess," I said and produced a uniform from behind my back. "It will adjust to your size and keep you cool. Awesome, right?"

The chin kept trembling. "Why are you so mean to me?"

"It was a joke."

"You're just like Dad."

"I'm not like him!" I yelled and threw the uniform at him. My heart was in my throat again.

"You are!" His little fists clenched.

I stormed toward him; my right hand raised.

"Wayne!" Juliet shouted, her voice echoing through the Raptor. She stood in the doorway, glaring.

Joshua stood defiantly, staring at my raised hand. "You are."

I lowered my hand and walked toward Juliet. "I'll never hit him. I wanted to scare him."

"What's the difference?" she said as I pushed past her.

"This!" I snapped, pointing at my scar. "I'm not like my fucking father."

She grabbed me by the arm as I walked away. "Then don't be like him."

"You saw the rest of my scars?" I glanced at Joshua, where he still stood, buck naked, glaring at me. "Look at him, perfect. He had it easy."

Juliet released her grip.

"Get dressed," I ordered my brother, and walked off. "And watch out for the zipper. You're not wearing underpants."

The Vortex glider settled fifty metres from the Johnson farmhouse.

"Lights off," Darius instructed the computer.

The full moon illuminated the farmhouse and surrounding desert as if covered in snow. Darius was six when he last played in the snow. His father fetched him from school and flew him hundreds of miles North to the last area covered in snow. That day, his father wasn't a general, he was much more. They build snowmen, had a snowball fight, and made snow angels. A snow angel made by a General – that was a sight, also the fifth anniversary of his mother's passing. The following day, his father turned into a grieving, vengeful husband. He blew himself up, taking with the CEO and board of directors of a pharmaceutical company – setting in motion a chain of events that had changed the course of human history.

"Any signs of life?" Darius asked the computer.

"Negative."

"Damn it!" He hit the steering wheel. "Search area one square kilometre for DNA strain, Johnson."

A small drone detached from the Vortex and shot into the moonlit sky.

"On screen."

The windscreen lit up with a blue grid, displaying an aerial view of the farm and surrounding area. The blocks lit up in red, one after the other, until a green block appeared over the farmhouse.

"There must be Johnson DNA within the farmhouse, but investigate."

"Affirmative."

The drone ascended and circled the farmhouse until it detected an open door.

"Activate light and enter," Darius instructed, eyes pinned on the windscreen. Light flooded the house as the drone entered, casting deep shadows as it investigated the scene.

Darius shook his head at the wretched living conditions, the flaking walls, empty shelves, and barren floors. "Enter to the left."

The drone turned, illuminating the room. The only evidence of this being a bedroom was the rolled-up blanket and pillow in the corner. A small section of the windscreen flashed green.

"Identify."

"Captain Wayne Johnson."

"Magnify."

"What the hell?" Captain Johnson's thumb lay on the floor in front of the cupboard. Darius' frown wrinkled out. "Show me the inside of the cupboard." He nodded as he saw the open safe. "You won't be able to access it, Wayne." He reclined. "Search the house for Captain Howard Johnson. Wait!" Darius noticed something in the cupboard. "What is that?" He leaned forward and pressed the windscreen.

"A whip, a strip of leather fastened to a handle, used for beating a person or urging on an animal, according to the Oxford English Dictionary."

"Whose blood is that on the whip?"

"The DNA matches the Johnson family strain."

"Is it from the same DNA strain received today on my calling card?"

"Affirmative. A hundred percent match."

Darius shook his head. "What happened to you, Howard? It is not the Johnson way."

"Match the strain to Wayne Johnson."

"Negative. General Wayne Johnson is already in my database and is not a hundred percent match."

Darius rolled his eyes. "I mean, save the strain received today as Wayne Johnson Junior."

"Affirmative."

"Proceed with DNA search of Captain Howard Johnson."

The drone exited the room into the lounge. The windscreen lit up green as the drone entered the kitchen.

"DNA match for Captain Howard Johnson," the voice confirmed.

"No shit," Darius whispered. "It's all over the room."

The drone stopped and hovered above a covered body.

"Is... is it the body of," he swallowed, "Howard Johnson?"

"Affirmative."

Darius closed his eyes. "I hope you are finally at peace my-"

"Incoming call from Captain Bryan Young."

Darius scratched his temple. "Accept."

"This is a secure call, Commander. We've got a situation."

"Proceed, Captain."

"It's the President's daughter, sir. She fled the Dome."

Darius frowned. "Nobody can flee the Dome, Captain. Somebody had to open a window for her."

"She attempted suicide by crashing into the Dome perimeter, but I convinced Commander Whitmore to open a window."

"Sadie was your responsibility, Captain," Darius said. "First the Gravity Room fuckup and now this!"

"I take full responsibility, Commander." Bryan looked down at the dashboard.

"Where is she now?"

"She's not tagged, Commander, but she escaped in the Presidential limo–"

Darius sat up. "The Presidential limo! How did she manage that?"

"Well, uh–"

"Never mind! Where is she now?"

"Thirty kilometres west of the Dome, twenty kilometres east of your location."

"So, I must sit tight, and she will find me."

"Affirmative, Commander, but I will upload the limo's tracking codes into your system."

"Very well. And Captain?"

"Yes, Commander."

"How did you know my location? I'm off the grid."

Bryan smiled. "Stacey tracked your heat signature. She owed me a favour."

"Seems to me Stacey owes a lot to many – going to have a word with her."

"Don't worry, Commander. The Council doesn't know your location." Bryan grinned. "Your secret is safe with me."

"That's what worries me," he said while disconnecting the call. "I don't enjoy owing favours."

"We're here," Juliet said as she stepped out of the cockpit.

It was the first time she'd said anything since my last outburst. Joshua was also ignoring me, following Juliet around like something freshly baked. Brock had regained consciousness. I kept my eye on him most of the time because I could sense he didn't like me either.

"Where's here?" I asked.

"You'll see in a moment," she muttered.

The monotonous sandy landscape or dead land as Captain called it made way for the mountain range I'd always longed for on the horizon. It was as I imagined it – captivating. Living. Different. Mother described the mountains as mesmerising and dangerous, like fire. The full moon lit up the peaks with a hundred shades of grey, like a frozen claw reaching for the stars.

My stomach wedged between my lungs as the Raptor descended. Joshua! I sprinted into the cockpit. He sat strapped in next to Fritz, eyes fixed on the lights and controls. Fritz wasn't wearing his mask. Strange-looking guy – words and pictures painted on his arms and neck. What bothered me most was the lonely streak of red hair in the centre of his shaved head.

"Scarface, the man of the hour," Fritz said in his strange accent. "Glad you could join us, laddie."

"I don't like it when you call him that," Joshua said, glaring at the pilot.

Fritz made eyes at me. "You better get used to it, lad. I told everyone bout yer brother, Scarface. He's a hero, destroying five focking Sweepers and that he's grandson of General Johnson. There will probably be a thousand fockers waiting for us."

"Why did you do that?" I snapped.

Fritz frowned. "What's the problem, lad?"

"I'm not a fucking hero! I'm just... just a farm boy. All those people–"

"We've never been around many people," Joshua interrupted.

Fritz smiled. "I don't know what yer afraid of. Yer built like a focking tank."

My heart started up again. It must be the small cockpit. I turned and bumped into Juliet.

"It wasn't five Sweepers, Fritz," she said, our eyes locked. "It was four and a half."

"She's lying," I said. "Juliet shot down all of them."

"Is that true, las?" Fritz smirked.

Juliet squeezed past me. "No, I'm just jealous." She wrapped her arms around Fritz and kissed him on the painted cross on his neck. "Can't wait to sleep in our own bed tonight."

I left; angered at what I saw. What was she trying in the bathroom if she already had a mate? A challenge popped into my head. He won't stand a chance. When I'm done with him, I will wipe my arse with that red strip of hair. I'll skin him alive and use his painted hide as a rug. I froze, shocked by my disturbing thoughts. I needed to be careful with them – women. They were as dangerous and unpredictable as the Sweepers out there. They stirred up such anger. Never let your guard down with them.

"Juliet told me what you did."

I heard Brock's voice as I glared at my brother's teddy bear. Brock was awake, slumped forward with his head in his hands. I clenched my fists, waiting for his next move.

"Sorry, I could have killed us all," he whispered.

"I was in your seat." I took a seat across from him.

Brock stuck out a trembling hand. "Let's start over," he said, looking at me through swollen eyes.

I hesitated. It was like trusting a snake begging you to pull its rotten tooth.

"It's okay, I promise," he said.

I reached over and shook his hand. "I'm not an idiot."

Brock smiled. "You made that clear." His eyes narrowed. "You're a strong boy – I usually win the fights. How old are you? You're not even shaving yet."

"Almost eighteen."

Brock frowned. "Shit."

"Where are we going?" I asked.

"Go look," he said, pointing at the cockpit.

I hesitated; perhaps Juliet was still kissing that painted asshole.

"Go! You will miss it."

I went back, against my will, and stood in the doorway. Juliet knelt next to Joshua, explaining to him what some controls did.

"You see the mountain in front of you?" I tapped Fritz's shoulder.

"Where?" Fritz asked.

"Don't joke with him!" Juliet warned. "He will knock you out and take over the controls."

"Don't worry, lad, I've done this a million times," Fritz said, flipping switches and pushing buttons. "Raptor One, in the slide, request clearance to" –he glanced at Juliet– "penetrate."

She shook her head while talking and pointing at the lights.

"Raptor One cleared for landing," a male voice responded. "Opening the barn door. You've got thirty seconds."

A horizontal slither of light appeared in the centre of the rock face, growing larger and larger. The Raptor sped up toward the light.

"Twenty seconds," the male voice said. Running green lights invited us in. "Ten seconds." The Raptor entered the tunnel and slowed. "Closing barn doors."

We went ahead until entering an enormous hangar lined with Raptors and other flying machines, some smaller, others bigger. People dressed in grimy red uniforms scurried around, carrying and pushing stuff. We were inside the mountain.

"Wow," Joshua whispered.

"Trust me, after a while, it feels like a tomb," Brock said.

I could feel his breath on the back of my neck. He could have knocked me out, but he didn't.

Fritz set the Raptor down next to another Raptor. "Raptor One, shutting down." He flipped switches above his head.

Joshua kept a close eye on Fritz's every movement.

A bunch of men in red uniforms approached, pushing a cage.

"Opening cargo doors and lowering ramp," Juliet said.

The Raptor shuddered while Fritz turned off the cockpit lights. "Bravo Zulu," he said with a flick of the fingers.

We exited the Raptor via the ramp. The red uniforms herded cattle and a few sheep into the crate. A bald, overweight man with a bushy moustache waited for us at the end of the ramp.

"That's Minister Buchanan," Brock whispered in my ear. "He's in charge of food collection and distribution. Be careful."

"Six cows, four sheep, and a cat," Buchanan barked, hands raised. "After six weeks?"

"A cat?" Joshua whispered.

"Just remember, those two are mine." I pointed at Emma and Fiona.

Buchanan's demeanour changed. "Of course, Mr Johnson." He smiled. "I will keep them in a safe place for you. But first, we allow no weapons." He glared at Grandpa's shotgun.

"The cat!" My brother ran down the ramp and followed the crate.

Buchanan lunged for him but missed. "Get him!" he ordered Fritz. "He will get lost."

"Joshua!" I yelled.

He stopped in his tracks and watched, shoulders slumped, as the crate disappeared into an unlit corridor.

"Don't touch my brother again," I warned.

Buchanan glanced at Brock. "What happened to you?"

"I touched him." Brock pointed at me and sauntered down the ramp.

"Is that a bite mark?" Buchanan squinted at Brock's neck.

"Yep."

"You better have that looked at – doesn't look good."

"Since when do you care?" Brock muttered.

"The shotgun, Mr Johnson," Buchanan said, holding out his hand.

I hid the gun behind my back. "Come and get it."

Buchanan's beady eyes narrowed. All froze as if captured in a paused image of a memory card. Then his bushy moustache lengthened as he smiled. "Very well." The smile didn't reach his eyes.

"Very well," I said.

"Follow me." Buchanan turned and headed for the corridor. "The General is waiting."

"Aren't you coming?" I asked Juliet.

The Raptor team looked at me with almost the same look Joshua gave the crate before it disappeared.

Juliet shook her head. "We will see you later."

"Well, later than." I shrugged and took Joshua by the hand. Something stinks, the way they looked at me, the way Buchanan reacted to my brother and my shotgun. I knelt and whispered in my brother's ear, "When I say run, you run and find Juliet. I will find you."

"Come, Mr Johnson," Buchanan called from the edge of the corridor.

I glanced at my brother, then at Juliet. She gave the nod. We followed him down the corridor and into another chamber filled with holes or caves. The smell overwhelmed even me. Joshua cupped his mouth and nose. Wooden staircases ascended the chamber from all angles, linking the caves like a spider's web. People dressed in filthy rags stumbled about as if four breaths from dead.

"Bad, I know," Buchanan said as he noticed Joshua's cupped hand. "Don't worry, we vent this section at midnight." He pointed at the enormous blades attached to the roof high above. "This is the inner part of our commune, so not much ventilation." He stepped over the body of an old man - such a small ration of meat would have angered the vultures.

"Only good for blood and bone meal," I whispered, shaking my head.

A woman sat next to the body, dazed, staring into nothingness. "We can only open the roof once a day for a minute, you know, to avoid being detected. This is also the section where we house the non-essentials."

Joshua knelt by the dead body.

"Don't touch him!" Buchanan said.

My brother looked at me, eyes wide. "He looks dead."

"I fucking hope so," I said. "If I'm that far gone, shoot me."

Buchanan nodded.

My brother's chin started up again.

"We all die one day, son," Buchanan said with a wave of the hand. "Don't worry. The cleaners come by every hour to remove the bodies and that." He pointed at a row of buckets.

"What's that?" Joshua whispered.

"Shit," I said. "What do you do with all the dead?"

"Everything gets recycled. Nothing goes to waste. The buckets are a sign if they get enough food – too many buckets, too much food. I try to minimise the buckets, if you know what I mean." He winked.

Joshua placed his hand on the woman's shoulder and whispered, "I'm sorry."

Her eyes flickered alive, and she smiled at him. I pulled him away before she could touch his face with her filthy hands. I didn't know why, because we looked and smelled the same a few hours ago. The only difference: these people gave up, and it might rub off.

"Did you see her face?" Joshua whispered as we snaked through the non-essentials. "I think she'll be fine."

Mom told him the crazy story that the paths tears made on a dirty face were when an angel had wiped it away. His angel pissed me off, visiting him so many times. Angels were afraid of me, except this afternoon – they caught me off guard.

It took my eyes a moment to adjust to the lit corridor. At the end stood two guards with heavy weapons, guarding a steel door.

"If you don't wear one of these" –Buchanan tapped a small shiny pin on his shirt pocket– "the force field will incinerate you."

"Force field? Where?"

He stopped two metres in front of the two guards and glanced over his shoulder. "You don't have one of these, so we need to disable it." He nodded at the guard, who pressed his thumb on a glass plate next to the heavy door. The section in front of Buchanan flickered blue, then disappeared.

"Hurry, you've got ten seconds."

I took Joshua's hand, and we walked through the invisible wall.

"Watch this," Buchanan said as the force field re-activated. He removed a piece of paper from his pocket and threw it at the force field. The invisible wall flickered blue as the paper burst into flames.

"This way." The heavy door slid open, revealing another chamber. The white walls were in stark contrast to the stone walls of the first chamber. Steel stairs and bridges linked living quarters and work areas. Clean people in white uniforms walked with purpose; rapid-paced, upright and chins raised – another stark contrast. There were no angels here.

We followed him through the chamber to another lit corridor, waiting for the invisible wall to disappear, and entered a similar chamber. People in black uniforms - like mine – occupied the hall. One section had a man screaming at a group of people, ordering them to run and crawl and climb walls. The man must be powerful for them to do stupid things like that.

"That is Captain Koonz." Buchanan pointed at the screaming man. "He oversees training. Watch out for him." He glanced over his shoulder. "And never look him in the eye."

A group of soldiers leaned against a railing, laughing.

"Another minute, and you could be part of our team," one soldier said.

"I-I c-c-can't!" A man tried to scream, but the words stuck to his throat.

"Come on, we've all done it. I tell you what, if you can say a sentence without stuttering, we'll pick you up."

The rest of the group burst out laughing.

Koonz looked up, stared at the commotion for a moment, then turned back to his training.

A small soldier, about half my size, dangled from the railing, fingers slipping.

"Please help him," Joshua whispered, squeezing my hand.

"This way." Buchanan pointed.

"But his death will have a purpose in this place," I replied. "There's no place for weakness." I started following Buchanan.

"Then what are you doing here?" He let go of my hand. "Shouldn't the powerful look after the weak? Isn't that your purpose?"

"P-p-please!"

"Only thirty more seconds!" A soldier mocked.

"What if I was hanging on and you weren't there?" The little shit fired back, flushed with anger. "And someone strong stood by and waited for my death to have a purpose."

I scratched my head. Fuck!

"Mr Johnson," Buchanan called.

Joshua smiled as I walked past him. I grabbed the soldier in the centre by his collar, yanked him away from the fence, and grabbed the little soldier's arm the moment he lost his grip.

"T-t-thank y-y-you," he said as I hoisted him over the railing.

The other soldiers stepped away, hands raised, staring at their buddy lying at Buchanan's feet twenty meters away.

Boots dangling, I held him up with one hand, studying the small man. He was skinnier and paler than the other cave dwellers. And about my age. "What is that?" I pointed at the red spots on his face.

"P-p-pimples."

"Is it contagious?"

"N-n-no."

I lowered him to the floor.

"Thanks," Joshua whispered as I took his hand.

"T-t-thank y-you," the small man repeated.

Buchanan stared at the man lying at his boots as we joined him.

"Is he alive?" I asked.

"He's breathing."

"He was also weak," I told my brother.

"Ye, but he was a bad weak."

I shook my head. "Let's go."

We stopped in front of a steel door guarded by two men.

"Wait here for General Ross." Buchanan stepped aside as the door slid open.

I ducked and entered the room.

"Wow," Joshua said. "Look at the bed."

The room was small, all white and clean, with a toilet, basin, and bed. A mirror covered the entire wall in front of us. What wowed Joshua were the clean white sheets.

He jumped around as the door slammed shut.

I closed my eyes. "Shit."

The mirror changed into a window, revealing a row of people - some dressed in black, some in white, and one in a brown uniform like my father had in his cupboard – this uniform had fewer medals, though.

"They look like us," the old man in brown said as he stepped forward. "What have we learned?"

"They are strong, General Ross, aggressive and analytical," Juliet said as she stepped into view.

"Ouch, you're hurting my hand," Joshua whispered.

"Sorry," I said through gritted teeth and let go, glaring at Juliet.

She continued, "The most disturbing fact is that they are natural fighters. He learned the firing and targeting systems in a matter of seconds and destroyed five Sweepers in under five minutes."

General Ross gave a nod. "And you're sure he had no previous experience?"

"Somehow, he knew about the Sweepers' weakness, but he could have learnt that from his father."

"What are they doing?" Joshua whispered.

"They have the same reproductive organs as humans." Juliet glanced at me. "Much bigger, though. As everyone knows, I have experience."

The General rolled his eyes.

"And they get aroused – just like us." She approached the glass. "And they get jealous,"–our eyes locked– "just like us." She turned away and continued. "What also makes them a formidable enemy is they never give up. Joshua, the younger one, told me the human father had beaten the older one frequently."

I glared at Joshua.

Juliet turned back to me. "He would refuse to go down or break. In fact, he hated his father more for committing suicide than for the abuse he inflicted on him."

"Why did you tell her all this?" I seethed.

"Sorry, Wayne, I-I thought she was a friend."

I felt as naked as when the door of the steamer opened.

"The son of General Johnson must have loved the alien woman?" the General said. "He gave up his life when he freed her and fled the compound to live in such conditions. Surely he must love their offspring?"

"This only started after they took the mother. As Joshua said, the beams took her. This was also when Wayne changed, according to his brother."

"In what way?" an old woman in white asked.

"It's like puberty in a human child, but what they become is very disturbing."

I took a seat on the bed, burying my head in my hands.

"Sorry," Joshua whispered.

"He would become like a wild animal, kill livestock with his bare hands and devour the raw flesh. His father would then attempt to control him, try to stop him from slaughtering more of their precious livestock."

"God help us," General Ross whispered.

"After his feeding frenzy, he could go weeks, even months, without food."

"Do they eat human flesh?" General Ross glared at me with open disdain.

"I don't know," Juliet said. "Ask the little one."

General Ross bowed to Joshua's height. "Tell me, boy, has your brother ever killed and eaten a man as he did with the cows?"

My brother stared at the old man.

"Don't worry," Juliet joined in. "Tell the General. He will give your brother something to make him never do it again. He won't be angry ever again."

I heard the gasps as my brother nodded. "Mom told me she saw Wayne kill and eat a man. And that I must never do a bad thing like that. She never told Wayne she saw him because she was afraid of him."

"Start the tests." Ross straightened and turned to an old woman with purple hair. "Find their weakness."

"But, General, the plan was to negotiate with them," Juliet said. "He can communicate with them. Contact his mother."

General frowned. "If they meant anything to their mother, she would have taken them with or came back for them. They feel no love or compassion. She left them behind like they were nothing."

"He's our only hope!" Juliet said, her voice strained. "We can't fight them!" She pointed at me. "On every level, they are more advanced. Imagine how deadly the ones are trained to kill? He's a child."

General Ross slammed his fist against the window. "Enough! Then join the cowards in the Dome!"

"I'm not a coward," Juliet seethed. "We can't win this fight."

What am I? I looked down at my brother, but he wasn't there. I peeked under the bed and found him curled up, wasting more water. He was more human than I was. The things I'd seen in chamber one, what humans did to each other. Did I want to be human?

"You heard that maybe mother is not like the dead cows outside," I said, still seated on the bed, watching the humans on the other side debate my fate – and theirs.

"Why did she leave us?" Joshua said, sniffing, peeking from underneath the bed. "Why didn't she come back?"

"Is that why you're pissing through your eyes?"

"Yes, no... yes," he flipped-flopped.

"Don't worry. I also don't know how to feel."

He shifted toward me and whispered, "I'm sorry for talking about you, but I had to."

"Don't worry, at least now I know I'm not all crazy."

"What are we?"

"From what I've heard and seen, better than humans."

The fighting died down on the other side of the window.

"We're stronger. We don't give up, and most important of all, we stand together." I stuck my hand out and waited for my brother. He accepted it with a smile.

"And that's why they're going to lose the fight," I said, glaring at the static row of humans. Their eyes filled with fear.

"Now that I've got your attention, I killed the human, ripped him apart with my bare hands" –I smiled, revealing my fangs– "but I did not eat him, you taste like rats, and I don't like rats," I lied.

General Ross looked at Juliet with a shocked expression.

"That's why he never smiles," Juliet whispered.

"It's not just our balls that's bigger."

6

"Fuel cell low." A female voice broke the silence. "Activating reserve cell."

Sadie maintained speed; eyes pinned on the two beams of lights piercing the darkness. As she glanced at the time – 19:09 – two lights appeared in the rear-view mirror. Her bare foot pushed down on the accelerator.

"Incoming call from Commander Darius Von Swartz."

"Cancel call!" Sadie said.

Darius appeared in the centre of the windscreen. "I'm here whether or not you like it, Miss Green."

"What do you want?"

"You late for another party?"

"Leave me alone!" Sadie yelled at the windscreen.

"Running away, never–"

"Oh, shut up!"

"Watch out!"

"Shit!" Sadie jerked the wheel to the left, skimming a dead pine tree.

"What amazes me is the driving capabilities of women have never evolved."

"Go stick your amazement up your arse."

"Please activate autonomous mode. Please," he said, without the sarcastic tone.

"Reserve cell at ten percent," the female voice warned.

Darius beamed. "The weight and size of the car deplete a reserve fuel cell faster than a vibrator in a brothel."

"Please leave me alone," Sadie whispered, wiping away tears.

"Autonomous mode activated, emergency shutdown initiated."

The limousine decelerated to earth.

"Emergency safety systems deactivated," the computer warned as the interior of Darius's glider lit up with flashing red lights. "Shut down procedure bypassed."

"I did not allow deactivation!" Darius said, swiping and tapping the touch screen in the centre of the console. "Shit!" he shouted as he looked up and saw the red lights of the limo. He pulled back, but the controls were unresponsive. "Steward, you fucking bastard," he shouted as the Vortex glider ricocheted from the roof of the limo. A split second before crashing into a dead oak, Darius grabbed hold of the emergency handle above the window, raised his legs and wedged his feet against the dashboard. The impact split the tree in half, pulverizing the nose of the glider. Warning lights and sirens filled the cockpit as it crashed to the ground. Dust and smoke enveloped the glider as it came to an abrupt stop against a boulder.

Darius groaned. "Activate emergency beacon... and open... doors."

"You have deactivated all emergency safety systems."

Sparks illuminated the cockpit, setting the control unit on fire.

"Shut down fuel cell and open doors!"

"Un-un-unable to comply." Lights blinked on and off as one panel after the other turned off.

Darius kicked at the cracked windshield, screaming as the flames engulfed the cockpit. "Extinguish flames!" he ordered.

"Stay down!" Sadie, wrapped in a blanket, stood by the window, aiming a handgun.

"Shit! No!" Darius covered his head, crouching down.

She fired three shots, picked up a rock, and hurled it through the window.

Darius leapt from the Vector, flames scorching his clothes.

"Run!" he yelled, grabbing Sadie by the arm. "The fuel cell is still active!"

Sparks and flames shot from the wreck, followed by a thunderous explosion. The shock wave charged through the desert, sending them to the ground.

Alarms erupted in the control room as a red dot appeared on the globe.

"What's happening!" General Steward shouted.

A young officer approached, out of breath. "A fuel cell erupted fifty-three clicks west of the Dome, sir. The signature shows it is Commander Von Swartz's Vector, sir."

A faint smile formed as Steward glared at the red dot.

"The Presidential limo was also in the vicinity, sir."

"What? Why did you not tell me that before?" he barked. "What's the status on it?"

"It was immobile, sir. The fuel cell depleted – and then the explosion. We don't know its status."

"A depleted fuel cell can't explode, so something else caused the explosion." Steward sighed, scratching his head. "Okay, send a team."

The officer turned on his heel.

"No, wait. I will handle this myself." Steward waited until the officer was out of earshot and activated his communicator. "Encrypted call." He leaned forward. "Retinal scan." Steward waited for the blue light to scan his left eye. "Voice only," he said. "Is it done, Mr Gray?"

He gave a nod.

"Let me know when you have confirmation. And get Miss Green back to the Dome if she's still alive."

Darius opened his eyes and smiled as he stared at the heavens. "So, I'm dead." His face distorted with pain as he tried to move. "No, I'm still alive."

"What did you say about female drivers?" Sadie said, lying beside him.

"You're the one who stopped dead."

"Ever heard about keeping a safe following distance?"

Darius smiled and turned his head toward her.

"Don't look," she whispered. "I've lost my blanket." She tried to cover herself. "Ah." She threw her hands up. "You've seen it all anyway – someone probably projected my fat body on every building in a galaxy far, far away from here."

"At least you're wearing underwear, and you're not fat."

She placed her hands over her face and whispered, "Not good enough to be displayed on every building."

"So, if you had the body of a model, you would have been okay with it?"

"No! Yes." She sighed, shaking her head. "I don't know."

Darius returned to the stars. "Well, don't feel bad. Billions of miles away from here, some alien kid is jerking off to your image. You made his two minutes."

Sadie gave a suppressed laugh. "Everything is so instant, so open. One mistake, and it's out there forever, haunting you for the rest of your miserable life."

"You shouldn't get upset about this bullshit. In an hour, there will be another mistake. Like you said – an instant – it only lasts a moment."

"You all right?" Sadie asked, mesmerised by the stars.

"Thanks to you. Where did you get the weapon?"

"Captain Bryan's – he left it on the front seat."

"For the first time, I'm glad he's such an idiot."

A moment of dead silence followed.

"Isn't it amazing?" Sadie whispered. "So real. Not scripted. Not twenty-four degrees all the time. And no stupid Halley's comet."

"Amazing," Darius replied. "I'm fucking freezing, and the explosion damaged my suit's climate control."

"I think to have lived, one must experience life without the shield."

"You know what you tried to do is permanent?" Darius asked.

"What?"

"Ending your life."

"My father and mother worked their entire lives for this day – and I fucked it up in forty-five minutes." She covered her face again. "When I called him, he was so, so broken."

Darius studied the troubled girl next to him. "What the fuck?" Darius sighed. "That's not why he was, uh, broken."

"What do you mean?"

"Imagine you were working your entire life to accomplish something, and then when you did, somebody comes to visit and tells you that-"

"What?"

"That it wasn't real. His presidency – the Council is in charge, and they organized it for him. They are in charge, like puppet masters sitting high in the Dome, pulling strings. If he doesn't do what they order him to do, they will kill him like his predecessor."

"What!" Sadie sat up.

"He wasn't even aware of your" –pointing at her body– "great reveal."

Sadie lay down again. "Who is the Council?"

"There are fifty-two members, four in each city, elected thirty years ago when they activated the shields."

"The time when the Great drought started?"

Darius hesitated a moment. "Yes, if one council member dies, the remaining members vote for a replacement. It's such a corrupt process because the replacement is a family member or someone who pulled the right strings. So, you see, my dear, your embarrassment is the least of his problems."

"How are we going to get back?" Sadie sat up. "My father needs me now."

Darius smiled. "I tried to send out a distress call before my ride exploded. But I don't think-"

"Isn't this cozy?" Mr Gray blocked Darius's view of the stars.

"Bloody hell," Darius muttered. "So, it was you fooling around with my glider."

Gray held up a palm-size oval-shaped communicator. "It's amazing the apps you can download these days." He slipped it into his suit inside pocket and scratched his temple with the barrel of his 13mm Johnson gas-propelled pistol. "What were you doing out here?" Gray said, circling him before pausing at Darius's feet. "You left the Dome before Miss Green's little stunt."

Darius pointed to the stars. "I came here for the view."

Gray smiled. "You're getting nostalgic in your old age, old friend. And deaf. You didn't even hear me coming."

Sadie stared at Gray, her knees pulled up to her chest.

"I'm sorry it had to come to this, old friend," Darius said. "But I always knew this day would come." The broad-shouldered, towering figure, dressed in his custom grey suit, seemed even more spectacular from Darius' view.

"How so?" Gray smirked.

"I question orders, and you don't."

"In life, you get the shepherd, the sheep, the wolf and the lion.

The wolf eliminates the stray sheep, but who eliminates the stray wolf?"

Darius rolled his eyes. "Be careful, Simba. Don't trust the shepherd. This old wolf knows." He tried to get up, but Gray pushed him back with his boot, aiming his pistol at Darius' chest.

"Get up, Miss Green," he ordered, not taking his eyes off Darius.

"Did Steward send you?" Darius groaned.

Gray shrugged. "Of course."

"Only Steward?"

"He gave me a message."

"Not a Hallmark card, I suppose."

Gray shook his head. "This is for not showing him respect."

Darius smiled. "Just a tip."

"What?" Gray's finger curled tighter around the trigger.

"Never turn your back on a scorned woman."

Gray peeked over his shoulder and looked down the barrel of a trembling gun.

"Drop your weapon," Sadie seethed.

"This is between him and me, Miss Green." Gray kept the weapon trained on Darius. "After I'm done here, my orders are to take you back to your father. Don't you want to go back?"

"He will take me back." She glanced at Darius.

"Darius can't return. The council wants him decommissioned. He served his purpose." Gray lifted his boot from Darius and stepped back. "He means nothing to you."

"Be careful, Sadie," Darius warned, eyes shifting from her to Gray. "He's quick. Take a deep breath and pull the trigger."

"I can see you don't want to do it, Sadie." Gray smiled and gave another step back. "You're not a killer like me – or him. Let me do this, and we go home."

"He's the one who visited your father today," Darius said. "Shoot!"

Gray swung round, pivoting on his heel. Two shots exploded into the silent night.

Sadie dropped the weapon and stepped back, shivering.

Gray's weapon slipped from his hand and plopped into the sand. He fell to his knees and muttered, "By a white bitch?" He tumbled over on his side, his last breath a drawn sigh.

Darius struggled to his feet and removed his coat. Sadie stood dazed, unflinching, focused on the lifeless body. He draped the jacket over her shoulders and whispered, "Thank you. Now let's get you home."

"Is it for us?" Sadie whispered as she slipped into the jacket.

"What?"

She pointed at two fast-approaching lights on the horizon.

"I'm not sure. I expected help from the east. That's coming from the north." He took her by the arm and sprinted away from the smouldering wreckage. "Look for Gray's ride," Darius said.

"I see nothing." Sadie panned the moonlit expanse.

"There!" Darius pointed at a silhouette behind a large rock formation.

The lights banked to the right and made a full circle around them. They kept going until the fifty calibre Johnson machine guns primed – the high pitch whistle unmistakable. He grabbed Sadie around the waist and dived for cover. The guns fired a deadly purr, spewing flames of destruction – like the devil's horns. A blinding flash lit up the expanse, followed by a loud explosion. Darius threw himself over Sadie, shielding her against the shock wave.

"They'd just destroyed our ride," Darius heaved.

The Raptor touched down between them and the burning wreckage, lowering its ramp.

"I guess I'm not going home tonight," Sadie said as four men dressed in black stormed toward them.

7

G eneral Ross and his entourage stood stagnant amongst the hive of red uniforms.

"Who intercepted the signal?" Ross peered down the runway. "That man must get a promotion or extra rations."

"It was a woman," Captain Koonz mumbled.

Ross rubbed his hands together. "Commander Von Swartz and the President's daughter. Luck or God is giving us a break."

"Some believe it's the same thing. Some believe human existence or life is preordained," Koonz replied.

"What do you believe?"

"I don't. Humans believe in a god to blame their current fucked-up situation on something. The only outcome that's preordained is human nature – we will not stop until there is nothing left to consume. Our demise is inevitable."

Ross glared at Koonz. "Always such an optimist."

"It is what it is." Koonz shrugged, then turned his attention back to the runway. "Who could have thought hacking into their least secure server would drive her into our arms?" He glanced at Ross. "The hacker was a man."

"I can't see a woman humiliating one of their own like that."

"I wouldn't be so sure of that, sir," Koonz said. "My wife killed my mistress with an axe. Dismembered her pretty little body."

"You mean your ex-wife?"

"You mean my axe-wife," Koonz smirked. "We're still happily married."

Ross frowned.

"She showed so much dedication and effort when she chopped her up, I realized how much she loves me. She then sent a little piece with a note to every good-looking girl in the commune, warning them to stay away from me."

"They're here," Ross said, placing his hand on Koonz's shoulder.

A swarm of red uniforms approached the Raptor as it touched down, securing landing gear and connecting cables. Two reds pushed a cage toward the lowering ramp.

"What's the latest news on the alien boys, Professor Santiago?" Ross asked as the elderly woman dressed in white took up position beside him.

"They have the same anatomy–"

"I don't want similarities," Ross said. "What's different?"

"Muscle tissue, bone density, and pain threshold. The tests I did on the elder brother would have killed any human being. They can also decrease their metabolism."

"Keep it up, Professor," Ross said as he approached the ramp.

Commander Von Swartz and the president's daughter stumbled down the ramp, followed by the Raptor crew.

Ross continued, "Like a princess plucked from her castle and tossed into the swamp."

The scurrying reds ceased work and started cheering, fists raised.

"Welcome, Commander," Ross said with a satisfied grin as his two captives reached the end of the ramp.

Darius studied the hangar. "I knew there was a resistance, but this is impressive." He shrugged. "Futile, though."

"We might be in the gutter, but we have our eyes on the stars," Ross replied.

"Oscar Wilde," Darius said as he glanced up. "I can't see any."

Ross kept his glacial expression. "Well, at least the stars we see are real."

Darius smiled. "Touché."

Ross held out his hand. "General Ross."

Darius shook his hand and pointed to Sadie. "This is Miss Green, but I think you already know that?"

"Indeed, I do." He studied her from head to toe. "Every nook and cranny."

Sadie threw her hands in the air. "Even here!"

Ross grinned and said, "Let's talk somewhere private."

"I trust that you're not," Darius glanced at the stone walls, "cavemen, so please take Miss Green to the infirmary for some care. We are, after all, all human."

"But some are more human than others," Koonz muttered, glaring at Sadie.

"You mean equal. George Orwell," Darius said.

"It's the same fucking thing, prisoner," Koonz snapped. "Now, you are less human and less equal than I am." He removed his handgun. "It all depends on who's holding this."

Ross nodded. "Indeed." He glanced at Professor Santiago. "Please take her to the infirmary."

"Come, my dear." She held out her hand. "And let's get you some clothes."

"And, Professor," Ross said with a fiery glare, "we're not friends yet, so take her to the prison infirmary."

"Do all the people in chamber one receive the same treatment?" Sadie asked nurse Seymore as she took a seat on the crisp hospital bed.

The young nurse ignored the question and handed her an orange hospital gown.

Sadie held up the garment with two fingers. "I'd rather go naked." She dropped it to the floor and fastened the top button of Darius' jacket.

"Suit yourself, princess. It is a prison ward, and that's what prisoners wear." She plucked a hot towel from a bucket and pressed it against the cut on Sadie's cheek.

"Take it easy!" Sadie slapped the nurse's hand away and snatched the towel. "I'll do it myself. And what's your problem with me, anyway?"

"We had to fight for survival," Seymore snapped. "You live in your crystal palace, pretending everything is perfect. Do you even know what your people did?"

"What do you mean?" Sadie asked.

The nurse stared at her, taken aback. "You don't know, do you?"

Sadie shook her head.

"What's the use?" the nurse whispered. "The chances are we're all going to die when they arrive, whether we inside Nirvana or not."

"Who's they?"

"The aliens, you idiot."

"Aliens?" Oh, please.

The nurse glanced over her shoulder and then whispered, "We caught two of them."

Sadie leaned forward and whispered, "How do they look?"

The nurse shrugged. "Like us."

She burst out laughing. "Now, how do you know they're aliens?"

"Because they are stronger," Seymore defended. "And... and they've got big teeth." She pointed at her groin area. "And I was told they have bigger... you know."

Sadie covered her mouth as she laughed. "I think you guys lived in this cave for too long."

The woman glared at her, cheeks flushed.

"So, someone hung with big teeth is an alien. I think the men here made it up because they're ashamed. What's next, a high IQ?"

"Okay!" she snapped. "I'll show you. You won't find it that funny anymore." Seymore scurried to the door, glanced up and down the corridor and waved Sadie closer.

Sadie jumped from the bed and followed her out of the room, barefoot.

"They just brought him in," the nurse whispered.

"Where's the guards?" Sadie glanced over her shoulder.

"It's barely alive. We caught the aliens yesterday," she said, tiptoeing down the corridor. "The father was human, but the mother was one of them."

"How did they catch them?" Sadie whispered, mimicking the cat burglar's approach.

"They were living on a farm with their father. The old man blew his brains out before we arrived – probably knew we were coming."

"And the mother?"

"The boys said the beams took her. That means they came and fetched her."

"The boys?"

"The aliens."

"How old are they?"

"Six and seventeen."

"That's sad. Why is he barely alive?

"We're doing tests on them, trying to find their weakness." The nurse stopped at the last door in the corridor and pressed her thumb against the security panel. "He's not going to last the night. Luckily, we still have the younger brother." The door slid open, and the nurse waved her closer.

Sadie gasped, covering her mouth. The smell of burnt flesh made her nauseous.

"Don't let his looks fool you – tough as nails." The nurse stared at the half-naked body in awe. "They don't make them like this on Earth." She nudged Sadie. "Let's see if it is as big as they say."

"What did they do to him?" Sadie's eyes welled up. Bleeding lacerations covered old scars all over the alien's torso.

"Everything. But the four hundred thousand volts finally brought him down." She pointed at his charred soles.

"Don't you feel anything for him?"

"Why? They're coming to wipe us out," the nurse scowled. "They'll do worse to us."

"They!" Sadie pointed at the ceiling. "Not him! He's half-human, lived on a farm all his life and lost both his parents."

The nurse walked over to the alien and raised his upper lip, revealing his fangs. "They are animals!"

"Seymore!" a voice called.

The nurse froze. "Shit, she will kill me if she finds you in here." She ran to the door and peeked out. "I'm coming, Professor!" She rushed back to Sadie. "Stay here. I'll fetch you as soon as she leaves."

"Wait! What if he wakes up?"

"Does it look like he'll wake up anytime soon?" She pointed at the heart monitor. "Forty-five over twenty."

Sadie studied the lifeless body. "But–" The door closed behind her. "Just fucking perfect." She backed into the furthest corner, keeping a watchful eye on the monitor, every beep elevating her heart rate.

"I knew about General Johnson, but I was unaware he did it on this bold scale," Darius said as they entered General Ross's office. He froze, soaking up every inch of the décor: walls clad with rich wood, brass antiques of the old world, and books filled shelf upon shelf. "We share the same taste, General."

"This was Johnson's office." Ross pointed to an old chair in front of his desk. "Take a seat."

The chair welcomed him with a pleasant creak. "I missed this," Darius whispered.

"Excuse me?"

"I mean, back home, everything is so artificial and impersonal."

"Here in our cave," Ross smiled, "we will never forget our heritage, our values," he made a sweeping gesture with his hand, "our history. In the Dome, they live for the moment – no values, no identity – a bunch of spineless cowards, preparing to give up." Ross straightened. "I'm not talking about you, Commander. Your reputation precedes you."

"The people in chamber one. Are they also part of your heritage?"

Ross laughed, throwing back his head. "I will humour you with an answer, Commander. Every society in human history had its non-essentials, rejects, the sick and the elderly who did not plan for tomorrow, but we do not have the means to implement a welfare system. The little we have must go toward the workforce. Otherwise, there would have been no one left to fight" –pointing at the ceiling– "them."

Darius nodded, deep in thought. "As one of the founding fathers of The Council, I heard he had an open cheque book, so to speak. He channelled funds and material away from the Dome project by elevating the price of the construction material – an age-old tradition. When the time was right, Johnson and his followers left, and none was the wiser. It was a crazy time. No one checked the finer details. To survive was a challenge."

Ross closed his mouth and swallowed. "You know more than I do, Commander. Why did he not work with the Council to construct this place?"

"Well," Darius shrugged, "I heard there were three reasons for this. One, our alien friends would also know about this place. And two, The Council deviated from his plan to make this world a better place for all. Use the shield to protect Earth. Instead, they used it to protect the rich and powerful. When he fought against their plans, they tried to kill him. He lost his wife in the attack but managed to escape with his five-year-old son."

"And the third?"

"The dome model was flawed. It would be like shooting at a goldfish-"

"Trapped in a teacup," Ross said.

Darius smiled. "Oh yes, you've also met his son."

The general's bewildered expression disappeared after a beat. "Oh yes, it was your calling card that made us catch up with the Johnson aliens." Ross reddened, glancing down at his polished mahogany desk.

Darius' chair creaked with excitement as he sat up. "That was embarrassing, General," he said, still reeling from the barrage of information in one sentence. "Wait before you ramble on and tell me all your secrets. So, Captain Johnson ran away from you" –Darius rubbed his chin– "because he'd saved an alien woman from your clutches and then had two children, which you now have." Darius fell back into the chair. "Wow!"

The general's cheeks had the same reddish tinge as an avid whiskey drinker. Darius' father had drowned himself in it after his mother's death.

He pointed at Ross. "There was something about that kid. I only met him the other day." He smiled. "I'm so relieved that they are safe. Their father always kept them inside the house when I visited. I thought the Sweepers got to them first."

Ross smiled wryly. "Well, the eldest got the Sweepers, five of them, on the way here."

"Good for him. The kid needed a break. Where are they now? Can I see them?"

Ross shook his head. "That won't be possible."

"Why not?"

"We're running some tests on them."

"Tests?"

"To find their weaknesses."

"What?" Darius flew from the chair. "But they are just kids – you just told me he helped you by destroying five Sweepers! They have

Johnson blood in them! The rightful owner of this desk will never approve of this."

Ross rose to his feet. "Might I remind you, you are a prisoner, just like they are." He slammed his fist on the desk. "And they are not kids! We need to know what we are fighting! And how dare you preach to me – what you and the Council did was unforgivable. These chambers would have been empty if it was up to the Council."

Darius rolled his sleeve up, revealing a scar. "Firstly, I don't agree with the Council. This cave would be dust if I were still tagged. Secondly" –he removed a calling card, hidden within his collar– "I could have activated this at any moment, but I didn't."

"Why not?" Ross paled as he retook his seat.

"Because I don't like the goldfish idea."

"So, what are you saying? You want to defect?"

"We're all human. We need to work together." Darius stood up and walked to the bookshelf. "But first, we need to get rid of this council."

Ross leaned back in his chair and folded his arms. "How do you suppose we do that?"

Darius removed a book from the shelf. "Before I tell you, I need three things." He paged through the book.

"Proceed."

"The brothers, the President's daughter, and" –he held up the book– "mine got destroyed in a minor bumper bashing."

"Which book is that?" Ross frowned.

"One you haven't read, The Art of War."

8

Professor Santiago was older than the captain; wrinkled skin, purple-grey hair and her movements slow and shaky - but calculated. She had the same wild, angry eyes as the captain, though. Again, I'd asked mom's God to give me the strength to keep me going because my brother would be next. I'd never considered asking the captain's god for strength because his god took mom with a beam. The final destination worried me - maybe it was the place called hell mom warned me about. She never warned Joshua. But mom was good. Why beam her to hell? Perhaps the beam-god took her to stop her from turning people good. Well, other people because she failed with me.

I played a game with the beeps, keeping it as far apart as possible; it helped with the pain. But the woman in the corner made it difficult; I felt her eyes on me, and after her fear subsided, I could almost taste her sweet, tender flesh. It was what the humans expected of me, and killing her would heal my wounds faster. I could then break out and rescue my brother. Or was it a trap? Maybe they wanted to see what I did with her. As my father tried to prove, nature will win. I will try not to give them the satisfaction.

My body shuddered as I tasted the water. The beeps were now uncontrollable. I licked my lips, swallowing, afraid to open my eyes; perhaps it was that old woman in white.

"Take it slow," the woman said.

Not that I had ever heard one before, but she had the voice of an angel. I clenched my jaw, fighting back the sudden rush of tears. Maybe she is an angel, making me cry just to dry it with her fingers. No, angels won't smell of fear.

I opened my eyes and said, "Go away."

"It's okay," she whispered, her big brown eyes filled with sorrow.

"You heard what I am," I said hoarsely. She had the same black hair as Juliet, but hers was longer and untidy. She'd been crying black tears – did the devil dry hers?

"Why are your lips black?" I asked. "Or did you kiss the devil? Or are you an alien too?"

She touched her lips as if she had forgotten about painting them. "It's lipstick. I painted it."

"Your nails too?"

The girl looked at her hands the same way she had touched her lips. "It's nail polish." She shrugged. "I don't know why I painted it black."

"There must be a reason. You decided on a colour, went out and got it. You painted both your lips, both eyes and ten nails." I shook my head. "And you don't know why?"

She stared at me long and hard, then said, "My dad hates it."

I looked at her long and hard, then nodded. "That makes sense." Maybe I won't eat her just yet. "Thanks for the water," I whispered. It had the desired effect. The anger drained from her eyes. She wasn't as small as Juliet or as pretty, but they had the same fire within.

"What's your name?" She poured more water into my mouth.

I swallowed. "Wayne. I think. I don't know what's my alien name. And yours?"

"Sadie. Sadie Green. Like the colour."

"Well, what happened to you, Sadie Green?" I asked.

She glanced down at her worn jacket. "It's not mine. The man who wore it was in an accident." Sadie grabbed the bottom part of the coat and tried to cover more of her scraped and bruised legs.

"You stole it from a dead guy?"

"No!" she scowled. "He gave it to me."

"So, what happened to your clothes and the guy that gave you his jacket after the accident?"

She frowned. "You're asking a lot of questions for an alien."

"How do you know? Have you met one before?" I shrugged. "That's what aliens do, they ask questions. How else would they get to know the planet they are visiting?"

She had a sweet smile. Nicer than mom and Juliet. Captain and I hadn't been smiling. I hadn't been because it increased the smell of fear, and he didn't because after mom left, there was nothing to smile about. Captain Joshua and I weren't funny together. I smiled when Joshua ate Snowy without knowing it. I didn't tell him because the captain would've fetched the whip.

I clenched my jaw and increased the beeps to one every three seconds. "Fuck."

She touched my arm in a panic. "What's wrong? What can I do to help?"

"The pain gets worse when I increase my heart rate."

"Don't increase your heart rate, then."

"I heal faster if I do," I groaned. "I need to get to my brother before they get to him. He won't last a minute."

"And then what?"

"We escape."

"Just you and him?"

I shrugged. "You can come with if you like." Like a takeaway, on Grandpa's memory cards.

Sadie frowned. "I'm a prisoner too." She soaked a cloth with water and wiped my face. "This is old." She traced the scar on my cheek.

"My father gave it to me." I turned my head away. "I deserved it."

She continued, gently wiping my wounds. The pain was disappearing faster than I'd expected. "It happened five days ago," I whispered. "But don't tell them."

"What do you mean?" Her hand froze on my pounding heart.

"My wounds heal faster if I, uh," I turned my head away, "never mind." She would know I'm a monster. What do I care what she thinks?

Sadie placed a hand on her hip and slapped me with the wet cloth. "Oh, please." She rolled her eyes. "That's the oldest trick in the book. Just tell me already. And you know you don't say that to a woman." She started wiping my legs. "If there's one thing we're good at is extracting secrets. Especially from a man."

"You talk a lot." I clenched my jaw, fighting back a groan – she wasn't wiping as gently as before.

"Well, you have stopped talking."

"Okay," I groaned as she reached my feet. "Before you fucking kill me."

She smiled, tickling my tender soul.

I burst out laughing and pulled back my foot. What was that? I straightened my leg, scowling at her. "Don't do that!"

"See, there's human in you." She reached for my foot but stopped short. "Tell me, or I will do it again."

"I heal faster if I drink fresh blood," I blurted.

Her big brown eyes grew even bigger as she asked, "Like a vampire?"

"What's that?"

"A man that seduces women so he can drink their blood. It gives him strength. They prowl at night. They don't like the sun, holy water and garlic. Oh yes, and crosses. And they are immortal." She shrugged, still with wide eyes. "Only in some of the movies. In others, they shine in the sunlight and don't care about garlic and crosses. But in all of them, they are immortal, and the woman they bite also turns into a vampire."

"Why do they hate crosses?"

She rolled her eyes. "Because they're evil, silly. They drink the blood of humans."

"Well, I only drink blood to heal faster. I don't have a problem with crosses and daylight. I don't know what garlic is. And I'm only seventeen, so I don't know if I'm immortal."

"Oh, my gosh!" Sadie placed her hands over her mouth. "Monique will not believe this." She fanned her face.

Why is she so excited? "Why are you so excited?"

"Am I going to turn into an alien, like you?"

I don't know; there wasn't much left of the man to turn into an alien. I played it safe as I needed her blood. "Maybe."

She took a few deep breaths, then held her wrist in front of my mouth. "Let's go save your brother."

"It will hurt."

She pointed at three cuts across her wrist. "I know. I've done it before. Just stop when I tell you to."

I took hold of her arm, bringing her wrist to my mouth.

"Just bite down quickly," she ordered.

I obeyed.

She closed her eyes and clenched her jaw, fighting the pain. That's when something stirred within me. Something I couldn't explain. Maybe it was her blood rushing through my body, healing my wounds. Or perhaps something else. But something good.

***

"How is it possible we can't detect your crafts on our grid?" Darius asked as he and Ross made their way to the infirmary.

"I will not tell you all our secrets, Commander. Our crafts are old, but not our scientists."

"Do they know about your location?"

"The aliens? Well, we're using their technology. We acquired it from the craft that crash-landed." Ross pressed his thumb against the security panel. "Remember the alien woman, the Johnson boys' mother?"

"Was she the only survivor?" Darius asked as he entered the infirmary.

"She was the pilot and the only one in the craft."

"Was she shot down?"

Ross shook his head. "Looks like we're not the only ones having problems with women drivers."

Darius nodded as he glanced down the corridor. "How long after General Johnson's disappearance did you capture the alien?"

"About a month. Wait." Ross turned to Darius. "How do you know about his disappearance?"

"I heard something. You just confirmed it."

Ross tilted his head, frowning. "Then tell me why he didn't take his son with?"

Darius shrugged. "We both met his son. He's as stubborn as they get. I think he tried, but the kid wanted to stay, settle, start a family."

Ross nodded. "That makes sense. He wasn't the adventurer type. An introvert, nothing like his father."

"Well, give him some credit. He did run away with an alien and started a family."

"Touché. We did find the General's body in the desert a few years ago. Someone double-tapped the old man between the eyes." Ross looked around the infirmary. "Professor Santiago!" He turned back to Darius. "To be clear, you can't have the boys. We need to find their weakness."

Darius shook his head at the stupidity. "You think they will climb out of their fighters, line up, and give you time to exploit their weakness. They will destroy you without laying eyes on them." Idiot.

Santiago and the nurse appeared around a corner. "General Ross, I wasn't expecting you."

Darius scanned the infirmary. "Where's Miss Green?"

"And the guards I posted at the alien's room?" Ross scowled.

"They were unnecessary and too bloody nosy," Santiago said,

walking to the nearest door and pressed her thumb against the glass panel. "Miss Green is in here. Nurse Mary cleaned her up." Santiago froze in the doorway. "Where is she?"

The nurse burst out crying, her hands covering her face. "I'm sorry, General, she didn't believe me about the alien, so I... I had to show her and–"

Ross grabbed her by the hair. "You left her in there with that animal!"

"I sedated him. She should be fine," Santiago said as she marched down the corridor, her white coat floating in her wake. Ross and Darius followed.

"Wait!" Ross drew his weapon, then gave Santiago a nod. "I'll go in first." He stormed into the room as the door slid open, gun trained on the alien. "Get away from him," Ross ordered Sadie.

"You can put the weapon away. He's out of it," she said and stepped away.

"I told you," Santiago said as she entered the room.

"You okay?" Darius asked, noticing Sadie's pale complexion.

"I'm fine," she said. "It must be all the excitement of the day getting to me."

Santiago approached the alien, eyes narrowing. "Look at his wounds." She bent over, studying his torso.

"What wounds?" Darius said. "I see only scars."

"We won't get much out of him now." Ross holstered his firearm. "Time to start with the brother."

"I already did," Santiago said.

The pulse on the heart monitor spiked.

I opened my eyes and grabbed the woman around her wrinkly neck. Her body discharged such a volume of fear that it burnt the back of my throat. The invisible wall protected her no more. Our eyes locked for six beeps before I threw across the room. Ross was slow as a cow. He also went down like a cow as I ploughed into him. I resisted the urge to bite down on his neck as Sadie was in the room. I grabbed nurse Mary by the ankle as she ran for the door.

"Help!" she screamed as she hit the floor, hands reaching.

I pulled her back and covered her mouth with my hand. "Quiet," I whispered in her ear. "Don't give me a reason to eat you."

Her anxious breathing slowed through my fingers. I lifted her from the floor and turned to the remaining threat.

"Darius?" I said, almost dropping the woman. He stood in the corner, shielding Sadie.

His Adam's apple bobbed. "Wayne."

"What are you doing here?"

"Don't worry," Sadie said. "They also took him." She stepped out from behind him. "It's his jacket. He's with us."

Darius frowned. "Us? You knew he was awake?"

"I helped him." She touched the bloody cloth wrapped around her wrist.

Darius glared at the cloth, then at me. "You took her blood!"

"I gave it to him!" She stared at him with those big brown eyes.

I lowered Mary to the floor.

"How did you two get to this point?" Darius said, his complexion paler than usual. "I turn my back for one minute, and you serve him your blood."

"Where's my brother?" I asked the nurse.

She backed away, her mouth opened, but nothing came out.

"Where!" I barked.

She jerked and pointed a shaking finger. "Room four."

"My bag and clothes!"

"The professor's office."

"Take off your suit."

She did the gaping mouth thing again.

"Now!" I removed the general's security pin as she unzipped. "She's got a pin on her suit," I said to Sadie and pointed at the nurse.

"I'll take Santiago's pin," Darius said, and approached the professor.

"No!" I seethed. "That's my brother's. You don't look like a prisoner, so you're staying."

"Hey, I'm here because of you, kid. I went searching for you when you activated my calling card."

Sadie grabbed the white uniform from the half-naked nurse. "He can fly the plane," she said and removed her jacket.

I'd never seen a woman in underwear, and now I'm in a room with two. The urge overwhelmed me as I ventured a peek from the corner of my eye. Without even touching their milky flesh, I knew it was soft and warm. Soft flesh filled their bras to the brim and covered their curved hips. I had the overwhelming urge to grab hold of those fleshy bits and lick it or bury my face in it or-

"Wayne!" Darius snapped.

I tore myself away from them and swallowed. "What?"

He looked at me with a shocked or confused expression – couldn't tell and then said, "Take it easy."

"What?"

"What about me? Where am I going to get a pin?"

"I don't trust you. You took the farm from us. If you try anything, I'll–"

"You couldn't wait to get away from the farm," he snapped. "Nobody took your precious farm. Think about it. There's nothing to take. The land is useless. Every time I visited, I begged your stubborn father to come to the city. He always refused. The last time you saw me, I told him they were sending out the Sweepers." He approached, seething. "You were so fed up. You blew your dad's head off."

I grabbed him by the neck and raised him off the ground. "He killed himself – ask my brother."

Darius clutched my arm and whispered, "O... Kay."

I dropped him to the floor. "I'll find you a pin on the way."

"He's waking up." Sadie rushed to the general, who was reaching

for his weapon. "I'll take that, dude," she said and plucked it away from him.

Ross's face distorted as he turned on his side. "I think... you broke... my ribs." He shifted back and rested against the wall. "You're never... going to get out of here," he said in shallow breaths.

"As we've discussed before, General, we need to stand together," Darius said. "I've got a plan, and I need them."

"You can't trust him."

"I think I can, but do you trust me?" Darius removed a card from his collar. "It's still not activated."

The general looked at him and then at me. "You think he will fight beside you when they arrive?"

Pointing at the ceiling, I said, "I don't know them." Looking at Ross. "I hate you. And the Council I despise for sending Sweepers to kill their own. But I'll fight for my brother and her" –I glanced at Sadie– "for helping me when all of you treated me like an animal."

"What about me?" Darius asked.

"Undecided." I turned to the nurse. "Get me a knife or something... Now!"

Nurse Seymore gave a step to the right, then left, turned once and sprinted out the room. "Follow her," I ordered Sadie.

Darius knelt next to Ross and waved his calling card in front of the general's nose. "You will let us go?"

"I will let you and the alien go," Ross said, glaring at the piece of glass. "But the girl is a valuable asset."

Santiago groaned, eyes flickering.

"Don't you understand that she's vital to my plan?" Darius begged.

"You can't let the alien go," Santiago whispered, clutching her head.

"I don't need your permission, old cow," I seethed. "I'm getting my brother out of here, even if I have to kill every human in this cave."

"You must carry him," she smirked.

I sprinted out of the room, searching for number four. Sadie and the nurse appeared at the end of the corridor. "Where's my brother?" I yelled. The nurse gave a step back, but Sadie stopped her, pointing the general's weapon at her head.

She gestured to a door a few metres from her. "It wasn't me," she cried, gripped with fear. "The professor did it!"

Sadie grabbed the woman's hand and pressed her thumb against the glass panel, opening the door.

I shoved the nurse out of the way and stormed into the room. My brother was lying on a table, motionless, eyes wide open. No beeps. I froze, afraid to go any closer. Sadia rushed past me. I held my breath, keeping my eyes pinned on his unblinking eyes, begging for a sign of life. Why hurt such an insignificant being? I'm glad I'm not human. From the most bottomless pits of my sandstorm memories, I saw another face. It was Joshua or something of him. I didn't call him Joshua. As Sadie worked on the tiny body, I prayed to mom's God and dad's beam-god; one must be listening.

"Joshua," I whispered after my plea and gave a step toward him. "Joshua."

"What did you do to him!" Sadie screamed over her shoulder.

"She... she injected him with succinylcholine," the nurse said.

"English!"

"It causes muscle paralysis, including the muscles used for breathing."

"Help him, or I will blow your brains out," Sadie said through gritted teeth.

"Please!" the nurse screamed. "We don't have the antidote here – it's too late!"

My heart gave a wild jolt as I heard a beep. I ran to my brother's side, grabbed his arm and whispered in his ear, "So you also know the trick. Make the beeps as slow as possible. If you stay with me, I'll get you your cat."

"Get my bag, clothes and his teddy bear," I said to Sadie, grabbed the knife from her hand, and sprinted down the corridor.

Darius stood in the doorway. "Don't kill them, please. I need them when the time is right."

"Get out of my way," I seethed.

"I heard what she gave your brother. We have the antidote, and if you think of giving him blood, he can't swallow. He will choke."

"Where's the antidote?"

"Nirvana. I'll help you, but then you need to help me."

"Let's go." I pushed him out of the way and knelt next to Santiago, baring my fangs. "I will kill you when the time is right, but for now, I need your help."

The fear in her eyes subsided until I grabbed her thumb. "Don't worry, I've done this before." It took longer than expected. She squealed like a pig until I stood with her thumb. "You also want a key?" I asked Darius and glared at Ross.

He shook his head and muttered, "I'm glad the doors do not open by retina scan."

I shoved the nurse into the room and closed the door.

"Wait," Darius said. "Smash the security panel. It should give us enough time."

Sparks and glass flew as I rammed my fist into the panel.

9

Dressed in my black uniform, I walked in front, while Sadie, in white, pushed my brother on a gurney, as she called it. Sadie's father would be pleased because she washed her face – no more black tears or devil-lips. I was also happy. Her lips were thicker than Juliet's, but not as red. More kissable. Softer. I think.

Darius followed, dressed more as if he belonged in chamber one. I held my breath as I pressed Santiago's thumb against the panel. The door slid open.

"Don't look anyone in the eye," Darius whisper. "And walk head bowed, you're the tallest man in this shit hole."

We started our journey in chamber three, the black uniforms. I heard Koonz in the background, training his men, but kept my eyes on the path ahead. Our escape went smoothly; people walked past, not even glancing our way. But then, Juliet appeared – walking and talking to another black uniform. I kept my eyes on the door, increasing the pace.

Juliet kept her eyes on Koonz as she talked to the man beside her. They were about twenty strides away. I stepped to the left and waited for the gurney and Sadie to pass.

"Keep going," I whispered. "That woman knows me." Sadie lifted her chin and pushed on without missing a beat.

I took a position behind Darius, using him as my shield. We kept up the pace, all eyes pinned on the exit door. The gurney caught Juliet's attention as it went by her. She stopped, eyes narrowing.

"Joshua," she called out and approached the gurney. "I'm sorry..." Tears welled up in her eyes. "What did you do to him?" she scowled at Sadie.

"You know what they did," I said, stepping out from behind Darius.

She took a step back. "Wayne... how... how did–"

I took her by the arm and whispered in her ear, "You turned your back on him after I begged you." She tried to pull free. "They poisoned him," I said through gritted teeth.

"Everything okay?" asked the man she walked with.

"I'll catch up, Vince," she said, smiling.

"You sure?" He looked at my hand, clutching her arm.

"Yes!" we barked in unison.

He gave a step back. "Okay, catch you later than."

"I doubt that," I said.

The man shook his head and walked off.

"We need to get out of here, or else he will die." I let go of her arm and stepped back. "This is now your decision – if he lives or dies."

"Where are you taking him?" she whispered, glancing at three black uniforms walking past.

"The Dome," Darius said. "They have the antidote." He looked at Joshua. "It might already be too late. He barely has a pulse."

"He will make it," I snapped.

"Heartless bitch," Sadie said as she pushed past Juliet.

I followed and didn't look back. The next obstacle was the two guards behind the door and then the force field. The thumb might work for the door, but if it didn't work for de-activating the force field, we would have a problem – Darius and the gurney could not pass. Carrying Joshua the rest of the way would draw too much attention. I glanced over my shoulder as I pressed the thumb against the security panel; Juliet was gone.

"Don't smile," Darius whisper as the door slid open; two guards blocked our path.

Sadie pushed the gurney and stopped in front of the guards. "Please open. I've got my hands full."

The door closed behind us.

"Where are you taking him?" the one guard asked, walking toward the panel.

"For more tests."

"Is this the alien?" guard number two asked, leaning over the body.

"No, it's just a kid with an infectious disease," Sadie said. "Lumatitus."

The guard backed away.

"We need to get going!" I snapped.

Guard one glared at me. "You know the procedure. Where the authorization to transport a patient from chamber three to chamber one."

"I'm so sorry." Darius strolled toward him, searching for something in his inside jacket pocket. "I had it here somewhere."

I moved toward guard two.

"Here you go." Darius struck him in the face with his elbow, plucked off his pin, and pushed him through the force field.

"No!" The guard burst into flames as he fell through the wall. Then exploded into a cloud of shimmering particles.

I rammed the other guard's head into the corridor wall, knocking him unconscious.

Sadie stood wide-eyed.

"I've got my pin." Darius clipped it on. "Throw him at the wall." Darius pointed at the unconscious guard.

"He's out," I said and glanced at Sadie.

"If someone comes through that door, all hell will break loose, and your brother will die."

I ran to the control panel and pressed Santiago's thumb against it. The wall flickered and disappeared. "We've got ten seconds. Go!" Smoke and the smell of burnt flesh filled the corridor.

Sadie covered her nose with one hand and pushed the gurney past the force field.

I grabbed the guard, tossed him over my shoulder, and ran down the corridor. On my first trip, I remembered the hatch somewhere in the centre. I laid the guard on the floor next to the panel.

"It's bolted in," Darius said in an urgent whisper. "We don't have time for this."

I grabbed the edges and ripped the panel from the wall. I know, but Sadie's watching. Idiot! I punched the guard once more before shoving him into the hole. "He should be out for a while," I said, and rammed the panel back. "Let's go."

Sadie's passing glance gave me that same feeling of satisfaction in my stomach I had felt with my first taste of human blood. Darius's passing glance was the complete opposite.

The journey through chamber two went without incident; the white uniforms were so busy working on their glass tablets, we could have walked through naked. We glanced at each other as I pressed the thumb against the panel, opening the door to chamber one.

Two guards approached, and one said, "The infirmary is back that way."

The door closed behind us.

"We know, silly," Sadie said, smiling. "Professor wants us to dispose of the body. The boy died of an incurable disease, Lumatitus."

The guard frowned. "But the incinerator is back that way." His eyes shifted from Joshua to Sadie, then to me. "And shouldn't you seal the body?"

I closed my eyes as the door opened behind us. Now I must kill.

"Hey, Mitch," Juliet said. "It's okay, they're with me."

"You know the procedure," Mitch smirked.

Juliet walked up to him and snaked her arms around his waist. "You know how I hate procedure." She stared into his eyes.

"We need to bury him in the desert," Sadie said. "He might infect the whole cave."

Juliet stood on her toes and kissed the guard. My jaw tightened the longer they stood lip-locked. She grabbed him by his butt and rubbed her body against his. I looked away.

"Get a cave, you two," the other guard said and pressed his thumb against the panel.

"See you later." Juliet winked at him. Of all of us, she was the most dangerous. Mitch was like clay in her hands, bending and stretching at her will.

"You took your time," I whispered to Juliet as we made our way through the dark tunnel.

"A thank you would be nice," she whispered. "I've just pissed away my life."

"Wow, what a life."

"Fuck off."

We entered chamber one and zigzagged through the buckets, the dead, and the dying. I took my brother's hand as we passed the old woman he had touched; she died at the same spot her husband did.

Sadie covered her mouth and nose, teary eyes pinned on the exit. Darius and Juliet also kept their eyes on the exit. Why stay here and die, consumed by the smell of death, when you can die out there, breathing fresh air while watching the sunset? Maybe that was my father's idea, I don't know, but it made sense to me, whereas to live in chambers two and three, knowing what was happening in chamber one.

I kept my eyes on my brother, feeling his anguish. Our slow pace had the opposite effect on my uncontrollable heart rate. I wanted to run to the flying machine and get to the Dome as fast as possible. For my brother's sake, I took deep breaths, squeezing his hand.

Juliet jumped back into the corridor. "Wait!"

"What?" I asked.

"Blacks searching the hangar. It's not normal. They must look for you."

"Shit." Darius peeked around the corner. "Shit."

"They're not looking for me. I hope," Juliet said. "I'll go first. Get the Raptor ready."

"And then?"

"Work your way toward me."

"Which one is yours?" I asked.

"The last one at the far end," Juliet said.

"Of course," Darius said. "Why would it be the nearest one?"

"If you can get me the hand of the pilot that flies that one," Juliet pointed to the Raptor nearest us, "we can use it."

"I don't want to play devil's advocate, but how are we going to get out of here once we're on the plane?"

"Leave that to me," Darius said.

Juliet stared at me for a beat, then grabbed me behind the head and pulled me down to her level. "I'm sorry," she whispered and kissed me hard - also with the tongue, as she did with Mitch.

The suit was a tight fit. That fucking farm! I missed a lot.

She pulled back and looked into my eyes. "I believe in you. You were sent for a reason." With that, she left me.

"Does she suck on every man's face she meets?" Sadie muttered. "She must be riddled with disease."

Darius elbowed me and whispered, "First kiss?"

Was it that obvious?

"Evacuate! Evacuate!" a voice boomed over the loudspeaker as flashing red lights and sirens filled the hangar. The reds froze, looked around bewildered, then charged for the exit.

"Now's our time!" Darius shouted. "Pick him up."

I threw Joshua over my shoulder.

"Stay right behind me!" Darius grabbed hold of the gurney and stormed around the corner.

"Go!" I pushed Sadie out of the corridor and followed close behind.

The sea of red uniforms parted as Darius ran toward them with the gurney.

"There they are!" A guard screamed above the chaos.

"Stay low!" Darius shouted and pushed into the wave.

"Fire!" A man shouted behind us.

I glanced over my shoulder. Koonz was sidestepping reds, aiming.

"Fire!" he repeated and pulled his trigger. A red uniform fell to the floor next to me, blood squirting from his head.

Gunfire erupted as the guards followed Koonz's order. A woman grabbed her shoulder to the left, and by the time the two men to the right had hit the floor, they were dead – both headshots. Fear permeated the hangar, infecting humans like a disease. Like Lumatitus – whatever that is. I sprinted past Sadie and Darius and threw Joshua on the gurney. "Take care of him!"

"Where are you going?" Darius shouted.

"Kill some humans!"

I jumped onto the moving gurney, waiting for the first guard in our path, and leapt on top of him. I sank my teeth into his neck and tore out his jugular. The blend of fear and blood fuelled my hunger for more. No dying animal tasted this good. Must be the human's distinct odour of fear they discharged when dying – the more afraid, the tastier. The human curse, I guess.

"Watch out!" Darius warned as he rolled by, pointing at a guard standing on the wing of a Raptor.

I wrenched the weapon from the dead guard's hands and fired – the rounds tore through his body and threw him off the wing. I aimed at the next guard, then the next, then the next, killing each with a single shot to the head. It all seemed so familiar; the icy steel in my hands, the killing. Exhilarating. Each life I took fuelled my rage and quenched my thirst for revenge. This is who I am. I became the man my mother feared I would become.

Darius and Sadie had reached the Raptor when two rounds struck me, one in each leg. I fell to my knees, searching for the shooter. Koonz. I pointed my weapon at him and pulled the trigger. Click. Nothing.

"Wait!" Koonz screamed at his fast-approaching men. "He's mine!"

Sadie and Darius ran up the ramp, both pushing the gurney. She kept her eyes on me until she disappeared into the Raptor. They went unnoticed, as all eyes were on me – the monster drenched in blood. My plan had worked.

"This will be fun," Koonz sneered.

His men surrounded me, closing the circle. "Never die on your knees," a voice echoed from the sandstorm. I struggled to my feet, using the weapon for support. Drive the pain from your mind. It's a human flaw... an emotion.

Koonz fired another round into my left leg, followed by another into my right. I remained standing, glaring. Blood seeped down my legs and into my boots.

"On your knees, or I can keep going," he said.

"I prefer standing," I lied. The pain pulsated through my body. Each pulse brought me to the brink of passing out.

"Suit yourself." Koonz aimed his weapon at my head. "The professor wants her thumb back." He held out his hand.

I kept my eyes on him and removed the thumb from my pocket. "This one?" I shoved it into my mouth. The taste of cold blood, the crushing nail, and bone almost made me vomit, but I acted as if it was the best meal since Snowy. Without fear, it tasted vile. I smiled, revealing my blood-soaked mouth. "Gamey, but delicious."

The shock on Koonz's and the guards' faces was priceless. A few heaved and gagged. The Raptor fired up behind me, but my audience seemed uninterested. The monster in their midst kept them mesmerised.

Koonz tightened his finger around the trigger. Everything in me wanted him dead, but my legs would fail. How you die is a choice. A bullet through the brain would be the end of me. I knew it. Santiago should have tried it from the start, but it would've been too quick for her. Humans gained strength by torturing. Especially if the thing tortured was not like them. I closed my eyes. My brother was safe. Sadie and Juliet would take care of him. I'm free.

I jolted as the shot echoed through the hangar, but felt no pain. Was I wrong? Koonz still stood in front of me, his weapon dangling by his side. He looked at me, but not with the same wild eyes. The guards' attention was not on me, but on searching for something. Koonz fell to his knees, his hand moving to a tiny hole in his chest. "Son of a bitch," he said under his breath and fell forward, facedown, into a pool of my blood.

The guards scattered as a volley of shots rang out. Then I saw them on the wings of our Raptor, Brock and Fritz, picking off the guards, one by one.

"Are you just going to stand there?" Darius was behind me, clutching the gurney. I fell onto my ride, grabbed the weapon he handed me, and didn't stop firing until we reached the Raptor. Brock and Fritz waited on the ramp, supplying cover.

"Close the ramp!" Brock yelled.

Bullets ricocheted off the metal ramp and into the Raptor, ripping through containers and seats. Sadie and Darius pulled me off the gurney and dragged me deeper inside. Everyone took cover, weapons aimed at the closing ramp. The Raptor shook as it became airborne, the whine of its engines pitching. A soldier leapt into the Raptor and took cover behind a container.

The ramp slammed shut. Darius and Sadie glanced at me.

"Don't look at me," I groaned. "I'm wounded."

"What's going on back there?" Juliet screamed from the cockpit.

"We've got a focking stowaway," Fritz replied.

"Who? I might know him!" Juliet said.

Darius shrugged. "What's your name?"

"R-R-River L-liberty!"

"River Liberty!" Darius called to the front.

"Liberty!" Juliet replied, surprised. "Shorty, is that you?"

"Y-yes!"

"Yes, it is!" Darius relayed.

"What are you doing here?"

"I'm w-w-with the g-giant. He s-s-saved my l-l-live."

"He said he's with Wayne! Saved his life!" Darius turned to me. "Did you?"

I sat up, fingering a hole in my pants. "It wasn't on purpose. Joshua asked me."

"Show yourself," Darius ordered.

"Don't worry, they won't shoot you." Sadie handed her weapon to me and walked toward the container. "It's okay."

Shorty appeared from behind the container and handed Sadie his weapon. He approached, hunched, with a sheepish smile, eyes darting between me and the floor. Red spots like flea bites covered his face.

"Now I've seen it all," Darius said and stood up. "This is like a fucking school bus."

Shorty knelt by my side and said, "Do you r-r-remember me?" He stuck out his hand."

"I heard it was you." Wouldn't call him a man, though, but I admired the shit for taking the leap, leaving everything he knew behind his family. If he had any, his friends, well, I doubted he had any of those. Maybe it wasn't such an enormous step for him.

"T-t-thank you."

"I knew they were too quiet!" Juliet yelled. "They're bringing out the big guns!"

Darius sprinted to the cockpit.

"Where's Joshua?" I asked Sadie.

"In the cockpit, strapped in." She sat next to me.

"Can you explain to Brock why I need his blood?" I said.

"What!" Brock gave a step back.

The nose of the Raptor dipped as Juliet eased the throttle forward. "How are we going to get out of here?" she asked, pointing at the closed hangar doors. The warning message flashed on the control panel: Missile Lock. "Why are they waiting?"

"We're trapped. I know Ross. He's playing with us," Darius said. "Do we have missiles?"

"The doors are blast-proof," Juliet countered.

Ross' voice blared over the loudspeakers in the hanger. "Commander, you know there's no escape. Turn on your comms."

Juliet removed her headphones, activated the cockpit speaker, and said, "Afternoon general."

"Juliet?"

"I'm sorry," she replied. "But you over-stepped the line. They are not our enemy – they're just children."

Ross sighed. "You've thrown away everything you worked for."

"You're wrong, General. You've thrown away everything you stood for."

"Let us go, Ross," Darius demanded. "Can't you understand I've got a plan?"

"No!" Ross's voice echoed through the Raptor. "I can use the President's daughter to negotiate–"

"They will laugh at you," Darius interrupted. "You know the President is not in charge. She means nothing to them."

Static filled the aircraft.

"You know I can't let you go. After what just happened in the hangar–"

"You ordered them to shoot!" Darius yelled at the comms. "We had to defend ourselves."

Another moment of static. Darius and Juliet stared at each other, waiting in anticipation.

"I will lose all respect if I open those doors," Ross said. "We have missile lock. You have thirty seconds to return."

Darius took off his jacket and handed it to Juliet. "Can I have the chair, please?" She hesitated. "I got my wings in one of these."

Juliet unstrapped and muttered, "God help us."

"Ross doesn't know who he's dealing with." Darius took a seat and flipped a few switches. "I played along, but no more."

Ross stood with arms folded, peering through the control room window at the hovering Raptor. "Prepare to fire," he said with a shake of the head. The Raptor turned a hundred and eighty degrees. "Wait," he said, grinning. "I knew he would come around."

The Raptor hovered back toward the hanger, increasing speed.

Ross's grin vanished. "What's he doing?"

Warning alarms and lights triggered in the control room.

"He's armed his missiles, General!" an operator screamed.

"Fire! Fire!" Ross bolted from the window as the missile left the Raptor.

Juliet covered her mouth, eyes focused on the line of smoke trailing the missile. The explosion ripped apart the control room, triggering every alarm in the cave.

"Hang on," Darius said, and pushed the throttle forward. The Raptor sped up down the runway and into the hangar. Juliet grabbed hold of Darius's chair as he raised the nose of the Raptor, higher and higher until it pointed at the fans mounted in the hangar's roof.

"What the fock are ya doing!" Fritz yelled from the back.

Darius fired four missiles before levelling out. The explosion rocked the roof of the cave.

"You missed," Juliet said.

"I never miss," Darius said and manoeuvred the Raptor away from the falling debris. "I didn't aim at the fans. Be patient."

A thunderous crack sounded as the weight of the massive fans brought down the damaged roof. Boulders and blades demolished and flattened half the Raptors parked in the hangar. Sunlight flooded the cavern and illuminated the carnage.

"Fuck me," Juliet whispered.

"I can't multitask, my dear," Darius muttered. "Let's go home, Dorothy."

The powerful engines pushed them back into their seats as the Raptor accelerated toward the gaping hole.

10

General Steward's eyes narrowed as he wheeled his way toward the globe in the centre of the control room. "What is that?" He pointed to a tiny flashing red dot on the hologram.

A female operator turned in her chair and said, "I just picked it up, General. It's static, not one of ours, and the scanners can't make out what it is."

"Show me a satellite image."

An aerial view of a cloud of smoke billowing out from a mountaintop filled the screen.

"Is that mountain active?"

"No volcanic activity detected, General – the heat signature is too low."

"Call back two Sweepers to investigate."

"What's wrong with them?" Gabriel asked, staring through a pane of glass at Whitmore and Grace lying side by side in a hospital room.

"We're still running tests, but their condition is deteriorating by the hour," Doctor Michaels said, flipping through a chart.

The tall, emaciated man fitted more the part playing by the undertaker than a doctor. With his pallid complexion, he should be on the other side of the window, occupying a bed.

He squinted at the page, readjusting his glasses. "It's not viral."

"You think someone poisoned them?"

Doctor Michaels kept staring at the chart.

Gabriel clapped once. "Hello!"

The doctor jolted alive, frowning at Gabriel, his bushy ash-white brows almost touching each other.

"You think they were poisoned?" Gabriel repeated.

He cleared his throat. "It's possible."

"Let me know once you get the results back."

The doctor nodded and shuffled into the room.

Gabriel shook his head at the departing fossil; most of the old man's ailments were reversible, from his eyes to ears to his arthritis. Why he decided not to ease or at least slow his deterioration was beyond him. He's still using a fucking clipboard!

"Where's my mother?" Ryan yelled, running down the corridor toward Gabriel, followed by two security guards. He halted by the window, heaving. "What happened?"

"They both came in early this morning," Gabriel said. "They still running tests."

"You think she will die?"

"Drop the act." Gabriel smiled. "It's only us here."

Ryan grabbed Gabriel by the arm and said in a frantic whisper, "But she needs to nominate her successor!"

"She can't nominate you because of your age," Gabriel said, glaring at Ryan's hand. "Careful."

Ryan let go. "But I'll be eighteen next month."

Gabriel shrugged. "Shit happens. Besides, last night she already nominated someone."

"Who?" Ryan snapped his head toward Gabriel.

"Darius Von Swartz."

"What!"

"Yep, he will be one of the four, and Steward will be Supreme Commander."

Ryan ran his fingers through his hair. "And Martha... who did she nominate?"

Gabriel smirked. "The bitch. She caught us all by surprise."

"Who?"

"I believe you've met his daughter," Gabriel said, chuckling.

"His daughter?"

"President Green." Gabriel burst out laughing.

Blood drained from Ryan's cheeks. "What will happen to me?"

Gabriel shrugged as he walked away, still laughing. "I think you need to apologise. With your blue eyes and good looks, she'll forgive you."

After the look Brock gave me while donating blood, I promised myself never to ask another man again. It felt awkward, sucking on a man. The pain was gone, wounds healed, blood washed away, but the scars remained – as always. Sadie sat a chair away, hands on her lap, staring at the cockpit. The invisible wall was back, separating her and me. Deep down, I knew why. She didn't smell of fear, but things had changed.

"I'm sorry you had to see that," I whispered. Shorty sat to my right on the other side of the aisle.

She glanced at me, then returned her gaze to the cockpit. "What?"

I swallowed. "The guard I, uh... killed."

She gave a slight nod.

Her silence angered me. Talk to me! "I lost control. I'm sorry."

"It's what you are. You can't help it." She gave an indifferent shrug.

She was right. "I will leave the city as soon as I know my brother is fine."

Sadie looked at me. She wanted to say something, but then returned to the cockpit.

I continued, "My brother is not like me. Mom kept him good. On the righteous path, as she called it. So, he won't cause any trouble."

My hand tightened around the armrest. I took a deep breath to settle my pounding heart. Damn women!

Shorty leaned over and said in his high-pitched voice, "H-he d-did what h-he ha-ha-had t-to do. He won't k-k-kill a good pe-pe-person."

I didn't like him; he talked funny, had a strange look in his eyes, and was weak.

"Shorty, why don't you go to the cockpit – see how they do things up front."

"I'm-I'm fine t-thank you, W-W-Wayne."

On the way, he said it, I have a shitty name. And how did he know my name? "My name is Scar, and go to the front!" I snapped.

Sadie waited until River left us. "Scar?"

"Maybe he can say it faster. Why does he talk that way?"

"I feel sorry for him," Sadie said. "It happens to someone with low self-esteem." She looked at me. "You better be patient with him."

Fritz and Brock sat together whispering, now and then glancing our way.

"What?" I scowled.

"Take it easy, W-W-Wayne," Fritz said, and he and Brock burst out laughing.

I glared at them, but as I noticed Sadie's stifled grin, I shook my head and smiled.

"Thank you for taking your time getting to me. Couldn't you have shot the bastard before he shot me?"

Brock glanced at Fritz and said, "Can you believe this guy? We left everything behind for him, and this is the thanks we get."

Fritz shook his head, "We did it for Juliet – she called us. Besides, when we got there, Koonz, the goon, was already dead. How'd ye manage that?"

"I didn't shoot him."

"Well, it wasn't us," Sadie said as she stood up. "We were still busy with Joshua when the shot rang out."

We all thought about it for a moment, glanced at each other, then at the cockpit.

"Nah," Brock said, but not convinced. "It couldn't have been him."

The Raptor went silent as Shorty returned.

"W-w-what?"

Fritz looked at Sadie. "Before our debate, we were talking about how familiar you look."

"Familiar?" Sadie said. Her cheeks flamed. "I can't see why?"

"Yes!" Shorty yelled; eyes filled with excitement. "You're t-t-the–"

"Shut up!" Sadie shouted and fled into the bathroom.

I glared at Shorty until he took a seat.

"You have never seen her in your life."

He gave a wide-eyed nod.

I struggled to my feet and limped over to Brock. "What happened?" I asked him because Shorty's version would take forever – I would find out if I were immortal – and Fritz talked funny.

Brock glanced at the bathroom, then said, "Some asshole left her hanging in a club called Gravity with no way of getting out. Then the other assholes recorded her half-naked body as she struggled to get out."

"Yer mot twisted and turned fir over a focking hour," Fritz added.

"Yer mot?" I asked.

"Your girlfriend," Brock said and leaned forward, whispering. "Then one of Ross' men on the inside hacked their system and projected her on every building in Nirvana."

I sighed. "Fuck."

"Bang on." Fritz nodded.

"Well, don't mention it again," I said.

Both nodded.

I made my way to the cockpit, where my brother lay strapped in.

"So," Juliet said in a challenging and cold tone, keeping her eyes on the horizon.

Strange, with just one word, a woman can say so much. And with no words can say much more. "There's no so. She lost her appetite with me when she saw my appetite."

"So." She glanced over her shoulder. "You eat people."

"Yes."

"Should I be worried?"

"No, you're too skinny."

"I'll take that as a compliment." She returned to the horizon. "Excellent incentive to watch my diet."

"Uh-huh."

The desert was behind us. Another invisible wall had held me captive my entire life – a wall as thick as the eye could see. The monotonous sandy landscape had changed into rigid shades and shadows of brown, scattered amongst lone ruins, bone-dry rivers and skeletal forests with trees looking like porcupine needles.

I looked at Joshua. Why him? Another good one.

"Sorry, Wayne," Juliet whispered. "I didn't know what they were planning."

I followed a ghostly river as it cut through a porcupine forest. "The coward said it's too late for me."

"The coward?"

"My father." The river snaked left as it cleared the porcupine. "He tried to poison Joshua before the farm turned him bad." I pointed at five tall structures, all leaning to the right. "What is that?"

"An old city. Downtown. You're not a bad person, Wayne. You need to learn how to control your anger." She shrugged. "Because your anger kills people."

I hunkered down and looked right through the squares of one building. "And how do I control my anger?"

"Take deep breaths and count to ten. It will allow your rational mind to catch up. If you still need to kill the person, then you can, because then you won't kill a good person."

I nodded and pointed at the remains of a massive statue - the bottom half of a naked man with four legs – two apart and two together. "And that?"

"What remains of the biggest statue ever created by man - The Vitruvian Man by Leonardo da Vinci. This city was like the science capital of the world. All the clever people came here to study and test their theories. They argued and discussed the best way forward on how to save humankind."

"So, I guess they argued and discussed you guys to hell."

"You guys?"

"Well, what I've been through and what I've seen, I'm happy to be an alien, especially when I saw the size of the statue's peepee."

She burst out laughing and said, "Your statue would have five legs."

I laughed because she laughed.

When she quieted down, she said, "They knew how to save the world."

I frowned. "Oh?"

"Back then, science always impeded greed and power, so nobody listened."

"And now?"

"We don't use money anymore, but power used science."

"I heard you guys laughing," Sadie scowled. "Your brother is lying next to you unconscious, and you laugh with the woman responsible."

Shit! She's right. For a moment, I'd forgotten about him. I turned around and looked down into those big, fiery brown eyes. "I can't help it. You said so." I walked out of the cockpit and said, "I'm a monster, remember?"

Rocks and debris still fell from the gaping hole when Ross stumbled into the hangar, face blackened and uniform torn. "Go after them! Go after–" The ray of sunlight beaming into the hanger distracted him. He walked, dazed, toward the light.

"General!" Major Corbin yelled, from where he assisted a soldier in lifting a boulder from a mangled body. "It will stretch our resources to the limit!"

Ross continued toward the light.

"General?" Corbin walked toward Ross.

The general took a deep breath as he bathed his face in the sunlight. "God, I've missed this," he whispered. "We are living like rats."

"But we have no other choice, General," Corbin said, also taking in the sun.

Ross stared at him for a moment. "You're right. It would be foolish to go after them now. Get the injured to the infirmary."

"How are we going to repair that?" Corbin asked, pointing at the gaping hole in the roof.

Ross smiled. "You know we can't."

"But it will detect us?"

The General shrugged and strolled off. "We can't hide in here forever."

"Why is your name, Blondie?" Gabriel whispered as he rolled her red locks around his finger.

She smiled, circling his nipple with her finger. "Why is your name Gabriel if you're not an angel?" Her finger left the nipple and made its way down his toned torso.

"Oh, but I am." He raised his head from the pillow and kept a close eye on the venturing finger. "The angel of death." Blondie's hand disappeared under the silk sheet.

Gabriel closed his eyes and grinned with satisfaction. "You're killing me tonight."

"Let's go again, Angel of Death." She mounted him, her red manicured nails digging into his chest. "Wicked boys make me so hot." Blondie thrust her hips forward, then backward. "How bad are you?"

"Very," he groaned, head digging into the pillow.

"Tell me, how bad?" She sped up, fingers clamping his chest.

"Terrible," he heaved.

She stopped. "It's not fun if you won't tell," Blondie said in a baby girl's voice, making a sad face.

He raised his head, smiling. "Oh, you so bad." He grabbed her slender hips and tried to force her, but she held firm.

"I will find myself a real evil boy," she said, trying to dismount.

Gabriel held her firm, his blue eyes cutting into her. "Kill everyone who will stand in my way."

"That's better," she smirked, grinding her hips. "Stand in your way of what?"

"Taking control of the Dome," he whispered through gritted teeth.

Blondie increased her rhythm, fingers clawing at flesh. "How... you... going... to... do... it... bad... boy?"

"Made... a... deal... with... the... devil," he grunted.

"Who's... the... devil!"

"Yes!" He threw his head back, raising his hips. "Darius!"

"Who's... standing... in... your... way?"

"That... fucking... Gen-Gen-General Stew-Stew-Steward!" he grunted, grabbing at her bouncing breasts.

"Yes! Yes! Yes! Yes!" And then she froze, back arched, groaning with pleasure as she reached her goal.

Gabriel's head rose from the pillow as he whimpered, eyes clamped shut. Both let out a satisfied groan as their tense bodies relaxed. Blondie collapsed on top of him. A moment of bliss-filled silence passed as the stacked bodies, drenched in sweat, calmed their breathing.

"You know what turns me on more than an evil boy? A powerful man," Blondie whispered. "I hope it will be soon."

"Sooner than you think." Gabriel wrapped his arms around her. "You will scream your lungs out within two weeks."

It took longer for the sun to settle because we headed straight for it. Everyone was asleep, except Juliet, so I made myself comfortable in the back of the Raptor, as far away as possible from the fucking fireball and my brother. A container was big enough for me to lie in. Not sleep, just rest - my new rock-of-reflection or box-of-reflection. Dad said, before he painted the ceiling with his wisdom, we must tell mom I tired him. So, father and Ross believed she was still alive. I can't see you starve to death, and I can't take you to the city. Why did he refuse to take us to the city? Why did he only try to poison Joshua? And why was Sadie so-

"So, you are a vampire." Sadie peeked over the edge of the container. "Because a vampire sleeps in a coffin during the day."

"Will you hate me less if I told you I was?" I said.

"I don't hate you," she said, grabbing hold of the edge. "I was just, uh, taken aback. I didn't know you were so uh-"

"Wild?"

She smiled. "It's still so unreal. And the thought of you meeting my dad scared the shit out of me. He is the president, and I, uh-"

"Don't want to introduce him to a monster that might kill him."

She stared at me, waiting, her frown intensifying with each passing second.

I rolled my eyes. "Don't worry, I won't eat the president."

She let out a sigh of relief.

"Unless."

Her frown returned. "Unless what?"

"Unless he's fat. I like fat people, good or bad." I licked my lips.

"Wayne!" She leaned over, trying to punch me in the stomach, but slipped and fell on top of me.

Sadie gasped, her body tense, eyes clamped shut.

"Don't worry," I whispered, smelling her fear. "You're too skinny." That line seemed to work with women. "I might chip a fang."

Sadie opened her eyes, her fear dissipating. "Are you trying to seduce me?"

Take it easy, Wayne. Shallow breaths. My body reacted. I didn't know what it craved; her blood or her. "I'm still new at this," I whispered. "I don't know what I'm trying to do. Or what you want me to do?"

Sadie held me captive with her big brown eyes as she inched her way up my body.

"I don't know what will happen next," I whispered, panting, heart-pounding. Rage and my prey's fear had fuelled my hunger for blood. It fuelled something else. I was afraid to let go, lose control, surrender to whatever boiled within. A familiar scent filled the coffin. Mom and Captain, under the sheets, popped into my head. I cringed; they weren't fighting.

"This is new to me too," Sadie whispered, her breath warming my lips.

She inched the last inch, pressing her soft lips against mine. It was more kissable than Juliet's.

I closed my eyes, surrendering. My alien half was about to explode from its confined quarters.

"W-W-W-Wayne."

We froze, lips locked.

"J-J-Juliet is calling y-y-you."

One, two, three, four, five, six, seven, eight, nine, ten.

We un-inched and looked into each other's eyes.

Sadie shook her head.

One, two, three, four, five, six, seven, eight, nine, ten.

"Okay," I whispered. "He's too skinny."

She gave the most beautiful smile. "Now, I know you can control your rage."

Thank you, Juliet.

And you're not The Vitruvian man."

"I thought you came when you heard the laughter?"

"W-W-Wayne-"

"Shorty!" Sadie shrieked over her shoulder.

I shook my head.

"Scarlet," Sadie whispered, in awe, standing in the cockpit behind Joshua's chair. "My first real sunset."

I stood between Sadie and Juliet, refusing to look at Joshua.

"I think it's more crimson," Juliet muttered. "And it loses its appeal when going to bed hungry."

I glanced at Juliet, then Sadie, before returning to the horizon. "I will see red if that's the only reason you c-c-c-c-called me."

Juliet pointed at her crimson horizon. "Look at the sun's reflection."

I squinted and noticed it as if another sunset. The Dome seemed on fire, illuminated by the sun's rays. I gathered the courage and looked at my brother. "Open your damn eyes and look at it." We were here – the big city, and he's... sleeping.

As the sunset, the other rose. "It looks like a drop of water."

"Cruel, right?" Juliet said.

"What do you mean?"

"The people not allowed in, starving, no water, looked at this creation every day. Some probably tried to drink from it."

From the corner of my eye, I noticed Sadie looking away.

"Have you ever been here?" I asked Juliet.

"Not this close." A red light started flashing on the control panel. "Shit."

"What?"

"Darius!" Juliet yelled. "We've got two Sweepers on our tail!" She glanced at me. "You think you can take them out?"

"It's only two," I replied.

Darius entered the cockpit and removed his calling card. "Open a channel," he ordered, and pressed his calling card. "Control, Commander Darius Von Swartz. Open a window."

A blond woman appeared on a small screen in the centre of the control panel. "Commander, where have you been?" she asked, almost whispering.

"Stacey," Darius said, relieved. "I've got the President's daughter and two Sweepers on our tail. Open a window, please."

"Commander," she said, glancing over her shoulder. "I've got orders not to let you back in."

"From whom?"

She hesitated.

"From whom!"

"General Steward."

I ran out of the cockpit toward the back, yelling, "Brock, we've got two Sweepers!"

<hr>

"Get Steward on the line. Now!" Darius seethed.

"It's not protocol," Stacey said, bewildered.

"Fuck protocol! The death of Sadie Green will be on your hands."

Stacey disappeared from the screen.

"Seems like you pissed off somebody," Juliet said and banked to the left.

"Excellent idea," Darius said. "Keep the shield between the Sweepers and us until I can sort out this mess."

The Raptor skimmed the surface of the water as it circled the Dome.

"Shit," Juliet whispered. "They've separated. One is on our six. The other is coming around the other side."

Darius glanced over his shoulder as he heard the guns firing. "I hope his luck didn't run out."

"He hasn't disappointed me yet," Juliet said.

"Just be careful – if you touch the shield, we die."

"Who the fuck is General Steward?" Sadie scowled, clutching the back of Joshua's seat.

"Him." Darius pointed at the screen as Steward appeared.

She leaned in, shouting, "Listen here, you fucking Neanderthal. My father will have your shrivelled balls–"

"As you can see" –Darius stepped in between– "I have the President's daughter with me. You going to let us in or not?"

"Where did you get the craft you're flying in? It's not one of ours," Steward said, eyes narrowing. "We also detected another eight life signs – you know I can't let you in."

Darius frowned. "You sure it's eight and not seven?"

"Yes."

Juliet glanced at Joshua, then at Darius, eyes filled with hope.

The Raptor jerked, almost diving into the shield. Juliet eased back on the controls.

"I've got one of them with me! They sent him down to negotiate with us. If you kill him now, they will destroy the Dome!"

Steward's smile disappeared. "You're bluffing."

"Hold on!" Darius interrupted and sprinted out of the cockpit.

Fritz stood between Brock and me, pointing and yelling, "Take the shot! Watch out! Where's the other one!"

Darius entered, out of breath, and placed his hand on my shoulder. "Come with me," he whispered in my ear.

"I'm a bit busy!" I said, and pulled the trigger. The rounds ricocheted off the Sweepers nose.

"Fritz, take over!" Darius said, and grabbed me by the arm.

Something was in his eyes I had not seen before – panic or excitement or a combination of the two – but whatever it was, I had to go with him.

Fritz leapt into my chair as I exited the gunner's station.

Darius started rambling as we made our way to the cockpit. "Your brother is still alive, but the general doesn't want to open a window for us, so I told him we have an alien. You came down to negotiate our surrender, and if he kills us, your people will see it as an act of aggression, and they, I mean your people, will destroy the Dome if he kills us."

Through the gunfire and bullets slamming into our Raptor, I heard Sadie scream, "Kiss this! You probably recognise it!"

She stood hunched over;, nurse's dress pulled up, her butt pressed against the small screen. Juliet tried to push her away with one hand. "Sadie, please! You're messing with my controls."

"Sadie!" Darius barked.

She blinked from her fit of rage, then looked at me, shocked. "I, I'm sorry," she whispered, lowering her dress. "I snapped."

"Count to ten," I said. "It helps."

Sadie gave an embarrassed nod and stepped away.

The old man on-screen shook his head, glaring.

"What's your name?" I asked.

"General Steward," he answered.

"My name is Wayne Johnson, grandson of the Great General Wayne Johnson. My brother Joshua, is sick and needs help. Will you let us in?" I wouldn't tell him I wasn't all human. This old man would do the same to Joshua and me, as Ross did to us. I chose death above being treated like an animal.

"Incoming Sweeper," Juliet whispered.

The glistening arrow appeared over the Dome horizon, heading straight for us. Our guns firing at the one behind us.

"What are you doing?" Darius whispered behind me. "I told you what to say."

"What happened to your brother?" Ross said.

"Poisoned by General Ross... your enemy."

He frowned. "Why?"

"Because he's a Johnson."

The old man mulled it over, his cold eyes shifting.

"Keep it straight," I said, not taking my eyes from him.

It sounded like rocks falling into a metal bucket as the rounds from the incoming Sweeper slammed into the Raptor. "Keep it straight," I repeated and took hold of Juliet's chair.

"There's no human in a Sweeper," Juliet said. "You can't play chicken with it."

"General, have you decided?" I asked.

"I'm not convinced," he said, and disconnected the call.

"Everybody, hold on!" I yelled.

The Sweeper approached faster than I'd expected.

<hr>

General Steward leaned back into his chair, rubbing his chin.

A redhead woman appeared on screen. "This is Lola from operations, General Stew."

He straightened. "How did you get through to me?"

She leaned in until her green eye and red eye patch filled the screen. "You don't have a choice."

"Who do you think you are, giving me orders?"

"I told you, Lola from Operations. Supreme Commander Whitmore and Secretary Martha Grace passed away two minutes ago. Whitmore nominated Commander Von Swartz, and Martha nominated President Green. Council Act Thirteen states that if any Council member harms or causes the quietus of another Council member or family-"

"I know the Act!" He yelled, hitting his desk with a fist.

"Will be removed from office. I will use your conversation with Commander Von Swartz as evidence that you knew he was on that flight if it's too late." She leaned back. "Also, Commander Von Swartz, as of two minutes ago, has the authority to open a window and call off the Sweepers. He has the power now. This is Lola from Operations, out."

"Get ready to pull up," I said, fingers buried in the seat.

The left engine of the Raptor blew apart.

"We're hit," Juliet yelled, hanging on to the shuddering controls. "I won't have the power to–"

The remaining engine disintegrated into a ball of flames.

"We're going down!" Juliet shouted, fighting for control. "If the Sweepers don't get us, the shield will."

I felt a strange sensation in my stomach as the Raptor lost altitude, plunging toward the watery surface.

"This is it," Sadie said, her voice shaking.

"I'm sorry," I said, holding her head tight against my chest.

She looked up and whispered, "Kiss me."

The incoming Sweeper was only seconds away, so I didn't hesitate. I placed my right hand on Joshua's head as our lips touched, first softly, then more intensely. The kiss Juliet gave me was nothing compared to this one – maybe it was the rush to beat death.

The sound of the firing guns in the rear stopped, interrupting our kiss. We both searched for the incoming Sweeper.

"They broke off their attack," Juliet said. "To watch us crash and burn."

The Raptor descended faster, nose-diving toward the shield.

"This is not how it's supposed to be," Darius said, standing behind me, wedged between the doorway. My arm tightened around Sadie as we plummeted towards death.

"Wait!" Juliet yelled. "There!" She pointed at a swirling hole expanding below the Raptor.

"They've opened a window for us," Darius said. "Are the landing jets still working?"

"I hope so." Juliet went to work, flipping switches and turning knobs.

"Slow our descent."

The Raptor shuddered as it fell through the window. Moments later, the city appeared below us – tall glass buildings, lit with thousands of lights and large colourful images, filled the Dome. Far below, flying machines and people scurried like ants. For a moment, I had forgotten about our situation, amazed by the beauty before me.

"There's a building below us!" Juliet pointed.

"Good," Darius said. "Land on the roof. The further we fall, the harder we land."

"Impact in five, four, three," Juliet counted. "Brace for impact!"

I grabbed Sadie around the waist, lifting her from the floor. The sound of crushing metal and shattering glass resonated through the Raptor. Darius collapsed as his legs gave way on impact. Juliet tried to unclip her straps as flames and smoke gusted from the controls. I lowered Sadie to the floor and rushed to Juliet. "Get Joshua," I said to Sadie.

The flames spread, blackening the cracked windshield.

"Wayne, help!" Juliet screamed, kicking at the flames.

I grabbed hold of the straps and pulled. "Come on!" It ripped apart.

Darius was still on the floor, groaning.

"Now we're even," I said as I tossed him over my shoulder.

"I'm not saved yet," he muttered.

Brock, Fritz, and Shorty were searching for something between the scattered containers and debris in the Raptor's rear.

"What you looking for?" I asked between coughs. Smoke filled the Raptor.

"Our weapons," Brock said and pointed to one of the side windows. "We need to shoot it out. It's over two inches thick. The ramp is jammed shut, and there's no other way out."

"But the gunner's room is just glass," I said, entering the room. Shit. I stepped back, dizzy; the glass-encased room was protruding over the edge of the roof. The Raptor shuddered, followed by a loud grinding noise.

"We're going over the edge of the roof!" I threw Darius against a container and ran to the window.

"What are you going to do?" Fritz asked and knelt, trying to get away from the smoke.

"He's getting us out of here," Juliet said, covering her mouth and nose with her arm.

I grabbed hold of a metal railing next to the window and slammed my fist into the glass. A slight crack appeared. Another shudder and a screech intensified my efforts. I punched the glass until it shattered. I stepped back, clutching my throbbing fist, and yelled, "Go!"

Sadie handed Joshua to Fritz. "Get him out of here."

Brock stared at my bloodied hand and turned to Darius lying on the container. "Let me get your skinny arse out of here."

"That would be nice," Darius groaned as Brock picked him up and stumbled toward the window.

The Raptor tipped as one after the other jumped ship. My lungs were on fire. "Go! I'm coming," I yelled at Sadie. "I'm looking for my bag!"

"Are you crazy?" She grabbed my arm and pulled me toward the window.

Another shudder resonated through the hull as the Raptor slid further over the edge.

"H-h-here y-you go." Shorty held up my bag, face blackened by the smoke. I grabbed him and Sadie as the Raptor lost its fight against gravity. Sadie was the first I tossed through the opening, and then Shorty.

Three or four pairs of hands reached through the window as the Raptor made its final bow. I grabbed hold of the hairiest arm. Brock pulled me to safety. We all needed a moment, laying on the roof of the building. I turned on my back, staring at the fading blue heavens.

Johan Thompson

There were no stars – at the farm, this time of day, Venus and Sirius would be glowing. Many a night, mom and I would lie on our backs and watch the night sky. She knew a lot about the stars. I love the stars.

A flying machine with whistling engines blackened the purple skies above us. It was bigger than a Raptor, with more guns under its wings, big and black, unblemished by war. A sin. Another appeared, then another, until the sky swarmed with them. One touched down on the roof, at once lowering its ramp. About two dozen men dressed in brown uniforms stormed out and formed two lines.

Darius sat up. "They will probably throw us in jail."

"What's new," I muttered.

A tall man in a blue suit and blond hair sprinted down the ramp.

Sadie ran toward him, crying, "Dad!"

The man wrapped his arms around her, kissing the top of her head, stroking her hair, eyes filled with tears. I'd never seen a man cry like that. She was his most prised possession. For a split-cycle, I longed for a bond like that. But then this voice from somewhere, deep within, warned, "She's his greatest weakness." What the hell is a cycle?

"Relax," Brock whispered, sitting up next to me.

"What?" I glanced at him.

"It looks like you're about to attack him."

I shook my head and stood up.

"Sorry for leaving you like that, daddy," Sadie sobbed.

"Don't do that again," he said, wiping away her tears before brushing away his own. "I thought I had lost you."

"Dad," she said and pulled him toward us. "These are my friends. They saved my life."

He smiled and stretched out his arms as if waiting for a group hug. "Thank you, thank you, thank you."

"This little boy needs urgent medical attention." Sadie pointed at Joshua on Juliet's lap.

Sadie's father waved the men in uniform closer and said, "Take them to the hospital. Make sure they are well looked after." He approached Darius and stuck out his hand. "Commander Von Swartz."

Darius reached out. "President Green. I apologize for not getting up."

"I believe we will be working together," he said as they shook hands. "Welcome to the Council."

Darius frowned.

"Martha Grace nominated you before she passed away."

I noticed something familiar in Darius's eyes, a flash from the sandstorm, not the physical eyes, but a mixture of emotions – a desire fulfilled, bordering on madness. I imagined the moment in my life, that first moment my fangs had sliced through soft skin and drew first blood... human blood.

Darius swallowed, so did I.

Two men, one standing, the other in a wheelchair, stood on the roof of Building Seven, looking down at the organised mayhem at the base of a nearby skyscraper. A tizzy of blue and red lights kept their distance as the swarming neon red firebugs doused the smouldering wreckage with foam.

"Why did you let him back in?" Gabriel asked with a shake of the head.

"I didn't," Steward said and turned his wheelchair away from the crash site. Oh, you're good.

"Who was that man Darius brought? You think it's an alien?"

Steward smiled and shook his head. "No, that was just Darius being desperate. Remember, outsiders close to the Council still believe the alien bullshit. That's the only way we could get them to do the things we wanted them to do."

"How could the Council allow outsiders to join?"

"The remaining council members respected Whitmore and

Martha." He shrugged. "They approved both appointments."

"I wonder what they will do when they find out the truth?"

Steward removed the green and black chequered blanket covering his lap, stood, and walked toward the edge, placing his hands on the stainless-steel railing. He peered at the rising halo the setting sun cast against the west side of the Dome. "What does it matter? They will accept it and play along, like all the chosen before them. Like you did. Like I did."

Gabriel took up position beside Steward. "I know we have our differences, but together we are stronger."

Steward nodded. "Do they know what killed them?"

"Both drowned in their blood. Lungs perforated."

"Who, besides us, wanted them dead?" Steward muttered, tapping his fingers on the rail.

Gabriel frowned. "You mean it wasn't you?"

"No – and that's what bothers me." Steward let go of the railing. "I know everything going on inside the Dome." He glared at Gabriel. "Even what's going on inside your head."

"What do you mean?" Gabriel said in a defensive tone.

"That's the reason I brought you up here." Steward swung around, elbowed Gabriel in the face, grabbed his legs, and flipped him over the railing.

"What are you doing!" Gabriel screamed, clinging to the rail.

"One of my little birdies told me." Steward smirked and removed a small container from his pocket. "A bird with red hair who goes by the name Blondie."

"Please, Steward," Gabriel cried, trying to pull himself up. "I'll do whatever you want... please!"

"Okay." He smiled. "Die for me then." Steward pointed the container at Gabriel and sprayed gas into his face. "This will paralyze you, but only for a minute – undetectable. You'll be just another dejected little sod who realised life s-s-sucked. Who thought by jumping off a high-rise would send a ripple through Nirvana. Make a point. Make a headline."

Gabriel gasped; eyes filled with fear.

"Nirvana is only meant for those who appreciate its privilege." Steward walked back to his wheelchair. "By the time you hit the ground, I would have forgotten about you." He took a seat with a satisfied grin, threw the blanket over his legs, ironed out the folds, and drove into the awaiting elevator. If it wasn't Gabriel who killed Martha and Whitmore, who then? Darius maybe? But they were working together. Or were they? Steward turned the wheelchair around and smiled as Gabriel's life slipped through his fingers. "I'm sorry, Gabriel. You won't be able to scream on your way down, but at least you'll see your apartment for the last time." He shook his head. "Oh, the fun you had there."

The 'dejected little sod' disappeared with an expression a tad disturbing – a snapshot of pure terror; his face puce with fear, bulging eyes fixated on death, and silent, gaping mouth. Steward expelled the image at once, replacing it with ensuing images of triumph and joy: granite statues of him – the world's saviour, bringer of rain, prosperity, and civil obedience. Crowds singing his praise, hailing his strength and wisdom. The world would indeed be a better place; no famine, no wars, no wicked sexual conduct, no addictions, no politicians, no correctional facilities, no asylums and no religion – the root of all evil. He would be the one to implement the last stage. For decades, humanity had the technology to create the perfect human, capable of being tracked and monitored. A human with conscience and empathy. Awakened. The Seven sins, weakness and disease sliced from its DNA. But, with all the fucking human rights groups and politicians, no one within the council had the balls or power to implement. Until now. As the 'dejected little sod' said, "We need to nip it in the bud." Any deviation from the norm terminated. Gradually, humanity would be cleansed. Strengthened. We can only be truly human when all flaws and shackles are eradicated. This time, we would do it right.

Steward was six when their family moved into the newly constructed Building Seven. The Haves had bought and renovated the thirteen city centres selected globally – in secret, of course. Each centre equipped to fulfil every conceivable need. The have-nots picked up villas and mansions for a fraction of its worth as the Haves moved to their new apartments. Land was dirt cheap and offered some yield. The timing had to be perfect; the have-nots still had to believe there was hope. Propaganda machines advertised the great outdoors, farming and off-grid-living. It worked, the cities emptied. Finally, Earth had enough – had nothing more to give. Destroyed by the Seven sins. Stage two came into fruition on a Tuesday morning at nine. The shields enfolded the Haves and only a few have-nots. The Haves still needed the have-nots for specific duties – duties automation couldn't fulfil. Like bolstering the Haves' ego. Make them feel special. Only those without Glitz and Glamour notice it. Robots could be programmed – but its fakery was known. When bolstered by humans, its fakery is uncertain.

The have-nots starved – oceans were a toxic mush of rubble and sewerage, the land unyielding - barren torture. Earth was ripe for stage three; hasten its demise. The only element of hope that had remained: Rain. So, a decade after the shields, a Wednesday, the Cloud-chasers embarked, crisscrossing the globe, spewing its cargo from the edge of the Stratosphere. The Council back then, one of whom Steward's father had thought it would take a decade to eradicate the parasites - the have-nots. Three decades later, on a Thursday, they implemented Stage Four. They dispatched Sweepers to eliminate the Earth of the few remaining diehards. The unplanned two decades took its toll on resources and civil obedience. The offspring of the Haves did not appreciate their privilege; spoilt, bored, highly opinionated and, for some reason, felt entitled – unaware of the sacrifices their parents made. Continually questioning the status quo. What's on the outside? We want to see the world. Why can't we leave? Is this life? When will the fallout of the asteroid dissipate? History had been rewritten to include a catastrophic event, a reason for Earth's demise. The truth is indefensible, a disgrace to humanity. The truth would also question the competency of the current rule.

11

My footprints disappeared over the horizon. An endless desert surrounded me. Where was I going? Back to the farm? I walked further into the unknown. Was I on my way out?

"Joshua!" I screamed, searching.

I was alone. My heart was like the expanse that surrounded me. I fell to my knees, fingers clawing at the cracks.

"Wayne."

A shadow appeared before me. I looked up. "Mother?"

Her white dress and long gleaming hair fluttered in the wind.

Joshua appeared beside her, beaming. "Goodbye, brother," he whispered and touched my cheek. "I will see you again – don't be sad."

Mother took his hand and said, "I love you, Wayne, and always will. You need to be strong, like always."

They turned and walked away, further into the desert.

"No!" I jumped up and ran after them. "You will not take him from me!" No matter how fast I ran, I could not catch up with them. "I need him! I need you!" They dissolved into the watery mirage.

I fell to my knees and screamed at the top of my lungs, "Bitch!" Again, she had left me!

A flying machine approached high above, in its wake a streak of white powder, which expanded until it covered the entire desert like a veil. The plane exploded in a ball of flames; its fiery chunks streaked across the blue.

I panned the desolate horizon – nothing.

The light breeze intensified, blowing away the powder. Thunder rumbled in the distance, becoming more robust, like an awakening beast. An expanding cloud formed on the horizon, covering the vastness. The rumble increased in intensity. As if riding on the wind, the clouds covered the skies and blocked out the sun.

"Joshua!" I screamed and stumbled to my feet.

The wind ceased as if controlled by an invisible force. Another bout of silence until a blinding white light thundered down to earth. My pounding heart, suffocating. Another beam followed, then another, each more intense, till the clouds wept. I filled my mouth, relishing the clean, unpolluted water, and washed my charred face. No scar! This was a dream. The pouring rain subsided to a trickle, as did my anger. Just a dream, I told myself, but had never experienced rain, never tasted it, never felt it against my skin. Another earth-shattering beam struck the soiled ground, jolting it alive. Trees and grass forced their way through the weakened shell as if it had waited for the perfect moment. The flat landscape morphed into a luscious jungle. Like on Krono, before we destroyed it. A fragile green bird chirped with rustling wings in an unfolding tree. The chatter ceased as it found me. It bounced off the branch and flew my way. I reached out, waiting...

"Wayne."

A gentle stroke on my hand coaxed me out of my dream. I opened my eyes and looked into Sadie's big brown tear-filled eyes. She kneeled before me, where I sat in the chair beside my brother's hospital bed. I sat up; it angered me seeing her like that.

"I'm sorry," she whispered.

I glanced over her head at the doctor standing beside Joshua's bed. The moment our eyes met, I knew it wasn't a dream.

He was with his mother; the vividness of my dream told me so. What if he had come back after I had woken? What if it wasn't as amazing as he had thought? But the flat line told me he liked it there. Coward. Why was I so angry with him all the time? Was it because he held me back? Because he thought he was my only reason for living.

I understood why the captain killed himself; he was human. He had experienced love and then had lost it. Mother tried to explain love once. She said it was like a bine seed planted in your stomach. The one you love supplied the water that made it grow and flourish until it reached all the corners of your body. But what if the one supplying the water dies. The bine will retract, wither, and die - leaving an empty shell. Like, father. So, it's wiser not to fall in love.

I felt bad admitting that I didn't feel a bine die with my brother's departure. However, he was my responsibility, and I failed. That emotion I didn't like.

But what now? Joshua was gone, and here I am in Nirvana. Just a farm boy. No, I'm not – that was what the captain and mother wanted me to believe. Sadie is my responsibility now. And this time, I will not fail. Her pathetic father doesn't have the balls to protect her.

It was only me, Joshua's shell, and his teddy bear in the room. I'd almost died in the Raptor searching for the bloody thing. Sadie had left. I had one last thing to do for Joshua - the voice in the sandstorm begged me. Sadie would help me. Krono? When or where was Krono? Did I destroy it?

Steward grinned as the green light to the left lit up. The door slid open, and Darius stepped out. The men in uniform formed a barrier in front of the wheelchair.

"Where's Green?" Steward asked.

"He... he still needs... a moment," Darius muttered in a daze, shoulders slumped.

"Close the door!" Steward ordered one of his men.

Darius shook his head as the door closed behind him. "You fucking bastards," he whispered, locking eyes with Steward.

"Leave us!" Steward ordered his men as he removed a pistol from underneath his green and black chequered blanket.

Darius kept his eyes on him until they were alone.

"Survival of the fittest, Commander," Steward said. "Our predecessors did what was necessary to survive the drought. Vegetation and animals were nearing extinction. We would have died of starvation. They gathered what they could before activating the shield."

"That I understand!" Darius yelled. "But to ionize the atmosphere to prevent condensation. To prevent the cycle of life from continuing!"

"Haven't you been listening?" Steward bellowed. "We're running out of power. We had thirty years. We need to exterminate any humans still alive out there before the shield collapses. We will be defenceless against the starving masses that will storm the city."

"Then stop with the cleansing. Stop ionizing the atmosphere."

"No!" Steward snapped. "Any sign of life, a raindrop, a sprout would give them hope – a reason to live. Scientists predicted humans would delay the earth's recovery by decades. They would interrupt the cycle, consume whatever the earth produces, preventing the next step."

Darius shook his head, disgusted. "Might I remind you, you're also human."

"You get human, and then you get human."

"And the alien armada on our doorstep?"

Steward shrugged. "We had to create a threat for the troops on the ground and air to follow our orders. That's why most of the Council members are high-ranking military officials. And that's why I didn't believe you when you said you had one of them."

Darius stared at him, unflinching.

"You were bluffing, weren't you?"

"Of course, I was bluffing! You were trying to kill me!"

He replaced the weapon under the blanket. "Let's put that behind us. You're part of the Council now."

"And the citizens, the truth will come out one day, and they will find out we deliberately destroyed the earth, that we cause billions to starve?"

"They are the children of the wealthy, the selected, who constructed this bubble. They were well aware of the masses that starved on their doorstep. Why did they not protest? Why was there no outcry? It's called self-preservation, a basic human instinct. That's why you activated your light." He glanced over Darius's shoulder. "And that's why his light will also go on – just like all the others before him." Steward turned his wheelchair around and headed for the elevator. "Just like all the governments before us." He entered the elevator and spun back to Darius. "No matter how hard we try, Commander, we're only human. We would have reached this point. We've just sped up the process."

Darius glanced over his shoulder as the door opened behind him.

"I told you," Steward said, beaming at the green light.

Things went crazy after Darius suggested we bury Joshua at the farm. He arranged a Vector G6 passenger carrier, a window to leave, and diverted Sweepers from our route. We were on our way back to the farm a week after my brother's death. What I also did not expect was the group who waited for us as we entered the flying machine: Juliet,

Brock, Fritz, Shorty and Darius, all dressed in black, all saddened by my brother's departure.

Juliet and Fritz sat at the helm, the rest of us in the back, periodically glancing at the small white coffin in the aisle, expecting it to open at any moment. But it never did.

"Darius seems different," I said to Sadie, seated next to me.

"My father too," she said, fingering a shiny cross dangling from her neck.

"What do you mean?" I resisted the urge to touch her, afraid of the bine seed. The last time we'd kissed was when we faced death, nine days and seven hours ago. Since then, Joshua and my dream occupied my thoughts. The Dome somehow changed us – pushed us apart. But I'm not relieved. My heart wanted her close, but something from within the sandstorm warned me. Women are like fire. Enjoy their warmth, but if you get too close...

"He went for a meeting smiling and came back crying. He's like the day I fled the Dome."

"Seems like being a Council member is not that... great. But give him some time." My words had nothing behind it – cold.

"I think they told them they are running out of time."

Is that such a terrible thing? "Don't worry, I will protect you."

She frowned, shaking her head. "That's great, Wayne, but what about the rest of the people? My father, my friends?"

Why should I worry about the rest of the people? Should I? "I mean, I will try to protect them too?" I cringed at the emptiness of my words.

She sighed and glanced at the coffin in the aisle.

Okay, I get it! I couldn't even protect my brother. "I'll be back." I had to get away from the fire.

She stared at an invisible spot on the cold grey floor, holding on to the cross around her neck.

I stood up and moved to the rear. Darius only noticed me when I took a seat next to him. "You've been staring out the window since we've left."

"I couldn't save your brother."

"You were not the one supposed to." We sat in silence, staring at the unchanging expanse. "I know you had a lot to do with this," I said. "Thank you."

He pulled himself away from his reflection and gave me a forced smile. "It's the least I could do."

"Your plan. I will still help you."

He turned in his chair, eyes piercing as if he tried to see inside my head. "What's your deal, Wayne?"

I knew what he meant. "What do you mean?"

"The Council made up the alien threat to justify their actions. Ross believes there will be an invasion." He shifted in his chair. "Let's look at the facts. Our satellites do not detect any spacecraft or anything. You were born on Earth. But you're not human." He waited for me to continue, his eyes begging for answers.

I shrugged. "And here I am. I'm sorry, Darius, but I don't have the answers."

He fell back in his chair with a sigh and returned to his reflection.

"I had a dream."

"Hmmm," he murmured, distracted.

"The day my brother died, I saw him and my mother. She said to take him back to the farm, but then, something strange happened in the dream. I don't know if it was them trying to tell me something or something else trying to tell me something."

"A lot of something," he muttered.

"I was in a desert, and a flying machine came overhead, spraying the usual white powder, then it exploded."

He turned his head toward me.

"Then there were beams and clouds, and water falling from the sky. I felt earth's anger. And then trees and flowers and stuff broke through the ground." I glanced over his shoulder through the window at the monotonous skyline. "It was the most beautiful thing I've ever seen." So was Krono. Why did I destroy it?

I couldn't tell if he was excited or confused, but life was back in his eyes.

"The problem is," I continued. "I've never felt rain or seen anything like that. I could smell the trees and flowers and–"

"Yes!" he sat up. "I knew it!" He jumped from his chair and shoved past me, pacing the aisle. "Screw the scientists. They said it would take years." He stopped and waved his finger at me. "It's a sign from somewhere. I don't know. But there's no way you could know about that."

"About what?" Sadie asked.

He glanced at Joshua's coffin and raised his hands. "I'll tell you after."

We all went back to our positions, but the static in the cabin remained. I felt my brother in the flying machine as if he had a part in Darius's reaction. Whatever Darius wanted to tell us, it had confirmed my dream; my brother would join my mother – wherever that may be. Ross was right; my mother didn't die – she left us. She left me.

I returned to my seat next to Sadie.

"What is it?" she whispered.

"I'll tell you later," I lied, because she wouldn't understand. I knew Joshua and mother weren't dead. However, the captain was dead because he was human. Thank the gods.

My stomach was in a tight knot as I stepped off the flying machine. Everything was how we left it; the lopsided cow enclosure, the rusty windmill, the battered tool shed and the weatherworn tunnels – as if a large cat shredded its cloth.

"You lived here?" Sadie asked, eyes wide with shock.

"I wouldn't call it living." For the first time in my life, I felt ashamed. I knew more of the world, how other people lived. Now, I saw my home through Sadie's eyes.

I stopped a fair distance from the farmhouse as if an invisible force pushed me away.

"Was he like you?" Sadie asked.

"No." I wiped my sweaty palms on my pants; Captain could, at any moment, emerge from the shadow of the doorway. "He's human."

"Why were you so afraid of him, then?" Sadie slipped her hand into mine.

Her warm, velvety touch sent a charge through my body like that first taste of human blood. I took a deep breath. "Because he was my father." I looked at Sadie. "Isn't it a natural reaction to be afraid of your father?"

Sadie frowned, then shook her head. "Nope."

Darius fell in beside me. "Your mother, did she look human?"

"No, I only realised she was different when I met Juliet. She didn't change when I angered her. I saw other women on grandpa's memory cards but never paid attention to the detail."

"How was she different?" Sadie whispered, her fingers caressing my palm.

"She had no ears but could hear. Her eyes were the colour of the setting sun, and her skin a curse."

"What do you mean?"

"She changed colour when her mood changed."

Sadie and Darius looked at me with impassive expressions.

"What?" I asked.

"You messing with us?" Sadie said.

"I'm not." I laughed. "She had the same skin colour as you. But when she experienced an intense emotion, her colour changed. It wasn't bright colours, more faded as if sprinkled on."

"Undertones?" Sadie said.

I nodded. "She turned reddish when angry, greyish when afraid and yellow when she kissed father or us. I once saw her purple, but only briefly. They chased me out of the room."

"We'll get him," Brock said as he and Fritz walked past, carrying the other coffin Sadie had arranged.

"Thanks." It was all I could get out, my throat as dry as the ground I stood on. What if they found nothing?

"I visited this place a few days ago and saw the whip," Darius said.

"So?"

"Was it your blood on it?"

Sadie glanced at me.

"I was... difficult."

"Stop blaming yourself," Darius said. "He was... difficult. Could never figure him out."

I nodded and walked toward the dead tree, where I would bury Joshua. Next to my Rock-of-reflection.

"What was in the safe?" Darius asked.

Shit, I had forgotten about the memory card. "Nothing." Was it still in my bag?

Fritz and Brock stumbled out of the farmhouse, as white as the coffin they carried, their eyes projecting the scene they'd just left. Fritz seemed as if he was about to pass out.

Brock looked around at the barren landscape. "Where you want to bury your father?"

"There." I pointed to the cow enclosure. "Under the shit."

Darius shook his head. "Wayne."

"Okay," I muttered and pointed. "There, next to the windmill."

"I don't want you to return later," Darius said. "Bury him next to your brother, please."

I gave a drawn-out sigh and yelled at the coffin bearers, "Okay! Bury him next to my brother."

"I know it's a focking sad day and everything," Fritz said. "But please make up yer bloody mind." They had reached the windmill.

I dug my brother's grave, and the rest took turns with my father's hole. The ground was unyielding, and the sun did not disappoint. I finished four hours later. Shorty, Fritz, and Brock shortly after - exhausted and covered in dust. As all gathered around the fresh graves, I experienced something unearthly – a camaraderie. Not one will stab me in the back. Unbelievable.

We stood a moment with our heads bowed, staring at our dusty boots. Somebody had to say something, and that somebody was me.

I cleared my throat. "This world is fucked." I received a few frowns, but all gave a slight nod. "However, none of you had to be here." I pointed at the piles of dirt. "They meant nothing to you. But you all came. Before I realised what I was, I hated all humans, I hated the world, I hated my life. I don't understand why we're here, what our purpose in life is, but what makes it bearable is this moment, you being here. Because of you, I hate humans less. Life is worth living, as long as you have someone or something to die for." I looked at the small pile of dirt by my feet. "So, for that, I thank you, brother." I know he couldn't hear me. "Sorry for being such an asshole with you. Goodbye."

Sadie took my hand and squeezed it.

Darius looked sad, a picture of sombreness – as if his face was melting away.

"You only long for something once you've experienced it and then lose it," I said, looking at Darius. He was a picture of sombreness – as if his face was melting away. "I never knew how the world was before, but I know now. And I know you can fix this fucked-up world."

Darius stared at me, eyes narrowing, then smiled. "Many people will end up like this," he pointed at the graves, "to fix this fucked-up world."

"I think saving the world is worth dying for." Something, a voice or a face, rebelled against the words.

"Wait a second," Sadie said. "Before we save the world, I think we all need to get pissed tonight." She nudged me with her elbow. "What do you say, farm boy?"

"I don't know what that means," I said, "But it sounds like fun."

"Just don't smile like that tonight," Darius said, pointing at my fangs. "You will scare away the ladies."

"Smile all you want," Sadie said. "I want you all for myself tonight."

"I need a break from that tiny apartment they shoved us in," Fritz said, glaring at Darius.

Darius shrugged. "Hey, it's all I could organise. Hopefully, somebody living in a bigger apartment will die this week."

"The apartment is okay," Juliet said. "It's the stuff they call food that's a problem."

"I like it," Fritz said. "It's better than the soup we had in the cave."

"Yeah, what's in those biscuits?" Brock asked.

Darius pointed at the graves. "Saw any of these in the Dome?"

Brock chuckled. "What do you mean?"

"That's the reason your father never wanted to come to the Dome." Darius glanced at me. "And that's also the reason your father," he glanced at Sadie, "is in such a state."

"What do you mean?" Brock asked.

"You probably had a little piece of the woman who had occupied your tiny apartment," Darius said, suppressing a smile.

"I'm going to be sick," Fritz said, and broke away from the group. "I emptied the whole dispenser yesterday."

"Don't worry, it's processed. They only extract the proteins," Darius said. "What do you think they put in the soup where you come from?"

"We're not so different," I muttered.

"Wake up, people," Darius said. "It's called survival. You can only grow so much in a tunnel. The real meat ran out decades ago. We're part of the cycle of life. We're all going to be flushed down a toilet one day." He glanced at Brock. "They can't wait for you to die – you'll fill six dispensers."

Steward smiled as the green light came on. The red door opened moments after, and a well-set man exited. He removed a handkerchief from the inside pocket of his uniform and wiped his forehead.

"No more biscuits for me," General Josef Keller said.

"Don't worry, Josef, Council members, get the genuine thing."

Keller shook his head and placed a hand on his bulging stomach. "You know how many biscuits it took to look like this? I consumed a platoon."

"More likely, a brigade," Steward muttered.

"So, no aliens?"

Steward shook his head.

"Good to know. So, who are we fighting?"

"Everyone outside."

Keller nodded. "We need to neutralise the threat before the shield collapses."

"Glad to have you onboard, General." Steward turned the wheelchair around and headed for the elevator. "We found General Johnson's stronghold – they are the only threat."

"When do we attack?" he asked, swaying toward the elevator.

"Tomorrow at dawn – after we get rid of the Council." He turned around and waited for Keller to enter. "We have complete control over the military now. Time to disband this silly council and let everyone know who runs the show."

"What about the Council members in the other Domes?"

"One city at a time, Josef. We will deal with them as and when their shields fail. For now, I piss in my pond, and they piss in theirs. Besides, I've never heard or spoken to anyone in the other cities. They vote, that's all. A tick on a big screen. I will simply cut comms." He glanced at his watch. "In one hour and sixteen minutes, the Council will be no more."

"What did you promise the other generals?"

He shrugged. "Each his own country." He threw off his blanket and stood up.

Keller retreated into a corner, shocked. "And this?"

"Defeat always falls on those who thought their enemy weak."

Keller shook his head. "You've been planning this for a long time."

"I will be in control of everything; resources, redistribution of land. They will remember me as the creator of New Earth, who brought it back from the brink of extinction. Who summoned the clouds to bring back life? Who brought order? They will remember me as a god."

Keller forced himself further into the corner. "And what country do I get?"

"After the Chinese had its way with Africa, nobody wanted her." Steward took his seat as the elevator doors opened. "Now, if you'll excuse me, I need to take a leak."

"W-w-why aren't you s-s-sweating?" Shorty asked Darius as we made our way back to the flying machine.

"It's a nitro-suit, keeps him cool," I answered.

"Same as our uniforms, which we can't wear anymore," Juliet said with a roll of eyes.

"I'll get you Dome uni–" Darius froze. "Did you hear that?"

It was a sound I'd heard before – in my strange dream and the other when Joshua's mother left. We searched the horizon, nothing.

Shorty pointed at the sky above us. "T-t-there!"

It resembled a Dome window, but instead of a whirlpool of water, it was swirling clouds.

"Damn it! Run for the Vector!" Darius ordered.

The cloud grew, turning faster and faster until a beam of blue light ascended from the centre, striking my brother's grave with the sound of a hundred shotguns. I grabbed Sadie and Juliet and shielded them from the rolling blue wave.

"What the hell?" Stacey whispered as her controls lit up. "Commander Darius, come in!" Static. "Commander–"

Captain Bryan ran into the control room. "What happened?"

"A massive energy surge fifty clicks to the west – Darius's location."

"From where?"

"Our sensors can't detect the origin."

"Try him again."

"Commander Von Swartz, come in." Silence. "Commander!" She glanced at Bryan. "I think you need to call the President."

12

H e woke, gasping.

"Relax," a woman soothed.

"Help!" His head struck glass as he tried to sit.

"Just a few more moments," she said. "Take deep breaths."

The blue light surrounding him dimmed. He filled his lungs, blinking. I can breathe again! "Wayne!" His voice was unfamiliar, deeper, grown-up. His heart rate was slower and more powerful - every beat pounced against his chest, like a blacksmith shaping iron. He balled his fists and grunted as his nails tore into his palms.

"You're safe," she pressed her hand against the glass cylinder.

"You're the woman in my dreams," he whispered, wide-eyed. "You're... you're..."

"Yes." She leaned forward and kissed the glass, her blond hair skimming the surface.

"Mother?" he whispered. "But how? Where am I?"

"I've thought of you and Malik every day since they took me."

"My teddy bear?"

She gave a loving smile and whispered, "Your brother."

His eyes lit up. "Is Wayne here?"

"No, he's not ready. He must stay a while longer."

He studied his naked body, fear clutching at his throat. "What happened? I'm a man!"

The woman glanced over her shoulder and said, "You will remember everything in a moment, but for now, we need to leave the transporter room."

The cylinder slid open, and she reached to embrace him, kissing him on his bald head. "I've missed you, Arden."

"But my name is Joshua?"

She cupped his chin and raised his head, staring into his eyes. "Yes, you must remember your human side, the Joshua inside you... the little boy." Then she wrapped him in a white cloth and said, "Come, let's go."

Heavy footsteps and the sound of rattling chains approached.

"Quickly," she whispered. "Hide!"

Joshua ran toward one of the many stone pillars in the room and hid behind it.

"We detected a memory transfer," a man growled in a strange language, but Joshua understood.

Only Amira was in view.

She bowed her head and said, "The time has come for Malik to be awakened, Lucius."

"Damn it, Amira! Alcantar did not approve it!" the man's voice thundered through the chamber.

Joshua stepped back as the man, Lucius, appeared, glaring down at his mother. He never saw such a frightful, towering figure; dressed in black, with chains dangling from his legs and arms. Taller than Wayne, with bigger arms... bigger everything. A deep scar ran across his bald head, also worse than Wayne's. Lucius also had no ears, just like his mother. Joshua reached for his right ear. *Just like me.*

Lucius grabbed Joshua's mother by the hair and jerked her head back. "What if he's not with us anymore?" he hissed. "He's been with the humans far too long."

"But this was our plan from the beginning," she said, her skin blackened.

"Malik's plan," he seethed, pulling her head further back. "Not mine."

"Stop!" Joshua yelled and stepped out from behind the pillar. "Leave her alone!"

Lucius released his hold. "Arden? I thought you were still with Malik."

"The humans killed his human body," Amira said. "I had to bring him back."

Lucius sniffed, nostrils flaring. "Interesting," he said, and exposed his fangs. "I can smell your fear from here." He strolled toward Joshua. "You've been with the humans too long – it's made you weak."

As Joshua straightened his back and wrapped the cloth tighter around his body, he realised his strength, bulging chest, and biceps. I'm taller than him. He looked around the room and remembered the day they had placed him in the transporter. The day Joshua was born on Earth, eleven Earth years after Malik had transported, and eighteen years after his mother started her mission.

"He's confused, Lucius," Amira said and stepped in front of him. "His human memories are still fresh in his mind. He's still just Joshua, the little boy."

Lucius shoved Amira out of the way. "How I've waited for this moment of weakness. That body means nothing without the heart of Arden."

Amira grabbed him around the leg and begged, "The Elders want to see him!"

"They failed!" Lucius shouted, wrenching Amira from his leg, tossing her across the room.

"You know, Malik," Arden said as he let the cloth fall from his body. "He never gives up... And you know if you hurt me," Arden approached Lucius, "which is unlikely. He will find you wherever you are and kill you. You're angry with her because she has awakened him, and you're afraid he will succeed." He stopped in front of Lucius, glaring down at him. "He will be hailed a hero and crowned ruler of our new world." Yes, he could feel it now. He was no longer Joshua; he was transforming into Arden once again.

Lucius stood, fists clenched. "You're still confused. You hated your brother and would never allow him to take your rightful place. He failed six Earth years ago. He had to be inside the Dome before his transformation. That's why Alcantar transported you to do what he couldn't." He sneered. "And here you are, also a failure."

"Malik could still succeed," Arden seethed.

"The humans will never allow him to enter. His impatiens and temper will give him away."

"He did not know what or who he was," Amira said as she struggled to her feet. The tinge of black on her skin faded. "We had to wait for the right moment."

"Fools," Lucius muttered.

Arden grabbed him around the neck with one hand and shoved him to the ground. "You're the fool," Arden hissed, exposing his fangs. "It would have been impossible to awaken him inside the Dome. We cannot penetrate their defences, and you know it."

Lucius gagged, his tongue searching for air.

Arden released his hold and stepped back. "My younger brother has formed a powerful bond with the humans and will be inside the Dome as planned. Awakened."

Lucius held his throat, turning on his side, heaving.

Amira walked up to Arden and reached for his hand, but he pulled away in anger. "The humans made you weak." He turned and walked toward the doorway. "The Elders were right to recall you — you were having second thoughts." He shook his head. "Of all the human males on that planet, you chose him to fertilize you."

Amira lowered her head, disappointed. She'd hoped Arden would have kept something of Joshua: compassion, empathy – humanity. The nightmare of her recall was still fresh in her mind. Her mission was to travel to Earth and infiltrate their defences, to plant the seed of its destruction, but instead she'd discovered love. Amira wanted her sons to experience the same before they awakened and set the wheels of human annihilation in motion. She hoped they would reconcile. But Arden's reaction confirmed her fears -the Leon race, especially the males, was dead inside, their purpose to conquer and destroy. The only pleasure was to see their enemy suffer. Although there were humans with similar characteristics, they were the minority. The majority craved love, companionship, fulfilment by doing good. Here she was, mother to the most feared conquerors, preparing to destroy the final speck of good left in the universe.

Arden reappeared in the doorway, glaring at Lucius. "If you touch her again, I will kill you. She's not just a female, but the only Dream-walker Malik approved to communicate with."

Amira turned away to conceal her smile and tinge of blue. There was hope still.

It was as if a shotgun had gone off in my head. An explosion of images reeled through my mind, pushing me to the brink of madness. I grabbed my head, afraid it might explode, and fell to the ground, gasping for air, fighting the tide of disturbing images. But the more I struggled, the deeper I sank - until surrounded by darkness.

The alarms were still blaring in the control room when an operator turned to Steward. "Incoming call from outside the Dome. Should I allow access, General?"

"From where?"

"The same location where we've detected the smoke, General."

Steward tapped his finger on his armrest, mulling it over.

"General?"

"I'll take it in my office." He turned to the operator. "On a secure line."

Static filled the screen in his office, and then the image of an elderly man appeared. He looked in his seventies, but his dense black hair threw him. Must be a toupee. "Supreme Commander Steward," he said. "Thank you for taking my call."

"You have me at a disadvantage, sir," General Steward said, approaching the screen. "You know me, but I don't know you."

The man smiled. "I'm General Ross, commander of the outcasts, remnants of the late General Johnson."

"I can't say it's a pleasure, General," Steward said.

"The feeling is mutual. But we have a common problem."

"And what is that?"

"We detected, and I'm certain you have detected, the surge of energy that struck Earth a few minutes ago."

"It's just a solar flare."

Ross's frown filled the screen. "No, General, the signature is consistent with the surge that struck Earth so many times before. Your shield is still operational, so I'm not sure why they struck prematurely."

"What are you trying to say, General?"

"This is their modus operandi, how they invaded all the other cities. The moment the shield fails, they hit the city with an electromagnetic pulse. Thereby disabling all defences and, most importantly, communication." He shifted in his seat. "They still want the planet to survive because they need to inhabit it. They sit and wait on the sideline, taking us out one by one. You see, when they had arrived, the cities were already protected. Most humans outside the domes had perished. So, Johnson's shield prevented a full-blown invasion. Their technology cannot penetrate the Dome."

Steward sighed. "General, this is the story we told the military to—"

"To do your dirty work!" Ross yelled, slamming his fist on the desk. "I know! And your lie became a reality!"

Steward leaned back in his seat. "We did what we had to."

"And we did what we had to, but now we need to stand together."

"Two things, Ross. Why did my predecessors not know about this, and how do you know about this?"

"While you were busy destroying the world, we captured one of them – over twenty years ago."

"And he just told you everything," Steward said with a hand gesture.

"It was her, a stubborn her. Human or alien, everything has a breaking point." Ross smirked. "And to answer your second question, I think your predecessor knew about the invasion long before they had arrived. That's why he invented the shield."

"Who? Johnson?"

Ross nodded. "As if he could see into the future. Unfortunately, the rest of The Council couldn't. Greed feeds on innovation. They only saw an opportunity. The puppet masters made plans to destroy what's left on the outside and start anew."

Ross smirked at Steward's silence. "I see that I've got your attention."

"I'm not convinced yet. Then why are there no mention of aliens in the Re-" Steward looked away, searching for a word starting with re.

"You mean the Reveal? Because there is no one left after the invasion of a city."

Steward leaned forward in his wheelchair. "How do you know about the Reveal?"

General Ross chuckled. "We've been hacking your system for years. We spread the image of the President's daughter."

"But we did not detect a breach?"

"We're using the technology retrieved from the alien ship. The same technology that allowed us to search for food without you detecting us."

Steward's face went ashen. "But that means they also—"

"They know everything about you, your plans, your secrets... everything."

"Why are you telling me this now?"

"Because our minor accident has left us exposed."

"We noticed."

"And we know that you are planning an attack."

Obviously, the fool is so bloody desperate. "What do you want, Ross?"

"I have over four thousand people who need a new home."

Steward shook his head. "We don't have space, and I doubt if any of the other Domes do."

"What other cities?"

Steward waved away the remark.

"I will hand you everything we've got – technology, food, intel, military, you name it."

"I can arrange for you, your family, and your scientists."

"Together, we stand a better chance."

"That is my offer, Ross. Take it or leave it." Steward's eyes narrowed. "And if you don't, I will attack and take what I need."

"If I go down," Ross moved towards the camera until his eyes filled the screen, "you will go down."

Ross ended the call and slammed his fist on the desk.

"I take it we need to prepare for battle," Buchanan said and stood up from his chair in the corner.

"Fuck him!" Ross shouted and grabbed a book from his desk, throwing it across the room.

Buchanan stared at the photograph of Wayne Johnson on Ross's table. "The alien story surprised steward," he mused. "So, that means Darius did not tell him about the one in their midst."

Steward looked at Buchanan through narrowed eyes. "That means Darius is working on his own plan. He doesn't trust Steward."

"Do the aliens know everything that's going on in the Dome?"

Ross snorted. "No, I made that up – thought Steward would let us in to get his hands on the technology."

"How do you know everything, then?"

"I've got my people on the inside – the same people who gave us access to humiliate the President's daughter."

"I think you need to call Darius. Tell him everything you just told Supreme Commander Shithead. He is now part of the Council. Maybe he can help us."

Ross picked up the photograph of Wayne. "Maybe the alien is on our side."

"With all due respect, General, after what you did to him and his brother. Juliet was right. He was our only hope."

Ross fell back into his chair. "I did what I thought was right."

Buchanan stared at the wall of books, shaking his head. "Maybe God is tired of us, after everything we've done to each other since the dawn of man. We never learn, do we? We always follow our stubborn ways of what we," he glanced at Ross, "thought was right." He walked toward the doorway and turned with the handle in hand. "We've never deserved this planet. Maybe they can do a better job."

Ross shook his head as Buchanan closed the door. "That from a man who denied food to starving babies."

"Wayne!" Sadie called me back from the darkness. I woke in the flying machine, surrounded by humans. Wayne's no more a weakling, an ignorant farm boy. Thank the gods he's dead. Alcantar is the name of my father – not the name of the god the humans pray to.

"Are you okay?" Sadie asked, placing her hand on my forehead.

"No, he's not," Darius said, looking down at me.

Leons despise a woman's affection – it shows weakness. We take what we want whenever we want – our terms. Women are not allowed to make the first advance. Great warriors had fallen prey to their magic.

"He looks confused and scared," Brock said, standing hands on hips.

I am Malik, destroyer of worlds, but I'm also Wayne, a farm boy polluted with human blood. For now, I'll be Wayne. My purpose was as bright as the sun: deactivate the Dome and clear the path for my troops. I will prove to Father that I'm next in line to the throne and not Arden. Finally, I will have his approval. He will see me as a warrior, not as his son. We had planned many Earth years for this moment, and I would not let him down. This would be my greatest achievement.

"W-W-Wayne?"

I closed my eyes as I felt the rage boil within me. We kill weaklings like him at birth. "Yes," I said through gritted teeth.

"A-a-re y-y-you o-o-kay?"

"I'm fine." I opened my eyes and noticed Sadie's troubled expression.

She removed her hand and stood up. "Let's give him a moment."

"Do you know what that was?" Darius asked, but his expression told me he wasn't asking.

"A blue beam."

"From where?"

I shrugged. "From the sky."

"Actually, Wayne, there were two blue beams: one hit your brother's grave, and moments after, another one struck you," Darius said. "That was not a coincidence. Another peculiar thing, you were holding onto Sadie and Juliet, and nothing happened to them."

"I took the brunt of the beam," I said.

Fritz stepped in. "Sadie is right. Let's give the lad a moment." He took Darius by the arm and pulled him away.

Sadie glanced over her shoulder as she walked back to her seat. She seemed hurt or afraid. I couldn't tell which. Shit! I still need her to complete my mission. Human females were hard to read – they remained the same colour whatever their mood. Leons weren't good at detecting emotion. That's why the gods made it easy with their women.

As I lay on my back, I thought of Arden, my older brother. So different to Joshua, and yet the same being. Why did they send him to Earth thirteen years after me? Did they think I wouldn't succeed? Or did Amira fell pregnant with the human by mistake, and they took the opportunity? That night, six years ago, when the Leons transported my brother, my mother and I were lying on our backs watching the stars. As the whirlpool of clouds appeared above us, she looked at me – her skin a cheerful yellow – and said, "Call your father. God answered my prayers." I was on the doorstep when the beam struck. My father knew something because he came running out of the house, stopped by my side and said, "I will meet your brother soon."

Did my father know about the invasion? If he did, why had he been so excited about another alien on his doorstep? Somehow, I already knew the answer: my mother had not intended to follow through. She'd tried her best to raise us as humans, show us love, compassion, and beauty. She had planned to convince us not to proceed after our awakening, or at least to fill us with doubt. The Elders had been aware of this, and that's why they'd recalled her. My human father turned into a different man then, a man without purpose, as if his soul had left with my mother.

Even after the recall, my mother continued to annoy me as she wandered into my dreams, showing me beauty at every turn. But she had forgotten it was humans who'd destroyed that beauty. Humans took our farm away, killed my brother – as far as they were aware – and they'd almost killed me. They were an emotional species, corrupt and driven by greed.

Yet, I admired Amira, her stubbornness. When she believed in something, it was challenging to sway her. Like me.

I struggled to my feet and made my way to the bathroom. The

humans were observing every move I made, their eyes filled with suspicion. Especially Darius. I had to try harder, be more like Wayne... for now. Sadie would be the most difficult to mislead. I stared at my reflection in the bathroom mirror, considering this strange combination of Malik and Wayne, stroking my blond hair, touching my ears, inspecting my hands. Am I more human or Leon? I had transported to my mother when the embryo was in its first stage before my human host received its consciousness - or soul, as mom had explained. It was the first time we had attempted it with another species. We had to because I had to look more human.

"What's wrong?" Sadie asked, standing in the doorway. "What happened out there?"

I turned to her and shrugged. "Nothing."

"Don't lie to me, please," she said. "You seem different – I can see it in your eyes."

I reached out to her because that's what Wayne would do. Sadie gave a step back. "You're afraid of me?" I asked, trying to control the anger in my voice.

She looked away.

"I'm still Wayne." I didn't know why I wanted to convince her, but it troubled me to see her like that.

"Why are you so angry? For a moment, when Shorty spoke to you, it looked like you wanted to kill him."

"He irritates me," I snapped and returned to the mirror. "He's weak."

"I saw what you saw," Sadie whispered after a moment's silence.

"What do you mean?"

"When the beam struck, I saw shocking images of a man, a violent man. And when you opened your eyes, I saw something of that man."

I slumped my head. It would be more difficult than I'd thought. I glared at her and whispered, "You better not tell anyone."

Her eyes pooled with tears as she retreated to the doorway. "I don't know who you are now, but I fell in love with Wayne. Don't forget why we are here. We did it for you, Wayne. And Shorty is not weak. He saved your life. Who do you think killed Koonz?" She would've radiated red if she was Leon. "He gave up everything for you," Sadie fumed. "So, think of that before you throw us away." She turned on her heel and stalked off.

"I didn't ask you to save me!" I yelled. What was going on with me? Malik would never stand for this – a woman talking to him like that.

I leaned my head against the mirror; I'd been Malik for an hour, and she'd already figured it out. Something took hold of my heart, shaking and squeezing it. I couldn't breathe. Take it easy, Wayne. Malik! I'm Malik! I needed to get out of this tin can. Even if it kills me. I stumbled to the back of the cabin, clawing at my collar, heaving, searching for the switch to lower the ramp.

The others turned in their seats, staring at me, confused.

"You all right, Scar?" Brock asked, rising from his seat.

I waved him off and whispered, "I'm... fine... I just need some... air."

"Looks like a panic attack to me," Darius mumbled.

"Yer right," Fritz said. "It's a focking panic attack."

Leons don't get fucking panic attacks. I noticed a red button behind a container and stumbled toward it.

"Wayne, no!" Darius jumped up and ran toward me.

"Juliet!" Fritz yelled. "Land! It's an emergency!"

I slammed the button with my fist – triggering every alarm onboard - lowering the ramp. Darius was about to grab me from behind when the flying machine started its rapid descent, throwing him to the front of the cabin. He landed on Brock. I dropped to my knees and grabbed hold of the grid covering the ramp. Sadie and Fritz clawed their way toward me, their screams drowned by the air rushing into the cabin. I could only see the blue sky and not the land below. Wayne's grip tightened the closer Sadie came to him. I had underestimated the farm boy. He is stronger than expected. As if she gave him more power.

I didn't know how high we were, but I didn't care. This is the only way. I would fall to my death, transport back to Malik's body, and tell Arden I had failed. We would never give up, though. That's what we do. That's what we are good at: our purpose. We had never failed before.

"We will fight this together!" Sadie shouted. "You're not that man I saw."

I turned and looked into her pleading eyes. "Stay away!" Malik will hurt her. For a moment, it was only her and me, no alarms, no screams. Can't fight it; I'm more human than Leon. "I'm sorry," I whispered and let go of the grid. Did Malik let go or Wayne? As I left the flying machine, the image of my father's headless corpse flashed through my mind.

And then I struck the sand less than two seconds later, knocking the wind out of me. Shit. The flying machine touched down nearby, its whining engines dying.

My escape did not help – I still felt the same. I was not the Malik I knew. Even if I transported back to my old body, I would again feel this way. This was me now, a bag of confusion. If I returned like this, they would kill me like a blind Leon baby. I sat up, heaving. A wall of eyes stared down at me.

"What the hell were ye thinking, lad?" Fritz asked, standing, hands on his hips, shaking his head.

"Trying to kill himself," Darius said.

I shook my head, biting my lower lip.

"I saw what you saw, Wayne," Juliet said, kneeling before me. "I hope that wasn't you." Her blue eyes burned right through me.

I looked at Sadie, searching for something in her eyes, but found nothing.

"Tell us everything," Sadie said, her tone cold as ice. "Otherwise, we will leave you here. I've got people I love back home, and I won't bring harm to them."

"This is it, Wayne," Darius said. "No more secrets." He also took a seat in the sand.

I buried my head in my hands and said, "I can't. You'll leave me here."

"I don't know who or what that thing was I saw when the beam struck," Juliet said. "But that is not the man sitting in front of us – we all can change."

I looked at her, then Sadie, then Fritz, then Brock, then Darius, and Shorty.

"Well, strap yourselves in then," I said. I can't tell them everything; it's unforgivable.

13

Arden's heavy footsteps echoed down the iron-clad corridor of the Leon's mother ship. It was a spear-shaped vessel, eight miles from bow to stern and half that size port to starboard. After regaining his memory and courage, he shuttled from the transporter ship. The Leon's captured the vessel over a hundred years ago from the Balthazars. The Leon's ship was in terrible shape; years of neglect and confrontation took its toll. They loaded what remained of their enemy into the Leon's decrepit ship and send it crashing into the nearest star. A fitting end for their vessel. Also, a fitting end to a pathetic enemy; negotiating their surrender before firing a single ion. Even their flesh tasted like the phallus of a Sumatra elder, a foul, bitter taste. The body's natural tendency was not to swallow. So keeping them as livestock was not an option. The humans named the star that had caused a species' extinction. Proxima Centauri. Such a waste of time naming things they never intend to conquer. That was also the moment the Leons had noticed their next melee. The radio waves and images the blue planet beamed into the depths of darkness were impossible to ignore. To voice one's presence in this universe, one must be an idiot or powerful. The Leons realised the former to be the case. The humans were like a blind youngling struggling through a treacherous forest, searching for a friend.

"I'm back!" Arden hollered, and slammed his chained arm against the wall. A loud bang ricocheted from the walls and disappeared into the belly of the spaceship. Down the corridor, the weak scattered into different chambers. The brave pressed themselves against the cold iron and bowed their heads in submission. No one made eye contact. Arden's piercing eyes spared no one. "This place reeks of fear... and piss! I turn my back for two cycles..." He halted halfway down the corridor and turned his head toward a shivering male, one with the wall.

"How old are you, boy?" Arden demanded.

The boy ducked his head and whispered, "Four cycles, Master."

Twelve Earth years. "This is your prime cycle. Have you converted yet?"

He nodded.

"What's your name?"

"Lyceum, Master."

"Then show me your fangs, Lyceum."

He hesitated.

"Show me!" Arden's voice thundered down the corridor.

Lyceum raised his head, eyes closed, and opened his mouth.

Arden grabbed him under his chin and studied his fangs. "Good size," he lied.

Lyceum opened his eyes, beaming.

"But as you know, size doesn't matter. It's what's in here." Arden pointed at his heart. "You must show respect, but never weakness." Arden pushed out his bulging chest. "Stand tall and proud."

Lyceum mimicked him.

"That's better." Arden smiled, exposing his fangs.

Lyceum hunkered down, petrified.

"I was smiling, not challenging. Show me your blade."

Lyceum drew his sword and handed it to him.

Arden balanced the tip on his finger, flipped it, and caught it by the handle. "Three rules if you want to survive until your seventh cycle."

"Why the seventh cycle?" Lyceum asked.

Arden looked up and down the corridor. "It's forbidden, and if you tell anyone, I will kill you."

The boy nodded.

"The Evocation Ceremony – when they transfer the memories of all your previous lives."

Lyceum's eyes widened.

"They want you to gain experience in this one, make it on your own and be powerful enough, mentally, to handle the overload. With each life, you gain experience, grow stronger."

"Why are you telling me this, Master?"

"I could smell your fear from my room. Remember, we can only rise in rank by challenging and killing our opponent. Now that you've had your prime cycle, they will challenge you around every corner. You're easy prey."

"What are the three things?" Lyceum whispered.

Arden swirled the sword around his finger. "I learned this in my previous life – the hard way." The sword spun faster and faster. "You need a back-plate, Enox lotion, and..." he released the spinning sword. As Lyceum's eyes followed the sword into the air, Arden removed a dagger from under his arm, pressed the blade against Lyceum's throat, and caught the sword on its return. "And you need a diversion."

The dagger scraped the boy's Adam's apple as he swallowed. "What's the Enox lotion for?"

"It neutralises the smell of fear." Arden holstered his dagger. "The back-plate is for your friends because they will be the ones who will stab you in the back."

One of those friends, Erich, appeared around the corner and froze. He raised his hands and yelled. "You waste no time! Slice him open, my friend!"

Arden grabbed Lyceum by his collar and tossed him down the corridor, away from Erich. "Go! You're not worth it."

Lyceum scurried away on all fours and disappeared into the nearest room.

"It's your lucky day, boy!" Erich approached Arden with one arm raised.

"Erich!" Arden marched toward his friend. "Surprise to see you still in this life."

They grabbed each other in an arm-wrestling hold and studied each other's bulging biceps.

"Two cycles in stasis have made your body weak," Erich said through clenched teeth, his arm trembling.

"Two cycles have taken their toll on yours, too," Arden said. "Time for a new one." He swung Erich around, threw him against the wall, and pressed his blade against his friend's throat. He stared at Erich's eye patch and lifted it. "What happened?" he asked and stepped back as blood seeped from the empty socket.

"A female." He shook his head in anger. "They have no respect." Erich glanced down the corridor. "Why did you let him go? We could have feasted on his bones."

"He was a bag of fear. You know it gives me heartburn." Arden burst out laughing, placing a hand on Erich's shoulder. "Feasting on his bones!"

Erich nodded. "I can still smell him."

Arden frowned. "You serious, my friend? Eating one's own flesh is forbidden. It's a universal rule."

His cold black eyes bore into him. "A lot has changed. The Elders proclaimed that one can consume the flesh of a lower-standing Leon. The gods gave their blessing."

"Let me guess, you are running low on food," Arden said, and slipped the sword into his scabbard.

He sighed. "Food outside the protected cities is few and difficult to target without raising suspicion."

Arden pointed the way and proceeded down the corridor. "What happened while I was away?"

Erich shrugged. "The usual – fighting, killing each other, waiting for you to open the door. We're going mad. We need a good fight, my friend, and food."

"Well, the wait is over. Malik will deactivate the shield within the cycle."

"You spoke his name as if you are brothers once more."

"We will always be brothers," Arden said, glaring at a passing Leon. He felt his friend's suspicious gaze, scrutinising his every move, his every expression. So tiring. "But I will never turn my back on that bastard again. I will have my revenge."

Erich tapped him on his shoulder, nodding.

Arden continued, "We need to set aside our hatred and do what's needed to capture the planet."

"Set aside your hatred." Erich burst out laughing. "Something happened to you on that planet."

Arden turned to him, placing a hand on his sword. "Say that once more, and I'll cut you from balls to chin."

Erich swallowed his laugh, bowed his head, and went down on one knee. "I meant no disrespect."

Arden released the hilt and walked down the corridor.

Erich caught up and said, "Your father is furious."

"Because I failed?"

"And that he had to send me to fetch you."

"Anyone challenged him?" Arden asked.

"Seven, all failed miserably."

"Pity."

"You still wearing your back-plate?"

"Why would I? Malik is not here," Arden lied.

A male's chilling screams sliced through the roars of a hungry crowd. Arden mashed the grip of his sword the closer they came to the gaping mouth of the Pit.

"A challenge?" Arden asked.

"We never had so many. They can already taste the blood of humans on their lips." Erich ran into the arena and roared, "Look who's back!"

Arden took a deep breath as he heard the roar of the crowd and entered with a raised fist. The arena erupted as all rose to their feet, chanting, "Arden! Arden!"

"It's a surprise, my friend!" Erich yelled above the roar of the crowd. "Your father arranged it."

Alcantar rose from his throne on the far side of the Pit. His throne, a claw reaching for the heavens. Massive chains dangled from the roof, groaning under the strain of iron fire pits. Torches, dripping with fire, lit up the iron walls, reflecting in the crazed expression of its spectators. Arden faced many a challenge in the Pit, but for the first time, the stench of rotting flesh and death overwhelmed him, almost too thick to inhale.

"Welcome home, my son!" Alcantar's booming voice drowned out the euphoria. "I transported you a present." He pointed down into the Pit.

Two human males, half-naked and covered in blood, huddled in the centre.

"Look!" Alcantar roared. "I told you I would surprise him."

The arena grew quieter the longer Arden took to respond. Another first for Arden was the sorrow he felt for the humans.

"Come on, Arden," Erich whispered through the side of his mouth. "Say something."

Arden placed his hands on his hips and looked around the arena with mock rage. "Who played with my food?" he screamed.

The arena burst out laughing, including his father.

"That's my Arden," Alcantar roared, pointing. "He's back!"

The wall of spectators parted with bowed heads as Arden made his way to his father. The older human kept his eyes on him as he passed.

He stopped and looked at the gaunt man. "You had your life," Arden said. "You're not afraid anymore." He almost added, "We have many, so that's why we're not afraid… why we have nothing to live for."

The old man gave a tired nod and closed his eyes, waiting.

Arden knew what the man wanted. The spectators had no clue. Otherwise, they would have perceived his next act – showing mercy – as being weak. He drew his sword and decapitated the man in one motion.

The crowd roared with satisfaction, edging closer, salivating from the smell and spill of fresh blood.

"No!" the younger human screamed and attacked.

Arden stepped to the side and grabbed the man in a chokehold. "I did him a favour," he whispered in his ear. "Take it easy, or you'll leave me no other choice." Arden released his grip as the man calmed down.

"What are you waiting for?" he screamed, tears running. "Kill me!" He stood, pushing out his chest.

"Ooh," Arden said with raised brows. "A human with balls wishing to die." He glanced at the salivating spectators. "You know me. I don't grant wishes."

"Fight! Fight! Fight!" the spectators chanted louder and louder.

Arden raised his hand, silencing the arena. "You also know I only fight warriors. There's no fun in killing a defenceless man – especially a crying one."

Alcantar smirked. "You've done it before."

Arden grinned. "Crying, but not defenceless." He glared at the man. "Prepare him for battle – tomorrow. Now, I want to convene with my father."

"Something to look forward to," Alcantar said, rubbing his hands.

Arden bowed before his father and took a seat next to him.

"Glad to have you back, my son," Alcantar said as he watched his men drag the human away.

"And remember, he's mine. I want him fit for battle," Arden ordered.

The human kept his eyes on Arden as they dragged him away. He frowned as Arden winked at him.

"You're not hungry?" Alcantar asked as he noticed the spectators edging closer to the corpse - growling, salivating, snapping.

Arden shook his head. "Let them have it. They need it more than I do."

Alcantar pointed with an open hand to the headless corpse. "But the head is mine!"

The males stormed the corpse, clawing and ripping at the flesh.

Erich approached, head bowed, holding the head by its tangled grey hair. Alcantar grabbed it from his hand and gouged out an eye. "Eat!" he ordered Arden.

"I'll feast on my human tomorrow," he said.

Alcantar glared at him, dangling the eye in front of him. "Eat!"

Erich looked at the eye and then at Arden, encouraging him with a nod.

Arden grabbed the eye and shoved it into his mouth. A wave of nausea and perspiration washed over him as he bit down; lukewarm pus exploded in his mouth. He kept a straight face as his stomach contents boiled into his throat. Vomit, and you die – simple. He kept swallowing, forcing down the eye and bile. The scene playing out in the Pit did not help his current situation; a group of males played tug of war with the old human's intestines.

"What happened on the blue planet?" Alcantar asked, and wiped his mouth with the back of his claw. "Why you back so soon?"

"The humans figured out I was not human," Arden said, focusing on the dancing flames of a torch at the Pit's entrance.

"How did they do it?" Alcantar raised the head above his, opened his mouth, licking at the dripping blood.

"Poison."

Alcantar lowered the head, shocked. "Barbarians." He shook his head at the head. "Killing a defenceless six-year-old boy."

Arden frowned.

"That's the worst way to go for a warrior," Erich said.

"They didn't kill Arden!" Alcantar snapped. "They killed a boy."

"Are we still hiding on the dark side of Jupiter's moon?" Arden asked Erich.

He nodded.

Alcantar took the head between his claws. "Watch this." He crushed the skull, and the remaining eye popped from its socket. "I would have loved to do it when he was still alive, but you spoiled all the fun. The look in their eyes when they see their organs devoured... priceless. And they taste better when oozing with fear." He licked the grey matter from his hands.

"I need a drink," Arden said and stood up.

"I'll join you in a moment," Alcantar muttered with cheeks bulging, pus dripping from his lips and down his braided beard. "No fun in drinking cold blood."

Arden pushed Erich to the side and kept his hand on his sword as he made his way past the gory feast. He wanted to run, but kept his pace until he was out of sight. *What's going on with me?* He started running as fast as his trembling legs could handle but slowed to a walking pace every time a Leon appeared. Halting by an iron door, he caught his breath before pulling the lever.

Amira stood at a window, gazing at the stars. "Arden," she said, and fell to her knees. "Please forgive me." Her skin shimmered grey. "Forgive me for what I did on Earth. My loyalties are with the Leon race. It was not my intention–"

He raised his hand, silencing her, and closed the door behind him.

"Please don't be angry," she begged, skin blackening.

Arden gagged and fell to his knees, the chains and sword clanging on the iron floor. He heaved his last meal.

Amira rose to her feet. "Arden?"

He fell onto his back and clawed at his clothes. "I must... get out," he whispered, panting. His long nails scratched his neck as he ripped open his collar.

"Wait! You're hurting yourself." She mounted him and forced his hands apart. "Calm down! Look at me!"

Arden's bewildered eyes locked onto hers.

"Take a deep breath," she ordered.

Arden obeyed. His rapid breathing and hammering heart slowed.

"What happened?" she asked and let go of his hands.

"I can't stand this place. I can't stand what we are. What I was. What happened to me?" He closed his eyes.

"Somehow, you still have Joshua inside you," she whispered, removing his hand. "You tasted what it was not to be Leon. And I'm afraid that once you've tasted it... you can't go back being–"

"–a monster?"

"We are a despicable race. Whose only purpose is to destroy. We are the cancer of the universe."

Arden studied his blood-stained hands and long reptile-like talons. "We must stop them."

"How?"

"Killing Father, and... Malik, if I have to."

Amira stood up and returned to the window, to her stars. "I thought you... I thought he would change with human blood in him." She turned to Arden. "But he wasn't the Malik we know, was he?"

Arden sat up, searching Joshua's memory. "No, he wasn't," he said. "Still as stubborn, but not hungry for power." Arden looked at his hands. "I caught him crying, something a Leon male can't do." He sighed, shaking his head.

Amira clasped her hands and gave a step toward her son. "See, he changed!"

He struggled to his feet. "That was Wayne, without Malik's memories." On Earth, without the memories of their earlier lives between them, they were brothers once more. "I will know when I see him. If he's Malik or Wayne."

"But if you cut off the head, another one will grow in its place and continue the invasion."

"I will be the head that grows back."

Amira looked at him, eyes filled with sorrow. "But that means you will have to–"

"Remain the head," Arden interrupted. "My punishment for what I did in my past lives." He took a deep breath. "I will return you to Earth – you must find happiness and peace."

She hugged Arden. "My happiness and peace are right here with my son." She tapped his chest in thought. "We'll find another way."

He stroked her cheek and whispered. "I've never seen you turn blue."

She smiled up at her son. "I'm relieved, happy, safe and content."

"It looks good on you." Arden smiled. "I guess blue is your colour."

14

As we sat in the Vector's shade, surrounded by the desert, I told them everything: Amira, Arden, Alcantar, the transporter, and how my race procreated. I also told them about Malik — what he did, who he was, and his purpose. My mind was like a boiling pot, spilling its contents until nothing remained. I wasn't fazed by the barrage of emotions that surrounded me. I owed it to them, especially Sadie. I could never be Malik again; the human blood flowing through my veins had stained my Leon side. Even if I die and return to my Leon body, my human memories will fail me. I was neither Malik nor Wayne. When I was done, all sat quietly, locked in their thoughts, processing every detail.

"So, if the shield remains, they won't invade?" Sadie broke the silence.

I nodded.

"But there's a problem," Darius whispered. "The underground river is drying up."

Fritz ran his hand over his red mohawk – Sadie called it so. "What does that have to do with it?" he asked.

"The city and the shield run on nuclear power. The water within the primary system that's heated by the fuel rods to generate the steam that runs the generators never leave the system. That water is radioactive and gets recycled."

Brock frowned. "Okay."

"The system needs cool water from a secondary source to turn the steam in the primary system back to water. We use the underground river for that. We had a second power source – solar power – but it was outside the shield and destroyed by Ross men."

"That was my plan," I whispered.

"What do you mean?" Juliet asked.

"I told you my purpose was to shut down the shield from the inside. It was not the only thing I had to disable, destroying the nuclear core was the other. We would then start the invasion, surround the city and..."

"And?" Sadie asked.

"Hit the city with an electromagnetic pulse, thereby knocking out all forms of communication," Darius said.

"T-t-then."

"Feast," I said.

"F-f-fuck."

Darius fell back with a heavy sigh, placing his hands behind his head.

"It will be a slow invasion."

"Why?" Brock asked.

"The smell of human fear increases the Leon's appetite." I swallowed. "Especially while feasting."

"Fear is the overture to a bloody bacchanal," Darius muttered, staring at the underbelly of the G6.

"Fear signals the beginning of a bloody drunken feast," Sadie repeated, noticing the frowns.

All eyes shifted to me. I jumped up, trying to get away from the silent disgust, and bumped my head against the fuselage. "Tsakfak." Brilliant! Cursing in Leon will win them over.

I walked into the desert, stroking my bump, then looked at my hand. I stopped; eyes focused on my blood-soaked fingers. The footsteps behind me stopped. I turned around and held up my hand. "My blood is red."

They stood in a row, uncertain, unapproachable, but thank the gods, unafraid.

I continued, "A Leon's blood is black. Black like their hearts. I'm human."

"How do we know that you won't change once you're inside the Dome?" Brock asked.

"Because I'm still Wayne." I shrugged. "And they would smell the human within me, whether in this body or my Leon body. Malik made a lot of enemies up there."

"I'm not convinced," Darius said, hand raised, shielding his eyes from the sun.

I gave a step toward him, blocking the sun.

He lowered his hand.

"You all came running without your weapons," I said.

Darius frowned, a hand reaching for his hip.

I glared at him until he straitened, chin raised. Typical Darius: he would face death before running. "If I were more Leon than human, you would all be dead. They would open a window, knowing you are on board, and I would destroy the core, kill myself and wake up in my old body – mission complete. So, the question is, do you believe I'm Wayne or Malik? I won't beg. The Leon within won't allow it. I'm asking you to trust Wayne." I stepped back and pointed at the G6. "You all get on that thing and decide. If it's Malik, then throw out a weapon and take off. I need something to kill myself with. I'd rather die fighting in the Pit." I pointed at the sky.

Darius nodded. "Okay, let's have a chat." He turned and marched toward the Vector.

"I-I'll w-wait here with W-W-Wayne." Shorty broke rank and scurried to my left, folding his arms.

Darius turned back, squinting at me with one eye, head cocked.

"I'll also wait." I winced, hearing her voice.

Sadie walked toward me. Her big brown eyes had turned into fiery ambers. "I believe in Wayne, but if I see Malik once, I'll fuck him up." She waved a finger at my nose. "Don't fuck with me, Malik. I'm not like one of your whimpering chameleons. You won't see me turn black with fear. You will only see red when you drown in your own fucking blood. Yes, it's red now." She pointed over my shoulder. "My people are in that city. My friends are in that city. My dad is in that city." She poked me with that same finger as she said each word, "Do... you... under... stand... me?"

Both of us nodded. Both of us hardened.

"We will also wait," Fritz said, glancing at Juliet, then at Brock. Both confirmed with a nod.

Darius placed his hands on his hips, shaking his head. "Well, what the hell you all waiting for then? Let's get back to Nirvana and work on that dream of Wayne."

Sadie took my hand as we made our way back to the flying machine. "You're not Leon," she whispered and rested her head against my arm.

"How do you know?"

"Because I would be dead by now."

My heart pounded in my throat, and my stomach felt as if I was still falling from the flying machine. What the hell is happening to me? My legs moved, but I didn't make it move – as if I levitated toward the craft.

Steward despised coming down to the cavern, it reminded him of their mortality. It didn't matter how hard they tried strengthening or beautifying their facade. They built all on a corroding foundation, slowly losing its lifeblood. Time, the constant enemy. He leaned forward, careful not to fall from his wheelchair, to get a better look at the ever-declining body of water flowing far below. Two years ago, the river flowed inches below the platform.

"How long do we have left?" General Steward whispered as if not to alarm the river.

"Worst case a week, if we're lucky... two," Dr Bowler, a pale, skinny man with white hair tied in a bun, replied in a dull tone. "So, only a week."

"What other options do we have?" The other reason Steward hated descending into the pits of Nirvana was Bowler; monotonous, expressionless, and impossible to read - even his eyes were glazed like a bloody corpse.

He scratched a pimple on his cheek. "Pray for rain."

Steward rolled his eyes. "You think, after everything that had happened to us, that there is a God? I thought you were a scientist."

"I didn't, but now I do."

"Keep me up to date." Steward reversed his wheelchair - glaring at Bowler - backtracking into the elevator. "And Dr Bowler."

"Yes, General," Bowler hummed.

"You need sunlight."

"I like to be alone."

The doors closed.

Steward stared at his contorted reflection in the stainless-steel doors, contemplating. He slid his hand in under his blanket and fished for his communicator. "Dammit," he murmured, standing up. A shot rang out as his weapon and communicator landed on the floor. The round ricocheted from the steel wall behind him and ripped a hole in the ceiling. Steward searched his body. He looked up at the hole and sighed, "Thank God." With shaking knees and pounding heart, he picked up the items and fell back into his chair. "Bloody idiot," he said, switching on the safety. After replacing the weapon under his blanket, he placed the communicator on his palm, facing up. "Call General Keller."

After six beeps, a hologram image of Keller's head appeared. "Yes, General," he answered with bulging cheeks.

"Call back the ionizing drones."

Keller frowned. "Isn't it too soon?"

"I'm afraid it's too late," Steward said. "Our water supply is dwindling."

"I thought you said there were no aliens?"

Steward hesitated. "What do you mean?"

"The surge of energy wasn't a solar flare, but originated from Jupiter's moon, Europa." He squinted. "There's something wrong with your communicator, General. Your image is shaking."

Steward loosened his collar and rested the back of his hand on the wheelchair's armrest. "Better."

"Much," he managed through the chewing.

"I'm on my way."

"And another thing, General, we found Ross's spy."

"Who?"

"A control room operator, Lieutenant Stacey Norman."

"You sure it's not Lola from Operations?"

"Who?"

"I will keep my eyes on you," Darius said as we touched down.

"Don't worry, I will be by his side all the time," Sadie said, squeezing my hand.

"And no one says a word of what happened out there," Darius said. "Or what he is. We'll meet up tomorrow at the Presidential palace."

Captain Bryan sprinted up the ramp of the Vector. "Darius," he heaved. "I mean, Commander."

Darius sighed. "What now?"

Bryan hesitated as he glanced with a bewildered expression at the group.

"It's okay," Darius said. "You can talk."

"Keller found Ross's spy."

"Who?"

"Stacey," he whispered. "He intercepted a communique she sent this morning to Ross."

Darius slumped his head with a sigh.

"But that's not all." He stepped closer. "Remember, you helped get some of her family members into the Dome."

Darius nodded. "So now they think I'm also a spy."

"Especially with you leaving the Dome every time you get a chance."

"I'm not a fucking spy," Darius seethed.

Soldiers streamed into the hangar and surrounded the flying machine.

"You want us to take them?" Brock whispered.

"No, it will be suicide," Darius said and turned to Sadie. "Tell your father everything."

Keller waggled into the hangar with a satisfied grin spread across his face. "Darius! As a member of the Council, I have the authority to arrest you on charges of espionage and murder."

"Murder?" Bryan asked.

"Supreme Commander Whitmore and Martha," Keller said. "The cigars he handed them were laced with poison."

"What?" Bryan gasped, taking a step back. "How could you?"

"He's lying. I smoked one of those cigars."

"We studied the surveillance video of the Operations room," Keller said. "It shows you removing one from the bottom of the cigar box. You were very selective."

"What the hell Commander!" Bryan scowled. "I mean Darius." He drew his weapon.

"I searched for one not covered in dust," Darius shrugged. "And how do you know the cigars killed them?"

"We had it tested," Keller said, chin raised.

"I was bloody lucky then. And how do we know you didn't lace it with poison after they had died?" Darius scowled. "They were my friends."

Keller's expression soured. "That's ridiculous," he said with a wave of his puffy hand. "Take Darius and that giant," Keller pointed at me, "to General Steward. The rest, except Miss Green, will be taken in for questioning."

Keller placed his hand on Bryan's raised arm and said, "Take her to the President. He's waiting outside for her."

Sadie kissed me on the cheek and whispered. "Love you. See you later."

That tingly sensation intensified. I gave her a nod but avoided those eyes; I couldn't say the same.

"Steward plans on taking control of the Domes!" Darius yelled as eight soldiers herded us toward the exit.

"Is there something you need me to tell your ex-wife tonight?" Keller smirked as we passed him.

"Yes, tell her to be at the bottom for once," Darius said. "Hopefully, her implants explode and kill both of you."

"Quiet!" Keller yelled, silencing the laughter of his men.

Four soldiers led us down a long corridor.

"What's an implant?" I asked.

"What women put in their breasts to make them," Darius pushed out his chest, cupping his hands, arching his mouth, "fuller, bigger... more noticeable."

I nodded.

"It's a joke," Darius said.

"What about Sadie?"

"She's the president's daughter. They will not touch her."

I frowned. "You mean they won't touch it?"

Darius looked at me, confused. "She's a woman, not a thing or an it."

"You two are clearly from different planets," Juliet said. "Wayne was referring to Sadie's boobs. She's got an impressive pair. I'll be careful if I were you."

"She's just focking with ye." Fritz nudged me from behind. "Juliet is jealous."

"You'll be safe with Juliet," Brock noted. "No implants there."

"Fuck off!" Juliet snapped.

"Give us another one," Brock asked as we turned a corner.

Darius glanced over his shoulder and nodded. "Before my ex-wife married fat Keller, she had to do a course in whale humping."

"Quiet!" a soldier in the back yelled, silencing another volley of laughter.

"What's a whale?" I asked.

Darius frowned. "It's a big fucking fish. You know very little for someone who has lived a few lives."

"The oceans were empty when we arrived," I said. "It seems the Leons and humans want the same thing."

"And what's that?" Brock said.

"Both want this planet destroyed.

He snorted. "We don't want it destroyed."

"Then humans are dumber than I had thought."

"Amen to that." Darius dropped back and took up position next to Brock. He whispered something in Brock's ear.

"You two come with us," the guard said, pointing at Darius and me as we arrived at an elevator.

The group divided into two. Four guards escorted Fritz, Brock, and Juliet further down the corridor while four waited with us.

"Where's Shorty?" I whispered into Darius's ear.

He looked at me, puzzled, and then glanced at the departing group. "We must put a leash on him."

"I thought it would be bigger," I said as we entered the Control room.

"What are you talking about? This is huge!" Darius said, extending his long gangly arms.

"Not where I come from."

"That's Steward," Darius said, glaring at the man wheeling toward us.

"I remember him," I said. "Let's hope he didn't believe the alien story you told him."

"He didn't."

The guards parted for Steward. "So, this is the alien," he said. "Keep your weapons on him," he instructed the guards. "If he tries anything, shoot him in the legs. I need him alive." Ten rifles turned my way.

"It was just a story to get in," Darius said.

"We've got lots to discuss, Malik," Steward said. "But first, I have to deal with another issue at hand."

How the hell did he know that name? Maybe Darius told him before I joined him in the cockpit. I glanced at Darius. His frown and shifty eyes told me he was just as puzzled.

Steward turned to the screen. "All staff members with a security clearance below Alpha, evacuate the Control room." Most of the people made their way to the sliding doors on the far side of the room.

"I'm not a spy, Steward," Darius said.

"Maybe, maybe not," Steward said over his shoulder. "But you are a murderer."

"Just like you."

"On screen," Steward said.

General Ross appeared on the screen, glaring.

"I apologise for keeping you waiting, General," Steward said.

Ross gave a slight nod. "Have you reconsidered? May my people enter the Dome?"

"Some of your people already entered the Dome," Steward said.

"What do you mean?"

"Bring her in!" he hollered, without taking his eyes off Ross. Two soldiers walked in, carrying a woman between them – dressed only in underwear - her feet dragging on the floor. The soldiers made her stand next to Steward.

The size of the screen magnified his shock; widening eyes – unblinking – ghostly guise and sudden sheen of sweat on his brow.

His black hair was in stark contrast to his pale skin. Ross cleared his throat and swallowed. "What is all this?"

"Don't underestimate my intelligence," Steward said. "We intercepted a communique she sent you last night."

"You are mistaken, Steward." He shook his head. "I don't know that woman."

Steward shrugged and looked at the guard standing beside Stacey. "Shoot her."

The guard removed his sidearm and pointed it at the woman's head.

"Stop!" Ross screamed, slamming his hand on the desk.

Steward gestured for the guard to wait. "That's better."

"What do you want?"

"We want your stealth technology."

Stacey looked up, showing life for the first time. "Don't do it, Father. You won't be able to search for food."

"So, they know?" he whispered, as if only them in the room.

She nodded. "I'm sorry."

"No, I'm sorry for putting you in this situation," Ross said. "I just thought life would be better for you in the Dome." He tried to blink the tears away. "Anywhere but here."

"I know," she whispered.

Ross turned his head away.

"The technology!" Steward snapped. "Or she's dead!"

Darius gave a step toward Stacey but froze as he looked down the barrel of a soldier's rifle. "We all need to stand together, Steward. Nothing of this will matter when the aliens arrive."

"Exactly," Steward said. "So, give me the technology."

"Only if you let us in."

"No, we don't have the resources to support your people. We barely have enough for–"

"The aliens have the technology," Ross interrupted, recovered; resolute and assertive. "The only reason you want it is to track our craft."

Steward rose to his feet and walked over to Stacey, weapon in hand. The few remaining staff traced every step with a shocked expression.

"I will count to three," he said and pointed his weapon at Stacey's head.

"Don't do it, father!" Stacey screamed.

"One!"

"Guarantee me, you won't attack our craft," Ross said.

"Two."

"Okay!" Ross jumped from his chair and disappeared. He returned moments later with a glass tablet and tapped and swiped at it with trembling hands. "Open a channel for me to upload the data."

"Don't do it!" Darius yelled. "You can't trust him!"

"Deactivate the firewall," Steward said, his weapon still trained on Stacey.

"It's uploading, General," a woman said, staring at her screen.

Ross straightened and raised his chin. "Thank you for your service, Lieutenant."

"Upload complete," the woman said. "Activating firewall."

"Open and verify the data," Steward ordered.

Lieutenant Norman stood at attention and saluted the General.

"Data verified, General."

Ross returned the salute.

A gunshot echoed through the control room, jolting the unexpected.

Ross shut his eyes and bowed his head.

As I watched the blood pooling around Stacey's lifeless body, I wondered what my mother would think – were humans still worth saving? They were like us. Steward had the same expression as we had after a kill: crazed satisfaction. The same expression Professor Santiago had as she tortured me. The same expression my father had as he flogged me.

Ross opened his eyes. "I knew she was dead the moment she

sacrificed herself." For a moment, I almost detected a smile. "Never let your guard down... ever." He said and disconnected the feed.

"Leave her!" Steward screamed as two soldiers tried to pick up the body. He waved me closer. "Please join me."

I glanced at Darius before making my way toward Steward. He showed no emotion where he stood, eyes fixed on the body.

"We tracked the energy surge and found its origin," Steward said as I joined him. "We sent a message, and to our surprise, someone answered. I believe you know him."

"What are you talking about?" I asked.

"We couldn't understand each other at first, so he brought in his wife and son to translate. On-screen."

Every particle in my body froze as Alcantar's image appeared on the screen. I shut my eyes and took a deep breath. Even with my eyes closed, I felt the weight of his presence. I went down on one knee. The darkness suffocated me, wrapping me in its veil; like a baby in a blanket. I couldn't move.

"Ech sag vag heek kleich, Wayne," a voice in my head said in a resonant growl. It was Malik. I understood – "I'll take it from here, little Wayne."

Where have you been?

"In the shadows, waiting."

"Stach och, Malik," Alcantar said.

Malik rose to his feet. I was a silent observer, hiding in the dark, peeking through his eyes.

Arden, Malik's elder brother, stood next to Alcantar, where he sat on his throne. I recognised them as our memories had interwoven – Malik's and Wayne's. My human emotions angered Malik. I could sense it – he tossed back every memory of Sadie, Juliet, and my mother. Malik's violent past frightened me – the only way I could block it was with pleasant thoughts: Juliet's kiss - our dancing tongues, Sadie's touch, her scent, which I always took in with one breath, and the feeling in my stomach whenever our eyes met. I didn't appreciate those moments. – or realized its importance; my shield against evil.

"Stop it!" Malik growled.

I will block my feelings if you hide your violent past.

"Jyk eechste," he replied, meaning you first.

It was difficult to clear my mind; Sadie and Juliet were stubborn – as in life, but I managed. Malik's past faded into darkness. Living only in the present made it bearable for both of us.

Malik or I took a deep breath. It was me that caused our shaking legs. Alcantar leaned forward, frowning, resting a limp wrist on the hilt of his sword. "I'm struggling to see my son in that pathetic body. Must be the hair," he said in Leon and leaned back. "I will reward the sacrifices you have made growing up between them, my son."

"Good to see you, Wayne," Arden said in the human tongue, straight-faced, glaring down at me.

"Ech Malik," he hissed, exposing our fangs. He restrained the beast of rage, trying to claw its way from the shadows.

Calm down!

"I'm in control!" An image of his claws crushing the head of a Krono female flashed through my mind.

I gave him the moment Sadie offered me her wrist, that feeling – unconditional sacrifice from a person I barely knew. We need to work together because giving you complete control would be the death of both of us.

"I'll be transported back into my Leon body, and you'll be dead."

Part of me will still be in your head. And that's something you don't want up there, and you know it.

Our pasts, once again, became one – a black slate. The beast settled for now.

Arden continued, but with half a smirk, exposing only one of his fangs. "You all right, little brother." Both of us hated him for calling us that.

"Yes," we shrugged. "We..."

"I – we don't want to sound crazy."

As if you care.

We continued, "The only thing I can remember of your time down here is your tears." We placed our fists on our hips. "I'm still down here... inside the city. I won, you lost. You are my big brother, but," we grabbed our groin with both hands, "I've got bigger balls."

Alcantar threw his head back as he roared with laughter, fangs glistening with saliva. He pointed, shouting in Leon, "It is Malik!"

Arden stood glaring, claws balled, both fangs now concealed.

Amira shook her head, turning green.

Mother is angry at us.

"No, she's disappointed. I know that colour."

I'm disappointed in her, leaving me like that.

"Leon females and humans sicken me with their emotions."

The beast stirred in the shadows of my mind. How long could I survive this constant barrage of anger and hatred? My rage was like Joshua's compared to Malik's. Now I understood why Amira transferred him into a human body, anything to calm the Leon beast. And why my fear for a father figure?

"So, fucking dramatic Wayne. Remember, I hear and sense every thought, just like you feel mine. We are one. And to settle one of your disturbing emotions, they took Mother. She didn't run away. Alcantar had realised Amira had prevented us from completing our mission. I will deal with her on my return."

I will not allow you to disable the shield.

"You know you'll not be able to stop me. The Leon side is stronger. Our human side will die. Soon we'll be one."

Never!

"Remember, in rage, we were one. We spoke as one, our actions coordinated. Who grabbed our nut sack, you or me?"

Everyone is looking at us! Did your father say something?

"Take it easy, little Wayne."

If you call me that one more time...

"As promised, I brought you your son," Steward said.

As my father spoke, Arden translated. "I told General Steward our plans, Malik. We come in peace, and we would help them rebuilt. We have the technology to revive the atmosphere and restore balance. In return, he will share the Earth's mineral resources with us. You will have free access to their systems and power sources to assess where our technology could improve their situation."

It surprised me how well my father lied. The only words he emphasised were power source and free access. Arden's translation had no focus and no conviction.

"Stop wasting your breath, Alcantar," Steward said. "I know your plans and why you send Malik here. His only mission was to disable the shield."

Alcantar smiled at hearing the translation. "Finally, a leader I will enjoy crushing."

"Your son failed. You failed." Steward pointed to Stacey's lifeless body. "This is what I do to spies, and I will do the same to your son."

Alcantar listened with an apathetic expression as Arden whispered in his ear.

"However, I will let him go if you agree to leave Earth and never return."

Alcantar leaned forward, resting his chin on his fist. "You think after fifty Earth years I'm just going to leave?"

Steward removed his handgun and pointed it at our head. "Agree, or I will blow your son's brains out."

"Why do you entertain humans like this?" Alcantar asked. "Allowing them to live – especially that well-matured one next to you. All you need to do is wipe his arse and nose. You can prove your worth to me. Take your brother's place." He smiled. "Like you've always wanted."

Arden did not translate.

"I will count to three!" Steward screamed.

"I can't wait to be back in my Leon body, Father." We looked at our hands. "The limitations in this human body are frustrating. So difficult to rip the flesh from their bones with these hands."

Alcantar nodded. "I can just imagine my son. Fortunately, the gods allowed you these." He tapped the hilt of his sword against his fangs.

"One!"

We scanned the operations room. "There's only a few of them, but if I fail, forgive me. I will return as Malik, and we will take this city together. As we should have done."

"As I've suggested from the start," Arden said in Leon, again with one fang exposed. "But as always, you wanted to go at it alone, to prove yourself worthy." Then he said in English, "Don't you understand? We will never be good enough for father. Stop trying."

Alcantar elbowed Arden, scowling. "Talk in Leon!"

"Tell me, brother, who won the fight within, the six-year-old human or the spineless Leon?" I asked in Leon.

"Two!" Steward shrieked.

Arden gave a step forward, wrenching the hilt of his sword. "Let him shoot you," he seethed. "I'll be waiting."

"Take it easy, you two," Alcantar grunted.

Arden gave another step and said in human, "Wayne, I know you're still in there. Convince Malik that this is not the way. We can live amongst humans. You have tasted love, and it tasted sweeter than hate. I love you, brother." He stepped back and took his place next to Alcantar. "It's in your hands."

The lines of suspicion deepened the longer Alcantar stared at Arden.

"I will never allow your scum to live amongst us," Steward seethed and pulled the trigger.

A soldier on the far side of the operations room fell to the floor. Steward was old and slow but screamed like a girl as we broke his arm at the elbow. We sank our teeth into his leathery neck and ripped out his jugular. I tried to throw Darius the handgun, but Malik held on. We need his help... for now! He didn't understand our conversation with Alcantar. He still thinks we're Wayne!

Darius was already venting his anger on a guard as we threw him the weapon. An explosion ripped a hole in the door on the far side of the room. Fritz appeared through the cloud of smoke, firing wildly in the air, screaming like a crazy human. Brock and Juliet followed, looking demented. The reaction of the remaining staff and soldiers in the Operations room surprised us; those who didn't run away through the opposite doors raised their hands in surrender.

Darius pointed at Alcantar. "Cut the feed!"

Whoever was in charge, with all the confusion, managed the order – the screen blackened.

A group of four men were the only ones showing some kind of bravery. We, Malik and I, ran toward them, using Steward's lifeless body as a shield. They took aim and fired. His skinny frame fulfilled its purpose until we reached them. It must be his tough flesh or stubborn soul that did the trick. We threw the body into the group, knocking two off their feet. We roared, revealing our blood-stained fangs. They tossed their weapons to the side and raised their hands.

They've surrendered! Stop!

The beast leapt from the shadows – the taste of human blood irresistible – their screams feeding the frenzy. One by one, they fell, frozen by fear. We feasted as one, unable to stop until satiated. We rose, satisfied. When the beast returned to the shadows, the savagery of our actions dawned. Limbs lay scattered in a reservoir of blood, heads severed with mouths contorted with silent screams, all interweaved with a web of intestines. The headcount revealed only the four soldiers massacred, however, by the carnage, it seemed a troop.

Is this me? We looked at our hands, our body – it seemed as if we had swum a river of blood. Our uniform stuck to our body. The smell of bile and excrement overwhelmed me.

"I told you. Accept it... Wait!" An uncontrollable wave of revulsion boiled from within. We heaved a torrent of blood, emptying our stomach.

I told you we can't go back. We are one. Half-human, half Leon. Fucked.

"Accept it! Accept it! Accept it!" I cried, falling to my knees. This is me!

Darius and Juliet's team had taken control of the operations room. My cry drew attention. Even from that distance, I could see the shock and revulsion of all present.

Keller entered the operations room, followed by a group of soldiers. "Lay down your weapons!" he yelled.

I moved in behind the globe.

Darius aimed his weapon at Keller. "Steward is dead."

"That doesn't change a thing!" he said, and took aim at Darius.

So ironic, the mocking question I had asked my brother stared me in the face. Who are you, Wayne or Malik? Whose side are you on? Did the seventeen-year-old farm boy win or the Leon? I took a deep breath. "Fuck."

"Leave and disable the shield."

Oh, shut the fuck up! You're not real. And then what - Alcantar destroys the city, devours everything, and we're back to searching for another world to destroy. My human side had taught me cause and effect – consequence. Arden was right; we can live amongst them. Build versus destroy. I wasted all my lives. Make this one count. The cruelty and destruction of my earlier lives escalated because I needed to feel something. Sadie made me feel without hate. She had planted the bine seed moments before Malik had leapt from the shadows.

"I'm still here, human."

"I'm going nowhere, Leon."

"That woman will be the death of you."

"The bine seed signalled the death of you. The more it grows, the weaker you will become."

"You talk too much."

"Wait until you hear a human female."

"So, are we going to disappoint our father once more? Like you did yours. Like I, mine."

"Story of our lives."

"What now, farm boy?"

"The only thing I'm certain about is Sadie."

"She is your weakness."

"I want those big brown eyes to control me. Not by hate. I want to taste her sweetness, hold her in my arms. Feel her warmth. Fill my lungs with her scent."

"I'm going to be sick."

"You're not real." Malik is a ghost from the past. Memories – that's all. I will bury it with new ones – ones with Sadie and Juliet... and moments with my human friends. I was born on Earth, raised by a mother who taught me love and a father who tried to control my anger. He was right; I wasn't ready to go back. Arden was.

I removed my blood-drenched boots. Keller and his men stood with their backs toward me, thirty to forty yards away. I leapt through Earth's hologram and sprinted barefoot. Darius's eyes flicked my way, but returned to Keller a split second later. Cut the head off, and the rest will fall. Arden's words flashed through my mind as I crashed into Keller's soft, meaty body. A feast for twenty Leons. His weapon slid over the floor and came to a stop at Darius's shiny boots. I had a flashback to a previous life, where Malik had wrestled with a Tafron giant with its four arms and two horns. He almost catapulted Malik into his next life if it weren't for Arden. The only comparison between the Tafron and Keller was their weight. I lifted Keller from the floor by his collar and groin and raised him above my head, screaming, "Drop your weapons or I will throw him to the ground. He will pop like a... like a–"

"Watermelon," Darius helped.

One soldier, realising how vulnerable I was, raised his weapon.

I squeezed Keller's small testicles and whispered, "Tell them to lower their weapons."

He managed a few words between his groans. "Lower... your... weapons!"

I tightened my grip even more and filled him with urgency.

"Now!" Keller's shrill scream filled the room.

Juliet, Fritz, Brock, and Darius took up position beside me, weapons raised.

Keller's men obeyed.

"Kick your weapons away!" Darius ordered.

Again, they obeyed.

"Okay," Keller heaved. "Put me down... please."

He crumpled into the fetal position the moment his feet hit the floor. His men didn't look at him as a general anymore but as the pathetic windbag he was.

A rush of drumming footsteps approached.

"Shit," Brock whispered. "Here we go again."

A dozen soldiers entered the operations room. The look of horror ran down the line as they passed the butchered bodies. President Green entered the room and removed a handkerchief from his suit pocket, covering his mouth and nose. "What happened?" He paled.

"They resisted," Darius said.

Green scanned the room, and his horror-filled eyes settled on me. I held his gaze.

"Steward tried to take over Nirvana," Darius said. "We had to stop him."

Keller stumbled to his feet, still clutching his groin. "Commander Von Swartz poisoned two council members."

"What!" Darius said. "You and Steward conspired to take over the city. What plausible motive would I have? Everyone knew I loved Whitmore." He crossed his heart.

"It's true, Mr President," a soldier said.

Keller's double chin wobbled as he shook his head, eyes wide with shock. "I-I did not-"

"You are a traitor!" Darius shouted, pointing.

Keller gave a step back, searching the room for support.

President Green replaced his hanky and straightened. "Arrest him!"

"You are the traitor!" Keller spat at Darius as a group of soldiers grabbed hold of him.

"Place him in solitary confinement!" Darius said. "Prevent him from colluding with his comrades. Minimum rations. And add mutiny and gluttony to his charges!"

"What! No! Please, Mr President!"

"Yes! Minimum rations." Green nodded.

It took seven men to haul Keller away – two on each arm and three pushing from behind. The fool underestimated Darius and his bond with the President; the man saved his daughter. Darius threw Green a lifeline, and he grabbed it with both hands. The President had no other choice but to believe Darius. I didn't think Green to be that ignorant - with the clouds of war gathering, I would also choose Darius above Keller.

When his cries faded into the belly of Building Seven, Green turned to Darius. "I am the President, elected by the people."

Darius gave a cautious nod.

"Do we all agree?" He barked at the troops.

They jumped to attention. "Yes, Mr President!" Their voices were echoing down the halls.

"Good. Now pick up your weapons!" He turned to Darius. "Do we all agree that we are in this together?"

"That was my point from the beginning, Mr President."

"The men need a General, and I believe you to be the one." He stuck out his hand. "What do you say, General Von Swartz?"

Darius beamed. "It will be my honour, Commander-in-chief." He had that same look in his eyes when Green had told him he made Council.

"The Council within this Dome, from this day forward, is no more. I will address the people and broadcast the Reveal. The people will overthrow the Council within the other cities and punish them for crimes against humanity. No more secrets."

"I wouldn't reveal too much, Mr President," Darius cautioned. "A government needs to withhold some secrets. Otherwise, it won't be a government for long."

Green frowned. "What do you-"

Johan Thompson

Four gunshots rang out from somewhere in the building, followed by screams, then approaching footsteps. "You will not silence me!" Keller burst into the room; weapon levelled.

I grabbed the President and shielded him – for Sadie. A shot echoed through the room.

I waited for the familiar stinging burn. Did he aim at Darius? I peeked over my shoulder - Keller lay face down, one arm wedged under his massive frame, the other sprawled to the side, clutching the weapon. Blood squirted from a gaping hole in the back of his head. "He's dead."

"What happened?" Green asked, his breath pulsated against my chest.

"Shot in the head."

"Who shot him?"

"Don't know."

"So, you can let go."

I released him.

The president looked at me, tight-lipped as he removed his hanky – his jacket and half his face stained with blood. "I guess I should thank you, but you ruined my suit," he said, wiping his cheek.

"Y-you a-all right, Wayne!" Shorty shouted from where he stood on a steel structure stretching the length of the roof, holding a rifle equal to his size.

"I don't know how he does it," Brock muttered, looking up, scratching his shaved scalp.

I gave him a nod.

"Can you talk to your father now?" Darius asked, kneeling next to Keller's body.

"Like this?" I gestured at my blood-drenched body.

"Yep, like that." He unbuttoned Keller's shoulder straps and removed the four stars from each soldier.

I took a deep breath. The farm seemed not such a terrible place; the quiet, my rock, the endless horizon, and the stars that were greater than the darkness of space. "Why don't you shoot yourself? It will be quicker - that's not a fucking life."

I turned to the screen suspended from the ceiling.

"Can we make it official, Mr President?" Darius said, handing Green the stars.

"Here are the two most powerful men in Nirvana, standing next to you – playing with stars. So easy. Father can see it. Imagine his admiration."

"You still with us, Wayne?" Brock said, emphasising my name. The thing I hated about my human body – the eyes; difficult to hide what's inside. In Brock's eyes, the lines of fear and doubt were visible. What did he see in mine?

"It's difficult," Juliet said, taking my hand.

One thing I loved about my human body - the hands, alive with touch, every nerve connected to my heart. The warmth of her hand sparked alive every human particle in my body. "What's difficult?"

"To remain human in this world," she said, focusing on Green struggling with Darius' shoulder straps. "The struggle for power is sickening."

"Let's step out of view, Mr President." Darius guided Green away. "On-screen."

"Malik," Alcantar said in a calm tone.

"To remain human in this universe is difficult." I turned and looked up at him.

"Are you Leon... or human?" His black eyes piercing.

"Both."

He sighed with a shake of his head.

"Stop this invasion, please, Father."

Alcantar waved to someone off-screen. "Maybe she can convince you."

Amira appeared on the left of the screen. A warm feeling filled my heart, the same feeling I remembered from childhood, when she woke me in the morning or when she hugged and kissed me. So many images of her flashed through my mind. I swallowed. "Mother." It was all I could say; anything more, and I would show too much emotion.

"Tell him to fulfil his mission," Alcantar said, glaring down at me.

"Have you met someone?" she asked, her skin drifting between grey and blue.

I nodded.

She smiled. "Then you know what to do."

Alcantar rose from his throne and approached my mother. Arden reached for his sword.

"She has poisoned your mind," my father said, stroking my mother's hair. "Our people are starving, Malik."

"We can send you food," President Green said behind me.

Alcantar smiled and draped his arm over my mother's shoulder. "Like feeding scraps to a Dresden wolf. Tell your friend how we feast, Malik."

Amira turned black.

"Humans and Leons can work together, Father."

"If you don't want to tell him, I will show him."

"No!" I screamed as Alcantar sank his teeth into her neck.

Arden charged my father with his sword raised. My mother fell to the floor as Alcantar drew his sword. Their blades crossed with a mighty clang that echoed through the Operations room. Arden roared with rage as he brought down his sword, again and again. My father blocked every blow with controlled ease, as if Arden was Joshua once again. Alcantar's back was toward us. His free hand removed a dagger from his belt.

"Arden, watch out!" I yelled, but too late. My father rammed the blade into my brother's ribs as he raised his sword.

Arden stepped back and looked at the dripping blade in my father's hand. "I'll get you in the next one, you bastard." He fell to his knees and stared at me. "Destroy it... stop them from–"

Alcantar's sword sliced the air and decapitated my brother. The pinging sound of the metal blade still resonated as Arden's body tilted over.

"There won't be a next time," Alcantar seethed. "I will cast you and your mother into the depths of space, your souls trapped in darkness for eternity."

"No!" I gave a step toward the screen.

Alcantar glared at me. "Their deaths are on your human hands. I can see why you want to stay amongst them. Down there, you're the tallest. Amongst us, you were a constant disappointment. So desperately trying to prove yourself. Pathetic. Every time we cloned you, I wished the gods would get it right. As a Leon, size matters." The screen blackened as a hand gripped my shoulder.

"He's right. It is your fault."

Yours too!

15

Green turned toward Darius. "How long do we have until the shield fails?"

"Two weeks."

"We have stopped with the ionization?"

"Steward already did."

Green rubbed his eyes. "When do you think it will rain?"

Darius shook his head and shrugged. "The scientist predicted months, maybe years."

"So, they don't have a clue."

"As always."

Green studied the soldiers. "How are you going to grow them a set of balls within two weeks? You noticed how we saw their backs."

Darius stared at the men for a moment, then said, "They have nothing to fight for. They need purpose... a leader. When they've got that, I can train them."

Green took a deep breath. "I will address the people within the hour, show them what's coming and who's in charge. You think the military will support me?"

"They will."

"What about the Sweepers and General Ross?" Brock asked.

"Call them back," Green ordered. "Tell Ross he's welcome. We need all the help we can get."

"Just like that, Mr President?" Brock asked.

He turned to Brock and said, "Simple, isn't it?"

Brock nodded, scratching at his groin.

Green leaned over and whispered in Darius's ear, "We're ignoring the monster in the room. I can't even look at his handy work." He removed his hanky and placed it over his mouth. "Don't you think we should arrest him?"

Darius leaned over. "He's not the arresting type, Mr President. And at this stage, we need a monster in our corner. I know he has issues, but I trust him."

"How sure are you?" Green whispered.

"We're still in one piece."

Green nodded, swallowing.

Darius grinned. "I'm just relieved I don't have a daughter he's in love with."

"Where is he?" Green asked, searching the control room.

"I will find him. Don't worry." Darius turned to his troops. "Protect the shield generators. If they go down, we all die."

"I thought you trust him?" Green asked.

"Just a precaution."

"Where's Juliet?" Brock asked.

Darius looked up at Shorty. "Where did they go?"

Shorty shrugged. "I-I d-don't know, General."

"You never miss nothing!" he snapped. "Find him and tell him I need him. In three days, we're leaving for the desert."

"What do you mean?" Green asked.

"You said I needed to make soldiers out of them," Darius said, and walked toward the exit. "Time to get their hands dirty."

Juliet led me to the barracks on the third floor of Building Seven. Besides a soldier groaning on a toilet, the barracks were empty. After jumping into a steamer and Juliet finding me a clean uniform, we merely walked out of Building Seven. The death of Steward and Keller spread like the smell of bile and excrement in the Pit. I sensed the fear and confusion as we made our way out of the building. People were running up and down corridors, not sure what or where to go, searching for orders. It was astonishing; the news had already reached the outside as we stepped into the street. They displayed images of my father with the words alien invasion on every glass building and screen. People stood gripped with panic; some stopped their fly mobiles in the middle of the street, climbing out to watch.

"Ross is doing this," Juliet whispered. "The file he uploaded must have contained a virus that disabled the firewall."

I had lost my brother and mother again, but this time I knew it was forever... how death should be. The life I lived now meant so much more, as this would be my last. I thought of my brother's last words: Destroy it... stop them from...

What must I destroy?

Ross's image appeared on the screens. "My name is General Ross, leader of the resistance. Life as you know it will end within two weeks. Your precious shield will collapse. Power failure caused by your dwindling water supply. Your leader's decision to ionize the atmosphere and prevent rainfall caused this. Their sole purpose was to starve the nations outside the Domes. Their actions will be your downfall. Aliens, known as Leons, will attack and destroy you as soon as the shield fails. It is a barbaric race that feeds on human flesh." Ross reclined in his chair. "Enjoy your last moments, and may death come quickly. God be with us all." Ross's image disappeared, followed by a woman advertising youth-infused laser masks.

The citizens watched the woman in stunned silence until the end.

"Does it remove scars?"

She frowned. "Don't be silly. I like your scar, it's sexy. Do you like anything you see?"

I didn't answer because that would betray Sadie. In truth, I liked everything about Juliet. I wanted to take her in my arms and hold her tight against me. Maybe in another life, but this would be my last. This life I want to spend with Sadie.

Juliet grabbed me by the arm and kissed me. She did the tongue thing. I wanted to pull away but couldn't. Maybe it was the Leon within who'd resisted. For that moment, I forgot about Arden, my mother, and the fact I had to confront my father.

"Wait," Juliet heaved. "Let's go."

We ran down the street, sidestepping the static scene, and entered a glass building.

"Hold it!" Juliet shouted at people waiting in an elevator.

The occupants shifted away as we entered, pressing up against the sides of the elevator, looking away, avoiding eye contact.

There was a moment of silence after the doors closed. We were still clutching hands, glancing at each other, excited.

"What are we going to do now?" an elderly woman asked.

I scowled. What did that have to do with her?

"We don't even know this, Ross," a young man with bulky eyeglasses answered. "He might be lying."

Then I realised what the old woman meant.

"No," she answered. "I could see it in his eyes. He was telling the truth."

The young man adjusted his eyeglasses. "In that case, I will take my grandfather's last bottle of rum, get sloshed and jump off a high-rise."

"No!" a woman snapped. "This is the time we must be with our loved ones, cherish our last days."

I glanced down at Juliet. Our excitement diminished. Our hands parted the higher we went.

"I'll visit my grandchildren," the elderly woman muttered. "I don't care what her asshole boyfriend says. I haven't seen them in years. They are always too fucking busy."

"I can't believe our leaders messed with the atmosphere," a bald, middle-aged man with a crooked nose said.

"It's true," I said.

"And how do you know that, sir?" the young man asked.

It was the first time anybody called me sir. And the guy was about my age. The doors opened, but nobody stepped out. I looked at him for a moment, then at the others; they were all staring at me with gaping eyes, hungry for the truth. "I lived outside the city my entire life. I heard the flying machines and saw the white powder. Birds fell from the sky, exhausted, searching for water, not stopping until their last breath. Animals walked until their hooves bled, not quit until their last step. I saw a man kill himself, not to see his children die. I saw drones, which your leaders called Sweepers, kill men, women, and children because they were still alive. Humans killed more of their own than the Leon race would ever hope to achieve. We are all the same."

The doors opened and closed.

The old lady shook her head. "If what you tell us is the truth, then we deserve what's coming. We let down our children and our planet."

"Ye, but it's never too late. I still have hope. This woman gave up everything for me." I placed my hand on Juliet's shoulder. "She saved my life more than once. I know a boy, half her size, who killed for me. Hell, Sadie Green saved my life." I shrugged. "All these people had no reason to do this for me, but they did."

"The President's daughter, sir?" the young man asked, fiddling with his bulky eyeglasses.

I nodded. "It didn't matter how hard your leaders tried to destroy this planet. It kept me alive with the little it had to offer. So, now is the time to return the favour. Don't you think? Let's use the little humanity left within us to save whatever good is still out there."

"Fuck," the old woman muttered. "What I would give to walk on the beach again, hand-in-hand with my Fredrick. Eat a rump and wash it down with a Cab Sav. Or watch the sunset with a glass of bourbon, shit-talk about our dreams. Most never came true, but at least we could see it."

"As I see it," I said. "You're the luckiest person in this elevator." I scanned the faces and settled on the young man. "I don't know about you guys, but I want memories like that when I'm her age. And when I dream and look to the future, I don't want it blocked by a fucking shield."

The doors opened on the ground floor.

"This is our floor," Juliet said and took my hand.

"What's your name, sir?" the young man asked as we stepped out. "Are you a soldier?"

I turned back. "My name is Wayne Johnson, and I'm a farmer."

"No, you're not, your Malik, destroyer of worlds."

The young man kept his eyes on Wayne until the elevator doors closed.

"You still going to get that bottle of rum?" the old woman asked.

He shook his head and removed his eyeglasses. "No, I'm going back to the office."

"What do you do?"

"I'm a journalist, and I've just recorded my greatest story." He held his eyeglasses up. "Never leave home without it."

Juliet unclipped a small square-shaped device from her belt as we stepped out of the building. She stared at the tiny display, frowning.

"What is that?" I asked.

"Dome communicator. Darius gave us all one."

"Why didn't I get one?"

"Probably doesn't trust you," she muttered, squinting at the display. "Or he thought a boy from the farm wouldn't know how to use one."

"Seems like a girl from the mountains also doesn't know how to use one."

"I've never called for a taxi before," she said.

I grabbed a passing man by the arm. "Help her with this. She wants to call for a taxi."

The man looked up at me, bewildered. "She just needs to talk to it." He leaned over. "Call taxi."

The device responded, "Calling for a taxi. Please remain where you are."

Juliet frowned at the man as he walked away, then at me. "Was that the alien in you that asked for help because human males..."

Just then, a small, dome-shaped vehicle stopped at the curb and slid open its doors.

"I Won't fit," I whispered. "And where's the driver?"

Juliet climbed in and slid to the other side. "Just try."

After several attempts, I squeezed myself into the taxi. I had to pull my legs up and force my head in between my knees. "I feel like a dung beetle in a flea circus."

Juliet burst out laughing.

"Like I'm back in my mother's womb."

"What do you know about a flea circus?" she laughed.

"My father tried it once on the farm." I groaned. "When he was still... before they took my mother."

"Tried?"

"The fleas wouldn't remain in their seats."

"You're not supposed to use real fleas. It's just called that."

"Well," –I attempted to shrug– "we had lots, and there wasn't much to do on the farm."

"Destination?" the taxi's voice asked.

"The Presidential palace," Juliet answered.

The taxi jerked forward, then stopped. "Maximum weight exceeded," the woman complained.

"I'll get out," Juliet said and opened her door.

"Why?"

"Like the woman said in the elevator," she climbed out. "Be with your loved ones."

"Where are you going?" I asked as I made myself more comfortable, utilizing the entire back seat.

"I'll be around," Juliet said, fighting back the tears.

The door closed, and the taxi jerked forward. At that moment, as I watched her through the back window, I hated my human side; things were so much simpler when I was a hundred percent Leon. She turned away and walked, head bowed, back into the building. I buried my head in the seat, praying for the guilt to go away. She had given her life for mine, and for what? So I could leave her on the sidewalk. I wanted to turn the taxi back, but I did not. Life was so much simpler on the farm. I concentrated on Sadie, her big brown eyes, her touch, her soft lips, her stubborn determination. It helped a bit.

16

"What do you want?" Bryan asked the boy standing on the other side of the steel gate.

"I want to apologise, please." The boy attempted to neaten his ruffled hair and dirty clothes. "Please, Captain, please."

Bryan studied the boy. His knee-jerk reaction was to draw his weapon and shoot the boy's balls off. "Funny how the wheel turns," Bryan sneered with a shake of his head.

"I was a dick," the boy said, teary-eyed. "But after my mother's death, I... I realised."

"That without her power, you are nothing."

Ryan wiped his tears away with his sleeve.

"The only reason I will allow it is for Sadie to get closure. Your apology would mean a lot to her." He removed his communicator. "Open the gate."

The massive steel gates groaned opened.

"I must warn you, she's not the Sadie you humiliated," Bryan said while scanning him for weapons.

Sadie wrapped a towel around her as she stepped from the steamer. She glanced at the antique digital clock above the marble fireplace - 2:32. If her father did not arrive with Wayne within half an hour, she would go to Building Seven and kick up a storm. Her father had promised her he would fight for his release.

A knock on her bedroom door startled her. "Someone is here to see you, Miss Green," a security guard said.

"Just a minute." She ran for her bed, where she had laid out her clothes. Her father had kept his promise. "Is my father also here?" she asked while slipping into a floral dress her mother had given her. It was the only thing in her closet that wasn't black.

"No, he's still at Building Seven."

She ran for the mirror.

"Your visitor is waiting in the formal lounge," the guard said.

"No, tell him to come here."

"Miss?" the guard said after a moment of silence.

"It's fine!" She glared at the door with a brush in her hand. "And leave us alone."

Sadie stepped back from the mirror. This was the first time she wore the dress since her mother's death. She could never wear something that didn't reflect how she felt inside. Today the dress felt right. A perfect match. She made an impulsive giggling twirl. A soft knock stopped her after the second turn.

"Come in." The door slid open. "You!" she gasped.

Ryan bowed his head and muttered, "I just came to say I'm sorry for what I did to you."

Sadie stepped back, hand on heart. The words, "Go away!" stuck in her throat.

"Can you find it in your heart to forgive me?" His ice-blue eyes melting.

She gave a slight nod, swallowing her fear. "What happened to you?"

"I lost my mother, my house, my friends."

She glanced past him. "I'm sorry to hear that."

"You look beautiful."

She crossed her arms, feeling the same emotions she'd experienced in the gravity room. "I'm over that now... I've moved on."

He gave a step toward her, and the door closed behind him. "Please give me another chance."

"I... I forgive you."

Ryan scratched his head. "I mean you and me." He gave another step. "I made a mistake. We can go to the gravity room and this time..."

She shook her head. "I have someone else now. I should have never gone to–"

"I will make it right," he said, his tone desperate. "Please!"

"We can still be friends."

Ryan's eyes narrowed. "You playing with me? First, you tried to screw me in the club, then you called me to your room, dressed like a slut."

"I wasn't expecting you," Sadie said. "I thought you were my boyfriend."

Ryan burst out laughing. "A boyfriend? You were so fucking desperate in the gravity room. Who would ever want to look at you?"

"Get out!" Sadie screamed. "You're drunk. I can smell you from here!"

"I will show you what you'd missed in the club."

"Are you crazy?" Sadie said. "The house is swarming with guards."

"I don't care." He leapt forward and grabbed her around the neck. "I've got nothing left to lose."

Sadie rammed her knee into his groin. Ryan fell to the floor and grabbed the seam of her dress as she ran past him.

"I can't believe the President convinced Steward to let you go," Bryan said as he arrived at the gate.

"Steward is not in charge anymore," I said. "The President is."

"How did he manage that?"

"I killed him."

Bryan looked at me long and hard and then smiled. "And Keller?"

"Dead."

"And Darius?"

"You mean General Darius."

Bryan shook his head. "Seems I've missed a lot."

"You going to let me in, or must I let myself in?"

"She's got somebody with her. A boyfriend."

My face lost all feeling. "Don't lie to me," I seethed.

"The President did not like you seeing her," Bryan said. "You being an alien and all."

"I don't care what he thinks."

He stared at me through narrowed eyes, scratching his chin.

"I promise I won't eat you."

He rolled his eyes and removed his communicator. "Open the gate."

I stepped through the parting iron and followed him to the white mansion with big pillars and small windows. It reminded me of a prison I had spent half of one life in. Arden destroyed it after he rescued me.

"She's in the lounge with the boyfriend," he said over his shoulder. "Just don't kill him. He's just here to apologise."

"For what?"

"Long story," he said as he walked up the steps. "It's better, she tells you."

I had to rein myself in as I followed him into the house. Every time I thought about Sadie, it happened – my heart was in my throat, my palms sweaty, my mind racing.

I almost bumped into Bryan as he stopped dead in a doorway. "Where's Sadie!" he snapped at a guard.

"She said I must send Ryan to her bedroom and leave them alone, Captain," a guard said behind us.

"She thought it was him, you idiot!" Bryan pointed at me and started running. "I told you not to leave that crazy kid alone with her."

———

Sadie kicked Ryan in the face until he let go of her dress. She was about to run for the door, but froze with her hand inches from the panel, then turned back. "No, this is my room," she said, her body trembling. Her rage smothered the same claustrophobic feeling she had felt in the gravity room.

Ryan stumbled to his feet, blood pouring from his nose. "Big mistake, bitch." He spat blood and lunged toward her with clawing hands.

———

I pushed Bryan out of my way as I heard the screams and slammed my fist into the security panel. The door slid open. I froze in the doorway, taken aback by the unexpected scene; Sadie was not the one screaming.

"Get– out– of– my– room!" With each word, she brought down a guitar on Ryan's head.

"Sadie, stop!" Bryan yelled as he entered the room.

I held him back with my arm. We watched in silence until there was nothing left of the guitar and Sadie's rage.

She stepped back, heaving. "No– means– no– asshole."

Ryan made strange whimpering noises as the security guards dragged him out of her room.

"What kind of weapon is that?" I asked, still in shock.

"We call it a guitar, and trust me, you don't want to hear her play it." Bryan placed his hand on her shoulder. "Are you hurt?"

Sadie shook her head. "No."

"I didn't know you wore dresses?"

"Seems to me there's a lot you don't know about me," Sadie said, her eyes burning with rage. "Where were you?"

I stared at the flowers on her dress and whispered, "Something happened."

She took a deep breath before taking my hand. "We've got a lot to talk about." The sharpness in her voice and the fire in her eyes faded. "I know a small café nearby."

Bryan broke his silence. "After what just happened, I–"

"I play saxophone as well!" Sadie snapped. "Don't follow us. You think anyone in his right mind will try something with him by my side?"

Bryan glared at me. "It's not the right-minded people I'm worried about."

"I agree," I said, and draped my arm over Sadie's shoulder. "I've seen more disturbing things inside the Dome than all my previous lives together."

"And don't worry," Sadie said. "I won't tell my father about your incompetence. This would be your third – no fourth in the last couple of weeks." She walked out of the room. "To be honest, I feel much safer knowing you're not looking after me."

Bryan grabbed me by the arm as I brushed past and whispered, almost pleading, "Please look after her."

"Don't worry." I patted his shoulder. "I'll do a better job."

17

Alcantar stood with his arms behind his back, peering through a window at the fifth planet from the sun in the human's solar system. They named it Jupiter. An enormous ball of gas. Useless and uninhabitable. However, the sandy rivers of gas circulating the planet were mesmerising. The Great Red Spot – a storm raging for over three hundred Earth years – fuelled the Leon's rage, their hunger for victory. "Let that be our inspiration," Alcantar instructed when they first arrived. "When weakness or doubt stalks you, draw your power from the Red Eye."

Erich had lost all hope in the Red Eye. In fact, he cursed it. Especially now with the bodies of Arden and Amira dragged away. Humans are stronger than initially thought. Not physically, but mentally. The mind of a six-year-old earthling corrupted one of the fiercest warriors. It cannot be the end of him! "Wait," he said and walked to Arden's head. Lucius glared at him as he picked it up with both hands. Erich closed Arden's glazed eyes with his thumbs and whispered, "Until we meet again, my old friend."

"There won't be a next time," Alcantar said, glaring at Jupiter, his back turned on his wife and son.

Erich nodded. "Human blood tainted him; it was not his fault." He placed the head on Arden's chest. "Arden was a great warrior, and I will miss him."

"Cast them both into space," Lucius ordered the young Leon holding Arden's legs.

"Including their clones."

"Yes, master," the boy said with a bowed head.

Erich trailed the bodies down the dark and lonely corridor. "You were the boy Arden spoke to," he said.

"Yes, master," the boy muttered.

"What's your name?"

"Lyceum."

"What did you talk about?"

Lyceum glanced at the Leon dragging Amira's body and then at Erich.

Erich peered at Lyceum for a moment. "Wait, I'll take her from here."

Ross white-knuckled the rail where he stood, peering at the black uniforms below him.

"You sure you want to do this?" Buchanan asked as he joined him.

"She was my daughter," he whispered.

"The Shield will collapse, with or without your help, and they know it now... after your speech."

"That's why we must act now, before its collapse," Ross said.

"We will have the blood of hundreds of thousands–"

"They have the blood of billions on theirs!" Ross screamed. The soldiers within the third cave looked at Ross for a moment. "I might save our people with this act."

"Look at them," Buchanan muttered. "You think they want us to save them? They're starving and without hope."

"Then I'll settle on revenge." He released the rail and walked into the control room. "Could you get hold of them, Major?" he asked the woman who had joined him.

"Uh, yes," she said.

"Yes, who?" he snapped.

"Yes, General."

Professor Santiago entered the room. "We made a mistake."

Ross glared at her. "What do you mean?"

"We should have trusted Darius." She rubbed her bandaged hand. "And Wayne."

He rolled his eyes. "Now it's Wayne."

"You saw the video of him. He's with us – the humans." She grabbed his arm. "Please reconsider."

Ross glared at her hand until she released her grip. "I've turned so many cheeks. They deserve what's coming to them." He faced the screens suspended from the ceiling and, taking a deep breath, said, "On screen!"

Alcantar's image appeared eyes flaming. Beside him stood an old Leon wearing a red robe and headgear resembling a priest's biretta.

"Bach snachs al ochroete vach Achte," Alcantar smirked.

The Elder cleared his throat. "Amusing. All these calls from Earth."

"I have something you want," Ross said.

The Elder translated.

"Your blood?" Alcantar said.

"We embedded a virus within the data I uploaded for General Steward."

"You mean the dead General Steward?"

"Dead?" Ross whispered. "Uh, how?"

"Killed by my traitor son, Malik." Alcantar shifted forward and leaned on his sword. "You were saying?"

"But, but who's running things?"

"Another insect. I don't care. Continue!"

Ross cleared the shock from his throat. "The virus or program enables us to open a window within the shield. Undetected."

Alcantar's eyes narrowed.

"I'm willing to hand you the code," Ross said.

"Why sacrifice your species?"

"Show us mercy. We are but a few and will never be a threat. With this code, you can infiltrate the Dome, disable the power source, and capture your son. Do what Malik could not."

"According to your broadcast, the shield will fail within two weeks, so why would I want the code?"

"I wanted to cause panic. I don't know how long they have." He shrugged. "Two weeks, six months, maybe another ten years."

Alcantar fell back into his chair. "You have yourself – as you humans call it – a deal."

"One more thing..."

Alcantar waved his hand to continue after the Elder had translated.

"Will you allow us to search for food?"

Alcantar rose from his throne and walked off the screen. Moments later, he appeared, dragging a human male behind him. "As long as you do not turn to cannibalism." He grabbed the petrified man by the hair and sank his fangs into his neck. Gasps and screams filled the operations room as Alcantar feasted on the screaming man.

"How can we trust you?" Ross said.

Alcantar tossed the body to the side and, with blood dripping from his mouth, said, "Dich ich wach ecg sach doe nigh coch krych."

"This is what I will do to you if you do not send me the code," the Elder said.

Alcantar stepped closer until his face filled the screen. "Jych hech ech cychle och diech ichvach bchin mech joch."

"You have one minute, or else the invasion will start with you."

"Send the code," Ross said as Alcantar's image disappeared from the screen.

"Don't!" Professor Santiago ordered.

"Send the code!" Ross turned toward Santiago and froze; the barrel of a gun brought clarity to his blind rage. "What... what are you doing, Sophia?" he said, blinking as if she sprayed him with a water gun.

"We will not allow you to do this."

"We?"

Santiago straightened. "If there is anyone in this room who disagrees with me, shoot me now."

Ross turned to Buchanan. "Arrest her."

"She's right. We cannot do this."

Ross searched the room. "They will invade! Slaughter us like pigs!"

"So be it," Santiago seethed.

Ross reached for his weapon.

"Please don't," Santiago whispered. "I know you lost your daughter, but the man who killed her is dead. We can't sacrifice all those people. We will be less human than them. This is not what General Johnson fought for."

"But what are we going to do?" he whispered, eyes searching for an answer.

"We must evacuate."

"And go where?"

"The Dome."

"But they don't want us?" Ross shook his head.

"Steward did not want us – and he's dead now."

Ross narrowed his eyes. "You want to go to Nirvana because of Malik? Because of a speech he gave in an elevator. He might have Johnson's blood in him, but he's not a Johnson."

"I don't know if it was Johnson I saw in him, but I saw a leader." Santiago readjusted her grip, fighting back her tears. "A leader who we do not have at this stage."

Ross looked around bewildered and found confirmation of Santiago's statement on the faces glaring back at him.

She lowered her weapon and wiped away the tears. "I'm sorry," she whispered.

"Yes," he muttered as he shoved past her. "You will be."

All eyes returned to Santiago as Ross left the control room.

Buchanan took a deep sigh of relief. "What now?" he whispered.

"Tell all they need to prepare," she responded. "We are evacuating."

"What about chamber one?"

"Everyone," she said, glaring. "Even if we need to make ten trips, we're not leaving anyone behind."

"You know we will make it easy for them," Buchanan said. "Everyone cooped up in one place."

"Together, we might stand a chance."

"Professor!" a female operator yelled. "The code is being uploaded!"

"From where!"

"General Ross's office!"

"Bastard!" Santiago ran for the door.

"Cut all communication!" Buchanan said and followed.

"It's too late, sir!"

Ross placed the photograph of his daughter on the desk in front of him. "The bastards will pay for what they did to you, my angel. Daddy will join you in a moment." He drew his handgun as he heard the footsteps and pressed the barrel against his temple.

The door flung open, and Santiago stormed in, weapon raised. "You coward! You think those animals will keep their word?"

"Of course not. Why do you think I'm doing this?" He smiled and pulled the trigger.

Buchanan froze in the doorway as Ross fell forward, half his head striking the desk, the other half oozing from the bookshelf beside him.

Santiago shook her head. "Finally," she muttered. "Revenge and hatred sealed the fate of humanity."

"We have received the code, master," Erich said.

Alcantar smiled. "Fools. They never learn, do they?"

"Your orders?"

He rose from his throne and approached Lucius. "Let the games begin. I want Malik out of the equation and their new leader. According to the images we saw, both of them have one thing in common."

Like a cockroach in a flea circus, sounds great, but the rides were too small, the circus inescapable, and the spotlight on me. The fleas kept their distance but couldn't keep their eyes off us. We strolled hand-in-hand down a paved road, passed glasshouses, empty shops, fake trees, fake flowers, and breathing fake air. We ignored our troubled past and uncertain future, pretending to be an average, carefree couple. Rushing to create memories. I kept blocking the taste and screams of the four soldiers.

"She will find out."

She knows what I am.

"You mean what I am."

Sadie led me into an alley lined with concrete buildings. It was the oldest part of the Dome, she told me, first constructed. The faded facade reminded me of the farmhouse.

"The farmhouse again, really? Why do you keep going back there?"

"Here we are," Sadie said, looking up and down the alley, then knocked four times on a weathered wooden door.

"I like this part of the Dome."

"This is the original city. Feels real, doesn't it?" Sadie said, touching the door.

"Original city?"

"The shield came down over an existing city, and over time, new replaced old." She looked at a glass eye above the door. "Take me to Kansas."

A dark-skinned man with curly grey hair and tired grey eyes opened the door. "Welcome home, Dorothy," he said with a smile, and wrapped his arms around her. "Where had you been, girl? I was worried about you after seeing-"

"Travelled the yellow brick road," Sadie interrupted. "Why are you answering the door?"

"Busy night." His smile disappeared as his gaze fell on my chest; it took him a while to reach my eyes.

"I see you found the lion," he said.

"But this one already found his heart," Sadie said, and wrapped her arm around my waist.

"You trust him?" the dark-skinned man asked.

"As much as you, Moses."

"What's your lion's name?"

"Wayne."

"They all taste the same. It's just a different wrapping."

He stuck out his hand and looked me in the eye. "Welcome to the Real-World café."

We followed Moses into a world I've never experienced before. A place filled with laughter, strange music with no rules, and it seems people unafraid of tomorrow. We made our way through the crowded room; people sat around tables, talking, drinking, eating, and laughing. I kept my eyes on the group of people on the raised floor that made the strange music.

"Where's your guitar?" Moses asked.

"I snapped a string."

"You must allow the music to take you wherever you want to go," Moses said. "Never fight the music. It's like fighting with your soul."

"You're right. I fought with it, but it helped my soul." Sadie glanced at me with a naughty glint in her eyes.

Moses stopped a few feet from the raised floor and clapped his hands. Two young men, dressed in yellow shirts and black pants, brought a table and two chairs. Moments later, our table resembled all the others, covered with red cloth and lit up by candlelight.

The glint in Sadie's eyes vanished as she noticed the three girls seated at a table a few feet from us, gawked and pointed our way.

"Yes, it's me!" Sadie gave a step toward them. "Mind your own fucking business!"

"Take it easy," the girl seated on the other side said. "Quite a catch you have there. And what Ryan did to you was fucking unforgivable. Just wanted to say."

Sadie nodded, "Okay. Thanks. Sorry." She returned to our table, red as an angry Leon female.

Moses glared at me. "Where's your manners, boy?"

"Manners?"

"You must pull a seat out for your lady."

"Why?" I asked. "It looks like she can handle a chair."

"Don't worry, Moses," Sadie said, head bowed, keeping her eyes on the red tablecloth. "He doesn't know what it means."

"And I guess with his size, nobody gon'na teach him some manners."

I took a slow seat.

"Don't worry, boy. It's genuine wood."

"That's what I'm worried about," I muttered. "There's an expiration date on all things natural."

"That's God's honest truth," Moses conceded, and placed his hand on Sadie's shoulder. "I need to get back to the door. I'll check up on you when it's quieter. Now that the people know they've got only two weeks left, everyone wants to start living." He shook his head, scanning the room. "Spending their credits because there's no tomorrow."

"Is he from here?" I asked as Moses blended with the crowd.

"Yep, but his ancestors were from Africa."

"Ancestors?"

She made a rolling motion with her hand as she said, "His great-great-grandfather and great-great-grandmother."

"I like this music."

"It's called Jazz," Sadie said, closing her eyes. "And I made a mistake. We shouldn't have come here. I thought with everything happening, people had forgotten about my..."

I reached over and took her warm, timid hands in mine. "Look at me."

The bine pierced my heart as a tear rolled down her cheek.

"Sorry," she whispered. Her tear-filled eyes glistened in the candlelight.

"With the memories of Malik's previous lives, all the worlds he had travelled, all the creatures he had encountered, not one could kill or hurt you with its eyes."

She smiled her hurt away.

"Show her how a Leon does it."

"See that man in the green shirt looking at us?"

Sadie glanced to her right and returned her gaze to me.

I turned in my chair and gave him the Leon death-stare. The man looked away, half turning in his seat, shielding himself with his shoulder.

"See."

She covered her smile with a hand, turning her head toward the stage.

"She is special for a human."

"And the frown?" Sadie asked. "You look worried."

I forced a smile, "Nothing. Now, you do it."

The strength in her eyes returned as she stared into mine. "Okay." She steeled herself, taking a deep breath. Her first adversary was a skinny boy with blue hair wearing a blood-red shirt and white pants – a nosy shit; he couldn't keep his eyes off her. She looked at him, eyes narrowing. He glanced away as if slapped through the face.

"We are ion cannons, and they are an asteroid field," I said. "But remember, before you fire, you must be fully charged."

Sadie looked at me with a victorious smile, eyes sparkling like Zelon rocks. "Otherwise, what would happen if not?"

"Your ion will ricochet off the asteroid," I said, leaning in. "The asteroid will get bigger and stronger, and it will take more power to destroy it the next time. Are you ready?"

"Is that you talking or me?"

She gave a determined nod, lips pressed, leaning in.

"On three," I said.

"What asteroid?"

The charged particles between us intensified. "Let's destroy all of them with one discharge," I whispered.

She gave a determined nod, eyes narrowing, nosing toward me.

We passed the point of no return – a self-heating reaction brought on by two beings or particles drawn to each other by an invisible force from different corners of the galaxy to form a single entity. No asteroid, black hole, or hellish beast could prevent fusion. "What?" What?

"One... Two..." I whispered and, on three, kissed her gently.

She kissed me back hard, slipping her tongue into my mouth. The taste of her strawberry lips, her godly scent, and our dancing tongues stirred the beast awake.

I pulled back.

"What's wrong?" she whispered, searching for answers in my eyes.

I cleared my throat, looking at our entwined hands. "I can't trust Malik. Not yet." I looked up, shifting. "I'm in control. It's just when I surrender to you, I can feel him inside my head, ready to take over."

She squeezed my hands. "We can take it slow until you feel you can trust Malik."

"That wasn't me, stirring. It was us."

Malik's thoughts withered as I drowned in her pools of mystic amber. She looked like a goddess in the candlelight – a ruler of a faraway world; untouchable, majestic, and pure. The flames danced in her eyes as if to the rhythm of the music. "You're beautiful," I whispered.

Sadie smiled and tucked her black hair behind her ear. "Bad lighting." There was something different in her eyes, the way she looked at me – shy but challenging – something that rustled the bine.

"Female magic."

"How did you find this place?" I asked, shifting.

"It found me... after my second attempt." Sadie rubbed her wrist. "Moses found me in the hospital." She shrugged. "That's what he does. He showed me a world that once was. He taught me to play the guitar and saxophone. Moses gave me something to live for." Her eyes hardened. "Then Ryan came along and destroyed it."

"Well, you destroyed him today."

She smiled. "I did, didn't I?"

"Yep." A moment of silence followed as our eyes locked. "Why try to kill yourself?"

Sadie crossed her arms as if to warm herself and glanced down at the red cloth. "Four years ago, they murdered my mother," she said, her voice strained. "My best friend died that day. My father was never there for me, always too busy." She broke her embrace and reached for my hands. "But I found myself again when I met you."

"Humans love touching each other."

Holding on to her hand was still a conscious decision. But the more she did it, the easier it became. "What do you mean?" I whispered.

She squeezed my hands. "I see a boy who fought for his survival all his life. That never gave up. No matter how hard life tried to turn you bad, you remained good. I found my strength in you again. I lived a privileged life, shielded from the harshness of it, like everyone else in Nirvana. Our lives centre around us. If things weren't perfect, we threw a tantrum. And when I mean not perfect, I mean not enough credits, clothes, boys, likes, size of my room and steamer time. So when something real happened that blew my bubble, I realised how alone I was. Their bubbles still protected them. I get it because, selfishly, my father wanted my bubble to last as long as possible." She shrugged. "I think every parent does. But bubble people bounce away from one another. Life popped both our bubbles." She smiled. "That and you're not bad looking."

"We were born without a bubble." Let that be our bond.

I shook my head. "I'm not a good person. I killed many in this life and the past."

"You're not Malik anymore. Forget your past lives. In this life, you killed the bastards that deserved it... who wanted to destroy Wayne?"

"My name is Beatrice, and I'll be your waiter for the evening," an underfed wrinkly grey-haired woman said, dressed in a yellow shirt and short black dress. "What can I order you lovebirds?" Her tone of voice did not match her impassive expression.

"She's got a lot of history-lines."

Sadie sat up. "Give my boyfriend the biggest steak you have. I'll take the three-hundred-gram rump with baked beans and eggs."

"Funny girl."

Sadie smiled. "I had to try. What's left to order?"

"Water with or without the twist and protein biscuits."

She sighed. "Just water then," she glanced at me, "with a twist?"

"And you?"

I shrugged. "The same, but bring me some strawberry flavoured biscuits."

Sadie gave me a look.

"I know, but I'm starving. And don't forget, I have tasted the real thing before." I winked at her.

"Who'll pay?" the server asked, removing a cylinder-shaped object from her pocket.

Sadie held out her arm.

Beatrice stared at the fresh scar on Sadie's wrist, caused by my fangs.

"It's pretty, isn't it?" Sadie scowled. "You want one around your neck?"

"Take it easy, girl," Beatrice said and showed Sadie her wrist. "It just brought back memories."

"You like mine?" I said and ran my finger down the scar on my face.

"A bit over the top," Beatrice said and scanned Sadie's wrist. "At least somebody did that to you. We did this to ourselves." She glanced at the device in her hand. "Looks like you folks are going to have a fun time tonight."

Certain things should not be imitated, like stars; it prevented you from reaching for it. Maybe that's why the people within the dome remained.

"What you looking for?" Sadie slurred, joining me in the alley. "You didn't go to the restroom once."

"My body uses everything."

Her eyes widen. "Lucky fucking you." She hiccupped and grabbed my arm as she lost her footing. "Maybe that's why the Leons could travel all over the uni-fucking-vers." She looked at the stars and made a sweeping gesture with her arm. "They don't have to take pee breaks."

Beatrice was right; we had a fun time. The best time of my life. "Not mine." The music was real, the atmosphere electrifying and the water, at first, horrible, but the more we consumed, the more I wanted.

"How's your wrist?" I asked, concerned. Her scars, old and new, were the colour of my strawberry biscuits after being scanned so many times.

"I can't feel my fucking legs... or face."

"You okay?" After four or five glasses, even Sadie had some biscuits. We also had a biscuit tasting competition, guessing the age, gender, and how the person had died.

"I'm fine!" she yelled, throwing her arms into the air.

I caught her just in time.

She seemed fine as our eyes locked. "I don't want the President to see me like this."

I nodded and picked her up.

"You had like two or three glasses more than me." She wrapped her arms around my neck. "I wanted to get you fucking drunk." She hiccupped and started crying. "Why?"

"It's the alcohol. Remember the humans with the red hair in the north? Alcohol took their fear away. And the livers of those that consume copious amounts are a delicacy."

"You need it?" she sobbed, her tears rolling down my neck.

I didn't call a taxi but carried her to my place; it was only eight blocks. Her warm breath burst against my neck. Soothing. I could hold her like this for ten lives. I glanced at the enormous clock on top of a building: 1:12. The streets were busy; people gathered in groups, staring at the big empty screen. I smelt their fear and sensed their uncertainty.

"We need to get out of this cage before they invade," a man said as I passed a group.

"There's nothing out there. We'll die of starvation," a woman answered.

"And what about our children?"

"Haven't you been watching the news!" a man snapped. "We need to do what that man said; it's our only chance."

Nowhere had I heard the word fight. But even if the humans decided to, they won't stand a chance. I glanced at the fragile body in my arms and pressed her tight against my chest. She moaned a bit, but I couldn't help myself. At least she cried no more, but made a funny snorting sound.

Another group stopped talking and stared at me as I approached.

"She had too much water," I explained.

"It's him," a woman whispered, elbowing the man next to her.

He nodded. "Can we help you, sir?"

I shook my head and walked through the group as they parted.

"But how can we fight them?" he asked. "Please tell us, Wayne!"

I turned back. "How do you know my name?"

"You all over the news," he said. "A reporter recorded you when you spoke to people in an elevator."

They waited for an answer. Sadie's snorting sound broke the silence. "You first need the will to fight. Something to die for." I glanced at Sadie. "Find that, then I can help you." I turned and went ahead on my path.

"He's so romantic," a woman whispered. "You never carried me like that."

"You crazy? With my back."

I went down on my knees beside my bed after I had tucked Sadie in, studying every line and curve of her porcelain face. So perfect, flawless. I took her hand in mine and kissed her palm.

"We won't be able to protect her. You know it. Unless we go back to Father and beg for our lives. He will accept us... and her. But we need to prove our loyalty first. Bring down the shield before its collapse."

I took a deep breath. It felt like Malik's third death when a Nuko giant had dropped a boulder on his chest—losing her terrified me. What the Leons would do to her horrified me. I blocked the disturbing images and jumped into the steamer, speed-cleaning. It was not out of choice, but because they only allow two minutes of steamer time every twelve hours before it shuts down. I wanted Sadie to have the next round. For the first time since I stayed here, I cleaned the apartment. One benefit of the little box I stayed in was I could neaten it in more or less the same time the steamer took.

I made myself comfortable on the barren floor next to the bed, using Joshua's teddy bear as a pillow. It still smelt of him. As I listened to the rhythmic snoring, I thought of the day's events:

Steward, the President, Juliet and the last moments of Arden and Amira. I shed some water as I fell asleep, the only comfort, the woman in my bed, and the teddy under my head. "You are so pathetic. Father will laugh himself to death if he sees you now."

Fuck off; I want to sleep.

———

Something yanked me from my nightmare.

"Shit!" Sadie yelled.

I jumped up and sprinted for the door.

"This bloody steamer!"

"They only give us two minutes," I said, standing by the door.

"Who's they! A bunch of fucking men! I'm covered in soap!"

I smiled. "Here's a towel and come with me."

The door cracked open, and she grabbed the towel from my hand.

"So, I take it you get over two minutes," I said as she stepped out of the steamer, wrapped in the towel.

"Don't start," she scowled.

"Come."

She followed me out of my apartment and down the corridor.

"What are you doing?" she whispered, tip-toeing behind me.

"A woman stays here," I said as we passed the first door.

"What do you mean?"

I stopped by the second door and knocked.

"What are you doing?" She glanced up and down the corridor.

The door opened, and a skinny pale guy dressed in dirty white shorts looked up at me.

"My girlfriend is not from here, and she needs another minute."

"I saw you on the news," he said, deadpan, scratching his crotch.

"Wayne," Sadie said, tugging my shirt. "I can't take this man's time."

"I'm sure he doesn't use it much."

"No, please." He stepped aside and waved her in. "Take the two minutes."

"Thank you." She sprinted past him and disappeared into the apartment.

"She's the President's daughter, isn't she?"

"Yep."

"Horrible what they did to her."

I nodded.

"I'm hungry. Nobody will miss him."

I shook my head. Look at him. "You live alone?"

"Yes, but I'm moving in with my sister over the weekend. A car or truck struck her husband while crossing the road. The details are sketchy, but the impact flung him into a billboard. Burnt him to a crisp. Can you believe it?" He shrugged, scratching his yellowy tangled hair. "The bastard deserved it, though. After his death, her seven-year-old daughter came forward, told my sister her father had visited her at night. His own daughter, can you fucking believe it? So, I'm moving in to help with the chores and stuff." He stuck out his hand. "Nathen."

"Wayne." I looked at his hand. "Since standing here, you'd scratched your balls twice."

"Unbelievable, as if that had ever stopped us."

He lowered his hand. "Sorry, bad habit."

"I can sense you have lost your appetite."

"Thank you," Sadie panted. "I think you have a few seconds left."

"That's more than enough time for me," he smiled. "Now I can say someone famous used my steamer."

As we made our way back to my box, the man yelled, "Thanks, Wayne! You gave us hope again. I know you'll get us out of this. Everyone knows it."

"What was that all about?" Sadie asked as we entered my apartment.

"Shit," I whispered.

"What?"

"I spoke to people in an elevator, and someone recorded it." I shook my head. "Now everyone thinks that I'm going to stop the invasion."

"What did you tell them?"

"I can't even remember." I took her hands as our eyes met. "The only thing I know is we need to get out of here. Tell your father we need to evacuate Nirvana as soon as possible."

"And then what?" Sadie whispered, frowning. "We're not as strong as you. We will die out there, and you know it."

"It will be more humane."

She let go of my hands. "This is not the Wayne I know?"

"Good idea, Wayne! They will be easier to find and kill in the desert."

Shut up!

"I know how they do things. It will be a slaughterhouse, the more brutal the killing, the more the satisfaction. It is what they do, it's just a game. It's like a hunter searching for the most efficient and most fun way to outwit its prey."

"So, we don't stand a chance? What if all the other cities stand together?"

I shook my head. "This is the last city still standing. They will destroy it as they had done with all the others. The shields of the other twelve cities had failed decades ago. After they'd conquered the cities, they retreated to Europa, one of Jupiter's moons, waiting for Nirvana's shield to fail. They thought if the humans did not detect them, they would disable the shield. After a decade, running low on food, they came up with a plan to infiltrate the Dome. The rest, you know."

Sadie shook her head. "That can't be true. Father said the council members in the other cities voted unanimously for the Sweepers to return. That was like a week ago."

"I don't know who's voting, but it's not them."

She took a seat on the edge of my bed, shaking her head. "You're making a mistake. We can't be the only ones left."

"I know it's hard to believe, but-"

"Stop it!" She jumped up. "You are making-"

"I'm not!" I screamed. "I have all these images in my head. It's driving me crazy! Malik shows it to me when I sleep. It's as if I was there. I can hear, smell and taste the fear, the screams. Mothers and fathers were trying to protect their children with knives and sticks and whatever they could lay their hands on. When they had realised their futility, they would plead for their children's lives." I wiped the tears away, whispering, "But that would just fuel their hunger. They kill the children first. They have waited decades for this moment, and the Leon race is not a patient race. Their hunger for what's coming will be brutal."

Sadie wrapped her arms around me, resting her head on my chest. "They have underestimated this city, and they will again." She looked into my eyes. "We have one thing that all the other cities did not have."

"What?"

"You." She poked my chest. "From what I've heard, you gave the people hope again. They believe in you. I believe in you."

"I lost my mother and brother yesterday," I said. "I don't want to lose you."

"Then you need to stay and help us because I'm going nowhere."

"We don't stand a chance."

We?

"I will rather die fighting for this human female than my Leon father. We will never be good enough for him. Let's accept it. At least our death will mean something to someone."

Step back into the shadows.

"Why?"

The only way this can work is for you to control yourself. Can you?

"Yes."

Prove it.

I kissed her softly. Her lips still tasted like strawberries. I was like a barrel of jet fuel, she the spark. The explosion instantly burnt off my clothes and her towel. She jumped into my arms and wrapped her legs around my waist, kissing me hard. I walked her to the bed, lip-locked, and laid her down gently. The warmth of her naked body, her soft, perfect skin, fuelled my desire. Almost to the brink of madness. I wanted to taste every inch of her body, starting with her delicate neck, full breasts, and the curve of her hips. She groaned as I entered her with my tongue. The rhythm of my heart was unnatural, uncontrollable, like jazz. She grabbed me by the hair and pressed me tight against her shivering body. Her taste filled my mouth, body, and mind. She pulled me up by the hair, and as our eyes locked, I knew what she wanted.

"Be careful," she heaved.

She clawed at my chest as I slowly entered her, arching her back, gasping for air. "You okay?" I whispered.

"Yes," she groaned, thrusting her hips toward me. Her groans intensified with each deepening thrust.

Malik remained in the shadows, cautious but curious. Repelled but aroused. As a Leon, he only witnessed the human emotion called love; he had never experienced it. Now trapped in a human body, they forced him to take part. The powerful feeling surged through his veins like a plasma coil, tainting each Leon particle and numbing his rage. The sensation was too powerful to resist, and now, too powerful to conquer. Only one option remained - surrender. As a Leon, the choice was inconceivable yet unavoidable.

It was as if she could read my mind, testing me, stopping me before I peaked. My self-control increased, taking it closer to the pinnacle with each pause. I had never experienced such euphoria and sensed neither had Malik, as their act was mindless, loveless, and without patience.

Her smell was overwhelming, her touch heavenly. I sensed every cell, every follicle within my body, on the verge of exploding. I had never felt so human in my life. The Leon was still present but tamed; no memory of Malik could overshadow this moment.

We knew when the time was perfect. As if one, we reached the edge, falling into a crystal pond filled with pleasure.

I fell next to her on the bed, exhilarated, my face buried in her tangled hair. She was still heaving, though, eyes shut and body trembling.

After a while, I whispered, concerned, "Sadie?"

She grabbed me by the arm and groaned, "W-o-w."

"Not bad for the first time as a human."

She opened her eyes and looked at me, surprised. "It was my first time... as well."

"It felt as if you knew what you were doing."

She smiled. "Amazing what you can learn online and from your girlfriends."

I circled her belly button with my finger and asked, "What else did they tell you?"

"They said it would hurt if..."

"If?" My finger moved toward her breasts.

"You know." She raised her head and glanced at my manhood.

I circled her nipple. "I'm glad that I'm not all human, that the most important part remained Leon."

She burst out laughing and climbed on top of me. We were both ready for more, and this time, she was in complete control.

"Your father wants to see you," Brian said as Sadie entered the Presidential Palace. "He's in his office."

"What happened to Ryan?" she asked.

"Prison, awaiting trial."

She nodded. "You told him what happened?"

"About your running off with the alien or Ryan?"

She looked at him, annoyed.

"Both."

She shrugged and made her way to the president's office.

Her father leapt from his chair as Sadie entered. "Where have you been?"

"With Wayne," she said.

He halted his advance with a frown. "So, you won't deny it."

"I wanted to be at the safest place in the Dome."

The president flinched. "That Ryan bastard will pay for what he did to you. I'm sorry for not being here." He wrapped his arms around her. "I've doubled security. It will never happen again."

"The only person I want to protect me is Wayne."

He took her by the shoulders and regarded her at arm's length. "I'm your father. I will protect you."

She shook her head. "You're never here."

Charles turned away and muttered, "Okay, I deserved that."

"I love him."

Her father peered at the revolving glass building through his office window. "You slept with him?"

"Yes."

He bowed his head.

"I'm turning eighteen in two weeks."

He nodded. "I thought you're going to wait until..."

"He's the one," she whispered. "And nothing can wait anymore. Our time is running out."

Her father was a different person when he turned back - as if deflated. "I don't want you to see him. Even if I must lock you in your room."

"What!"

"It's the only way I can keep you safe. I don't know when they'll attack, but when they do, I want you by my side."

"Then let him stay here!" she screamed.

Her father's life force returned. "He's one of them!" he screamed. "Killed five men yesterday! Tore them apart! He's an animal!"

The door opened behind her, and Captain Bryan walked in.

"Don't let her leave the house," Charles ordered. "And keep that thing away from her. If you catch him anywhere near her, you have my permission to do what's necessary."

"I will see him again!" Sadie stormed toward her father. "Not you or anybody in this fucking city will stop me."

"Then you leave me no choice." Charles sighed. "Bryan."

"Yes, Mr President."

"Put Wayne Johnson in jail. If I can't keep my daughter away from him, I'll keep him away from her."

"No, Father... please!" She fell on her knees with praying hands.

"On what charges, sir?"

"Murder." He looked at Sadie at his feet. "And rape."

Tears of anger filled her eyes as she rose to her feet. "Fuck you," she seethed.

"No, I believe an alien did that to you last night," he said without missing a beat.

Sadie winched; her father's words hit her like a gut punch.

Charles walked to his desk. "And remove all sharp objects from her room. You know how she gets when things don't go her way."

Sadie looked at her wrists, then at her father. Her tears evaporated. "You know who they will come for first?"

"What are you talking about?"

"They'll first go for the head, and I hope your human guards can protect you." She turned for the door.

"You think your boyfriend will do a better job?"

"I'll bet your life on it," Sadie said. Bullshit. She stomped down the stairs. Grownups fucked up this world, and now they want to tell me how to live my life - who to love. The only thing real in this fake world is my love for Wayne. I'll even take Malik.

Sadie rubbed the fang-marks on her wrist – feeling closer to him – sensing him. It burned her fingers as he did her heart. She felt safe touching it. Shivers ran through her body as she recalled the morning's events.

A guard hovered in the entrance hall and smiled at her as she approached. She forced a smile.

"I have orders not to let you out of the house, miss," he said.

"I forgot something in the limousine," she said, smiling.

"Tell me what it is, and I'll fetch it," he said, blocking her escape.

"Okay." She smiled. "It's that time of the month, and my menstrual cup is in the limo. My flow is quite severe with everything happening, so please hurry."

"I think it will be better if you fetch it," he mumbled with flaming cheeks, and opened the door.

"You sure?" She frowned.

He nodded.

"Thank you." Sadie skipped down the stairs to the limousine parked at the base.

"I told you she's not allowed to leave!" Captain Bryan shouted as she reached the limousine. The driver's door was unlocked, as always. Bryan and four guards were already halfway down the stairs when she slammed the door shut.

"Lock doors," Sadie said, and placed her palm on the biometric security panel.

"Good afternoon, Sadie," the AI greeted.

"I hope it will be," she said. "Start vehicle."

Bryan banged his fist on the window. "Get out, Sadie!"

She inserted her middle finger into her mouth before flipping him the bird. "Manual override." Déjà vu, she thought, as Brian tried to open the door. But this time, she wasn't that frightened, pathetic little girl. Today I'm not running away but running toward my new life, and nothing will get in my way.

Brian slammed on the bonnet, veins bulging. "You will not get away this time!"

"Proximity alert," the onboard computer warned.

Sadie waved at him. "Activate shield."

"Affirmative... security barrier to activate in three... two..."

"You can't es–"

A burst of energy enveloped the car. It propelled Brian and the other men several metres through the air before they hit the pebbled driveway. They lay motionless, stunned.

Sadie stepped on the accelerator as her father appeared in the doorway. He shook his head, deadpan. She felt nothing for him at that moment, as if she passed a stranger on the street. The limousine sped up toward the wrought-iron gates. This time, she would keep her eyes open.

"What?" she whispered, shocked, as the gates parted. She could not hold back the tears. It was her choice; if she crossed that bridge, there would be no return. She raised her foot from the accelerator, staring at her father's lone figure in the rear-view screen. How distraught he'd been when her mother had died. And now his daughter was leaving him, too. Her foot danced between the accelerator and the brake. The bridge was upon her. Decide! She glanced at the bite mark on her wrist and moved her foot toward the accelerator. Her father turned away; head bowed.

She slammed her fist against the steering wheel. "Fuck! Fuck! Fuck!"

The limousine slowed to a stop. Sadie burst into tears, caught between love and compassion.

Charles turned back.

She exited the limousine, made her way back to the house, and halted at the bottom of the stairs.

Bryan and the guards stumbled to their feet but kept their distance.

"I will stay," she said. "But if you arrest Wayne, you will lose me forever."

Her father nodded. "Thank you."

I was lying in bed, hands behind my head, reliving the morning's events. Not once did I have to fight Malik. She released the human in me and banished the Leon. Or Malik was also in love with her. But Leons can't love. Or could they? Maybe nobody taught them to love. Can you teach someone love? Like a Sukra beast, untamed. They would puncture your stomach and suck your intestines from your body, then defecate on your face before you drew your last breath. They would keep you warm at night and lick you clean if tamed. Only the most powerful and fiercest Leon could accomplish such a feat. Malik tamed four. The voice in my head was gone, but not the memories. The path forward would be challenging. Would I base the decisions I made on my experience or Malıik's? The result must always benefit Sadie because the reward is so... Wow! I searched Malik's memories for a way to defeat them, their weakness, their secrets, but slammed the lid shut – the images of the fallen cities, the massacres overwhelmed me. My head started to hurt – as if I was back on my Rock-of-reflection.

Three knocks at the door shoved me off my Rock.

"Yes!" I yelled.

"It's m-me."

"Itis open."

Shorty entered, beaming as if he were the one who had sex. He dragged in a bag.

"Good afternoon." I sat up before he noticed my excitement.

He frowned, surprised by my greeting. "G-g-good afternoon, W-Wayne."

"Killed anyone today?"

He thought about it for a beat, then shook his head. "And y-you?"

"No, it's been a quiet day." He remained in the doorway, staring at me as if I visited him. "Can I help you with something?"

He nodded. "D-Darius wants you."

"Where?"

"The s-south gate."

"Where's the south gate?" I frowned.

He pointed. "S-s-s-"

"If you going to say south, I will kill you."

He swallowed, still pointing. "A-at the edge o-of the city. T-t-today at s-seventeen h-h-hundred hours."

"I'm not into this military thing you have going" –I gestured at his soldier's outfit– "but-"

He showed me five fingers.

"Five o'clock today. Why?"

"T-training."

I burst out laughing. "I don't need training."

"No," he shook his head. "You m-must train us."

I swallowed my laugh and shook my head. "I don't know how to train humans. They're weak and cowardly."

Shorty marched in with his oversized boots and halted by my bed. With me sitting, he was at eye level. His sparkle was now a fiery pit. "I'm not a coward."

"I-I know that. I-I was talking about the people in the city."

"Darius said if you're not at the south gate by seventeen hundred hours, you must leave the c-city. Your u-u-uniform and w-w-weapons are inside the bag."

I remained seated. "How can I give them false hope? No matter how well I trained them, they will lose."

"They? I thought y-y-you were one of us?"

"But we've got only a week or two left?"

"So?" He shrugged. "S-s-somebody said that it's never too late to fight, that there's still h-hope. We must fight for the little human that's still left. That the planet had kept him a-alive, and that it is time to return the f-f-favour."

"No." I frowned. "I said we must fight for the little humanity that's still left in us."

Shorty smiled. "So, y-you can remember?" He placed his hand on my shoulder. "It's all we've got, Wayne."

I slumped, feeling the weight of the world on my shoulders. It was our only option. The only hope in this hopeless battle would be humanity. "I will see what–"

Shorty had left. Another thing, I only told Sadie I couldn't remember the conversation in the elevator, and that was right before we had sex.

Where the fuck was he?

18

I left my apartment at four-thirty, dressed in my military kit. One human characteristic I despised was doubt. A Leon doesn't have that problem. I was as strong as a Leon, but that means nothing on a slippery path with unsure footing, on my way to a battle already lost. What the human hell do they expect of me? Another human thing I hate is the heightened awareness of consequences.

I reached for the elevator button but couldn't press it.

I can kill myself and wake up as Malik.

What about Sadie?

No Leon would dare touch the property of Malik.

I studied my human hands, recalling the morning's events. If I can't touch her with these hands...

Love makes me more Leon. It takes away consequences. What does it mean? To act blindly to keep love alive. No matter how foolish or illogical the action. Whatever it takes to keep the bine alive.

Fuck! I'm asking and answering myself. Who am I?

Malik, if you're still in there, it's the Leon in me that's the coward. He's the one afraid of going into battle.

"I'm not!"

My knees buckled as a sharp pain exploded in the back of my head. "Yes, you are," I seethed, leaning against the frame of the elevator.

The beast within fought for control.

"You only want to go into battle when victory is certain."

The words startle him; he gave a step back into the shadows.

It is more courageous to go into battle when victory is uncertain. The pain in my head subsided. I straightened and took a deep breath. "So, are we going to do this or not?"

I was as strong as a Leon, with the heart of a human, on the right side of the battle – must mean something in the greater scheme of things.

I straightened and pressed the button. The doors opened to a packed elevator.

"I'll take the next one," a man said and stepped out.

I stood uncertain as one after the other slipped out until only a short white-haired woman remained.

"Go get 'em, farm boy!" someone in the group yelled as I stepped into the elevator. All started cheering and clapping as the doors closed.

"Thirty-five," the woman said in a raspy voice. "I missed my floor, and I can't wait for the next one.

I leaned forward and pressed the button. "No problem," I sighed.

"Any pearls of wisdom for a failing bladder?"

"Never give up," I said under my breath.

"Don't worry," she said as the doors opened. "Just the fact you're nervous comforts me." She shuffled out of the elevator.

"What do you mean?"

"You take the job seriously." She turned around. "And don't worry. If you fail, there won't be anyone left to judge you."

"You know I didn't ask for those pearls of wisdom," I said as the doors closed. I could still hear her crackle as the lift started its descent.

My feet were glued to the floor as the doors opened. I thought we are going to do this?

"It's him!" A youngling ran into the lift and grabbed me around my leg.

The little shit startled me. "Who do you think I am?" I barked.

"The mighty Wayne Johnson?" the boy said and stepped back. "My mom said you would save us from the evil aliens."

"Your mom is wrong!"

His innocent blue eyes filled with fear. "But who's gonna save us then?"

"Uh, what I meant to say was, your mom is wrong. It's not just me. I have an entire army that will help me kick their butts back to the Andromeda Galaxy. We called it, I mean they called it Drachtoch."

The fear in his eyes vanished as it had appeared. "W-o-w."

His mother stepped inside the elevator. "I'm so sorry, Mr Johnson." She grabbed the boy's hand. "Come, Joshua, Mr Johnson is a busy man."

My brother's name.

"Wait!" A man struggled through the crowd in the lobby. It was the man with the strange glasses who'd been in the elevator with Juliet and me.

"My name is Tyrone, I was with–"

"I remember you."

"Can I have a picture with you and the boy?"

Joshua looked at me with a smile that almost circumvented his head.

"But you have to pick him up. Otherwise, I won't get him into frame."

This would be my last time in an elevator, I promised myself. I plucked the boy from the floor and glared at Tyrone.

"I didn't know you are a captain," he said, pointing at my shoulder.

For the first time, I noticed the three stars. It was Darius's doing;

out of all the ranks, he chose Captain – Captain Johnson, my father's rank. I remembered the dusty old uniform with three stars in my father's closet. I had despised it.

Joshua grabbed me around the neck and kissed me on the cheek – on my scar. I swallowed, blinking; I would fail this boy, as I had failed my human brother.

"How about a smile?" Tyrone said, adjusting his glasses.

"Don't push your luck," I said and handed Joshua to his mother. If I smiled, they would notice I was not one of them. And I'm not in the mood.

I pushed through the crowd, astonished by their hunger for a hero. As I stepped out of the building, I took a deep breath of the filtered air and longed for home.

A gush of air and a loud whining sound brought me back from the farm – people scattered in all directions, looking up at the sky. Cars veered off the road, clearing a landing space for the Vector G6. The ramp was lowering before it touched down. A soldier jumped from the craft and halted in front of me.

"Captain Johnson," he said and made the strange gesture with his hand. I'd last seen it back at Ross's cave.

I did the same, placing my four fingers above the right eye. "Yes."

"General Von Swartz sent me, Captain. He wants to make sure you're coming."

"Let's go then," I muttered.

As I made my way to the flying machine, I glanced at the gathering crowd. Joshua stood in front, giving me the four-finger gesture, his chest bursting with pride. With our eyes locked, I returned the gesture. The crowd went wild, cheering and clapping. Tyrone broke through the crowd carrying a case.

"You Tyrone Bradford?" the soldier asked.

"Yes," he said and showed the soldier a piece of glass with his photo and name.

"Get in!"

"Why is he coming along?"

"General's orders, sir. He will document life in the camp, non-secretive stuff. He won't document our training methods or equipment."

"They call it propaganda," Tyrone said. "Get some patriotism going."

The flying machine took off while we were still on the ramp.

"Shit!" Tyrone yelled as he lost his footing, waving his arms as he tried to keep his balance. I grabbed him by his hair and jerked him back to his feet.

"Ouch... fuck! Why didn't you grab me by the shirt or somewhere else?"

"It was that or your balls."

He scowled at me as we took our seats. "What's your problem with me?"

"You're the reason I'm sitting here."

"What are you talking about? You would have sat in that chair with or without my video."

"You gave the people hope when there's none," I shrugged. "Everyone is looking at me as if I can piss fire."

"No, Captain," Tyrone said. "I just showed the people you. It's not about the speech, which was not that good, I might add. They saw something in you that gave them hope. I saw it too." He shrugged. "What else do we have? Without hope, there would've been widespread panic, looting, mass suicide." Tyrone snorted. "Hell, I wanted to jump off a roof, remember?" Tears welled up in his eyes. "So, let us remain human until the last, please." He removed the glasses, leaned over and first pressed his left eye against my shoulder, then his right. "Enjoy your moment, your last fifteen minutes." He cleared his throat as he replaced the glasses.

I glared at the wet spot, shocked at what he just did. "If you do that again, I'll totally go Leon on you."

He nodded, still emotional, and wiped his nose with the back of his hand.

I unstrapped myself and walked to the cockpit. "I want you to make a quick stop." I tapped the pilot on the helmet.

He raised his visor and glanced over his shoulder.

"Juliet!" I hugged her around the helmet. The flying machine veered to the right, almost slamming into a building.

"Wayne! Dammit!"

"Sorry."

She shifted in her chair. "I've got orders to take you straight to the camp... Captain." She said my rank in a strange tone.

"I didn't choose the three stars."

"Well, you're here, and you're wearing them."

"I can take them off."

She shook her head. "I know where you want to go, and no."

"I just want to say goodbye, please."

"No."

"Please."

"No!"

"Then I'm leaving," I said. "I know how to get out."

"Wayne!" Juliet yelled as I left the cockpit.

I walked toward the back, straight to the red button I had used before.

"What's going on?" Tyrone asked.

"I'm leaving!" I called toward the front.

"Sir, take a seat," the soldier said, placing his hand on his sidearm.

"I found the button!" I yelled.

"Captain!" the soldier drew his weapon and aimed it at my head.

"I will press it now!"

"What the fuck is going on here?" Tyrone said, glancing up and down the cabin.

"Can the little boy in the back please take his seat," Juliet said over the loudspeaker. "Mommy will take him to his playmate."

I shoved the soldier out of my way and took a seat.

Tyrone stared at me for a moment. "That's not very Captain-like."

"When you pull a gun, you must be prepared to use it," I said to the soldier.

"I was," he muttered.

"No, you weren't," I said. "I could see it in your eyes, your trembling hand, the sweat on your forehead." I grinned. "All because you didn't get the order to shoot. If you were a Leon, you would've been dead."

"You mean you would have been dead," Tyrone smirked.

"No, I would've known that you would pull the trigger, so I would've killed him. Simple."

"So, what you're saying is no one should follow orders?" the soldier asked.

"In battle, never hesitate. Follow your instinct."

Tyrone rolled his eyes. "Well, we're not in battle now."

My first instinct about him was correct; he was a dickhead.

Juliet touched down in front of the Presidential Palace. In the same way, she fetched me – vehicles swerving and people running. No one waited for me at the gate, so I forced it open and entered. Bryan and six guards stormed down the stairs, weapons drawn.

"You again," Brian said as he holstered his firearm.

"I just want to say goodbye to Sadie."

He shook his head, frowning at my shoulder. "So, they made you a captain?"

"I want to see her," I said.

"The President does not want you near her."

Charles appeared in the doorway.

"After everything I did for you," I shouted. "Saving your daughter's life."

"I know what you are, Malik," Charles said, standing with hands in his pockets. "If you were in my shoes, you would've done the same."

"Wayne!" Sadie called as she ran out the front door and down the stairs.

"Sadie!" Charles snapped. "You promised me!"

She stopped halfway down the stairs and turned toward her father. "I promised you I would not leave you. Now, allow us a moment."

He threw his hands in the air and disappeared into the house. Brian and his men stepped away, but kept their eyes pinned on me.

Sadie flung her arms around me. "I missed you."

We kissed as if we were back in my room, as if we were all alone.

"I'm going away," I whispered.

"Where to?"

"They're taking me to the South gate. Darius wants me to help train the men."

"For how long?"

"A week or two," I averted my eyes, "until the shield fails."

Sadie buried her head in my chest. "You mean until the end?"

I hugged her and whispered, "I promise you I will be by your side when the time comes."

My uniform soaked up her tears, just like Tyrone's, her grip tightening as if she never wanted to let go. I didn't want to either, but the image of that little boy haunted me, forced me to go. The bine had spread to all my extremities – flesh, bone, even the shadows. My body ached, every cell – human and Leon.

"We need to leave!" Juliet ordered, marching down the ramp.

I waved Bryan closer. "Look after her, please."

"You need not tell me that," he snapped.

I let go of Sadie and pushed her away. It hurt, like wrenching my heart out of my chest. "I will see you again. You need to be with your father – keep him strong and focused."

She nodded.

"Does the Dome have an underground facility?" I asked Bryan.

"It's classified."

"Take the women, children, and as much food you can–"

"It's not big enough."

"Then you've got some work to do."

He snorted. "I won't listen to some–"

"I will tell my father," Sadie said, wiping away her tears. "Now go."

I gave her a quick kiss and made my way to a very impatient woman.

"Give Malik a chance," Sadie called.

I didn't know who I was anymore. But she was right; the boy from the farm needed to retreat into the shadows. Are you ready? "This is what I do." I was relieved she stayed – Malik would scare her. "Don't be too certain. I see Dresden in her."

Sadie waited until the Raptor disappeared beyond the glass towers before running into the Presidential Palace. Her father appeared in the doorway of his study, shoulders slumped, cheeks puffed, and hands behind his back – defeated.

"I told you I was staying, so you can stop your moping," Sadie snapped. "We need to evacuate the city and take as many women and children to the underground facility. We need to create as much space as we can. It will give us more time when the shield fails."

"Only for a while," he muttered.

"It will give our troops more time to fight them instead of wasting time protecting us." She held out her hand. "So, are you going to stand around feeling sorry for yourself or are you going to be the President the people voted for, the man the people fell in love with, the father I love? I know you feel that all your hard work was for nothing. But fate chose you for this moment. I believe it with all my heart."

"You know what's down there? What we need to do to create space."

Sadie shook her head.

"Animals, insects, our own Noah's ark. The Council planned to set them free after they had" –he swallowed– "cleansed the earth. So, by opening the gates too soon, before the rain, we will condemn humanity."

"You know who condemned humanity, Dad? Us humans, by trying to plan our future, our destiny. We planned ourselves to death. It's time to throw open the gates and start believing again. Creation will evolve." She wrapped her arms around him and whispered, "The time is now."

He straightened himself and took a deep breath. "I love you, my angel. I'm so proud of you. I wish your mother were here to see you now."

"She is, Dad, she is."

———

"Open a window in sector six," Juliet said as we neared the south gate.

"We're leaving?" I smiled.

"Yep."

"We will be exposed. They can attack at any moment, monitor our training, our hardware."

She shrugged. "We have no other choice. Firing live ammo within the Dome is not advisable. And there is not enough space." She sped up toward the whirlpool. "Hang on."

I closed my eyes as we burst into the clear blue sky, basking in the sun's warmth. A surge of energy exploded inside me as I saw the troops and military hardware below us. Thousands of men scurried between tents, flying machines, and strange-looking vehicles fitted with long pipes or barrels.

"Where did all this came from?"

"Not all is as it seems," Juliet said, circling the training ground. "As a Leon, does it look impressive?" I glared at her. "Come on, listen to Sadie... Malik."

I looked out the window. "They might offer some resistance, but..."

"But what?"

"We don't look at the firepower. It's irrelevant. We look at the ants scurrying behind the firepower. Their size and determination. The more impressive, the more excited we get."

Juliet levelled out the Raptor and headed for a patch of sand near the biggest tent in the camp.

"I need to see Darius," I said as the Raptor touched down.

"He wants to see you," Juliet said, shutting down engines. "And call him General in front of the troops."

I walked to the rear. "First time outside?" I asked Tyrone.

"Yep." He stood and threw his bag over his shoulder.

"Brace yourself." I hit the red button, and the ramp lowered. A wave of scorching air filled the fuselage – as if opening a furnace. I closed my eyes and filled my lungs.

"Bloody hell," Tyrone mumbled. "How can anything survive out here?"

"I did, for seventeen years." I stopped at the bottom of the ramp, holding out my hand.

"What's wrong?" Juliet asked.

"Do you feel it?"

"What?"

"It's cooler than usual."

"You mean it was hotter than this?" Tyrone said behind me.

"I felt it too," Juliet said and pointed at the big tent. "He's waiting."

"Brock!" I called and approached him where he stood, talking to a group of soldiers. All jumped to attention.

"Captain Johnston." Brock did the hand thing and winked at me.

I understood and returned the gesture. "Where're Fritz and Shorty?"

"Fritz is trying to make pilots out of some of these pee stains, Captain." He smirked. "And Shorty is doing sniper training."

I studied the men behind him and shook my head.

Brock walked up to me and whispered, "I know, but it's all we've got."

"They're kids," I whispered. "I've never smelled so much fear."

"You can smell it?"

I nodded. "That's what fuels our hunger to feed."

"What about me?" he frowned.

"That's why they smell of fear." I tapped him on his shoulder and made my way to the tent. We had already lost the war. We just needed to show up. "Still want to be on the right side of the war?" Oh, shut up!

Darius's authoritative voice drowned the generators in the distance. He stood on the far side of the tent, slamming a stick against a big whiteboard.

He froze with the stick still pointing at the board. "Captain Johnson, glad you could join us."

The room turned toward me.

I made the hand gesture. "General."

He nodded. "Please join me."

Men and women, some dressed in plain clothes, some dressed in uniform, cleared a path for me. I was back in the Pit; the only difference was the dress code.

"Those who do not know, Captain Johnson is part Leon, part human," Darius said as I joined him on stage. A few people frowned at each other. "I trust Captain Johnson with my life. He saved my ass twice. And he's more human than Leon." He turned toward me and said, "I cleared all personnel in this room, so hold nothing back. Tell us anything that might help."

The racket of the generators reverberated through the tent. I cleared my throat and started at the most pressing issue. "Do we have satellite surveillance – something that can track objects in space?"

"We have searched our solar system but couldn't find them. We also couldn't track the incoming signal from Alcantar," Darius said. "It's like searching for bat shit in the desert."

"We... they're in orbit around one of Jupiter's moons. You call it Europa."

"Why there?" a Captain asked.

"It's the nearest planet or moon from Earth that we could find, which contains water. They should still be there."

"But that's like five hundred million miles away," Darius said. "It will take them years to reach us."

"It will take them between forty-three and fifty-two–"

"Years?" a soldier interrupted.

I glared at him for a moment. "Minutes."

Chaos erupted as all made known their disbelief or shock – I couldn't tell.

"Silence!" Darius yelled, slamming his fist on the whiteboard.

The amount of respect shown toward the new general surprised me. The generators were my only competition as I continued. "They need a line of sight before jumping to light speed, so they can't attack at once. It all depends on where the planets are in orbit. Earth needs to be visible to them, so to speak."

"Raven!" Darius called out.

"General!" A skinny boy with spikey black hair, a red t-shirt and jeans raised his hand.

"Find them!"

"He needs to find his pubic hair first," I muttered.

"Trust me, if they're out there, he will find them," Darius said.

"The other problem we have is their transporter beam. It also works with line of sight. They can, at any moment, transport a person or object to and from their location." I smiled. "So, I wouldn't wander too far from camp if I were you. They find it difficult to select a target within a populated area. Leons use the beam for another purpose, but for now, it's not relevant."

A bald man with a bushy moustache and dressed in a brown uniform raised his hand. "I don't want to sound rude, son, but I've studied the footage of Alcantar, and the Leon race seems too primitive to have developed these technologies themselves."

I nodded. "You're right."

"So, how did you get it?"

"The same way you get some of yours – by stealing it. They select their prey, study their technology, strength, weaknesses, whether the civilization has something they want. So, the Leon race grows stronger with every civilization they invade."

"What do they want from us?" the bald man asked.

I hesitated, glancing at Darius.

He gave me a nod.

"This time, the Leons do not want the technology. They have whatever technology this planet offered from the other cities they'd destroyed. They want food and a place to stay." I stomped my foot. "Solid ground."

"But there's no food left," the old man countered.

The hum from the generators, once again, saved me from hearing a pin drop. I took a deep breath. "I'm not talking about fruit, veggies, and cows."

It took a moment for the confused faces to realise what I had meant. One after the other, the expressions turned to shock. They murmured amongst each other.

"God, help us," the bald man muttered and stumbled to the nearest desk, waving a woman from her chair. He took a slow seat, scratching his head, bewildered eyes pinned on me.

"It seems to me your God left you a long time ago. They will slaughter you like–"

"Outside!" Darius ordered and rushed toward the exit.

I found Darius standing by Juliet's Raptor, hands in his pockets, kicking at the ground. "What was that all about?" he said through gritted teeth.

I shrugged. "You said, hold nothing back."

"You knew what I meant." He turned away and stared at a group of soldiers running across the dusty plain. "I'm trying my best here, Wayne – or is it Malik?" He glared at me over his shoulder. "Don't take away the fragment of hope we have left." Darius pointed at the big tent. "If those people in there have no hope, then we may as well switch off the shield now." He turned back to me. "I know you've lost your brother and mother. I know you're just as scared as we are. Even more, because you know what's coming. But what I need now is a solution." He placed his hand on my shoulder. "I want you by my side."

"Now, you want me by your side. Remember how you treated us at the farm?"

Darius kept his eyes pinned on me until I took a deep breath and whispered, "Okay." He turned back to the horizon. "The Sweepers we dispatched to the other cities confirmed your story. All are abandoned or destroyed. How did the Leons do it without us receiving a distress call or footage or any warning? And we received their vote when the council voted. How was that possible?"

"The shields failed one by one, not all at once. The moment a shield failed, we jumped to light speed, blasted the city with an electromagnetic pulse and invade. Humans are nothing without power. The only thing the cities wanted from each other was the vote. Nothing more."

"And how did you manage that?"

"I was not involved, but Gelman explained it to me. One of your own set it up: a simple program, a computer and a small power source left at each city. It duplicated Nirvana's vote. So, if one of the four voted no, one would vote no in all the other cities. I guess the traitor did the same with the recent election."

"Do you know why he did it?"

"Promise a human a new life, and he will hand you the world on a platter. He was also badly fucked by his fellow humans. According to Gelman, the human also fed Alcantar the deactivation codes to each city. A demand for a city. One of his demands he made at the end of his life. He wanted a new body."

"Do you know who it is?"

"Only Alcantar and Gelman know. But when we also wanted Nirvana, the city, he traded for another. He broke off all communication. Two things about Leons, you can't silence their hunger for victory, and you can't trust them." I frowned. "Shit, just like humans."

A loud bang, like a gunshot, rang out.

The troops dived for cover, burying their faces in the sand.

A black cloud rose from one of the big machines.

"It was just a tank backfiring!" Darius yelled at them, his face red with anger.

The troops leapt to their feet and dusted the sand off their clothes. "Relics of the past," Darius said after a while. "We're trying to get some going."

"Some?" I frowned, my eyes trailing the lengthy line of tanks. "So, the others are just for decoration."

"Yes." Darius sighed. "It looks impressive on a satellite image." He turned to the big tent. "I hope the people in there are still standing. Let's go."

A soldier exited the tent and ran up to us. "General!"

"What, Corporal?" Darius said as he halted in front of him.

"General Ross's people are on their way."

"Took them a while," Darius said. "Instruct them to land here first. I need all capable men and women before they enter the Dome."

"Yes, sir!" The corporal saluted and ran back into the tent.

"Ross," I seethed. "This will be interesting."

"Ross is dead," Darius said. "Committed suicide after he gave Alcantar a way into the Dome."

"Why would he do that?"

"Payback for what Steward did to his daughter."

"Now both are dead, and we sit with the—"

"There they are." Darius pointed toward the east.

At first glance, only a few black dots danced on the horizon, but the closer they came, the more appeared, like a flock of crows. I counted close to sixty flying machines of all shapes and sizes. The whining noise of the engines overwhelmed the sound of the grinding generators as the first crows touched down in a cloud of dust.

"I wonder how many you destroyed when you blew the roof of their cave?"

"Let's not go there," Darius said.

"Who's now in charge of them?"

"I am." He turned to me. "I need to show you something I found in your bag."

"My bag?"

"You know what I'm talking about."

"I wasn't sure if I could trust you." Now I was the one kicking at the sand.

"When I'm back, you need to tell me every detail about your Leon father's fleet," Darius said, and walked off toward the gathering flock.

19

"Settle down!" Darius shouted as he entered the big tent.

Several blacks and whites from Ross's bunch followed him inside. My heart rate and breathing increased as Santiago entered. She refused to look at me.

I had kept my distance from the tent's occupants, sitting in front, devouring one strawberry flavoured biscuit after the other, listening to the generators. I had a few challenging stares while enjoying my processed human flesh, but had won every stare-down. They're so weak.

I stood and dusted the crumbs from my uniform. "What is she doing here?" I said, as Darius joined me.

"She's part of their leadership."

"I can change that as I did with Steward." I turned to him. "You still need to thank me for that one."

"Not now," he scowled and turned his attention to the restless audience. "Those who can't find a seat just stand in the aisle!"

"I helped you with your plan."

Darius turned his back on the crowd. "What plan?"

"You wanted to poison the entire council." I glanced over his shoulder. "Don't worry, they can't hear a thing with this fucking generator."

Something flickered in his lifeless grey eyes. A steady smile formed, revealing his perfect teeth.

I continued, "How did you know that one of them would nominate you?"

"You're not just a farm boy, are you?"

"Not anymore." I winked. "You always get what you want, don't you?"

He placed his hands on my shoulders. "Remember that last day on the farm? I told you I could need a boy like you in the Dome." He shrugged. "Well, here you are."

"How's the rest of your plan turning out?"

"This is how far I planned." He winked and turned back to the audience. "Captain Johnson will tell us more about their fleet."

All eyes focused on me as Darius took a seat behind me. "They have only three ships, excluding the transporter, shaped like arrows or Sweepers, not shiny, but black as night. The biggest is the size of the Dome and about..." I thought of measurements they would understand. "A hundred stories high. The rest are half the size. The mother ship houses the fighters, disc-shaped and difficult to shoot."

"What about the Transporter?" Darius asked.

"It's shaped like a cylinder, the length of the mother ship. Not as robust as the rest of the fleet and no defences. The race we took it from was a peace-loving nation."

"How many soldiers?" a general asked, slumped in his chair.

"You mean warriors? Roughly a hundred and fifty thousand."

He glanced at Darius, shaking his head.

"How many do we have?" I asked Darius.

"Fifty thousand."

I nodded; no need to point out the obvious. A Leon warrior could take on ten humans, and it would be a quick fight.

"How do we kill a Leon?" Darius asked.

I shrugged. "Bullet through the brain or heart, just like a human, I suppose. The only difference is, he won't stop fighting until you hit your mark."

"Firepower of the fleet?"

"Enough to wipe us all from the face of this earth with one blow," I said, glaring at the frightened faces. "But they won't. Alcantar will call for a fair fight, hand-to-hand combat. For a Leon warrior to move up the ranks, he must prove himself in battle. The other reason they won't destroy us in one blow, they don't like their meals cooked."

Gasps of horror filled the tent.

"Don't you remember our brief chat outside?" Darius scowled.

"Wait!" I said, raising my voice. The tent settled. "That's not the worst of it. Every Leon has a clone waiting. The higher your status as a warrior, the more clones you have. If you kill a Leon, they will transport his soul to his new body, keeping him away from the gates of hell. With each transfer, he grows stronger, learning from his mistakes to become the perfect warrior. We gained the technology from the Argillian race over five hundred earth years ago." I raised my arms. "This is my thirteenth transfer and probably my last." More gasps. "So, they are not afraid to die. The energy beam I spoke about earlier includes this technology."

"What if we offer them something?" Darius said. "Land and whatever food we have?"

I shook my head. "Nothing prevents them from beaming humans from the city once the shield fails. But they won't do it. It's all about the fight, to show their power, move up the ranks – to quench their thirst." I focused on the old general. "They are a primitive race."

"What about Leon children?" the bald general asked.

"The technology to transfer our souls has its drawbacks. The Leon males became sterile. And most of our females chose not to transfer their souls. One lifetime with a Leon male is enough," I smirked. "They develop or grow the Leon clones into the second cycle. Then they await transfer."

"How long is a cycle?" Darius asked.

"Three to four Earth years."

"How did you become more human, son?" the general asked.

"For me to look more human, we decided that a human male must impregnate my mother. One of the few women left. They transferred my soul to the embryo within my mother at twelve weeks, but without my memory. The plan was to grow up amongst you, infiltrate Nirvana and disable the last remaining shield."

"When was your memory transferred?" the general asked.

"Two weeks ago," Darius said. "When they retrieved his brother's soul."

"Why didn't you go through with it?" a woman asked, somewhere in the back row. It was a familiar voice.

"I realised I was more human than Leon." I wanted to say fell in love but decided not to.

"I'm sorry for what I did to you and Joshua," Professor Santiago stepped into the aisle.

"And when I met that woman, I realised that we're all the same. Get her out of here." I seethed, exposing my fangs.

"Take it easy, Wayne," Darius said.

"He was a casualty of war," Santiago explained.

I stormed toward her.

She shielded herself with her arms and cried, "Show us you're more human!"

"Human!" I yelled, grabbing her by the arm.

"Leave them!" Darius ordered as men in black rushed toward me.

"What you did to us, you call it human!" My fingers dug into her flesh.

"I did it for humanity!" she cried out in pain, falling to her knees.

"Because of you, my brother is dead, drifting in space for eternity." I stormed out and stopped a few paces from the tent, tilted my head to the sun, and filled my lungs.

I'm not Leon or human or a farm-boy or a warrior. The proof reflected in the eyes of Alcantar, the humans in the tent, Charles Green and the Captain.

A cool breeze helped dry my tears – a flaw from my human side. Santiago did not awaken the beast; that was all Wayne.

Shirtless soldiers were training near me, their bony sunburnt bodies glistening with sweat. I unbuttoned my uniform.

Juliet stopped halfway down the Raptor's ramp. Wayne stood by the large tent. She could almost feel his anger as he unbuttoned his uniform, eyes focused on a group of soldiers, like a tiger stalking its prey. Don't do something stupid, Wayne. He walked toward them, throwing off his jacket and shirt. She stood in awe, admiring his body, every muscle toned. The image of him stepping out of the steamer still haunted her; a moment of regret – missed opportunity. I should have stepped into that steamer! She took a deep breath, cheeks flushed after she imagined following through with the act. She lost him the moment he laid eyes on Sadie. And he lost out on me. Miss Princess will never satisfy him the way I would have.

One by one, the men ceased training, watching the approaching figure with a confused expression.

"What the hell are you looking at?" Brock barked and turned around.

Juliet placed a finger on her lips, showing to Brock to butt out.

He stepped back.

"It's only fair to prepare you for what's coming," Wayne shouted.

More groups ceased training and approached.

Darius emerged from the tent and waved Juliet closer. "What's going on?" he asked.

"Training, or he's hungry."

"You have your stun gun?" Darius asked.

"Highest setting?"

"Yep. What happened in there?" Juliet asked.

"Santiago."

"You should have kept her away from him."

"And miss this?" Darius smirked.

Tyrone came running toward them, adjusting his glasses. "Can I record this, General?"

"Only for my entertainment," Darius said.

"Thanks," he said and ran off.

Darius and Juliet approached, cautious not to interrupt.

"I can hardly breathe," Wayne yelled. "Your fear covers this desert like a blanket. I'm certain your girlfriends, children, and mothers can smell your cowardice in there." He pointed at the shimmering shield. "You know what the Leons will do after ripping the flesh from your bones? They will go in there and rape your women, then feast on the tender meat of your children."

The troops' faces darkened with anger.

"I'm a Leon," he screamed, slamming his chest with a fist. "Today, I'm not a captain!" He pointed at a tank two hundred metres away. "The general will send you into the desert without food or water for four days if I touch that tank." Wayne pointed at Darius. "Do you agree, general?"

Darius gave a nod.

"You knew about this?" Juliet whispered.

"Nope."

"Some of you will die," Wayne said and started walking toward the tank.

The first row of four men gave an uncertain step forward but parted as Wayne reached them. A man in the second row stood his ground and placed his hand on Wayne's chest.

Tyrone adjusted his glasses with shaking hands, moving in between the troops like a fly searching for its next meal. He zoomed in on Malik's fangs as he smiled, staring down at the soldier's hand on his chest. The scene paused; the air charged with anticipation. Only the smallest of a spark needed.

Blood drops spattered Tyrone's glasses as Malik's head struck the man on the nose. Tyrone followed the man as he fell to the ground like a sack of potatoes. The spark.

The troops ascended on Malik, like piranhas on an injured animal. Tyrone ducked as a screaming man flew over his head. He wiped his glasses clean, moving in closer to capture every image. Malik advanced, step-for-step, closer to the tank, breaking limbs, busting noses, and fuelling their rage. He left behind a streak of groaning men, their blood absorbed by the sand.

Tyrone turned his focus on the tank. "Fifty metres!" he yelled. "Come on, take him down!"

"He's only one!" Darius shouted behind Tyrone. "Think out the box." He turned to Juliet. "Stun him before he reaches the tank."

"That's not fair!"

"I'm a man of my word, and I can't send these men into the desert."

Tyrone focused on a group of men approaching with weapons. "General!" he shouted at Darius, pointing.

"You crazy!" Darius yelled at them. "No weapons! Put that away."

Tyrone turned back to Malik, zooming in on his blood-soaked torso and the men hanging on to his legs. The relentless onslaught had taken its toll on Malik's body, but not on his determination. He brushed off the men as if they were toddlers.

A group of men climbed on top of the tank, jerked open the hatch, and leapt inside.

Tyrone turned to Darius. "What are they doing?"

"I told them to think out the box." Darius smiled. "I think they're getting it now."

Malik disappeared under the next wave of men. Tyrone focused on their expressions: blind rage. Something he had never captured before.

"I think they–" Darius swallowed his words as the men flew in all directions, crashing to the ground in a cloud of dust.

Malik was only ten paces from his aim, reaching forward.

Juliet aimed her stun gun.

Bang! A cloud of black smoke billowed from the exhaust of the tank. This time, no one ducked for cover.

Malik was only five paces away, elbowing a trooper in the face. Blood streamed down the man's face, but he did not go down; he slithered up Malik's back, sinking his teeth in Malik's neck. A wall of men moved in between Malik and the tank, hooking into each other. They roared, edging forward like a bulldozer.

Bang! Another cloud of smoke, but the engine failed to ignite.

More and more men barricaded Malik's path, screaming, edging forward, pushing him back. As if the entire camp had converged to the area, men and woman, with only one objective: The Leon would not touch that tank.

The fresh arrivals surrounded the tank, and as one, started pushing. At first, the tank refused to move, but as the screams grew louder and the faces reddened, it stirred. The tracks clanked on the torrid soil, screeching forward, faster and faster.

The troops roared as Malik's legs buckled and he fell to the ground.

Tyrone turned to Darius; the mighty general stood in awe; eyes filled with tears.

<hr>

We might just stand a chance, I thought, as the bodies piled on top of me. They were one. My rage extinguished, and theirs ignited.

"Get off him!" I heard Brock yell.

The weight lifted until the chilly breeze soothed my wounds. I rolled onto my back and sat up. "Where's the tank?" Soldiers surrounded me, all with the same victorious grin.

My first victim approached and stuck out his hand, blood still gushing from his nose. I grabbed hold of his hand, and he pulled me to my feet.

"Where's the tank?" I repeated, wiping the blood from my mouth.

The group behind me parted. I trailed the deep track marks to the beast's last destination, a hundred metres further away.

"Remember this moment," I said. "Together, we can beat them! Remember your rage!" I pointed at the Dome. "That is your tank. Protect it... whatever it takes. Even if you have to fucking move it!" I sniffed the air and smiled. "I smell no fear."

A defiant roar erupted, thundering further and further away until reaching the edge of the camp.

"And just remember, you were lucky. I stumbled over a body."

My back was on fire as I reached Darius; it felt like every trooper in the camp had slapped me.

"I don't know what to say," Darius said, placing his hand on my shoulder. "What's wrong?"

His hand weighed a ton. I couldn't take a step, no matter how hard I tried.

"Did I kill any of them?"

He shook his head, smiling. "Cuts, bruises, some broken bones, and a lot of broken noses. You okay?"

My knees buckled under the weight of my body.

"Wayne!" Darius tried to keep me upright, but fell on top of me as I hit the ground.

"I always knew you had a crush on me," I whispered. His face blurred, then everything darkened. "Tell Sadie I love her."

"I'm not your fucking messenger..."

The presidential limousine, with its security detail of four vehicles, hovered at a stop at the southern edge of the city.

"What is this place?" Sadie asked, hunkering down to see the top of a pyramid-shaped glass building. A security guard opened her door.

"Ever been here before?" her father asked as he joined her. She shook her head. "You and everyone else. Including me up to two weeks ago. This is the Museum of Natural History. The Council's idea – figured no one would be interested."

"What if someone visited?"

"They have some permanent exhibitions, but just enough to satisfy the nosy."

Sadie drew her hair back and tied it into a ponytail. "Sad, isn't it?"

"What?" Charles said, "Your dirty hair?"

"Not out of choice," she snapped. "The steamers weren't working this morning." She walked up the stairs. "I mean sad because we've forgotten our past, our purpose."

"Purpose?"

"God placed us on earth to look after it." Sadie glanced over her shoulder. "And we fucked it up."

"Sadie!" Charles said, glancing at Bryan.

"Don't look at me, Mr President," Brian said. "Her mother read the Bible to her."

"I'm talking about her language, idiot."

Sadie smiled as she entered the museum. They're like an old married couple. She froze as the doors slid open, almost walking into the gaping mouth of a grizzly bear.

"Don't worry, this one is dead," a burly man said, walking toward her, dressed in khaki clothes and a Stetson hat.

"I know," she whispered in awe. "I've never seen one in actual life."

"The name's Ben," he said, removing his hat and giving her hand a firm shake.

"Ouch." Her right leg buckled.

"Sorry, miss." He scratched his black beard.

"It's okay." She opened and closed her hand. "The name's Sadie."

"I know," he said with a wink. "An honour."

He saw my video.

"Not many people–"

"Wow," Sadie said, her eyes glued to the majestic animals on display in an African bushveld setting. She rushed toward the rhinoceros and climbed over the rope, ignoring the no-entry sign.

"That's a white rhino," Ben said behind her. "One of the many species we couldn't save before..."

She placed her hands on the thick, folded skin and whispered, "So sad."

"They went extinct a long time ago... killed for its horns." Ben joined her inside the display. "Even this one had its horn cut off one night." He pointed at the stub. "The fucker didn't know it was a fake horn."

"What about this animal?"

"The African elephant. No, also extinct. Killed for its tusks. Even this one had its teeth removed one night."

"Also fake?"

"Yep."

"It's massive," Sadie said, wrapping her arm around its leg.

"Thirteen feet high and weighs up to seven tons." He shook his head. "They will never walk this earth again."

"I read once you could repopulate a species by using their stem cells."

He raised his bushy brows. "That's correct, we can create an embryo, but we don't have a surrogate – we need a live female elephant."

"Excuse me," Ben said as the President entered the museum.

She continued with her depressing tour, understanding why so few visited the place; it was a reminder of how brutal, greedy, and self-obsessed humans are. Tears welled up as she paused at the feline display of tigers, leopards, and jaguars.

She jerked as her father placed his hand on her shoulder.

"Maybe you will feel better after you see what's downstairs," Charles said and hugged her.

She followed the group in silence, ignoring the rest of the exhibitions.

"I only dress like this for the few who visit the museum." Ben gestured for Sadie and Charles to enter the elevator. "I'm a scientist specialising in cryogenics. My actual name is Tobias Royston." He smiled. "I prefer Ben, though."

"Cryogenics?" Sadie repeated.

"Cryo-conservation of samples in liquid or gaseous nitrogen."

"What samples?"

The elevator doors closed and a few moments later, opened.

"You'll see in a moment." Ben stepped out into a long corridor.

"Are you the only one working here?" Sadie asked as Ben placed his thumb against the security panel.

He smiled. "No."

The green door slid open.

"My God," Sadie whispered, wide-eyed, stepping into the massive chamber. Square glass containers lined the room, stacked on shelves like books in a library. People in white lab coats walked on platforms, inspecting its contents. Sadie counted twenty rows before reaching the roof.

"Not as He intended." Ben smiled. "But we're trying our best to look after them."

Sadie walked to the nearest glass coffin on the bottom shelf and studied the panel. The temperature fluctuated between 28.2 and 28.6 degrees Celsius. She frowned at the name - Panthera Leo – and turned to Ben. "What's in here? I can't make out." She turned back, squinting at the figure sprawled in the yellowish liquid that filled the container.

"A lion," he said, pushing out his chest.

"Why don't you just" –she pointed at the panel– "call it that."

Her father smiled. "You know scientists, my dear." Charles gave her a peck on the cheek. "If you would excuse me, I have to check on something."

Ben continued as her father walked deeper into the chamber. "My predecessors considered captivity but decided against it because then you wouldn't be able to release them back into the wild. The animals need to hunt and fend for themselves. The other reason is food. To keep all awake for all these years," he shook his head, "impossible."

She looked around the chamber. "What are you doing to all these animals?"

"Induced torpor." Ben nodded; eyes wide with anticipation, as if she would know what it meant.

Sadie stared at him, brow furrowed.

He smiled. "It's a deep sleep hibernation-like state, like bears in winter or astronauts in space on a lengthy journey. We lower the core temperature of the animals, reducing their metabolism. The body still functions, but just at a much slower rate. My predecessors attempted cryogenic freezing, but the animals didn't survive. However, we use cryonics with embryos and larvae."

"How many species do you have?" Sadie asked, walking from one container to the next.

"A hundred years ago, there were over eight million species. We saved two million three hundred and sixty thousand. The scientists argued about flies and mosquitoes." He stared at her for a few seconds, then smiled. "I'm just kidding. The bastards are still out there." He pointed at the roof, shaking his head. "We'll never get rid of them."

"And the ocean species?"

He sighed. "Only a few hundred. When they started this, most had already died from pollution. As you know, the oceans are a toxic cesspool. We can never release those species." He shrugged. "Well, never say never, but not in my lifetime."

"Why release the other species, then?"

"I hope man has learned his lesson."

Sadie snorted. "Ye right. Man is the one that must go extinct."

He raised his brow and muttered, "Well, your wish might just come true."

She looked up at the steel roof. "Are we still inside the Dome?"

"Nope, when we wake the animals by raising their core temperature, the roof will open. We will then raise each level above the ground by a hydraulics system. We call the whole procedure The Awakening."

"But the animals will starve if we release them now. There's nothing out there."

"I know." Ben sighed. "The plan was to keep them in here long after the first rainfall, wait for the vegetation to grow, and then move each animal to its natural habitat. But we ran out of time."

"You mean power," Sadie mused.

Ben raised his arms. "The Ark has a fail-safe. If the power drops to a level not capable of sustaining life, it will trigger The Awakening."

"We need to keep this going as long as possible. We can't allow the people in here."

"And the invasion?" Ben countered. "You're willing to sacrifice human lives for animals?"

Sadie placed her hand against a glass container. "Yes. We sacrificed this for us."

"I was hoping you would say that, but" –he placed his hand on her shoulder, his eyes filled with sorrow– "a week or two will make no difference. Most of the animals will perish out there."

She shook her head. "You think God will allow that to happen?"

"After what we've done, I think so. If you search the night sky" – he made a sweeping gesture– "under Orion's belt, you will notice a constellation in the shape of an upside-down fist. It appeared about two hundred years ago."

"Really?"

He nodded. "Look carefully, you'll see the middle finger raised. They call it the Flipping-bird constellation." Ben bent backwards as he roared with laughter.

"Ha-ha, hilarious," Sadie said.

He shrugged. "Hey, that's all we've got left to laugh at humanity's stupidity."

She took a deep breath and searched the room. "Where's my father?"

"Come with me."

She smiled at the eccentric-looking man as she followed him past the endless rows of glass containers; woolly socks covered half his hairy legs and bulging calves, his khaki shorts fitted tightly around his muscular thighs - not the look of a scientist.

He stopped at the door at the far end of the glass rows and inserted a security card into the slot. The door slid open, revealing another chamber similar in size.

"What the hell is that?" Sadie gawked at the towering steel structure. It resembled the shape of a telescope, with a massive chrome ball attached to the end of the scope.

Her father was talking to a group of scientists at the base of the steel giant.

"A weapon," Ben replied. "We could never test it because to turn it on would consume about half the city's power."

"You need to turn off the shield."

"Yes. And the roof above it also opens."

Charles broke away from the white coats and approached. "We need to get going, my love. I need to address the people."

I woke in the desert once more, the sun's rays harmless. I touched my cheek, no scar.

"Malik!"

I turned around, and there she was, dressed in white, her skin an anxious grey.

"Mother?"

"They're on their way!"

"But you're–"

"No, we're not." She rushed toward me.

"But I saw you die?"

"Protect the President and his daughter!" Amira grabbed my arm. "They will take them as soon as they reach Earth."

"From the Dome?"

"Go! Wake up!"

I jerked awake, still feeling her hand clutching my arm.

"Nightmare?" Juliet asked, standing up from a chair beside my bed.

It was just me and Juliet in a small tent. "What's in there?" I asked, pointing at the bag with red liquid hanging above my head.

"You know what's in there," she smirked. "Santiago's plan."

I had never felt so strong. "How long was I out?"

"Just a day."

I sat up and ripped the thick needle from my arm.

"Take it easy," Juliet snapped, stepping back to avoid the blood squirting from the needle.

"They're on their way." I stood up, clutching to the bedsheet, realising I was naked. "Where are my clothes?"

"In there." Juliet pointed to the cupboard beside my bed. "How do you know they're coming?"

"My mother told me." I opened the cupboard and stared at the new uniform with three stars. "I want a black one."

She smiled. "Darius wants uniformity, but I have one in my Raptor."

"Fuck that," I muttered and wrapped the sheet around my waist. "Let's go."

The sun had cleared the horizon, shedding its red mantle as we rushed toward the big tent. The generators were silent. Half-naked men and women stumbled from their tents, coughing, scratching, and rubbing eyes.

"Is he in there?" I asked, adjusting the sheet.

"Yes, from this morning." Juliet started running toward her Raptor. "I will fire up the engine."

Darius was talking to Raven as I entered the tent.

"They're coming!" I said.

"How do you know?" Darius asked. "He searched the location you mentioned, but found nothing."

"My mother sent me a message. And they're going for the President and Sadie the moment they're in orbit."

"But they're in the Dome?"

"They will use Ross's technology."

"You sure about this?" Darius asked.

"Trust me."

"I will let the President know."

"I'm going," I said and turned for the exit.

"No! I need you here!"

"Try to stop me. Sadie means more to me than a tank."

20

The blast from the Raptor's engines ripped the sheet from my body as I exited the tent. I darted the thirty metres to the awaiting ramp, one hand shielding my eyes, the other attempting to hide my Leon part.

"Prepare for the invasion!" Darius's voice over the loudspeaker dampened the cheers from the gathering crowd.

I burst into the cockpit. "My clothes?"

Juliet pointed to the co-pilot's chair, eyes focused on my hands.

I grabbed the suit and stormed out of the cockpit. As I slipped into my favourite attire, I felt the Raptor ascended and turned. I carefully zipped up and returned to the cockpit.

"What are you waiting for?" The Raptor hovered a scant distance from the water-like wall. It filled our view.

"I asked Darius to organise a window for us, but he's taking his time."

"Let me talk to him."

Juliet flipped a few switches. "He can hear you."

"Please open a window for us, General," I said, calmly as possible. "They're coming for the President. Alcantar will execute him to create panic. He'll broadcast it on every screen in the Dome."

"Since when do you care about that coward?"

I ripped the headrest from the chair. "For Sadie then!" I yelled.

We glared at each other for a moment, a moment I couldn't afford to waste, my heart thumping in my ears.

"Bring them here then... I want you back. And remember, they can't take you back to the fleet." His image disappeared.

"The bastard," I said. "He wants the President dead."

"Why?" Juliet steered the Raptor toward the whirlpool.

"To be in charge." I threw the headrest onto the floor. "We're not that different –humans and Leons." I turned for the door and froze. "What the fuck are you doing here?"

"My job," Tyrone said with a smug grin. "The people want to see every move their hero makes."

"I'm not a hero," I snapped.

"I think you'll want to see this, Mr Hero," Juliet said.

"What?" I turned back. "What the–" My tank episode was playing on every tall building in the Dome.

"The best part is coming," Tyrone added.

"Remember this moment. Together we can beat them! Remember your rage! That is your tank. Protect it – whatever it takes."

"Powerful stuff." Tyrone nudged me with his elbow. "My boss told me people were forming human chains in the street, chanting your name." he raised a fist. "Malik... Malik... Malik."

"Malik?" I frowned.

Tyrone shrugged. "My idea. It sounds better than Wayne, Wayne, Wayne."

Juliet laughed. "Darius will be so pissed."

"Why?" Tyrone asked. "I gave the people hope... a fighting spirit."

"No." I shook my head. "You showed Alcantar one Leon could defeat a hundred men... and I'm half-human."

An uncertain frown appeared behind Tyrone's glasses. "S-s-shit."

Raven's biscuit dropped from his mouth as the dots appeared on the radar screen. He glanced over his shoulder, searching for Darius in the crowd of uniforms.

"General," Raven called, but the relentless bombardment of screamed orders drowned his voice. "Dad!" he shrieked. The screaming stopped as he grabbed everyone's attention.

Darius walked over and placed his hand on the boy's shoulder, leaning in for a closer view. "Take it easy," he whispered. "We knew they were coming. How many?"

"Four."

"Malik told the truth. Remember where I want you to go when they break through our defences. Don't try to impress me." Darius squeezed his trembling shoulder. "You already have."

Raven nodded, trying to swallow the fear crawling up his throat.

Darius gave his shoulder another squeeze before walking out of the tent.

Raven was even more confused when he heard Darius's Vector fire up and sped away.

Alcantar and six of his warriors marched into the transporter room. The blue planet blocked their view on the starboard side. He turned toward Earth and raised his arms. "Our feast awaits!"

"We should have attacked all the cities at once," Lucius seethed.

Alcantar swung around and grabbed him by the throat. "You doubt my decision!" he said. "There were fifty million combined, protected by impregnable shields... against our hundred thousand."

"Now we are only twenty thousand," Lucius hissed. "We turned on ourselves... and most of us have no replacement, as we have no more resources to create our clones."

Alcantar released his hold. "And now there're only five hundred thousand of them, with no planetary defences functioning." He placed a hand on his sword. "We will enslave them after we had our fill. They must continue to breed. We need a constant food supply. Their males will build our cities. Soon, we will be able to create our replacements and increase our numbers."

"We cannot increase our numbers because we are sterile!" Lucius said.

Alcantar smiled. "Oh, but we can. Malik is proof of that. We will take the seed of the strongest human warriors and impregnate our females."

Lucius stepped back, horrified. "What! And infect our blood with human–"

"Malik is still as strong as us!" He pointed at the blue planet. "You saw the images. He defeated a hundred men."

"Strong... maybe, but Malik's human emotions have made him weak. We will create an army that will question our decisions, driven by emotion."

"We will rule them, use their fear." Alcantar stepped forward and placed his hand on Lucius's shoulder. "What other choice do we have? We cannot conquer civilizations with our numbers." Lucius bowed his head. "You are my strongest warrior," Alcantar whispered. "The only one I can trust. Will you bring them to me?"

"The only reason you want them is because of Malik."

Alcantar turned back to the blue planet. "That's the only way, kill their leader and take away their hero."

"That is, if the program Ross gave us works. If not, the shield will vaporize me. And how do we know they will be at the coordinates he gave us?"

Alcantar glanced over his shoulder. "Do I detect fear?"

"Unlike you, I have no replacement."

He turned back to Lucius and placed his fist on his heart. "I will give you my clone if the program does not work."

"Welcome back, President Green," the woman said as Charles and Sadie stepped through the front door.

"What are you going to do, Dad?" Sadie asked.

"Pack a bag," he muttered. "We're going camping."

She froze, shocked. "You cannot send the animals out there now!"

Charles stopped halfway up the staircase, hand clutching the railing. "It's life. We're higher in the food chain." He proceeded up the stairs. "The strong will survive."

"I think you'll want to see this," Bryan said as he entered the house. "Sadie?"

He handed her his tablet. "It's all over the news. Your boyfriend is a hero."

She covered her mouth, shocked.

"Don't worry." He smiled. "He survives."

"What do you say now?" she said. A barrage of emotions welled up inside her – love, pride, longing, lust. Her heart was about to explode.

"I'm sorry," Bryan said. "I was wrong about him."

The lights in the house flickered and died, followed by a loud crack.

"What the hell was that?" Bryan whispered, searching the ceiling.

"An explosion?" Sadie asked.

He shook his head.

Sadie's father appeared at the top of the staircase. "The power is out," he said.

"The shield," Bryan gasped and ran out of the house.

Sadie followed close behind and almost bumped into Bryan as he stopped, staring at the sky.

"What's–" Sadie looked upward, also noticing the hole in the shield. At first, it shrunk, but then grew in size. Blue lighting rippled outward from the edge of the expanding void. She shielded her eyes from the natural sunlight flooding the Dome.

"But we still have power left," Charles said, running his fingers through his hair.

"Something triggered it," Bryan said.

The edge of the Dome disappeared behind the surrounding buildings.

Charles searched for answers in the crisp blue skies before he settled his gaze on his daughter.

"Why are you looking at me like that, Dad?"

"You know, it's the first time I've seen you in sunlight." He stepped closer and caught a strand of her hair blowing in the breeze. "I know it sounds silly." He smiled and filled his lungs with the fresh air. "Captain Bryan?"

"Yes, sir."

Charles kept his eyes on Sadie. "Sound the alarm. It's time to evacuate."

She nodded and wrapped her arms around him.

"Run!" Bryan yelled. "They–"

Charles and Sadie turned toward him. A blade protruded from his chest.

"No!" she screamed as it vanished. Bryan's eyes rolled back as he fell to the floor, revealing his attacker – a giant dressed in black with blood dripping from his fangs. She searched for the guards; all lay at the bottom of the stairs at the feet of six more Leons.

"They were admiring the light," Lucius said and ascended the last four steps.

Charles stepped in front of Sadie and whispered, "Hide in the panic room. You have access."

"No! Not without you."

"Go!" he yelled and shoved her into the house.

Sadie ran as fast as her trembling legs allowed, but not to the panic room, but to the study. She first activated the alarm under his desk and then removed the handgun from his top drawer.

"Welcome back, Mr President," the woman's voice greeted.

She peeked around the corner and saw the seven Leons with her father enter through the front door.

"You've got me!" her father said as they made him kneel. "Why do you want my daughter?"

"Show yourself, or your father dies," the biggest of the seven ordered and raised his sword above her father's head.

"She can't hear you," her father said. "She locked herself in a place. Not even you can break into."

"Let him go!" Sadie shouted, pointing the weapon at the giant. "I've activated the alarm. Every soldier in the Dome will be here in less than a minute."

The Leon lowered his sword. "You're not in the Dome anymore." He licked his fangs. "And we all know where the soldiers are."

"Sadie, I told you to go!"

"Get her!" The Leon pointed his sword at one of his men.

"Stay back!" Sadie screamed as the Leon approached. She flipped the safety catch, just as Darius had taught her. "Stay back!"

Her trembling hands tightened around the grip.

"Shoot!" Charles yelled.

She obeyed, squeezing the trigger once. The weapon recoiled, awakening the memory of Mr Gray's surprise expression. However, this victim exhibited no surprise. She was sure she hit him, but he kept coming.

The weapon recoiled another four times, spewing smoke before he twisted it from her hands. The Leon smiled while inserting his talon in one of his chest wounds. He licked his bloody finger. "Can't wait to taste yours."

"Let's step outside," the big one said, grabbing Charles by his blond hair.

"Have a pleasant day, Mr President," the woman said as he left the house.

Sadie followed, dazed. She stroked the bite marks on her wrist as she thought about him; he was not a Leon. Just their vile smell alone made her sick to the stomach. She placed her hand over her nose and breathed through her mouth. She had to slow them down, she thought, even for just a few seconds.

Charles paused halfway down the stairs, staring at Bryan's lifeless body. He glanced at Sadie before grabbing the weapon from Bryan's holster.

"Let her go!" he said, and pressed the barrel against his temple.

"Dad! What are you doing?" Sadie cried.

"They want me alive," he said. "Alcantar won't be happy if they bring me to him dead."

The Leons burst out laughing, their fangs glistening in the sunlight as they threw their heads back.

"Go ahead," the giant mocked, leaning in closer. "Shoot!"

Charles stepped back, bewildered. "Let her go!" His finger tightened around the trigger.

"Pull it!"

"Dad, no!"

"Pull it, you coward!"

A shot rang out.

"No!" Sadie ran down the stairs, her view blocked by the giant. She halted her descent as she heard the weapon discharge another six times.

The giant went down on one knee and grabbed Charles by the throat.

"Fuck you," Charles seethed and pressed the weapon against the Leon's head. He pulled the trigger until it clicked.

The rest of the Leons descended on him like a pack of wild animals.

Sadie covered her mouth with a trembling hand and took a slow seat on the stairs. "This is not happening," she whispered and collapsed backwards, staring at the blue sky. She crawled into a fetal position, body shivering.

The wind picked up, blowing strands of hair across her face.

"Lower the ramp!" I shouted as I saw the carnage in front of the presidential palace.

"Go!" Juliet handed me her rifle.

I knocked Tyrone from his feet as I ran down the aisle toward the lowering ramp.

"We're still too high," Juliet yelled.

"It doesn't matter!" I leapt from the ramp. "Yes! Now we are one!"

The fall lasted only a second or two, but the image of Sadie on the steps would haunt me for a lifetime. Charles Green was dead; his blood cascaded down the stairs as I fell toward the feasting Leons. The final snapshot before blacking out was of his vacant grey eyes.

I startled awake, gasping, entwined in a blood-fest of limbs, growls and curses. "Come on! Kill!" I shook the stars away and sank my fangs into the nape of the closest Leon, severing nerves. The taste of Leon brought back a flood of memories. I crawled to the next, grabbed him by the head, and broke his neck. The element of surprise was my only advantage; I could not allow them to regroup. I searched for my rifle, then only noticed the hilt of a sword protruding from my stomach. "Leave it!" I grabbed my first victim's sword.

A Leon sank his fangs into my leg, and another clawed at my chest. I raised the sword above my head with both hands and rammed the blade into a skull. The remaining two crawled away and stumbled to their feet.

Sadie was still on the stairs, eyes open but not awake. I stood up and grabbed the hilt protruding from my stomach.

"Malik," one of them snarled.

That's when I recognized him, Khan. He had challenged me eleven times before in the Pit and ones on Earth. "Thirteenth time lucky?" I forced a smile, resting my hand on the hilt. Every nerve the blade touched awoke.

"You were lucky the last time," Khan said.

"Chasing a ten-year-old boy up a broken windmill and falling to your death was not very warriorlike. Did my father approve the challenge?"

"No, but I had vowed never to tell. Alcantar killed me when I transferred back into my clone and tortured me the second time."

"You made quite the meal," I said.

"I was still alive when you started," he seethed.

"I know." I smiled. "I was hungry, and I like my meals hot."

"You're still half-human, and there's no broken windmill to save you."

"I wouldn't say half, more like a third."

He leaned over and whispered something in the Leon's ear beside him.

I clenched my teeth as I extracted the sword. The blade was never-ending.

"I will challenge you another day," Khan said. "But now, I must complete my mission." He reached behind his back and removed a transport activator – a cylindrical-shaped device the size of his hand.

"You running away?" I smirked.

"See you soon, Malik," Khan said and broke away, sprinting toward Sadie.

The other Leon attacked, wielding a sword. I had no choice; turning my back on him would be fatal. Our swords crossed with a clang. Khan already stood over Sadie, pointing the device at the sky. The transporter beam would take thirty seconds to calibrate before activating. I went into a defensive stance, moving toward Khan with every blow from my attacker. He was like a crazed animal, growling, snarling, salivating, a hundred percent Leon. I waited, feigning defeat as I went down on one knee. Blinded by the taste of victory, his attack became uncontrolled. The moment I waited for...

I jumped to the left and rammed my sword into his ribs. He

lowered his sword, eyes wide. I extracted the blade, spun round, and decapitated him.

"Come on!" Khan yelled at the heavens as I ran toward him. Sadie lay by his feet, shivering, unresponsive. I dived the last few feet as I heard the thunder.

The mountain was in stark contrast to the desert. The sheer grey rock appeared like a canvas, painted with ash and charcoal in an upward stroke, two-dimensional and never-ending. Darius sped up toward the wall.

"The President is dead!" Juliet said as her image appeared. "Why did you not warn them?"

"I'm sorry to hear that," Darius replied.

She swallowed. "The shield has collapsed."

"I know. But it was inevitable."

"They said that you'd left the camp. Where are you?"

"You and Wayne must return to camp," Darius said.

"He's gone," she whispered, tears welling up.

"What do you mean?" Darius snapped.

"After the second beam... he was just-"

"What!"

"Gone."

He shook his head. "He's got about an hour before..."

"Before what?" Juliet asked.

"Before we... Just get back to camp." He disconnected the call.

A slight crack appeared at the base of the canvas and swallowed the Vector.

21

The bridge was a hive of activity as Alcantar entered.

An Elder, dressed in a purple robe, scurried toward him, black eyes glistening with excitement. "The shield is down, Master."

Alcantar walked up to the observation window, glaring at the blue planet. "You're certain."

He bowed his head. "Yes, Master."

Alcantar turned to the Elder, a deep wrinkle appearing between his black eyes. "But they still had power left," he whispered and turned back to the blue mass. "What are they planning?"

"It seems our transporter beam disrupted their power supply. Our good fortune."

He shook his head. "Good fortune is the fool's illusion of victory. Death always follows." He turned back to the Elder. "Scan the planet for any power fluctuations. They are channelling it for a different purpose."

"Do you want to postpone the attack, then?"

He made a gesture with his claw. "No, instruct the troops to embark on the carriers. I will join them."

The Elder stared at him for a moment. "You're not pleased, Master?"

Alcantar's eyes flashed, but then softened. "This would be the first attack in countless cycles where my sons won't be joining me."

"You feel sorrow?"

"No." He turned back to Earth. "That is a human characteristic. It must be anger. Or is disappointment a human feature?"

"I believe sorrow and disappointment to be the same."

He nodded. "Then, I'm angry."

"You think he will come?"

Alcantar placed his hand on the window. "Humans have a strange effect on us. I've seen it."

"Amira."

He pointed at the Elder, seething. "Don't speak that name again."

"But she did what you ordered?"

He placed his hand on his sword. "Falling in love with that human was not part of the plan. Poisoning Malik's and Arden's minds were also not part of the plan."

The Elder bowed and turned for the exit, whispering: "And jealously is also a human characteristic."

"Elder," Alcantar said under his breath.

The old Leon stopped and slowly turned around. "Yes, Master."

Alcantar drew his sword and sauntered toward him. "I can hear you're tired of your old body."

He bowed his head and said, "I don't know what came over me, Master."

The control room fell silent; all observed the developing skirmish with eager anticipation.

Alcantar rammed his sword into the Elder's chest and grabbed him around the throat. "You have the mouth of a woman," he seethed. "I will transport you into one of Amira's clones."

The Elder's eyes widened, blood spilling from his mouth.

"I will have my way with you every night. You will know what came over you." The Elder collapsed in a heap of purple and red as

Alcantar pulled the sword from the limp body. He licked the blood from his blade before replacing it in the sheath. "Well matured," he muttered and bowed down. "You would think with age comes wisdom."

Erich ran into the control room, heaving, "Master, Khan had returned."

Alcantar straightened, looking around the room. Anger welled up inside him as he realised he was too afraid to ask. "Did he... succeed?"

Erich smiled, revealing his yellow fangs. "He more than succeeded."

The Vortex glided to a stop; its reflection visible on the white floors. Darius exited and made his way toward the lone elevator.

Professor Santiago scurried out as the doors slid open. "General, general, we've detected smaller vessels emerging from the mother ship."

"Have you maintained radio silence?" Darius entered the elevator.

"Yes."

"So, Professor, what do you think?"

She shook her head. "Unbelievable. You said you only discovered it a month ago. How?"

"Our hero, Malik." He smirked. "His father had a memory card in his safe, given to him by his grandfather, the great General Johnson. I removed it from Malik's bag when he was in the hospital."

"Does he know about this?"

"I don't think he had the technology to access the card. The data was encrypted, and only a military class biometric scanner can access it."

"Biometric? Whose DNA?"

"Johnson DNA."

"Malik's?"

"I visited Johnson's grave at the farm. I wasn't sure if Malik's DNA would work."

"Because he's only part Leon?"

"Yep." Darius opened his mouth to unblock his eardrums caused by depressurization. Santiago mimicked.

The sound of people yelling orders echoed in the elevator shaft as they neared their destination.

"Have you diverted all the power?" Darius asked as the doors opened.

None of the military staff acknowledged them as they entered the room. A dozen rows of computers cascaded down to a glass wall that overlooked the expanse. Nirvana's shimmering silhouette interrupted the monotonous vista.

"The moment their beam struck the Dome," Santiago said as she stepped out of the elevator. "As you ordered."

"Let's hope they've bought it," Darius said, walking down the stairs that divided the rows of computers. "You managing the old equipment?"

"It's just bigger and slower, but it still works the same."

Darius placed his hands behind his back as he reached the glass wall, eyes focused on the city in the distance. "The President is dead, so I will give the order."

"There's widespread panic in the streets... riots, looting," Santiago said.

"I expected it." Darius shrugged and turned to Santiago. "When will it be operational?" He pointed at the digital clock, counting down above the glass wall. "Is that the time – thirty-two minutes?"

"Yes."

"And you said smaller vessels are disembarking?"

"They are not approaching yet," Santiago said. "But..."

"What is it, Professor?" He turned around.

"According to our calculations, we've got power for two, maybe three attempts with a recharge period of five minutes between each."

"Then we need to make the first one count."

He turned back to the endless view and looked up at the blue skies. "You've got thirty minutes, Malik. Thirty minutes."

"Sadie!" I yelled, waking. Pain shot through my body as I tried to move. I was not in the transporter-ship anymore, but in the flagship, in the Pit, hanging from the roof, meat hooks impaled my shoulders, and chains tied to my ankles, preventing me from unhooking myself. Alone. "Sadie!"

Three silhouettes appeared in the Pit's entrance.

"Where's Sadie?"

"For now, still alive," Alcantar said, slowly approaching. Khan and Erich flanked him.

"Please don't hurt her," I begged. My anguish for Sadie overshadowed my pain.

"You see!" Khan yelled, pointing at me. "He's not Leon anymore. It was all for nothing, the men we've lost to get him here–"

"Silence!" Alcantar roared. "We have killed their leader, captured his daughter," he walked toward me, "and taken their only hero."

"Please, Father," I cried. "I'm still your son. Take me, but please let her go."

He shook his head. "Now I'm your father."

"The mighty Malik, crying like a baby, pathetic." He turned to Erich. "Are you capturing this?"

He nodded, adjusting the lens covering his left eye.

"This will break the human's spirit." Khan turned to Alcantar. "Your son is dead. Accept it."

"No, I'm not," I whispered. "I've just tasted love and seen what our lives are without it. How fruitless and aimless our existence is." I shivered as the meat hooks tore into my flesh. "Our only purpose is to destroy. We thought we could fill the emptiness inside us with hatred and death, but how many worlds have we destroyed and it remains?"

For a moment, it seemed as if something had awoken within my father. "But we are born this way, son. Without love."

"No, we're not. We just need to feed it. You sacrificed seven of your best men to see me again."

"It wasn't for love," he seethed. "It was for revenge."

"The transporter destroyed us."

"The transporter saved our lives," Erich said.

I fought to stay conscious, not to submit to the pain. "The transporter took our fear of death away. It fuelled our hatred to become the perfect warrior. Our purpose. We didn't evolve. We reverted with every transfer. Now you are nothing more than a parasite. You can't even remember why you wanted Earth."

"You know why," Khan said, "We need food."

"Then why did we not produce our own?" I shook my head. "No, because we are envious of what they have. Because without taking, we have no purpose – just a fucking parasite."

Khan grabbed me by the legs and pulled me down. I screamed in pain, losing consciousness for a moment.

"Wake up, you coward!" Khan yelled. "This is your last fucking life! What, according to your newfound wisdom, was the meaning of this one?"

I clenched my jaw and looked him in the eyes. "I found my true love. All my lives before this one, all my empty conquests, this one was my greatest victory. I'm the luckiest fucking Leon alive."

The three Leons frowned at me in stunned silence.

"I'm ready," I whispered. "Just get it over with."

"So, you surrender?" Khan said. "Do you think the humans have a chance?" He pulled Erich closer. "Make sure you get this."

"The question is, do you?"

"What do you mean, Malik?" Erich asked.

"If you surrender now, I will beg for your lives. You can join us to rebuild. For the first time, the Leon race can create something."

"It's the pain," Khan laughed. "He's gone mad."

I focused on my father. "If I don't give them an answer soon, they will destroy us. Our species will be extinct."

Alcantar turned away, and after a few moments, turned back. "The shield, that's why they disabled the shield. They're using the power for some kind of weapon." He ran for the exit. "We must attack now!"

"What about him?" Khan asked.

My father halted in the doorway, and with head bowed, said, "I lost Malik a long time ago. Kill him."

Just like that, a true Leon. At least he looked sad.

Khan seemed almost human as he looked up at me, barely able to contain his excitement. He drew his sword and sliced air, inspecting his blade. "I will kill you quickly," he said, aiming for my heart. "But your woman will not be so fortunate."

"Wait!" Erich said.

"What?" Khan lowered his sword.

"I want to ask Malik something."

He threw his hand in the air, turning away.

"You saw what they did to their planet," Erich said. "Where's the love in that? How are they different from us?"

"There's evil in every species." I clenched my jaw as I felt the hooks grinding against my shoulder bones. "They were in charge. Greed dictated their actions. But I believe the scale has tipped toward the good. We owe them another chance."

"You think they will let us live amongst them?"

I nodded. "Don't you want a home? A family?

"Enough." Khan pushed Erich out of the way. "Time's up, Malik."

Darius glanced at the clock. "Time's up." He took a deep breath. "Open the mountain."

Santiago nodded and turned to the rows of men and women staring down at her. "Open her up!"

Darius glanced at her with a raised brow.

Santiago shrugged, lips pursed.

"I saw the Chinese made this," he said.

Santiago gave a wide-eyed nod. "Let's pray," she muttered.

The room started trembling as a deep, grinding roar erupted from the belly of the mountain.

Santiago grabbed Darius's arm as she lost her balance. "I'm sorry, General."

"It's okay. Call me, Darius." He pushed out his chest. "Do we have a visual of what's happening?"

"Is the drone in position?" she asked.

"Yes, Professor," a control room operator said.

"So, what are you waiting for?"

A visual of the mountain appeared on a screen suspended from the ceiling. A large slit appeared in the centre of the canvas. The trembling intensified as an enormous chrome sphere appeared from the shadows of the gaping crack.

Santiago held on tighter. "What's the target?"

"Let's level the playing field," Darius said. "Target their transporter. We don't want to kill the same Leon twice. It's the fourth-largest ship. Cigar-shaped."

"I know," Santiago said. "I was also in the briefing." She walked up to a petite twenty-something woman dressed in a military uniform seated in the front row. "Let's see what she can do, Lieutenant Orr." Santiago stood behind her. "That should be the transporter." She pointed at the screen and patted the woman on the shoulder.

"Acquiring target," the Lieutenant called.

A slight tremor reverberated through the room.

"Target locked." Lieutenant Orr looked at Darius.

He closed his eyes and took a deep breath. "Fire!"

"Malik!" Sadie yelled as she heard the screams. Where am I? Panic gripped her as she crawled around in the dark. She covered her mouth and nose, almost vomiting from the vile odour. The last thing she remembered was her father's death. Am I awake? Or dead. Is this hell?

Sadie reached a cold, sticky wall and struggled to her feet. She tapped the wall as she moved along until she reached what felt like a door. She searched for a handle but found only a small square in the centre of the door. Sadie tried to open it, clawing at it with her fingers.

"Shit." She stepped back as she heard the approaching footsteps. It stopped in front of her door. It would be a wonderful time to wake, she thought. However, her pounding heart and trembling body told her this was not a nightmare.

Sadie stepped further back as she heard a loud clang. Light streamed into the room as the door slid open. It took a moment for her eyes to adjust. Then her throat slammed shut as if throttled by an invisible hand. She recognised the Leon from the images flashed on the tall buildings within the Dome. He was scarier and taller in real life.

"Alcantar," she wanted to say, but the invisible hand prevented.

"You want to see Malik?" he asked, holding out his claw-like hand.

She managed a nod.

Sadie shuffled forward, taken aback by his strange behaviour, almost cordial. It must be a trap, but I'll play along.

"We need to hurry," he said. "Our time is running out."

Juliet walked into the big tent, heading straight for Raven, seated at his desk, chewing. She grabbed him between his legs and whispered in his ear, "Tell me what Darius is planning or..."

He gasped, eyes widening the tighter her grip.

Khan's blade pierced my skin as he inched it into my chest.

"Khan, wait!" Erich pleaded. "Malik is right. We can live with humans. Earth could be our home!"

"Goodbye, Malik," Khan sneered. "I trust I won't see you again."

"I fucking hope so," I groaned.

Erich drew his sword and lunged forward, the blade raised above his head.

Khan ripped his sword from my chest and went down on one knee.

Erich froze, staring at the blade disappearing into his heart. He dropped his sword and keeled over.

Khan turned back to me. "He was turning more human by the day."

"Khan," a woman called from the Pit's entrance.

He swung round. "Show yourself!"

She sauntered into the light.

"Amira," he whispered. "But... but you're dead?"

"Alcantar brought me back. Release my son!" she said.

Khan tilted his head. "If Alcantar did send you, why are you grey with fear?"

My mother gave a step forward, turning red. "Release him!"

"I changed my mind," Alcantar said as he walked into the Pit. "Let him down!"

"But..." He looked at me, then Amira, then Alcantar. "I don't understand what—"

"Are you disobeying my orders?" Alcantar's hand tightened around the grip of his sword.

I was as confused as Khan. My father had never changed his mind before.

"Wait," Khan said, eyes narrowing. "Where's your scars?" He raised his sword. "And I believe that sword belongs to Arden."

I screamed in pain as the ship shook and tilted to one side. My father's throne toppled over, crashing into the Pit. Waves of liquid fire spilt over the edges of the massive bowls suspended from the roof, igniting everything in its path. Khan and Arden crossed swords, hissing, fangs exposed.

That's when I saw her. My pain and all the havoc within the Pit for that moment diminished. Sadie covered her mouth as her eyes met mine.

My mother, trapped between rivers of flames, yelled at Sadie, "Release the chains!"

Sadie stood frozen, caught in a nightmare of disbelief.

"Sadie!" I cried. "Release the chains!"

She startled into action and ran toward the lever my mother pointed at.

Khan evaded my brother, also running toward the lever.

Everyone in the control room stared at the skies.

"F-fuck," Darius whispered.

"My thoughts exactly, General," Santiago whispered. "Lieutenant. Tell me what I want to hear."

She leapt from her chair, punching the air. "Target destroyed!"

Cheers erupted in the control room, followed by high-fives and back-slapping.

"Settle down!" Darius yelled. "Target the flagship and fire when ready!" He walked over to the line of operators. "Open a channel to the camp."

"Channel open, General."

"Are the Sweepers re-programmed?"

"Affirmative, General," a man answered over the loudspeakers.

"Release all the Sweepers and target the incoming vessels!"

Silence followed.

"Sweepers released, General."

"Activate the Ark's plasma cannon and target the vessel on the flagship's starboard side when ready. You have enough energy for one strike, so make it count."

"Affirmative, General."

"General," Orr called Darius over to her targeting system. "The flagship. I think we damaged it when we struck the transporter."

"How do you know that?"

She pointed to the flashing dot. "It's breaking formation and moving in an uncontrolled trajectory toward Earth."

Darius smiled. "So it will overshoot and disintegrate upon entry."

Orr nodded. "Also, General." She pointed at the two dots. "These ships on the port side of the flagship are in line with one another. If I do this right, I can damage both with one strike. Not destroy, but disable."

Darius focused on the two dots. "They will follow the same fate." He tapped Orr's shoulder. "Just don't fuck it up."

She straightened in her chair, took a deep breath, and whispered, "No pressure, sir, no pressure."

"They have target lock, Darius!" Santiago yelled.

"Who? On what?"

"The approaching fighters."

Her shocked expression told him what the target was. "Whatever happens, stay at your posts!" Darius ordered. "We only need one more chance." He turned back to Orr. "How long?"

"Two minutes until recharged."

"Open a channel."

"Channel open, General."

"I want everything that can fly in the air, target the incoming fighters. Now!"

Sadie stopped in her tracks as Khan slipped in between her and the lever. She felt a wave of heat as flames shot up behind her, trapping her with the crazed Leon.

He snarled while raising his sword. "This is where it ends."

She glanced at his feet and made a rolling dive through his legs. "Not yet!" she screamed and pulled the lever. The chains rattled loose, dropping Malik to the floor.

"Bitch!"

Sadie hunkered down, shielding herself with her arms, waiting for the final blow. She heard a sword fall, opened her eyes and stared into the glazed eyes of Khan by her feet. His decapitated body keeled over into the flames past Alcantar.

He held out his claw. "I believe you will remember me as Joshua... Wayne's brother."

She grabbed his hand. "Wayne's dead brother?"

"Get on!" he said and knelt before her.

Sadie jumped onto his back, wrapping her arms around his neck.

"One... two... three!" Arden leapt through the flames and ran toward Malik and his mother.

22

B en almost dropped his glass tablet as a loud crack resonated through the Ark. He sprinted to the door at the far end of the building and, with a trembling hand, tried to insert his access card. After the third attempt, he stood back and took a deep breath. "Take it easy, Ben." The door slid open with the fourth attempt.

"What's going on?" he shouted at the stunned group of scientists, staring up at the parting roof.

"We did nothing," one replied. "It," gesturing with open hands, "just turned on."

"Watch out!" Ben hollered as sand, rock, and boulders tumbled over the edges of the roof into the cavern. Everyone ran to the centre of the cavern, arms shielding their heads.

The colossal metal gears at the base of the structure clanked into gear, pushing the chrome sphere through the gaping mouth of the ceiling. It locked into position with another deafening crack. White lightning spread over the surface of the sphere, covering it like a spider's cocoon.

"It's time," Ben whispered.

Darius peered through the window at the mayhem in the skies. Raptors and Sweepers swarmed around the incoming black dots. "How many of them?" he yelled.

"Too many to count, General."

The Sweepers' shiny hulls reflected the sun's rays, like flashing lights, as they defended their airspace.

"Incoming!" Orr yelled.

A streak of white smoke pierced the skies and hit the mountain below the control room, knocking everyone to the floor. Boards dropped from the ceiling, crashing onto computers and operators. Wires dangled from the roof like snakes, spitting sparks.

Darius jumped to his feet and pulled Santiago to her feet. "You okay?" he asked, coughing.

She nodded. "Is the weapon still operational?"

The dust and smoke settled, revealing the carnage.

"It was fully charged." Orr crawled from underneath her desk. "It was ready the moment we got hit." She stumbled to her feet, dusting off her uniform.

Darius stared at the silent machines for a beat. "Why did you not fire?" He grabbed Orr by the collar.

"I told you it was the mo – wait." Eyes narrowing. "I think we only lost power to the control room. If it's still charged, I can fire it from below."

"Let's go." Darius released her. "Everyone else must evacuate!"

"Run!" Santiago scrambled away from the windows.

Darius grabbed Orr by the arm and sprinted toward the exit. The explosion catapulted them through the door, burying them in debris. They lay quiet for a moment before Darius asked, "You okay?"

Orr threw half a ceiling board from her legs, sat up and dusted her uniform. "My dad said iron ore is not the most precious, but we use it to protect the most precious."

Darius smiled. "Your father is a smart man." He stumbled to his feet and held out his arm.

"Was." Orr grabbed his hand and pulled herself up. "He died, protecting his most precious." She froze, staring at the control room behind Darius. "It's gone," she whispered. "I can see the city."

Darius didn't look back. "Where to!" He grabbed her by the arm.

"The stairs." She pointed over her shoulder.

"Go!" Darius turned Orr by the shoulders and pushed her toward the door.

"We destroyed their control room," Alcantar said and turned his fighter away from the mountain. "Do not destroy the weapon," he ordered. "It's mine. Target their fighters."

A million needles pricked my arms as life returned. I pushed my mother's wrist away and wiped my mouth with the back of my hand. "Enough. You also will need your strength. Besides, it doesn't feel right."

Amira rolled her eyes and hugged me. "I missed you."

Sadie leapt from my brother's back and joined in. With a gritted jaw, I wrapped my arms around the woman. I looked up as I felt a hand ruffling my hair.

"I miss mine," Arden said, and glanced at his claw with regret.

"Who brought you back?" I asked.

"Erich. Thanks to you, I ran out of bodies," he said, glaring.

I struggled to my feet and stumbled to Erich sprawled on his back.

"Malik," he whispered.

I placed my hand on his chest wound. "Thank you, my friend."

Arden rushed over and sliced his palm with his sword. "Drink."

"No." Erich pushed Arden's hand away. "Take this." He removed the lens and handed it to me. "Show our people." He coughed, blood seeping from his mouth. "They will join the fight against Alcantar." Life drained from his eyes. "Let them see the light," he whispered with his last breath.

A group of Leon's ran past the Pit's entrance, but one stopped in his tracks and entered, confused.

"Extinguish the fire!" Arden ordered.

"Master? I thought you were leading the attack," the Leon said with a bowed head.

"Does it look like it, fool!" Arden snapped. "Where's everyone running to?"

"We have lost power to the engines, Master. We need to evacuate."

"What's the hurry?"

"We are caught in Earth's gravitational pull."

"Shit," I muttered. "We need to get out of here."

"Are there any carriers left?" Arden asked the Leon.

He frowned. "I don't know, Master."

"Go! Save yourself."

His frown intensified.

"Go!"

He bowed and disappeared around the corner.

"It's so strange to hear you speak their language," Sadie said. "What's going on?"

I explained our predicament as we left the Pit. Arden took the lead, posing as Alcantar, women in the middle, and me covering the back. I gave Sadie and Amira strict instructions not to show any affection toward us. No holding hands, no smiling, and no hair-ruffling. The latter only applied to me. The rules were pointless; no Leon gave us a second glance – all were searching for an escape, like rats trapped in a maze. The problem was we were also part of those rats. The corridors were thick with fear – Leon fear – never had I seen our race like this.

"Shit," my brother said as we arrived at the landing bay.

"Shit," I repeated; besides the scurrying rats, the hangar stood empty. "Let's get to the control room."

We spoke Leon, but Sadie understood; she took my hand and squeezed it. "We're together, and that's all that matters."

The bine filled my heart.

"Wait!" Orr gasped, clutching the rail of the stairwell.

Darius turned back and grabbed her by the arm. "Only five more floors... come on!"

She took a deep breath and lumbered the last of the floors with gritted teeth.

Darius burst through a door at the bottom of the stairwell, holding it open for Orr. "Where to!"

She pointed with a limp hand down a long corridor lined with pipes and cables. Darius grabbed her by the arm and hauled her the rest of the way.

"Here we are," Orr gasped as they reached a door halfway down the corridor.

Darius shouldered the door and froze, gaping at the towering structure protruding through the hangar doors.

"This way." Orr pushed past and ran to a terminal at the base of the structure. She flipped open the screen and yelled over her shoulder, "There's still power."

"I'm right here," Darius said, eyes focused on the monitor.

Orr's hands played over the keyboard. "I'm in."

"Targeting?"

"Should still point in the right direction."

"Let's hope." Darius took a deep breath.

She raised her dust-covered hand, pointing an index finger at the "Enter" button, and looked at Darius.

"Fire."

"I have charged The Ark's weapon," Raven said.

The tent fell silent as everyone turned their attention to him.

He turned to the eldest person in the room, waiting for confirmation.

"The order must come from General Von Swartz."

We entered a room overflowing with panic and fear, its occupants scurrying amongst flashing screens, keeping a watchful eye on the approaching planet. Earth seemed more beautiful than ever; the copper-coloured landmasses were in stark contrast to the blue oceans. No, Earth was more impressive when we first arrived; then, it still had the streaks of white and patches of green. However, back then, I did not see beauty.

We edged forward, leaving the two ships on our port side behind.

Amira grabbed Erich's recorder from my hand and walked over to a console.

"Damage report!" Arden yelled.

The room came to a standstill; panic-stricken expressions turned to confusion.

"Master?" An Elder was the first to break the silence.

"I'm not Alcantar, I'm Arden."

Confusion turned to relief.

"Thank the gods. You're alive!" the Elder called, claws raised. "Please help us!" He grabbed Arden's hand and fell to his knees.

Arden smiled. "Stand up, Gelman."

The old Leon rose and saw Sadie. "What's a human doing here?" he asked, eyes filled with contempt.

"She's my friend," Arden said.

"The humans have a mighty weapon, Master. They have destroyed our transporter and damaged our vessel. We have no power to the engines."

"Thrusters?"

He shook his head.

"Our re-entry trajectory?"

"We are coming in too steep, fifty-two degrees, we should be–"

"Coming in at forty," Arden interrupted. "Instruct one of the other ships to use their tractor beam and pull us away from Earth's gravitational pull."

"Yes!" Gelman cried. "Why didn't I think of that?"

"Because you're too busy dying," I muttered.

An alarm blared, lighting up the control room in red.

"No!" Gelman cried. "They're firing again!"

I pulled Sadie closer and wrapped my arms around her. Arden approached the window, fists clenched. A white beam blasted from Earth and barrelled past our port side. Cries of relief echoed through the control room.

"They've missed!" Gelman yelled.

"No, they didn't," Arden said, glaring to his left.

The two ships on our port side disintegrated. I watched with mixed emotions as one after the other exploded, hurling debris into the depths of space. Our ship shuddered as the shock wave hit us, tilting us further forward and increasing our momentum. Flaming debris shot past our window toward Earth. Sadie looked away as the upper body of a Leon flew past, trailed by its intestines.

"Plan B. Anyone?" Arden muttered.

Khan appeared on the screens. "Your son is dead. Accept it."

"We are broadcasting it throughout the fleet," Amira said as she joined me.

"You mean this ship," I said. "The fleet is gone."

"No, I'm not. I've just tasted love and seen what our lives are without it. How fruitless and aimless our existence is. Our only purpose is to destroy. We thought the emptiness inside us could be filled with hatred and death, but how many worlds have we destroyed, and still that emptiness remains?"

"Is this necessary?" I asked, embarrassed at seeing myself like that, dangling on chains, shivering with pain.

I felt Sadie's hand tighten when Khan had his fun with me.

"We are about to slam into—"

"Quiet!" Arden snapped, pointing at the Leons watching.

They all seemed mesmerised by my words. I had forgotten that I was the youngest brother. I'd been the oldest for six years, giving my brother hell.

"Are our fighters also seeing this?" Arden asked Amira.

"Yes, even the humans. Elder Siya is translating."

"I experienced love. All my lives before this one, all my empty conquests, this one was my greatest victory. I'm the luckiest fucking Leon alive."

Sadie reached up and placed her hand behind my head, pulling me toward her.

"I love you," Sadie whispered as our lips parted.

Arden turned to me. "Who's in charge down there?"

"With the President" –I glanced at Sadie– "not with us anymore, General Darius Von Swartz."

"I want to talk to the ship and our fighters below," Arden said to Gelman.

"What are you planning?" I asked.

"You may proceed, Master," Gelman said with a wave of his bony claw.

Arden cleared his throat. "My fellow Leons, don't let my appearance fool you. I'm Arden, son of Alcantar. Let's end this madness. Our hatred and rage have brought us to the brink of extinction. We have a decision to make, proceed with our fruitless quest for destruction, or join the humans, live amongst them in harmony, rebuild Earth, start a family, build a legacy. In a few moments, I will contact the humans and ask for their help. But in return, we must fight Alcantar and those who remain defiant. I want a representative within two minutes in the control room to give me your decision. It's a simple one: live or die!"

"You and I know that without human blood in them, they're not just going to turn good," I whispered in human tongue to Arden, keeping a watchful eye on the Leons in the control room.

"You don't have to be human to realise that continuing on a certain path will lead to death."

"What do you say, Gelman?" I asked.

"I'm with Arden," he mused. "A change is as good as a holiday."

"He's lying," Mother whispered in my ear.

I took Arden by the arm. "Can I talk to you for a moment?"

He stared at my hand for a moment. "Just make it quick."

We walked to a secluded part of the control room. "Let's say the Leons go for it, and we survive," I said. "What prevents them from turning on us? We will add three thousand men to Alcantar's forces."

My brother shrugged. "What's to lose? Father will win with or without their help."

"I don't like it."

"Okay, Wayne, how do you suppose we save your precious girlfriend?"

My brother called me Wayne, and I had no answer.

"I decide now." Arden glared at me. "I'm not your little brother anymore."

I stepped back with my hands on my hips. "Is that what this is about?"

"What?"

"The six years on Earth, the way I treated you. I did what I needed to do to keep us alive."

"So, you remember how you treated me?"

"You had it good. You had a bed, always the best portion–"

"It wasn't my fault. He liked me more!" Arden yelled, shoving my chest.

"Stop it!" Mother stepped in between us. "Now is not the time! You are carrying on like two younglings."

Sadie and the rest of the control room were staring at us.

"You two haven't changed a bit," Mother continued. "Leon or human, you are always at each other's throats."

"He's the reason I ran out of bodies and now's stuck with this one."

"Oh, please." I rolled my eyes.

"He's right," Mother whispered.

"Now you're taking his side?" I said.

"You know why I volunteered for the mission?" Amira said in the human tongue, reddening, a flash of anger in her eyes. "The last time you challenged Arden, you killed him! I saw Alcantar in you. I wanted you away from here. I wanted to give you a fresh start because I knew you would challenge your father next, and then I would lose you forever. I thought Earth would change you."

"It did," I whispered.

"You know why I went to Earth?" Arden said. "Because Alcantar reminded me of you every day, what a warrior you are, that you will lead one day." He pointed at the approaching planet. "I send Khan to Earth to kill you. When he had failed, I convinced father to send me down. I told him I wanted to help you bring down the shield. Lucky for you, I lost my memory."

I smiled, shaking my head.

"What's so funny?" Arden scowled.

"You know what father told me behind your back every chance he had?"

"What?"

"That I will never be as good as you. And that you will lead one day." I lowered my head in shame. "I deserve it. I owe you a life." I raised my hands. "Finish your mission."

"There's no time for a challenge," Arden said.

"No challenge." I turned my back on him. "I'll make it easy for you."

"That defeats the purpose of a challenge," he seethed.

"You better do it this way, because I will never fight you again."

"Just like that?"

"Just like that."

I heard his sword slide from its sheath.

"Arden!" Amira yelled, blackening.

"Malik!" Sadie ran toward me.

"Goodbye, little brother."

I closed my eyes as his blade sliced the air. A shiver went through my body as the icy steel touched my neck. Sadie had halted her approach, letting out an audible sigh of relief.

"I'm sorry, Arden," I whispered. "For being such an asshole. I was like our father."

"You're right," he said after an eerie silence. "You were an asshole."

I started breathing again after the sword returned to its sheath.

A Leon entered the control room and bowed. "We will fight for you, Master."

The Vector sped back to camp, full throttle, leaving in its wake a column of dust.

"I liked him," Orr whispered, watching the images of Malik on the console.

"I warned him not to go," Darius said, eyes trained on the aerial battle ahead. "Damn it!" He hit his fist against the steering column.

"He was a Leon," Orr remarked.

Darius glared at his passenger. "He was my friend."

She shifted in her chair. "I'm sorry, General, I didn't know."

Darius pushed a button. "Give me an update."

Raven's image appeared in the centre of the windscreen, chewing on something. "The flagship will enter our atmosphere in about twenty-two minutes. We destroyed the rest of the fleet."

"Good. And our fighters?"

"Not good, General. They're dropping like flies."

"That's our men we are talking about! And stop chewing!"

Raven spat out the mushy contents into his hand. "I'm sorry, General. Of the seventy-two Sweepers, we only have thirty left."

"Fighters?"

"Of the fifty-two, we've lost twenty-nine." Raven stretched his neck as he looked at the off-screen monitor. "Correction, thirty-two."

"Have we downed any of theirs?"

"Five or six, General."

Darius rubbed his eyes. "We can't beat them in the air."

"We still have power in the Ark's weapon for one discharge."

"Then target the flagship. We're not sure how damaged it is."

Raven nodded. "I was hoping you would say that."

"Fire when ready. I'll be back at the camp within two minutes."

"Another thing, General," Raven said, looking around before leaning in. "The battle is almost overhead."

Darius stared at his son for a moment, then took a deep breath. "You know what to do, then."

Raven shook his head. "No, and hide out with the animals, like animals. No, father, this is it, our last stand."

Darius gave him a stern nod. "Spoken like a soldier."

Raven's image disappeared.

"He's cute," Orr whispered.

Darius glanced at the blue-eyed brunette. "How old are you?"

The console lit up in red once more, alarms blaring.

"It's that fucking Darius," I seethed, walking towards the window.

"Get me comms!" Arden yelled.

"Just a moment, Master," Gelman said, his claws swiping at the console. "We don't have a–"

Raven's image appeared on the screen. "Yes," he said, shifty-eyed.

"Raven, it's me, Malik!" I stepped in front of my brother. "Tell them not to fire."

I could see his hand moving away from the keyboard. "Uh... I will tell them." He fell back into his chair, wiping his brow with the sleeve of his shirt. "Fuck, that was close."

"I don't see you telling them!" I scowled.

He glanced away and shouted, "Don't shoot!"

"Our sensors are still detecting the weapon is active," Arden said behind me.

"Just a second." Raven turned the camera away, and a few moments later, the alarm went silent. "I saw what they did to you, Captain," he said as the camera turned back to him. "Are you okay?"

"Nothing your blood won't fix," I said. "We need to speak to Darius... now."

"I'll patch you through."

A hand touched my shoulder.

"I'll handle this, Malik," said Arden.

"Let me introduce him to you. The first thing he'll see is Alcantar."

He gave a slight nod.

"Malik?" Darius said behind me.

I turned back to the screen. "We're in deep shit, General."

He raised a brow. "Join the club. Glad to see you're still with us."

"My brother Arden, wants to speak to you," I said. "He resembles someone you might know, but it was the only clone available." I stepped away.

"General." My brother nodded.

"Arden?"

"Our engines and main thrusters are down. We're coming in too steep."

"I'm sorry to hear that, but we have problems of our own. Your father is kicking our butts and will soon be able to attack the city."

"I have three thousand men willing to join your forces – if you can help us."

Darius shrugged. "How can I possibly help you?"

"Do your Sweepers have tractor beams?

"No."

"Do you have any ships with the technology?" Desperation filled his voice.

"Only in our movies. But why?"

"We need vessels that can latch on and act as thrusters, calibrate our entry into Earth's atmosphere."

"I'm sorry, Arden. Even if I had, I can't spare any. We are barely hanging on as it is."

"You need my men to win the battle."

Darius' eyes narrowed. "What guarantees do I have that they won't turn against us."

I took a position beside my brother. "Please, Darius, trust my brother. They will fight for him."

Another wasted moment passed. "Let me talk to my people, maybe there's another way." Darius' image disappeared.

My brother lowered his head. "I'm sorry, Malik."

Sadie's hand slipped into mine.

"Master," Gelman said.

"Yes," Arden muttered.

"We have a ship approaching. Human. They're hailing us."

"On screen," my brother ordered.

Juliet's image appeared. "Who's driving that bucket?"

"Uh, I am," Arden said. "It's me, Joshua." He glanced at us and shrugged. "That's the name she knows." I'd never seen a Leon blush before.

"I know." Juliet smiled. "I've been eavesdropping. You grew into a handsome... Leon."

He hid his claws behind his back. "Did Darius send you?"

"No, I bust someone's balls to find out where you were. What can I do to help?"

"We need something bigger or more of you," Arden said. "We're coming in too steep."

"I'm usually more than anyone can handle. Ask your brother."

Now it was my turn to blush, as Sadie looked at me.

"See what you can do to raise our nose, twelve degrees," Arden said.

She beamed. "I'm brilliant at getting a rise out of something."

"There she is!" Sadie said, pointing at the incoming Raptor.

"I didn't know your bucket could fly into space?" I said.

"They built it for hauling cargo to the space station," Juliet replied.

The Raptor dipped from sight.

"I will move in under the nose and use my thrusters."

My hand tightened around Sadie's as the seconds passed. I could feel the tension in the control room – no one moved, even breathed.

Juliet's image flickered as the Raptor made contact. "Here goes," she said, wiping the sweat from her brow. I could feel a slight vibration as Juliet activated the thrusters.

Arden turned to Gelman. "What's happening?"

The Elder squinted at the control panel in front of him. "It's not working, Master."

"Anything?" Juliet asked.

"Nothing," my brother said.

"I'm pushing thrusters to a hundred percent." An alarm activated in the Raptor's cockpit. "Come on! Give me more!" Juliet seethed through gritted teeth.

Arden glanced at Gelman. The Elder shook his head in despair.

"Juliet... stop!" Arden yelled. "It's not moving. You'll damage your engines."

"Shit!" She eased back on the throttle. "Open a door, I can at least play taxi."

"Hangar four... port side," Arden said. "It's empty. We don't want a stampede."

"Let's welcome our guest." I turned for the door.

"Master," Gelman whispered.

"Yes."

"I can handle things from now on."

Arden gave a sympathetic smile. "I'm the captain of this ship. Keep my seat warm." He glanced at me, Sadie, and Amira and said, "Your taxi awaits."

23

I
t was a phenomenon I did not expect. A sudden change, almost an awakening. Was it possible? Could a leader have such an impact? Was it all we needed, a spark of empathy, igniting the flame of humanity within us... them? Did Alcantar and his sons wield such fear and power that we could suppress those emotions? Had we fooled ourselves?

Or was it the fear of dying, knowing this was the last chance that brought about the change?

As we made our way to hangar four, the Leons we met in the corridor stepped aside, eyes filled with hope. All made eye contact. Some even smiled. Arden tapped some of them on the shoulder, bringing forth a flood of emotion. Their manner seemed awkward, almost as if they were still learning their unfamiliar expressions. They only knew three: rage, hatred, and fear.

Juliet sat in the cockpit as we arrived in the empty hangar. Only when I gave her the thumbs-up did she lower the ramp.

I expected only her, but to my surprise, four sets of boots stumped down the ramp: Brock, Fritz, and Shorty emerged behind her.

"You thought you're gonna have all the fun by yourself?" Brock said as he grabbed my hand and slapped my shoulder.

I smiled. "Can't seem to get away from your sorry asses."

"This big ass just saved your ass." Brock turned to Arden. "I believe this is Joshua." Arden gave a smiling nod. "Must be nice to trade in your old body for a new one."

"I don't like the one I ended up with."

"I like it," Juliet said, scanning Arden from head to toe.

"Thank you for coming," my brother said with flaming cheeks.

"H-hi Malik," Shorty said with a reaching hand. I pulled him closer and hugged him. He pulled away, embarrassed.

"Thought a spider caught you by now," I said, glad to see the little guy. "And what's with the blue hair?" I asked Fritz.

"Seen too much red. I needed a change."

"Let's get out of here," Juliet said.

"I think now would be a good time." Brock peeked over my shoulder, his hand reaching for his sidearm.

The hangar filled with Leons. But they did not approach.

"I won't be joining you," Arden said.

I nodded, whispering, "I know, that's why I'll be—"

Sadie pushed in between us and buried her finger in my chest. "Don't do this, Malik! We need you down there. I need you." No tears, just rage. She grabbed my hands, showing me my palms. "You are human." She glanced at my brother. "Sorry, Arden." Then back at me. "I've lost everyone I loved, and I will not lose you now. We've come too far."

"She's right, Malik," Arden said. "You gave them hope. You can't turn back now." He placed his hand on my shoulder. "And to make you feel better, I think I have a better chance up here. You're not jumping ship, you're just jumping onto yours, which is already on fire."

"Well, thank you," I muttered.

"Never thought I'll ever do this." He wrapped his arms around me. "Love you, little brother."

I cleared my throat. "Me too."

Arden smiled. "Who's more human now?" He removed his sword and handed it to me. "End it."

I took a deep breath. "I was hoping you would."

"I'll always be with you." My mother took my hand and kissed me on the cheek. "Love you."

"Aren't you coming with?"

"You know I can't leave him."

"Mother?" Arden asked, taking a step toward her.

Amira raised her finger at him, eyes flashing. "Don't even try." She turned to Sadie and stroked her cheek with the back of her hand. "Look after my boy. He needs you now more than ever. He can be stubborn and unforgiving sometimes."

Sadie nodded, wide-eyed. "He's not the Leon you once knew."

"Then nurture his human side." She glanced at me. "There is still Leon in him. They crave power."

"Yes, Mother, I'm standing right here." I looked at Arden. "Fuck."

"What?"

"Say it."

"No."

"Just say it, damn it!"

He shook his head, smiling, fangs glistening.

"Just checking."

My mother and Arden took their place in front of their followers as the Raptor took off. The strange thing was I didn't feel sorrow. I cried for them so many times.

"You okay?" Sadie asked.

I nodded. "I'm where I belong."

"What's happening, Pete?" Darius asked General Ford as he entered the big tent.

"We're not sure, General, but our fighters report some of their fighters have broken away from the fight. Some even turned, fighting for us now."

"Arden," Darius said with a pensive stare. He turned to Raven. "Call off the Sweepers and reprogram. They must only attack when fired upon."

Raven nodded and took a bite of a biscuit before working the keyboard.

"Shit," Darius whispered. "We need to get them on the ground. Draw a line in the sand and see who's on our side."

"General," Raven said, still typing. "I have an idea."

"About what?"

"About Arden's ship."

"Spit it out."

Raven leaned forward and spat out the rest of the biscuit.

"No, damn it!" Darius snapped. "I meant, tell me your idea."

"What are you waiting for?" I asked Juliet as we remained in orbit around Earth.

"The Dome is almost on the other side of Earth," she replied. "We will reach it faster if we remain in orbit."

"W-o-w," Sadie whispered as she glanced through the cockpit window.

"From here, it looks so peaceful," Juliet said. "Can't believe all the shit going on down there."

"Let's just stay on this side of the planet," Brock said from the rear.

"F-f-fuck, yeah!"

"The shit will find us wherever we go!" I said.

"Wherever you go!" Fritz said.

"What about an island?" Juliet asked.

"We would never enjoy the sunset," I said.

Brock appeared in the cockpit doorway. "Conscience is what

people think of you after letting them down. In another day, maybe two, there would be nobody left to think about us."

After a thought-filled moment, Juliet said, "What difference will another ship make?"

"She's right," Brock said.

"T-then d-d-drop me off before you g-go to your island."

"I was wrong," Brock whispered. "Conscience is a stuttering dwarf."

"I need to clean myself up." I ran my fingers through my tangled hair. "Get me Darius."

"Does it still hurt?" Sadie placed a hand on my chest, where Khan stabbed me.

"Ouch!"

She pulled away, wide-eyed. "I'm sorry!"

I leaned over and kissed her.

"Malik!" Darius said. "Sadie! Glad to see you're still alive."

"No, thanks to you," Juliet muttered.

"Let's not go there."

Darius's image flickered as I heard an explosion in the background.

"I need your help." Darius glanced over his shoulder. "Some Leon fighters are on our side, but it's not enough to turn the tide. Our camp is under attack. Call Alcantar out. We need his troops on the ground." Another explosion wiped his image from the screen.

"Darius?"

Juliet leaned over and flipped a switch. "We've lost transmission."

"How can I talk to Alcantar?"

"I'll broadcast on all channels," Juliet said. "Tell me when you're ready." She pointed at the co-pilot's seat.

Brock tapped my back as I took the hot seat. I took a deep breath and gave Juliet the nod. "You're on."

"I'm still here, Father," I said in Leon. "You have failed. If you want to kill me, do it yourself. Show your men you're not a coward. Show the humans how a true Leon fights, blade against blade. That's why your men are turning on you because of your cowardice. It is not how we fight."

My father's image appeared. "You are not my son."

"Then prove it."

"I will drink your blood before the end of day."

"I will send you the coordinates and instruct my troops to withdraw. Don't be late."

Alcantar's image disappeared.

"Did he take the bait?" Darius asked. "For me, it sounded like two cats getting rid of a fur ball."

"Yes, send us the coordinates where you want him to kill me."

"Can I also send the way how I want him to kill you?" Darius added.

I showed him the middle finger. "Why don't you come and sit on your throne, General?"

"I'm a hard-ass. It will break." He winked and disconnected the call.

Juliet shook her head. "Incredible."

<hr>

"You heard him," Darius said. "Withdraw the troops."

Raven crawled from underneath his desk. "Let's pray they do the same."

"It's never too late to start." Darius pulled him to his feet. "Take Lieutenant Orr to the Ark's weapon and do what you can. Three thousand men will come in handy."

"No pressure." He dusted off his pants. "Who's Orr? And where will you be, General?"

"You think I'd miss the opportunity to watch a good fight?" He checked his sidearm and slipped it back into its holster. "Lieutenant Orr is helping with the wounded in section three."

Raven stuck out his hand. "It was an honour to serve with you, General."

Darius took his hand and pulled him closer. "Stop with this General shit," he said, hugging him.

"Did I do good?" he whispered.

"I couldn't be prouder."

Raven looked away as he tried to hide the tears.

"I'm sorry, son, for everything."

"And Mother, you forgive her?"

Darius stared at the tear-filled eyes of his son and nodded. "Tell her I'm sorry. I know why she did it."

"Thank you," he whispered and wiped away tears.

"Now go."

Raven turned for the exit.

"And son..."

"Yes, Father?"

"After you've done what you can, don't come back. Go to Mom. She needs you. And take Orr with you."

He frowned.

"You'll see." He winked at his boy. "And be careful of the lions."

"You too, and we'll be waiting for you."

***

"Well, your speech worked, again," Juliet said as I returned to the cockpit. She glanced over her shoulder. "Did you save some steamer time for me?"

"No, you don't need it."

"I'll take that as a compliment."

I leaned over and kissed her on the cheek.

"You even cleaned your teeth."

"Thank you... for Sadie."

"I didn't do it for her," she whispered.

The Raptor shuddered as if struck by a Sweeper.

"It's just turbulence." Juliet pushed down on the controls and glanced at me. "Did you see that?"

I smiled. "The clouds." We stared at the fine droplets covering the window.

"It's good luck."

"Sadie!" I yelled over my shoulder.

She still wiped the sleep from her eyes as she entered the cockpit. "What?" She froze, staring at the window. "Am I still dreaming?"

"No." I draped my arm over her shoulder.

The Raptor broke through another white blanket, shuddering as we descended.

"It's a sign," Sadie said. "Why today?"

"Let's hope it's a good one," Brock said behind me. "You ready for this?"

"To face my father? I'll never be ready."

He placed his hand on my shoulder. "I have your back."

"Me too," Fritz said.

"M-me t-too."

***

Darius walked through the camp, kneeling next to one of the many corpses scattered amongst the smouldering tents. He searched for a pulse. "Shit." A quarter of the camp was annihilated. Medical staff scurried from one body to the next, yelling and waving as they found some breathing.

A Second lieutenant ran up to him and saluted. "We've got incoming, General." He said, heaving.

"Where the hell are you, Malik?" Darius muttered, searching the skies.

"The troops are awaiting your orders, sir."

Darius nodded and proceeded to the edge of the camp. "Let's hope they keep their end of the bargain. With all our men gathered in one place, it'll be like shooting at goldfish in a teacup."

"Sir?"

"Nothing."

As they walked through a wall of smoke, Darius stopped, overwhelmed by the scene; to the left, a chain of humans as far as the eye could see had taken a defensive position in front of the city. Civilians poured from the gates and joined the troops, strengthening the chain. To the right, Alcantar's forces landed. Leons leapt from their fighters, joining the black mass of terror. As the numbers grew, so did the roars.

"To fight and conquer in all your battles is not supreme excellence, supreme excellence consists in breaking the enemy's resistance without fighting." Darius looked up at the heavens. "Sun Tzu." He pointed at the clouds forming. "You see that, lieutenant?"

"Yes, Sir."

"Don't be afraid," Darius said. "Today, we are not alone."

"Sir?"

"There's more to this."

Cries of panic went down the chain on the left as several Leon fighters approached from the north.

"I knew I couldn't trust him," Darius muttered.

"Must, must I give the order to retreat?" the lieutenant asked.

"Wait, they're coming in too slow." Darius squinted. "Isn't that a Raptor amongst them?"

The chain stood their ground, but the cries amplified as the fighters circled above them. The roars to the right died down as the first fighters touched down in the centre of the battleground. One after the other, they landed in a straight line, forming a barrier until the Raptor touched down a hundred yards from Darius.

"You're right, General. There is more to this."

In succession, the engines shut down. The grey clouds shattered the silence, like a lion's roar rising, carried by the wind.

"The scene is set," Darius whispered.

Tyrone appeared from the wall of smoke. Flushed. He cleared his throat. "A few words, General."

Darius shook his head and pointed at the Raptor. "Go ask him. He's in charge now."

Tyrone frowned. "What do you mean?"

"You'll see. And do it live."

He nodded. "It could backfire on us."

"I want his image projected on every screen and building in the city. Let's hope he can keep the momentum going."

"Give me the chief. Now!" Tyrone spoke into his communicator as he ran toward the Raptor.

"I'm scared," Sadie whispered as we walked down the ramp of the Raptor.

"Go back to your house, please," I whispered as I rested Arden's sword on my shoulder.

"It's empty."

The crowd cheered as I stepped off the ramp. Tyrone circled me like a vulture. How had it come to this? My stomach churned, my heart clawed its way up my throat, and I lost all feeling in my legs. And worst of all, I couldn't show it. "Pull yourself together! Those that had turned will smell your fear and return to Alcantar." The defiant Leons joined us one by one as we made our way to Darius.

"I can smell the rain," Brock said after the clouds murmured above us.

"How do you know how rain smells?" Fritz replied.

"It's like knowing how your fart smells. I just know."

The crowd burst out laughing as Brock's remark boomed over the loudspeakers. He glanced around, confused, then smiled and waved as he saw his image projected on the glass buildings in the distance.

The wind picked up and covered the desert in a thick blanket of dust. I halted and turned to the group of Leons following. "I don't smell the rain, but I smell something else." Alcantar's forces had gathered upwind from our location.

"I can smell it too, Master," the Leon to my left said, exposing his fangs as he grinned.

"What?" Sadie asked.

"Fear. They are just as uncertain of the outcome." I stepped back and yelled. "And I'm not your master. I'm Malik, your friend. I know the sacrifice you've made, but it will be worth it. There is more than enough land for all of us - humans and Leons. It is not the end for us It's an awakening. You felt it too" –I hit my chest with a fist– "in here!" I pointed at the sky. "That is our sign. Just as Earth is preparing for a new beginning, so are we. Hatred and rage only bring pain and destruction." I wrapped my arm around Sadie. "We have lost our immortality, but love is eternal. We will live on through our children and what we create – no more hiding our emotions. You can smell my fear. I know it. It's normal. Embrace it. However, do not confuse fear with cowardice. Fear creates caution. To walk with caution into war is better than running into battle fearless. You might as well be blindfolded."

A child broke through the chain and ran up to me.

"Joshua!" his mother shouted and gave chase.

I handed Brock my sword and picked up the boy. It was the one I had met before. "Good to see you again, kid."

He traced my scar with a tiny finger, as he did in the elevator. "Does it still hurt?"

"Not anymore." I smiled. "You have magic fingers."

His face lit up. "Mother said so too."

I looked at Tyrone, staring into the lens. "Humans have the technology to help the Leons have children again. True immortality," I lied. "Only for those who will help in the fight against evil." I kissed Joshua on the cheek before handing him back to his mother. "Turn it off for a moment," I said to Tyrone.

"How are we going to do this?" Darius asked as he reached us.

"With caution," I muttered. "I need to cut off the head. Alcantar is the only thing preventing them from joining us."

"You think?"

I nodded. "Keep everyone back. If I die, get our fighters in the air and destroy theirs." I took Darius by the arm. "Don't let them get back in the air."

"And then?"

"Do whatever it takes to kill him and don't waste your men on defending the city."

Darius nodded.

Our eyes locked. He had the same look the day he visited the farm, the day he handed me his calling card. "You don't think I stand a chance?"

He pushed out his chest as he straightened and gave me the salute. So did everyone else; a wave of hands rolled down the chain. Even my Leons, although they had never seen it before, intuitively knew the meaning: It was nice knowing you, but... sorry.

Sadie wrapped her arms around my neck and pulled me toward her. We kissed until Darius cleared his throat. "I'll be waiting," she whispered, but her tears were telling me she was not expecting me back.

"Love you." I mouthed.

She placed her hand on my chest. "Take care of my heart."

24

"What's your plan?" Lieutenant Orr asked Raven as they rushed into the Museum of Natural History.

"I've studied the schematics of the weapon and realised it's not just a weapon."

"Shit! What do you mean?" Orr froze in her steps, then lifted her boot off the ground.

"What?"

"I just stepped in shit."

Raven studied the pile of animal excrement and then at the felines on display. "Maybe it's a disgruntled employee?" he mused.

"A big, disgruntled employee. Damn it!" She wiped her boot on the floor, leaving three streaks on the polished marble, before limping on. "Bought these before we went on training. What were you saying?"

"It has another two functions."

Orr waved her hand in front of her face. "Ugh..."

"We can use it like a tractor beam if you lower the power output."

"And the second?"

"It reverses the damage done. The ionization of the atmosphere."

"Like kick-starting nature?" Orr caught up as her leg had healed.

"Exactly."

"Now why the hell didn't they use it earlier?"

"According to the memory card the General, my father gave me, the Council wanted to wait until they had cleansed Earth."

"Cleansed?"

Raven entered the waiting elevator. "Where's the security in this place?"

Orr joined him and scrutinised the sole of her boot with flaring nostrils.

Raven continued, "Earth's resources couldn't support the eleven billion people because of global warming. So the rich constructed thirteen Domes sped up global warming, starved the unworthy, and waited for the right moment to kick-start nature."

"Wait, a second." Orr frowned. "I can't believe it. You want to tell me General Von Swartz is your father?"

"Yep." Raven pressed a button on the control panel. "But he wasn't as bad as my mom's boyfriend, Keller. Wait, no, I'm lying. My dad was a total dick up to about two years ago. Then suddenly, he changed, became a different man. I think after the divorce, he realised what life was all about."

The doors closed.

"Why did she go for Keller?"

"To piss my father off." Raven shrugged. "The age-old story. Work was more important." He glanced at Orr. "What about your sad story?"

"In comparison, peachy. I was the ripe old age of twelve when my parents died."

"Lucky you."

"Yep, an only child. No worries, no divorce."

They glanced at each other as they heard high-pitched shrieks echoing up the shaft. The screams amplified as the elevator neared its destination.

The doors slid open.

Both stood frozen, wide-eyed, until Orr said, "I guess it wasn't human shit I stepped in."

People in white coats scurried from one glass container to the next, punching and swiping at the control panels. One chased after a screaming monkey.

"Now there's something you don't see every day," Raven whispered as a man wearing shorts and hat ran toward them.

"Which one of you is Raven?" the man shouted.

Raven raised his hand, still in shock. "Me."

"I'm Ben. Your father told me you're coming." He grabbed Raven by the arm and pulled him out of the elevator. "You need to hurry before the rest of them wake up."

"What's going on here?" Orr asked as they ran toward a door at the far end of the room.

"The failsafe triggered when the weapon activated. We tried to keep the carnivores asleep for as long as possible. Something went wrong. We should have raised the containers above ground before the animals woke."

"Carnivores?" Raven said, glancing over his shoulder.

"They will be hungry." Ben stopped at the door and removed his access card, but before he could insert it into the slot, the door slid open. "That's strange."

"What?" Raven heaved.

A siren went off for a few moments before a computerized female voice said, "Lockdown started."

Ben looked over Raven's shoulder, eyes narrowing.

Raven turned around. "What?"

"The elevators."

"What-what about the elevators?" Orr said, frantic.

"It's locked."

Red lights flashed above the row of steel doors in the distance.

"Nothing went wrong," Ben seethed. "The bastards who designed this want us to be their first meal. That's why the herbivores are still fast asleep." He grabbed Raven by the arm and shoved him through the door. "Get going. I'll stand guard."

Raven entered the room, followed by Orr. At the very top, a sphere, covered with dancing white rays, pointed at the cloudy skies.

Orr ran past him, leaping over rocks and debris. "Come on!" she shouted. "The computer terminal is at the base of the structure!"

"Cool," he whispered. She's just like Rumour in Cavern Raider. His favourite VR game. He followed close behind, for a moment caught up in the wake of her tight behind. At the base, he removed a laptop and cable from his backpack and placed it on the console. He searched for a connection port and found it behind the terminal. "Thank you," he whispered, glancing at the sphere.

"Where did you get that old thing?" Orr asked, keeping her eyes on the door.

"The laptop? It's easier to interface with the weapon," he replied, and started working the keys.

"You need line of sight before–"

"I know. We need to wait until the ship is in range."

"You want me to do it?" Orr peeked over his shoulder. "Having three thousand people's lives at your fingertips..."

He turned his head and could kiss her if he wanted to. She smelt so good. "I can handle it." He smiled, staring into her blue eyes.

She pulled back, just a little. However, after a moment, she smiled back. A flicker of recognition in her eyes also increased his heart rate. His stomach mimicked the charged sphere above.

"I meant, do you know the angle of entry and velocity?" she whispered, keeping her eyes on his.

Raven swallowed the lump in his throat and nodded.

A growl and screams emanating from the next room destroyed their moment.

"I need to go help," Ben shouted from the doorway and disappeared.

Raven typed away. "I'm in." He rubbed his hands before continuing.

"Shit," Orr whispered behind him.

"What?"

"I think it's a gorilla."

"Is it big?" Raven said, eyes pinned on the screen.

"F-fuck, yes."

"Get rid of it."

"How?" Orr replied in a frantic whisper.

"I've just logged onto the ship," Raven said and turned the laptop around. He moved in behind the terminal to face the beast.

The gorilla sniffed the air, its black eyes following each movement with dubious curiosity.

"What's it doing?" Raven whispered, eyes shifting from the screen to the doorway.

"I think it's just checking us out." Orr stepped back until she stood beside Raven. She reached for something inside her uniform jacket.

The gorilla snarled, revealing its three-inch fangs.

"Okay." Orr removed her hand.

"Activating beam in ten seconds."

"Take it easy," Orr said and smiled.

The gorilla took up the challenge, slamming its chest with a deep growl, and stormed.

"Run!" Orr shouted.

With the rumbling above and the wind in my face, I made the journey that would decide my fate. Not to sound dramatic, but also humanity's future. It would be the first time challenging my father. Not even when I was a hundred percent Leon had I tried it. Now, weakened by human blood and overwhelmed by emotions, I knew the chances of defeating him was slim.

You still there?

Nothing.

Shit! I'm finally one, called Wayne or Malik. Lately, everyone called me Malik. Even Sadie. Strange how humans need either, depending on their situation. Today they need Malik. Hopefully, the need for Wayne is not over.

I took a deep breath; I might not see Sadie again. Hold her in my arms. Get lost in those big brown eyes and forget my past.

Ahead, the roars grew louder as the chanting of my name faded behind me. I rammed my sword into the earth a hundred yards from the wall of Leons, placing my fists on my hips.

"Alcantar!"

A heavy silence fell, the only sound that of rattling chains as the crowd parted. Even the skies were silent. My father emerged like a demon from hell, slowly approaching. It was hard, but I didn't flinch.

"We don't have to do this, Father," I said. "Join us."

"Fool." He shook his head. "They will pay for what they did."

"We did it to ourselves. They only defended themselves."

Alcantar drew his sword. "Let's get this over with. I still need to take the city before nightfall."

"You mean my city." I smiled as I drew Arden's sword from the earth. "I have accomplished my mission. You have failed."

I jumped back as my father struck. "You're getting slow, old man," I mocked, dragging the point of my sword through the sand as I circled him. Blind rage always allowed for opportunity... I hoped.

Alcantar lunged with a growl, aiming at my heart, but I turned sideways, arching my back. The blade poked air inches past my chest. I ducked down as he withdrew his sword and made a rolling jump to create distance between us. That infuriated him even more.

"Stand and fight like a Leon!" he yelled, running toward me.

"Oh, but I'm not Leon. You said so yourself." I arched my back with my arms stretched out as he wielded his sword. The blade grazed my chest, slicing through my uniform.

I jumped back and stumbled over the only rock in the desert. Sudden gasps went through the Leon crowd. My father had tasted blood, stabbing at me, snarling, eyes blackened by rage. His sword pierced the ground to my left and then to my right as I rolled from side to side. He raised his sword and brought it down, like an axe – my head on the block of wood. I held my sword above my head by the hilt and blade, blocking his attack. As he raised his sword, I struck. My blade tasted blood above his right knee. Not serious, but enough to encourage his retreat. I leapt to my feet, stepped back, and dusted the desert from my shoulders.

He stood rigid, eyes boring into me, saliva dripping from his fangs. "You are nothing like Malik," he said under his breath. "You disgust me."

"I'm still Malik." I shrugged. "I have just woken up."

"Well, then it's time to put you back to sleep."

"Once you have awakened, it's impossible to go back."

Alcantar took his stance, sword raised above his head. "Enough talk. If you don't stand your ground and fight, I will instruct my men to attack."

I mimicked his stance and gave him a nod. Playtime is over.

He charged with a bloodcurdling roar. Our swords crossed; the impact reverberated into my spine. I had forgotten how powerful he was. Each blow pushed me back. The clang of exploding steel stung my ears – his rage unstoppable, uncontrollable. Again, and again and again, he struck until my blade gave way under the onslaught. The sound of a blade snapping was a warrior's worst moment. It was the sound of defeat. Death.

I watched as if detached from my body – Alcantar's blade sliced through my right shoulder down to my chest.

"I'll feast on your woman first," Alcantar said as he extracted his blade and rammed it into my stomach.

I gasped, clutching my father's shoulder, staring into his dead eyes.

"You still think I'm slow, human." Alcantar extracted his sword.

"Father?" I whispered, retreated a few feet, and fell to my knees. He had no remorse.

"You see!" Alcantar pointed at me. "He's not a Leon, because

Leon's can't cry. Therefore, he's not Malik." He smiled. "Therefore, he's not my son."

A claw grabbed me from behind, by the shoulder, and raised me to my feet. "A gift," the Leon whispered.

A sharp pain exploded through my body as he stabbed me in the back. He shoved me forward with the 'gift' still lodged. I gritted my teeth, hand tightening around the hilt of my broken sword.

"I will make it quick, human." Alcantar approached, sword raised but froze; a grey wolf crossed our path, trotting over the plane as if unaware of our presence. I remembered seeing one of those, many years ago, searching for food on the farm. I killed and devoured its flesh. We all watched in silence until the blanket of dust covering the desert swallowed it.

"Beautiful," I muttered.

The clouds surrendered their precious cargo. At first, only a taste as large drops vanished into the sand, and then more followed, compressing the dusty blanket.

I dropped the sword, fell to my knees, and opened my mouth. My father walked up to me, sword dragging behind him. "Quench your thirst, as I will mine with the blood of your human friends."

"Finish it," I said, my palms turned to the heavens.

A white beam of light shot from the horizon behind Alcantar and pierced the clouds. The light differed from before – a constant beam, less blinding.

"Look, Master!" the backstabbing Leon called out, pointing at the horizon. Alcantar glanced over his shoulder. The Leon gave me the nod.

I pulled the dagger from my back and plunged it into my father's heart, twisting the blade. He staggered back, wildly wielding his swords. I went in low, repeatedly ramming the knife into his stomach.

"Kill him!" he roared, trying to push me away.

I raised his one leg from the ground and pushed, roaring. He succumbed to gravity and keeled over, taking me with him. The soil parched as it eagerly swallowed what the heavens offered. My actions weren't dictated by emotion or rationality anymore, but by blind rage and adrenalin. I lugged myself on top of him, my fingers digging into his battle worn breastplate, and plunged the dagger into his heart. He finally cried out, "Stop!"

Stumbling to my feet, I looked at the dagger in my hand; the pouring rain washed away the blood.

My father reached for his sword and picked it up by the blade, pointing the hilt at me. "Take it," he groaned. Diluted blood poured from his mouth as he turned his head toward me. "Take... it."

With a trembling hand, I accepted and knelt beside him.

"You are a Leon... I was wrong... only a Leon can kill me. I'm proud of you... my son. You are worthy... Take my place." The darkness left his eyes until they flickered and closed.

I stumbled to my feet, glaring at the line of Leons... still silent. "Is this what you want?" I yelled, pointing the sword at my father's body. "No more killing!" I threw the sword to the ground.

One by one, with bowed heads, they went down on one knee, placing their swords beside them.

—

"Run, damn it!" Raven yelled, hands frozen on the keyboard.

Lieutenant Orr drew a pistol from her jacket and fired three shots into the air.

The gorilla halted his charge, fangs exposed, glaring at them.

She pointed the firearm at the gorilla and shouted, "I'll fucking extinct your ass!"

After an intense twenty-second stare down, the gorilla backed off and exited the same way he entered.

Raven swallowed the lump in his throat. "Will you marry me?"

"Take it easy," she said, slamming the weapon down next to the laptop. "We need to finish our job here first."

Raven jumped into action. A few keystrokes later, the beam had found its target, pulling the ship toward Earth.

A crack of lightning illuminated the cavern, signalling the start of the rain.

"Now we have to wait and see," Raven said, glancing at Orr.

They heard more screams from the Ark.

"Wait a second," he whispered. "I remembered when searching for access to the weapon that I could also gain access to the Ark's mainframe."

The scientists huddled together in the centre of the Ark.

"Don't turn your back on them," Ben ordered.

A lion ran past the group, chasing a screaming monkey. He noticed a stalking Siberian tiger inching its way toward the group, eyes pinned on the petite woman beside him.

"Tiger to my right!" he screamed, pointing. "On three, just as I had told you!"

The tiger was only ten feet away, crouching, every muscle tense, preparing to lunge.

"One... two... three!"

As one, the group bellowed with raised hands and gave a step toward the tiger. The animal broke off its attack, scampering away. Ben shoved the woman in behind his back, searching for the next attack.

"Bear!" someone screamed to the left of him. "One..."

A bloodcurdling cry echoed through the chamber, followed by hysterical screams as a grizzly bear pulled professor Martins away.

"Leave him," Ben shouted as another tried to save the man. "Stay in the group!"

They watched in horror as the grizzly sank its fangs into Martin's neck, silencing his screams.

"Keep your fucking eyes open!" He felt a hand clasp his arm.

"Silverback!" the woman cried behind him, pointing at the gorilla to the right of Ben.

"One..." Ben started the count. "Two... three!"

The group screamed with waving arms. The gorilla towered, slamming its chest and charged, fangs exposed. Ben stepped into the path of the charging animal and shut his eyes, preparing for impact. The siren blared once more, followed by a loud metallic clang, shaking the Ark's foundation. Ben peeked through his left eye. The gorilla stood upright, just a few feet away, his head tilted upward. The roof parted like a drawn curtain, allowing in the rain. Animals and humans stood in awe as if the downpour washed away their fear and hunger.

Ben closed his eyes and opened his mouth, quenching his parched mouth.

The Ark's foundation rocked once more as the roof locked in place.

A slight tremor beneath their feet intensified with each passing second. The gorilla glanced at Ben as if searching for an answer.

"The entire room?" Ben said as the floor and containers ascended.

The rest of the closed containers drained their yellowish fluid and unlocked. One by one, the glass fronts fell open.

The Ark ground to a halt, waiting...

"You know the drill," Ben shouted. "We need to release the animals on the top row before the Ark elevates the next row above ground."

The group, still wary of the roaming carnivores, splashed their way to the bank of awaiting elevators.

The animals emerged from their glass coffins, like a newborn, dazed, confused, and unsteady. Ben approached a deer and herded it with arms stretched out toward the end of the steel ramp, to freedom. The majestic animal stepped onto the muddy earth, sniffing at the grey clouds, its pelt soaking up the rain. The other scientists follow suit, clearing the top rows.

Orr stepped out of an arriving elevator, clutching a puppy, smiling. Raven excitedly clutched his bag behind her.

"I guess I have you guys to thank for this," Ben said, placing his hand on Orr's shoulder.

She kissed the puppy's head. "Always wanted one... read about them."

"A wolf?"

Her brow furrowed.

Ben burst out laughing, slapping her shoulder. "Just messing with you. It's a dog. Consider it a gift from a grateful friend."

"Thank you, she's beautiful." She wrapped her arms tighter around the drenched animal.

"It's a him," Ben corrected. "Thought about a name yet."

"Well, I must change it now," she said.

"What about Mika?" he said, ruffling the drenched pelt.

Orr mused, with an arched mouth.

"It means new moon in Japanese." Ben draped his arm over Raven's shoulders and pointed at the city. "Because tonight, the city will sleep under a new moon."

"I like that," she whispered.

"Just one thing," Ben said. "You need to visit because I need him for breeding."

She shielded Mika with her hand. "You won't hurt him?"

Ben chuckled. "He will enjoy it."

"We'll take good care of him," Raven said, wrapping his arm around Orr's waist.

"Take it easy." She wriggled out of his grasp. "One step at a time. You still need to take me out on a date."

Ben looked at the city. "Let's hope there's time for that."

Orr frowned, then looked into Raven's eyes. "Technically, we were on a date."

"Technically, you're right," he whispered, placing his hands on her slender hips.

"Wait!" Ben plucked the puppy from Orr's hands. "Don't want it squashed to extinction," he said and walked off.

Orr shoved Raven back into the elevator and kissed him hard on the mouth. She grabbed him by the hair and pulled his head back. "Now you're all mine," she whispered through clenched teeth.

He swallowed, wide-eyed. "Maybe I must introduce you to my mother first."

The doors closed.

The human chain stood in silence; eyes focused on the horizon. The last thing anyone saw was Malik on his knees, but then came the rain. Visibility turned to zero.

Sadie started walking toward the murky horizon. She wiped the wet strands of hair from her eyes.

"Come on, Malik. Please save Wayne." First, her mother, then her father, and now... She bit her lip, fighting back the tears.

"Sadie!" Juliet shouted.

"I'm not just going to stand here?" she cried.

Juliet looked at Brock and Fritz, then at Shorty.

Brock shrugged and broke rank. "No use waiting for death."

Shorty followed. "W-wait."

"Wait for me!" Darius yelled, and removed his sidearm.

"What are you going to do with that?" Brock smirked.

"For Alcantar."

Joshua pushed through the chain and ran after the departing group.

"Dammit, Joshua!" his mother called out.

Like a dam wall breaking, the chain gave way. The marching crowd's roar grew as their momentum increased. The wave swept across the battleground until the ghostly line of figures appeared, creeping toward them.

"Stop!" Darius yelled, hand raised. The call repeated down the line.

"It's over!" I yelled above the roar of the approaching crowd.

Alcantar's Leons, again, went down on one knee, signalling their surrender. Sadie ran into my arms, almost knocking me over. I picked her up with my good arm, hiding the pain of my father's assault.

"You think I can go home and lick my wounds?" I said.

She nodded, running her hands through my drenched hair.

"You saved many people, farm boy," Darius said.

We ignored him, our lips locked until I felt two arms clamped around my leg; Joshua looked up at me, squinting from the rain.

"To be continued," I whispered to Sadie as I let her down.

I knelt in front of the boy. "How did I do?"

"I knew you were gonna save us." He wrapped his arms around my neck. "You wanna come over to my house and play?"

"Play?" I smiled. "I'll tell you what. Come to my place in a few days and help me."

"With what?"

"Farm... I've got a lot of things to do there."

He nodded, excited.

"Come, Joshua," his mother said. "Let's get you dried up. You're going to catch a cold."

As I watched them go, I thought of my brother. I struggled to my feet, using Darius's shoulder for support. "I hope you didn't attack the ship," I said, glaring at the beam spearing the clouds.

"I was tempted." He winked. "My son is trying to break their fall."

"You think it will work?" I asked.

"It's worth a try."

My eyes narrowed. "Wait a second–"

"Yes," Darius interrupted. "Raven is my son." He glanced at the line of Leons. "What are we going to do with them?"

"Feed them before they get hungry."

"I will arrange something, but for now, they must be happy with what we have."

"I know."

"Another thing. I can't let them into the city," Darius said. "It will be impossible to defend ourselves if they turn on us. I will set up a camp—"

"So, we are going to do this all over again," I snapped. "Only the worthy can enter."

"I can't trust them! You warned me!"

"We need to show trust for them to trust us. We are the same, human and Leon."

"Sorry, Malik." Darius removed a communicator from his drenched jacket. "Is it done?"

"Yes, General," a man replied.

"Do it."

The skies behind the Leons lit up, followed by a series of explosions.

"You told me I must do whatever it takes not to get them in the air again," Darius said.

The Leons became restless. Grunts rippled through the crowd of aliens.

"The war is over!" I yelled. "The camp is yours. Get some sleep. We will send food and clothes."

"Incoming!" someone screamed.

I glanced over my shoulder; my brother's ship broke through the clouds. The beam deactivated as it cleared the city.

"Now they're on their own," Darius whispered.

The ship left a trail of black smoke in its wake as it disappeared over the horizon.

"Let's go!" Juliet ran to her Raptor.

"We need medical supplies and food at the crash site," Darius spoke into his communicator.

One of the Leons stepped forward. "Dacht och boght."

Darius looked at me.

"It's their ship," I translated.

He nodded. "We will take as many of them as we can."

"Their fighters would have been helpful," I muttered.

"I did what I had to do."

————

We followed the trail of smouldering debris for miles before reaching what remained of the ship. It ploughed through miles of earth before grinding to a halt against a rocky incline, its last resting place. The black hull was in stark contrast with the desert hue. Humans and Leons ran from the fleet of ships as they landed at the crash site. The rain had stopped, but the promise of more to come lingered in the clouds.

"I'm sorry, Malik," Sadie whispered, taking my hand as we made our way to the ship.

We joined a mixed crowd, all staring at the wreck with the same hopeless expression.

"This is a gigantic ship," Darius said. "About a hundred storeys."

"Our pride," I whispered. "Stole it from the Balthazars."

From the corner of my eye, I saw him shake his head.

My hand tightened around Sadie's as a small hatch opened at the bottom of the ship, close to where hull and sand fused.

We stormed the hatch as the first survivors stumbled out. Humans and Leons worked together, attending to the injured.

"Where are they!" I asked Gelman as he emerged.

He smiled, pointing over his shoulder with his thumb.

"I never thought I would see your ugly face again," Arden said as he helped my mother from the ship.

Sadie joined in as we all locked in an embrace.

"You're not allowed to park here," Darius said.

"I believe I have you to thank for this," my brother said, shaking his hand.

"It was my son's idea."

Arden frowned.

"Why is it so hard for everyone to think I've got a son?"

I grinned. "Because you need to have sex before you can become a father."

"Ha ha ha, a half-Leon with a sense of humour." Darius searched the motley crowd of Leons and humans.

"Who are you looking for?" I asked.

"One of my men," he muttered as his gaze settled on the escape hatch. "Can I board, Captain?" he asked Arden.

Arden smiled, exposing his two-inch fangs. "Don't touch anything." After Darius stepped through the hatch, my brother turned to me and said, "I'm proud of you, little brother. It could have turned into a bloodbath... for all. Did he say anything? Any last words?"

"No."

He took a deep breath and bowed his head.

"You are our leader." I placed my hand on his shoulder. "And you look the part. I feel like Shorty amongst all these Leons."

"It is the size of your heart that counts. And you challenged him and won."

I gave a step back and kneeled in front of him.

"What are you doing?" he said.

The humans and Leons fell silent, circling us.

I spoke Leon, "With this, I pledge my allegiance to our great leader Arden, eldest son of Alcantar. I do this with all my heart." I held out my hand. "Brother to brother. Leon to Leon. Blood to blood."

Arden straightened, pushing out his bulging chest. He reached behind his back and removed his dagger. "Warrior to warrior." He sliced his palm, then mine.

"Warrior to warrior." I grabbed him in an upright wrist grip, and he pulled me to my feet.

The roar of the crowd was infectious, spreading to the outskirts. Leons and humans shook hands, slapping each other's back, nodding as if they understood each other.

Arden gave me an appreciative nod, then looked at his palm. "I forgot our blood is black."

"But not your heart. You will be a great leader."

He smiled, pointing at his fangs. "Finally, it's bigger than yours."

I grinned. "It's not that size that matters."

"H-h-here you g-go, Arden." Shorty held out Joshua's teddy.

"I've asked him to bring it," I smirked.

Arden glared at the teddy bear, then at me. He grabbed it and shoved it in under his arm.

"I thought with all the wild animals running around, you might need it."

Epilogue

One year later

Against Darius' will, Sadie and I had returned to the farm and rebuilt it with the help of my friends – human and Leon. A man named Tobias Royston, also known as Ben, provided us with the seeds for our first crop. We went big; enough fruit and vegetables to support our household and the Leons. Buchanan oversaw food security in the city – he converted old factories into hydroponic farms and donated the food dispensers to the Leons.

Earth gave us a second chance. It rained, we harvested, and the deserts receded. My love for Sadie grew as my child grew within her. In the ninth month, she brought my son into this world. We called him Charles. She promised me with our second, if a boy, that we could name him Howard, after my father.

My brother stayed with the ship, as it was big enough for all Leons. It didn't take Juliet long to join Arden. A town named Leonville had developed alongside the ship. Humans, especially women, found it in their hearts to help the Leons with their day-to-day chores. Women fell pregnant. The Leon males thought I had something to do with their sudden fertility. I had nothing to do with it, but I didn't deny it.

The people elected Darius President. A disputed result because Leons could not vote. He now lived with his wife, son, and daughter-in-law in the Presidential Palace.

Brock remained with the military and was now head of the Presidential guard. Fritz opened a tattoo parlour and married one of his first clients, a redhead woman named Angel. Shorty, as always, surprised me; he found his mate in Arden's ship, a Leon called Lyceum. My brother knew him. After he found his true love, Shorty lost his stutter.

Mother moved in with Sadie and me after the birth of her grandson. Not our choice, but an army of Leons couldn't keep her away. I suggested she could stay with the ship, with her people, and then visit my son in his dreams at night.

She responded, radiating violet, "And miss the mighty Malik, conqueror of worlds, change a diaper! How the mighty Malik had fallen. Defeated by love. My mission a success."

Darius stepped onto the balcony, dressed in a black slim fit suit and red tie, clutching a glass of bourbon. He smiled at the images of Malik and Sadie as they twirled and tumbled and laughed in the gravity room.

It was a chilly night, and the incessant blanket of clouds obscured the full moon. He removed the chiming communicator from his inside jacket pocket and glanced over his shoulder before accepting the call.

"Voice only," he said. "Yes, dear."

"Are you showing it again?" Carla Von Swartz asked. "Malik will have you for breakfast."

"It's their first anniversary. And showing the people a good ending is never a bad thing."

"When are you coming home?" Carla asked.

"I'll be home before ten."

"I'll be waiting, Mr President."

He slipped the communicator back into his pocket and raised his glass at the images on the adjacent building.

Angel stepped from the shadows.

Darius smirked. "I heard you like a bloody steak and a spicy, full-bodied red wine."

She sauntered toward him, twirling a lock around her finger. "I heard that you always get what you want."

"You know it." He took a sip.

"Do you want to flavour everything I offer?"

"Before I flavour anything" –he wiped a strand of hair from her cheek and tugged it in behind her ear– "if you betray me like you did Gabriel, they will find a piece of you on each continent."

"I was working for Steward. I never betrayed him." She took the glass from his hand. "Who's the enemy?"

"If I knew that, you would not be here. What about Fritz?"

She took a sip. "We have an open relationship."

The city lights flickered.

"What's going on?"

Waves of blue rays rose from behind the skyline.

"The shield."

She took a frowning sip, swallowed hard, and asked, "Why?"

"Soon, the Leons would want what we have. And they are not like us. They will grow tired of broccoli and potatoes and come looking for the real thing."

She pointed. "Wayne will not be happy."

Darius shook his head. "Malik is not a farmer. I told him he could make some serious credits in the city. He'll come around. He's more Leon than he thinks."

"You are-"

"How can I make some serious credits in the city?" I said, lying with my hands behind my head on the king-size bed, its canopy draped with heavy gold and blood-red curtains.

Darius gave her a nod and reclaimed his drink.

"See you later, Wayne," she said as she opened the door. "Do we need to bring anything for your party tomorrow night?"

"Just your pretty self and your focking husband, Angel."

She blew me a kiss as she closed the door.

"Increase brightness by thirty percent." Darius fell into a leather couch, glass raised, careful not to spill. "So, the guards just let you walk in, Malik?" He took a sip.

"It's Wayne." I sat up and scooted to the edge of the bed. "I'm a hero, remember? Untouchable."

He raised his glass. "Cheers. Can I get you something?"

I shook my head.

"Did you know the shield was going up?"

I nodded. "I'm a hero. People want to tell me things." He was hard to read – like trying to read a corpse.

"Sorry, I didn't visit, but I was so busy campaigning. I heard the house you build was bigger than mine."

"People want to do things for me because..." I shrugged.

"You're a hero." He took a sip. "How can I help you... my hero?"

"My brother discovered the skeleton of an old friend while renovating and cleaning the ship. A human killed him. You might know him, an Elder called Gelman?"

He frowned pensively, then shook his head. "I don't believe I do. But how do you know a human killed him?"

"He was double tapped between the eyes with a human weapon. And before you ask, Juliet explained the term. With their claws, Leons can barely handle a gun. So, firing a weapon with such speed and accuracy is impossible. Gelman was alive after the crash, and the only human that had entered the ship at that time was you. So why kill Gelman? To find the answer, I went to my Rock-of-reflection."

He sipped – deadpan.

"I sat until my ass and head hurt. I found the answer, but it was so inconceivable that I kept on sitting and reflecting. Until, finally, I had to accept it. Alcantar and Gelman were the only two Leons that knew the identity of the human supplying them with the codes. Alcantar didn't want any other Leon to find out he was negotiating with a human. So, with Alcantar dead, only Gelman remained."

Darius rolled the glass between his palms, staring at the contents.

"That day in the desert, below the Vector, you slipped up. You said that the Leons hit the city with an electromagnetic pulse, knocking out all communication. The only human that knew that fact was working with Alcantar."

"I knew the moment I said it." He emptied his glass, stood up and walked to the solid wood liquor cabinet.

"When I figured who you are, everything fell into place. I then understood why you kept on coming back to the farm. You tried to convince your son to go with you."

His eyes darted to me, then back to the drink he was pouring. "I told you so. But he never knew I was his father."

"But my old man was between a rock and a hard place. You didn't know about his alien wife and two half-breeds, because you never returned to the resistance after you had left. After Alcantar had fetched my mom, my father still couldn't escape to the city because his two boys might awaken and deactivate the shield."

General Johnson took a slow seat on the couch. "The cities I had sacrificed were on the brink of running out of power. Alcantar did not know, so I used the intel to my advantage, trading the codes of a dying city to save the lives of others. Alcantar knew where all the hideouts were for the unworthy and forgotten. You think Ross' resistance was the only. There were hundreds of camps. I bargained for their lives as long as I could, as long as I had failing shields. But your race always wanted more and more." He spilt his drink.

"I know," I whispered, avoiding his piercing eyes.

"So, I promised them Nirvana if they gave me a new body. I was ninety-five and still had so much to do. Because I had always delivered, Alcantar trusted me. I needed the body of a well-respected man, someone who had already moved up the ranks but was still young. So, Lola, Nirvana's AI, which I had helped developed back in the day, chose the thirty-five-year-old Commander Von Swartz. She sent him out on reconnaissance, claiming she had detected the heat signature of a wild animal. Darius helped capture animals for Ben's cryo-farm." He closed his eyes, bowing his head. "We met in the desert. They transferred our... souls, or memories, or whatever makes us who we are at the same time. Something that still haunts me." Johnson filled his lungs and let out a long-drawn sigh. "Commander Darius Von Swartz died an old man in the middle of a desert, killed with his weapon. I went to the desert unarmed."

"You could've occupied the same body, like me."

Johnson shook his head. "And risk losing the battle, like Malik. Darius was one strong-willed individual."

"A century ago, just before the Leons boarded the Balthazarians ship, they sent all their data to this solar system and erased everything on their ship. Was it the blueprints for the shield and weapon? Because humans still struggle to cure piles. The shield doesn't fit."

He nodded. "My great grandfather was a scientist working for SETI at the time. He had spent years deciphering and translating the data. The alien data came with a warning, 'Beware, you are not alone.' My great grandfather kept the data a secret and passed it on to his son. He knew that governments would abuse it. Every Johnson generation created something from those blueprints, as and when the technology on Earth became available." General Johnson stood. "I want some fresh air. The weather is much nicer with the shield up."

I followed him out onto the balcony. The city was asleep – no more flashing images. It was a windless, cloudless night, full moon, and Haley's comet snaking across the Milky Way. The city lights morphed into the starry skies at the edge of town.

The General peered at the city below, one hand clutching the railing, the other his drink. "My dear mom died of cancer because of greed," he said. "My wife died when they tried to kill me because they wanted the shield for themselves." He turned to me. "I took this body because I wanted a second chance. This time I will do it right. All humans will benefit, not just the rich and powerful. To be honest, I did not lose any sleep after handing over those codes to Alcantar."

"You handed the codes over to Ross to breach this shield," I said. "You handed Sadie and her father over to Alcantar."

He gave a step toward me, scowling, "I gave it as a sign of goodwill. The last thing I expected was for that senile old man to hand it over to Alcantar."

A chill exploded through my body, elevating my heart rate. He spoke the truth; they transferred his soul, or memories, or whatever made him who he was, to this body. I looked into the eyes of a Johnson – all-devouring grey and cold. The captain had the same eyes.

"You send it to Ross when you heard Steward caught his daughter spying. You gave the codes to Brock when the guards escorted us to the Operations room. Brock trusted you. He did not know what he was sending. Human nature dictated the next step in your plan. You bargained on Alcantar striking because you needed the diversion."

He leaned against the railing with his hip, glaring. "I worked my entire life for this moment," he seethed. "I gave so many people the chance to rule, but all of them fucked it up. Yes, I knew they would first go for the head, but I needed the time to prepare the weapon. I'm a leader, I decide for the greater good. And Charles Green," he shrugged, "and at that stage, Sadie wasn't part of the greater good."

He was tall, drunk and, because of his ego, top-heavy. I flipped him over the railing without spilling his drink. He held on with one hand, and after a sobering moment, let go of the glass. "Malik! No!" he screamed, trying to grab the railing with his drinking hand. "We're a team! Why!"

"I'm Wayne, just a farmer. And when you handed Alcantar the codes, you took away the chance."

He grabbed the railing with his other hand. "The shields were failing! Malik, please!" His voice echoed against the surrounding buildings before being swallowed by the night.

"You did not know that. And one thing that I admire, being human and all, is resilience. The men, women, and children in those cities would have kept the shields going. You sacrificed millions because of revenge. Simple. Every day, I fight against Malik's memories. Memories you had helped create."

The full moon illuminated the Johnson within, a pale, power-hungry ghost, which would never be satisfied. I saw the Leon in him.

"Fuck you! I made you!" he seethed, teeth glistening like fangs.

"No, you didn't. I'm still Wayne, just a farm boy."

Johnson's bony fingers clawed at the railing.

"Your past sealed your fate. Now that I know your secret, I won't be part of your greater good. And we both know what happens to those. I'm so tired of humans and Leons playing God."

"Malik!" The name trailed off into the night as the great General Johnson plunged to his death.

"The name's Wayne."

I removed the two-way radio from my pocket. Untraceable and simple. "Vulture is dead. Proceed."

"Affirmative," Brock replied.

"And don't damage the power to the city."

"Yes, Captain."

I walked back into the apartment and cracked open the door. The guards were still unconscious. The gas that Angel had released in the corridor's ventilation system knocked them out before I arrived. It was safe to take the elevator because Building Seven was the haven for the Haves; no cameras or tracing in or around Building Seven. No security guard or scorned employee or hacker to leak footage of their promiscuity, wicked deeds, and unusual habits. Whatever happens in Building Seven dies in Building Seven. They value anonymity more than their safety. Sadie's unfortunate incident only strengthened their resolve.

A crowd already gathered around Darius' body as I stepped out of the building. The fast-approaching sirens disturbed the sleeping city. A tiny brown bird bounced in the street, pecking at crumbs. I stopped and watched it. It tilted its head and looked at me with its shiny black eye. I held out my hand – waiting, testing fate. The bird bounced and fluttered into my hand. Shit! The shield was still up, but the air tasted lighter, and it felt as if I was back in the gravity room.

A slight tremor disturbed the bird; it pooped before flying away. I flicked it from my palm and continued down the street. Blue rays danced in the skies before the whirlpool appeared. It expanded, washing away the starry skies and exposing the clouds. The full moon cast like a white border or a silver lining around it. That's it! Silver lining! An excellent description - I need to tell Sadie before I forget.

"Okay, Malik," I muttered. "I completed your mission. Now leave me alone."

I filled my lungs with the fresh breeze rushing through Nirvana. Tomorrow would bring a new dawn. No more blisters, no more shit between my toes, no more trudging dust because Sadie bought me a hat, a fresh pair of gloves and boots. This time I'm prepared... well... until fate happens.

About the Author

Johan Thompson is a writer by night and manager of a law firm by day. He lives with his wife, two boys, and two dogs in Johannesburg, South Africa.

After studying creative writing, screenwriting, and watching every science fiction film created, he decided to draw on his interest and imagination to create his first novel.

The Monster Within is his fifth book.